SCOTLAND

As the feud between t...
the Maxwells threatens to consume the land,
a young woman sets out to find the treasure
that can bring peace to them all. . . .

Mona Graham was an outsider, even within her scheming family. As the only one who knew the location of the legendary Clachan Fala, she had been held a virtual prisoner in her own home—first by her husband, who wanted the treasure for himself, and now by his vile son . . . who wanted Mona as well. . . .

Patrick Maxwell was the lone wolf of his warlike clan. Cursed by his father for his recklessness, Patrick had ventured out to make his mark as a warrior-for-hire, living as free as he wanted, unbound by anyone or anything—until a raid into Graham lands led to his capture. . . .

Together, they embark upon a perilous quest to find the Bloodstone and end the enmity between their families. But the closer they get to the prize, the harder it is to contain their own passions for freedom, for honor, and for each other.

Brides of the Bloodstone
Praise for the first novel in this thrilling trilogy

TEMPTED BY YOUR TOUCH
"A tender triumph that tempted me to keep reading all night long."
—Teresa Medeiros, author of *A Kiss to Remember*

Books by Jen Holling

Tempted by Your Touch
Tamed by Your Desire
Captured by Your Kiss

Available from POCKET BOOKS

BRIDES of the BLOODSTONE

Captured by Your Kiss

JEN HOLLING

SONNET BOOKS

New York London Toronto Sydney Singapore

This book is a work of fiction. Names, characters, places and incidents are products of the author's imagination or are used fictitiously. Any resemblance to actual events or locales or persons, living or dead, is entirely coincidental.

An *Original* Publication of POCKET BOOKS

 A Sonnet Book published by
POCKET BOOKS, a division of Simon & Schuster, Inc.
1230 Avenue of the Americas, New York, NY 10020

ISBN: 0-7434-3804-3

First Sonnet Books printing January 2003

10 9 8 7 6 5 4 3 2 1

SONNET BOOKS and colophon are trademarks of Simon & Schuster, Inc.

For information regarding special discounts for bulk purchases, please contact Simon & Schuster Special Sales at 1-800-456-6798 or business@simonandschuster.com

Front cover illustration by Lisa Litwack; back cover illustration by Gregg Gulbronson

Printed in the U.S.A.

To Mom and Dad,
For never giving up on me, no matter what the endeavor.

PROLOGUE

❧

West March,
England, 1531

Mona Musgrave gazed out over the crowd at unforgiving
faces, her lips threatening to quiver with the strength of her
terror. She stiffened them, refusing to weep or beg. She'd
done enough of that already. If she was to die, she'd die
with dignity.

Her hands were bound tightly behind her back, the
hemp rope coarse against her throat. They'd dragged her to
the gallows on a litter full of holes; her gown was torn, her
arms and thighs chaffed raw from the ground. The drying
juice of rotten vegetables and fruit matted her hair to the
sides of her face and stained her clothes. A fiddle and a
flute spun a wild reel that made her head spin. Children
danced to the tune, singing, *"The witch is dead! The witch
is swinging by her neck!"*

Even now, moments from the end, the villagers hissed
at her, called her a witch and a murderess. They believed a
dead man over her, these people she'd cared for, healed,
helped. Her chin quivered again, and she clenched her jaw
against it, her vision burning and blurring.

The priest bellowed prayers at her, the *slap, slap* of the

back of his hand against his open palm punctuating his sermon on the dangers of the devil and how women are so much more susceptible to his wiles. The boards creaked beside her as the executioner stepped forward to kick the stool from beneath her feet. Mona's muscles clenched, her heart hammering painfully, waiting for the sudden drop, for the noose to tighten.

A bright blob swayed and jiggled before her eyes, her tears distorting it. She blinked rapidly, sending tears cascading down her cheeks, but clearing her vision. It was Arlana Musgrave, a white witch and the rumored Keeper of the Clachan Fala—the Bloodstone of legend.

Mona inhaled sharply. The priest fell silent with a final slap. The fiddler stopped on a screeching note. Parents hushed their children's singing. The crowd turned away from the spectacle of Mona to view Arlana with awe. It had been years since the witch had left her cottage. The crowd parted to allow her fat pony to pass, bearing its enormous burden.

No one knew what Musgrave grayne Arlana sprang from. Many people on the border bore the same surname and had no blood attachments, so this was not unusual. Mona had not seen the white witch since she was a child, and she had never spoken to her. Arlana looked no different than she had a decade ago.

Hugely fat, her bulk was draped in bright, rich cloth. Yellows, reds, greens, painted with odd shapes and symbols. Silver chains and colorful beads draped her thick neck, bangles clinked on her wrists. Her gray hair hung loose down her back, flowing wildly over her shoulders and mingling with the pony's mane. Her face was beautiful. Round and pale as a moon and for all her many years—no one knew exactly how old she was—she had not a wrinkle. Her blue eyes were penetrating and bright, framed by long black lashes.

Her pony, its sides heaving and lathered with sweat, stopped before the gallows.

Mona remembered to breathe and the air whooshed out of her. Dizziness nearly overcame her, but she steadied herself. Arlana looked up at her. Why was she here? Had she come to watch the execution? That would be Mona's luck—the notorious recluse emerged from her hermit hole for a bit of diversion.

Arlana's gaze fastened on Mona, assessing, judging. The silence drew out interminably. Mona could hear her heart pounding against her ribs, her breath laboring with fear. The villagers were unnaturally quiet, everyone waiting for Arlana to reveal her purpose in venturing out of the wood.

"My apprentice is dead," Arlana called out, her voice cracking as if she hadn't used it in years, never taking her eyes from Mona. "I need another." Her gaze swept Mona from head to toe. "She'll do."

A soft murmuring began in the crowd and washed through them like a wave. Mona stared at the old woman incredulously. Though Arlana was much revered by the village, she couldn't seriously expect them to release Mona just because she said so.

The priest stepped forward, distressed. "B-but she is a murderess—"

"I know what I know and you're wrong." Her sharp gaze pinned the priest. "She was telling the truth. Her husband was possessed."

The crowd gasped and the priest swung around, wide eyes on Mona. His lips flapped, but nothing came out. Without orders the executioner swiftly removed the rope from Mona's neck and cut her bindings, helping her gently down from the stool.

Mona looked out at the crowd, confused, trembling from the sudden reprieve. They eyed her differently now.

She'd always been known as a healer, and yet all knew she was human, fallible—and of late, they believed her depraved. Arlana was viewed as something else, something otherworldly, beyond understanding. And she was *good*. A *white* witch. This was what Mona saw in their eyes now as they gazed at her. Wonder, as if seeing her for the first time.

Legs shaking, Mona descended the gallows steps. No one tried to stop her. As she neared Arlana, the villagers reached out to touch the old woman's skirts and her pony. Mona reached Arlana's side and gazed up at her. A small smile curved the witch's lips.

Mona's head shook slowly, unable to give voice to the emotions welling up in her chest, choking her. "Thank you," she finally whispered.

Arlana let out a short, breathy laugh as she tapped her pony's sides and gestured for Mona to follow her. "You'll be cursing me afore this is over."

It was a fine cottage—bastle house, really—with a spacious upper floor and the lower floor devoted to livestock. It was precious few that didn't live intimately with the cows and chickens. The floor was not dirt but clean wood planks. The wood creaked and groaned as Arlana walked on it, and Mona feared it would give way under her bulk. But it held and the old witch lowered herself slowly and painfully onto the rug before the hearth. She waved a fat-fingered hand for Mona to build the fire back up. The silver rings on her fingers glittered in the dim light, shafts of weak sunlight from the open windows catching the cut edges of her jewels.

Arlana had spoken little to Mona on the long ride into the woods. Mona had tried to question the white witch about why she'd been chosen as the apprentice, for Mona had always thought Arlana's apprentice had to be a virgin.

But Arlana only shook her head and bade her to have patience.

They'd had to stop frequently to rest the pony, and Mona had been forced to help Arlana from her perch on the poor creature's back. Mona had never seen the like—Arlana's ankles were as big as Mona's thighs—and her feet were small, plump things, encased in silk beaded slippers. Mona knew well where all the finery came from. Scots and English alike traveled to her for healing remedies and fortunes. So far as Mona had heard, Arlana was never wrong. Though she never asked for a penny in payment, she was always well rewarded.

"You should have come to me long ago," Arlana said as Mona piled logs onto the cold embers.

Mona turned, frowning. "Come to you?"

"When you first suspected your husband was . . . not right in the head."

The slithering returned to her belly as it always did when reminded of Edwin Musgrave. "I couldn't. He wouldn't let me out of his sight."

Arlana nodded sagely.

Mona leaned forward. "Is it like you said? Was he possessed by the devil?"

Arlana scowled. "How should I know? It isn't as if the old horny ever showed hisself to me." She cocked a dark brow. "Not the Almighty, either—and me a white witch. Don't you forget it."

Mona shook her head. "But you said—"

"Never you mind what I said. What's the matter with you, girl? Have you never told a lie?"

Mona placed her hands firmly on her hips. "I don't lie."

"That much is clear. That's why you found yourself on the gallows with a noose about your neck." She snorted, shaking her head and pulling a wooden bowl near. "She doesn't lie! Imagine that!" She pointed the pestle at Mona before smashing it into the bowl. "Thank the good Lord that I do lie, or you'd be swinging in the breeze, lassie!"

Mona's hand crept up to her neck and she grimaced, massaging the suddenly sensitive skin. "I am to be your apprentice?"

Arlana glanced meaningfully at the cold logs. "Not if you cannot even get a fire going."

Mona leapt into action. Once the fire was blazing, she lowered herself onto the floor beside Arlana. "I owe you my life. I will do anything you wish, but please tell me what you want from me."

Arlana set the bowl aside, the contents—herbs or roots Mona was unfamiliar with—now ground to a fine red powder. Her round cheeks were flushed from the exercise of pulverizing the substance. "I have long watched you, Mona Musgrave."

Mona put a surprised hand to her chest but didn't speak. Since she was a very small child she'd heard stories about Arlana. She was the keeper of an ancient stone, the Clachan Fala. She was a white witch, immortal. She'd been alive forever. She was feared and respected in the village, her name spoken in hushed whispers. That Arlana had been watching Mona Musgrave was a shock.

Arlana's penetrating gaze took in the play of emotions across Mona's face, and she nodded slowly. "Yes. I had my eye on you when you were but a wee lassie. I'd marked you as the one to take my place. But then you fell in with that foolish Edwin and ruined my plans."

Mona had the strangest urge to apologize, but held her tongue. How could she be sorry for something she'd never been aware of?

"But now he's gone. The union scarcely lasted two years. You're seventeen, a good age to begin—better than fourteen, methinks, which is when I became the apprentice Keeper. I understand now that Edwin was part of the plan."

Mona blinked. How could being married to Edwin be part of anyone's plan? Visions of his twitching face, his fierce eyes, his impassioned outbursts—him holding her under the water until she went limp—all these things bombarded her, and she shook her head incredulously, her face twisting with the effort to shut the memories away.

Arlana's lips only pursed and her eyebrows raised. "Oh, yes. It is a solitary life I lead, you see that. But it must be that way. No men are allowed to know the secrets of the Clachan Fala—except the chosen one. You . . ." Arlana waved a hand, gesturing at Mona's body. "Men are drawn to you. You would have eventually been tempted, and then all would have been lost. But now, after Edwin, I suspect you want nothing to do with men."

Mona shuddered, a trembling revulsion filling her. But it was accompanied by a deep ache. She desperately wanted a child. Just one. And for that, she needed a man. But Arlana was right, Edwin had convinced her that it wasn't worth it.

"You're right. I have no interest in ever marrying again."

Arlana smiled and nodded, content. "Ah, good. You are right to reject that life. It's not for you—I saw that long before you did." She pointed a fleshy finger at Mona. "Men are responsible for slipping a noose about your neck. Men fear a woman strong enough to take matters into her own hands and rid herself of a worthless, abusive husband. You terrify them—so they tried to kill you. If there is a devil, he lives in the hearts of men. Oh, they don't know it, and some of them look to be angels in the flesh, but they will suck your soul away and throw it out like trash. To be the Keeper, you must have your soul intact. Is your soul intact?"

Mona frowned, unsure how to answer. She searched

within herself, feeling certain that Edwin had taken nothing but her innocence and trust, and they were not her soul. They were only remnants of the child she once was. "Yes, my soul is intact."

"Good. Do you want to be my apprentice? To one day be the Keeper of the Clachan Fala?"

Mona opened her mouth to give an affirmative answer, then closed it, confused. The gratitude she felt toward Arlana was enormous, but she wasn't sure what the Clachan Fala was, or what, as the Keeper, she would be expected to do.

Arlana gave her a cynical smile. The fire, now blazing, cast her face in a red light, making her resemble a grinning goblin. "Not so grateful now that the noose is gone."

Mona's head snapped up, deeply insulted that Arlana would doubt her integrity. "I will be the Keeper. I will do all that you teach me."

A cold smile spread over Arlana's face and her eyes grew flat. "Good. Now forget everything you've ever learned about right and wrong. It no longer matters where I will take you. It is a world that only women can understand. Men have no place in it. The men of this world think only they understand loyalty, courage, honor, duty—but they know nothing. I've given my entire life to protect the Clachan Fala, and if I had my life to live over again, I would repeat it."

Mona leaned forward, entranced by Arlana's words. "The Clachan Fala . . . what is it?"

Arlana smiled and leaned back, settling her enormous bulk about her, adjusting the colorful skirts over her round knees. "This is how it begins. My master, Merry Musgrave, first told me the story, and now I pass it on to you. There are two rules you must never forget. The first is that nothing I tell you is to ever be written down." Arlana tapped a finger against her forehead. Her nails were stained bright red. "It all must be in here. You will commit it to memory, every word, and when I'm gone, you will find an apprentice and begin anew."

Mona nodded. "What is the second rule?"

"You tell no one but your apprentice what I teach you."

"No one?"

Arlana's eyes narrowed. *"No one.* There are many who think they already know a great deal and they'll want to know more. They'll try to make you tell them. You mustn't give in."

Mona nodded, chilled by these rules.

Arlana reached into her bodice and brought forth a beaded necklace. She cradled it lovingly in her palms, gazing down at it with soft eyes.

"This, my child, is your new lover. The *iuchair.*"

Mona was surprised to find herself reaching eagerly for it. As the cool beads slid between her fingers, she closed her eyes. The air about her instantly chilled, as if a cold breeze whipped about her, stealing her breath. In her mind she opened her eyes and saw things—the mountains and valleys of the Highlands. Heather covered peaks, standing stones . . . a bleak and unforgiving island blasted by wind and the sea. It was as if she were a bird in flight, soaring high above the land. Mona gasped, an inexplicable longing welling up inside her. She'd been there, a thousand times, though she'd never left the English West March in her entire life.

Mona opened her eyes and met Arlana's knowing gaze.

"Do you now understand?"

Mona smiled slowly, realizing she'd finally come home.

1

Lord Ridley Graham searched Graham Keep for his step-mother, growing increasingly frustrated at his fruitless efforts. She was supposed to be watched at all times, but the man he'd set on her had only trembled and whispered that she'd escaped him hours ago and he'd yet to locate her. She was making this too difficult. He'd finally managed to rid himself of his brother and sisters, however temporarily. He'd hoped that without their interference he could finally convince Mona that she truly was better off with him.

Stepmother. He nearly sneered at the thought. She was five years younger than his three and thirty and the most exquisite creature he'd ever laid eyes on. He'd never accepted her as his stepmother. Ridley had found her first. He'd wanted her first. But his father had staked his claim, and like everything else, Ridley had been powerless to do aught but stand aside and watch.

But his father was dead and he was no longer powerless.

He stepped into the cook's garden, the sight of Mona settling his agitated soul. He stood back, wanting only to watch her for now. She'd always shunned the finery Hugh

Graham had tried to bestow on her. Even now, when she should be in mourning, she disdained Hugh still. Ridley loved her for it.

She wore a dun-colored kirtle smudged with green stains and a forest bodice. The long, creamy sleeves of her shift were rolled to the elbow, and her fine hands encased in leather gloves as she dug industriously in the garden.

Her hair, a silken ebony so dark it shone nearly blue in candlelight, was piled on top of her head, fat curls spilling down to nuzzle her cheeks and nestle against her neck. Ridley longed to run a hand over the smooth soft skin of her nape. It called to him and he stepped forward. But he stopped, hands clasped hard behind his back.

She would not welcome his touch. She never did. He didn't understand it, though he tried very hard. Part of him wanted to blame it on his father. Hugh had ruined her for all men with his violent lusts. But he knew that wasn't entirely true, for even before Hugh had met Mona, she'd rejected Ridley. And she did not fear his displeasure—in spite of all Hugh had put her through. She had the heart of a lion and yet she was nothing. A commoner, a widow, a healer. Ridley had lifted her out of her common life and tried to give her something better, and she resented him for it.

He was young, handsome, and a lord. Why could she not return his love? He'd given her everything, with promises of more. He worshipped her, treated her like a queen. How could she reject such a life? A life sought after by the daughters of lords, dreamed of by lesser women.

As he watched her, she seemed to sense his growing enmity. She turned hesitantly, enormous black eyes resting on him. Pools of deep water at midnight. The long black lashes that framed her eyes made her look innocent, a startled doe, not fully aware of the danger he posed. Her full pink lips tightened imperceptibly. Most wouldn't notice, she guarded her feelings so well, but Ridley had studied her for many years, openly and covertly. Hiding in her chambers to see her naked body. Following her wherever she went. He knew every expression, every blemish, every scar on her body intimately, and yet her heart was closed to him.

She didn't rise as respect demanded. Instead, she rubbed her gloves together. Dirt sprinkled to the ground. She removed the gloves methodically, still kneeling in the dirt and herbs, and laid them purposely on her lap.

"What is it, Ridley?" she asked, not looking at him. She caressed the leaf of a plant with her bare fingers. He would give anything for her to touch him in such a manner.

"You're hiding from me."

He watched her profile for some reaction, but her eyes never left the plant. Her nose was small and straight, her delicate features ethereal in their beauty.

"How is tending my herbs considered hiding?" She stood and faced him. The air was chill but she wore no cloak. The odd beads she wore about her neck peeped out from the embroidered neckline of her shift. They were important to her, these beads. They belonged to someone she once cared for a great deal. Ridley hated them, wished he could destroy them. But he wasn't a fool. She'd not just disdain him then, she'd hate him.

She wasn't far from hate now, he feared. She loved Ridley's brother and sisters deeply. She'd tried to mother them all after being forced to marry their father—and she'd succeeded with Caroline, Wesley, and Fayth. She'd even tried to befriend Ridley. But Ridley hadn't wanted her friendship—not unless it came with her body and her heart and soul. He'd scorned the scraps she'd thrown him, and so she'd stopped trying.

"You're angry at me," he said.

"What you're doing is wrong." She tried to walk past him, into the keep, but he caught her arm, reveling in the feel of her soft flesh beneath his hand. This close he could smell her hair. Rosewater. The faint scent of herbs clung to her clothes. Even in the weak sunlight her hair shone like a polished stone. He touched a curl that nestled against her neck, letting it twine about his finger.

"Leave off, Ridley."

She always said that. She always denied him what should be his right. His father had taken it from him. But Hugh was gone and she should be his. He refused to release her. They were alone. The servants knew better than to disturb him when he was with his stepmother. Only his siblings dared, under some mistaken idea they were protecting Mona from him. As if she needed protecting. He would never harm her, would never allow anyone else to harm her. He *loved* her. Why could no one see that? Understand it?

"I thought you agreed with my decision to marry Caroline to Lord Annan."

She'd been the only one who had. It had been an ugly time at Graham Keep. The Eden Grahams had been in a blood feud with the Annan Maxwells for centuries—since the disappearance of a disputed family jewel, the Clachan Fala. Hugh Graham had kept the feud thriving in his lifetime. But when Hugh passed on, Ridley proposed a peace to the new laird, Robert Maxwell. They sealed the peace with a marriage, Ridley's sister Caroline to Lord Annan. Caroline had been opposed; she'd always planned to enter a convent. Fayth and Wesley had fought him as well for defying Father's wishes.

But Ridley was their lord and his will was done.

Mona's lush black lashes rose until she pinned him with an accusing stare. "I agreed because I knew Caroline would find happiness with Lord Annan. But I don't agree with your reasons. You care nothing for Caroline's happiness or peace. You only want one thing."

She was not entirely wrong. It was true he'd not married off his sister for peace. He'd married her because according to legend, it was a condition that must be met. A Graham of the Eden grayne must wed a Maxwell of the Annan grayne. Only then would the Keeper bring the Bloodstone forth. And like his father before him, Ridley believed Mona was the Keeper.

But the Clachan Fala was not the only thing he wanted.

"You're wrong," he said, pulling her in front of him and placing his hands firmly on her shoulders. "I want you."

"I am your stepmother. What you propose is a sin." It was the same response she always tossed at him. Meaningless.

"My father forced you to marry him. You never loved him, nor he you. You bore him no children. I think that was God's judgement on the union. It was wrong." He pulled her closer, forcing her against him, pressing his cheek against her fragrant hair. "What we could have is right. God would bless us with many strong children."

"Bastards, you mean. You cannot wed me."

"I would defy the king and the church if you would have me."

She planted her palms firmly against his chest and pushed, putting a few inches between them.

"I am a widow and I mean to remain one. Forever." Her mouth was set in a firm line, but it was still beautiful and he wanted to kiss her. He lowered his head, halting when she grabbed his ear and twisted.

He released her abruptly and stepped back, yanking his throbbing ear from her fingers. He scowled down at her, but her sternness disappeared.

"Ridley, I beseech you, let me go. I cannot help you. I cannot give you what you want." She took a step toward him, palms out in supplication. "Be the brother I know you could be. It's hidden somewhere in your heart. Do not force Fayth to wed Lord Carlisle, he will abuse her. She will never be the same."

"Good!" Ridley's youngest sister was the most unruly, contentious little harridan ever born—and Father had adored her. Ridley hated her for that alone.

Mona shook her head emphatically. "No, not good! You already hurt her heart by forcing her to deceive her sister—and the reward you promise is naught but a castle in the air."

Ridley grabbed his stepmother and shook her. "Did you tell her this?"

Too much of his plans rested on Fayth trusting him and doing her job. If she even suspected Ridley had lied to her, it could ruin everything.

"I tried, but she wants to believe you. *I* want to believe you."

The disappointment in her eyes and voice struck him to the heart. "I will honor my promise if you give me the Clachan Fala. I will let her marry the stable boy if that's her fancy. It's within your power to make that happen."

She shook her head, averting her eyes as if she couldn't bear the sight of him. "I have no power. I wish you could understand that."

She had more power over him than she knew, more than he would ever admit to her. If she had shown him a shred of the love he felt for her, he'd fall at her feet and give her anything she wanted. But she couldn't even do that.

"When Hugh died, I promised to take care of his children—that was the last thing he asked of me." She met Ridley's gaze again. "And that includes you. I want nothing more than your happiness. Fayth's happiness. Caroline and Wesley's happiness." Her hands came up to grip his forearms. "You don't know what you seek. The Clachan Fala will not bring you happiness. It will not fill the hole inside you. Only you can fill it, through kindness to others."

"I have always been kind to you."

She rolled her eyes and spun away from him. He let her go.

"No, what you show me is not kindness. It is obsession. Manipulation. It is selfish."

He couldn't argue that. He'd first discovered her seven years ago. Hugh had always had a keen interest in the legend of the Clachan Fala. He loathed the Annan Maxwells—especially the then-laird, Red Rowan. He'd wanted to find the Bloodstone and flaunt it in his enemy's face. He'd been collecting tales over the years, which had led them to a small village that the Keeper was said to frequent.

Hugh had sent Ridley to investigate. It had been Ridley's lucky day. He'd only had to ask a few people before he was directed to the bakers, where Mona had been speaking to the baker's daughter. There had been women before Mona, but none after. She was all he wanted. He'd tried to court her, but she'd wanted nothing to do with him. He'd finally taken her to Hugh. It had shocked no one more than Ridley when Hugh raped her and forced her to the altar. And he hadn't even loved her. All he'd wanted was the Clachan Fala, and he'd believed that as his wife she would eventually give it to him.

Ridley had never loved his father, but Hugh had lost his respect that day. Seven years later, his feelings for Mona had only grown. And now she was free and he was Lord Graham. And still it changed nothing.

This time, when she passed him, he let her go. He stared blankly at the herb garden for a long while, his mind filled with thoughts of Mona, thoughts of the Bloodstone. She was wrong, it could bring him happiness. According to legend, the stone protected all who possessed it. He would be fearless and undefeated in battle. He would be honored by the king and grow rich in lands and titles. Then she would not refuse him. He would keep her as his mistress—refuse to marry her as punishment for her rejection.

It was slow in coming, but his calm was finally restored. Someone cleared his throat behind him, and Ridley turned. The man he'd set on Mona stood beside him, wringing his hands, sweating in the cold.

"M-my lord? I found her. She's in her chambers."

"Really?"

The man's head bobbed hopefully.

"You're removed from that duty. I will find someone more competent."

The man's face paled, his eyes filling with tears. *What a weak piece of dung.*

"I have a new task for you." Ridley turned to the herb garden and gestured to it. "Rip up all the plants and trample them."

Escape. Mona had to escape somehow—but not alone. A woman alone would never survive where she must journey. She needed protection. She needed a man. The irony was not wasted on Mona. She prided herself on being needed—not needful, and certainly never needful of a man.

But this was an extraordinary circumstance and it called for unusual—and perhaps repellent—tactics. She toyed with the beads around her neck, her mind turning back to the enormous Scotsman rotting in the bowels of Graham Keep. Sir Patrick Maxwell. He was a great knight, she'd been told. She'd visited him on a few occasions, to assess him. He seemed worthy enough. But Ridley had set a new spy on her, and he was more diligent than the last.

Mona left her chambers. She passed the empty chambers of her stepchildren, and her heart ached. How she missed them. She'd come to them seven years ago, one and twenty and fresh from the loss of her own mother figure. She'd needed them as much as they'd needed her. And now they were gone. She would see Caroline again, of that she was certain, but she might never again see Fayth and Wesley, and it broke her heart.

Mona hurried on to the highest point in the castle, a high turret, and waited until she saw Ridley ride through the gates with a host of men. Gone to work off his aggression. Just like his father, though both men would be loath to admit it. It was why Hugh had despised his son. He'd believed that Ridley contained all his faults and none of his virtues. Her heart ached for the poor boy deprived of his father's love. Hugh had been wrong about his son, but it was too late to change anything. Hugh was dead, and Ridley refused the comfort of friendship.

Mona strode back to her own chambers and retrieved a key, hoping she wouldn't need it. *Let the prisoner be honorable.* Hidden beneath a floorboard with the key were a clean set of clothes, a loaf of fresh bread, a fat candle, a blanket, and a book. She placed them in a canvas sack and threw on her hooded cloak. The new man followed her, but no more skillfully than the last. She lost him in the kitchens and took the secret ways through the castle until she reached the entrance to the dungeons. She waited in the shadows until she was certain her new shadow was truly gone.

A man-at-arms guarded the door, alert, lance held at his side.

Mona stepped out of the shadows. "Greetings, Ned."

"Good evening, my lady," Ned said, bowing and blushing beneath the shag of his dark beard. " 'Ere to see the prisoner again?"

"Yes, may I?" She always asked, though she knew he wouldn't refuse her. His wife was pregnant now after years of a barren womb, and Ned attributed it solely to a philter

Mona had given them to partake of together. He felt he
owed her a great debt.

"For you, anything."

Mona smiled though she knew that for a lie, even if he
didn't. His gratitude had limits. He might let her see the
prisoner, but he would not aid her in releasing him. He
opened the door.

As she passed him, she placed a hand on his sleeve.
"You'll tell no one I was here?"

"On my honor."

Mona descended the stone steps. Torches placed at in-
tervals lighted the stairs. Mona removed the bottom torch
and took it to the nearest cell, fitting it in the sconce beside
the door. Sir Patrick was currently the sole prisoner in the
dungeons. Others came and went, but he remained.

As she expected, by the time she turned, the Scotsman's
dirty bearded face was pressed to the bars.

"You again," he said, his voice cracking and raw. "Why
do ye keep coming?"

"I brought you this." She held up the sack.

The eyes narrowed, their color clear even in the dim
torchlight. The finest cerulean, like a gemstone. Misty as a
morning sky. The eyes of an angel. The kind of eyes Arlana
had always warned her about.

"He's different," Mona assured her mentor, long dead
now, but always with her in memory.

"Who's different?" the prisoner demanded. His beautiful eyes were at such odds with his face—masked by a
wild curling beard that must have once been blond but was
now brown with filth. If he proved to be the one, she would
have to clean him up.

Mona flushed, embarrassed she had spoken aloud and
glad for the hooded cloak that shadowed her face. "There
is food in here and a book—are you lettered?"

"Why do you keep bringing me things?" he growled, ignoring her question.

He was very suspicious, though she knew that if she turned to leave, he would beg her to return and be very civil. He was always like this in the beginning. The solitude made him difficult.

"I need something from you."

"Oh, aye?" He cocked a brow wickedly.

"Sir Patrick Maxwell," she said sternly, attempting to remind him of who he was and his place in the world. His knightly title impacted him not at all—the lascivious gleam didn't disappear. "I need a lock of your hair."

He frowned. "My hair?"

"And nail parings, too, if you please."

"What? Why?" His big fists released the bars as he stepped back, receding into the darkness of his cell. She could no longer see his face through the bars.

No doubt he considered her the worst of witches and thought she meant to cast a spell on him. Well, there was no help for it. She did not intend to explain herself. If he did indeed prove to be the one, she would reveal much to him. But she wouldn't know until she got his hair and nails.

She opened the sack and began to pull the items out, holding them up for his inspection. "I brought many things to ease you."

He still didn't return to the bars. She replaced the items in the sack.

"If you come to the door, I will cut your hair and nails, then pass the sack to you."

There was a long silence, then he said, "If you want my hair, lassie, you'll have to come and get it."

So he would make a game of this? She tried not be annoyed. He'd been a prisoner of the Grahams for nearly a year and kept in the dungeon for six months of it. He was bored and angry. And yet something told her he could not hurt her. Still, this was nothing more than a bid for freedom.

"I'm not a dolt. If I go into your cell, you will incapacitate me—perhaps even kill me and try to escape." She cocked her head, listening to his silence. "But you won't get far. I've friends here who know what I plan. They wait."

"Then why didn't you bring them—to help you take my hair?" His voice was sarcastic. He knew she bluffed.

"Very well," she said, sighing. She gathered up the sack and returned to the steps. She was halfway up the stairs before she turned, angry he wasn't calling her back. The window of his cell was dark.

Her heart beat wildly with fear, but something deep inside didn't believe he was capable of hurting her. He was a knight. He was honorable. So he had debauched a servant? He was only a man after all, incapable of controlling his lusts. So he had nearly killed the woman's husband? The man had tried to kill him first. It was only instinct to defend oneself. Mona believed all these things, even though Ridley had condemned him as dangerous and stuck him in this hole. He was not dangerous.

She removed the key from her bodice and returned to the door. It was locked with a heavy chain and a padlock. Mona had made this key years ago in case she ever locked down here.

"I'm coming in. If aught happens to me, Lord Graham will see you gutted like a pig."

"Think you I'd hurt a mere woman?"

Mona hesitated. "No. But I think you want freedom very badly. I can give it to you if you show patience. That's why I need your hair."

"You'll help me?"

"Yes."

"When?"

"Soon, I vow it." And saying that, she knew she would free him even if he wasn't the one. She did not make promises lightly.

He came back to the door, eyeing her suspiciously. Relieved, Mona hid the key in the folds of her cloak. He would cooperate now. No need to enter his cell.

His eyes narrowed. "What are ye hiding, lass?"

Mona shook her head innocently.

His face closed up and he receded into the darkness again. "Go away."

Mona's shoulders sagged. He was too clever by far. "I'm coming in. Will you give me your word that I will come to no harm?"

"Aye," the voice drifted to her through the door.

"Then give it."

"You have my word I'll not harm you."

Mona slipped the key into the lock. When the chain and lock were on the floor, she pulled the heavy oak door open as wide as it would go.

"There's no way out of the dungeons," she called into the shadowy darkness, "but for the door at the top of the stairs, which is locked and guarded. If you will help me and be patient, I'll arrange your escape."

There was no answer from the prisoner. The skin on Mona's arms prickled, unwelcome memories of her first husband, Edwin, invading her thoughts. He used to hide like this. *Just like Edwin, he is. They all are,* Arlana's voice whispered in her head. *Sir Patrick is not like Edwin,* Mona insisted and stepped into the cell.

A hand seized her neck, another snaking around her waist. Her face and chest were crushed against the wall, a body solid as granite pinning her there. Her cheek pressed against the damp stone, her eyes staring wide into the dim light from the open door, breathing in the faint, metallic odor of the mold that coated the stones. The blood pounded in her head, a scream lodged in her throat. *Just like Edwin.*

"You're verra trusting, my lady," Sir Patrick's smug voice whispered in her ear.

"You gave me your word!" she choked out. She tried to control her fear. Boldness and courage disarmed most men.

"I'm a desperate man."

"You are a knight! Have you no code of honor?"

That made him laugh. "Oh aye—my code is The ends justify the means. The end is freedom and you, my sweet lassie, are the means."

"I *will* help you escape. I gave you my word."

"Then help me now."

Mona shook her head. "I can't. The guard will never help me . . . but I can arrange it if you'll just let me."

He was quiet behind her, his muscles quivering with violence. Mona closed her eyes, praying he would do the right thing. She must assert her authority before this went any further. She forced herself to speak.

"Give me the hair and nails."

He laughed, his breath stirring the hair beside her ear, the sound rumbling through his chest and into her back. "And do ye plan to rip it from my head?"

No, she'd brought a knife, strapped to her thigh. But he was wise to her, his hands already rucking up her skirt, one large hand sliding up her knee. She grabbed at his wrist, trying to stop him, but he found the knife.

She trembled now, truly afraid. He slid the knife slowly from the sheath on her thigh, his fingers trailing unnecessarily against her bare skin. She shuddered, unused to being touched so intimately. The silver blade glittered before her face, orange in the torchlight spilling through the open door.

"Are ye afraid?" he asked.

"No," she said, pleased her voice was steady and clear.

"Ye should be."

"You gave your word I would not be harmed."

He was quiet behind her, the even rise and fall of his chest against her back. He pushed away from the wall abruptly, freeing her. Mona turned cautiously only to find the knife offered to her, hilt first.

She looked from the knife to his eyes, but his expression was unreadable. Faced with him, she was intimidated. He was enormous—nearly a head taller than her and broad and solid as a mountain. His hair was shoulder length and his beard a thick tangle. He wore a doublet, torn and stained, with no shirt beneath it. His breeches were in similar condition, and he had no shoes.

"It's a wonder you aren't ill," she said, accepting the knife and shaking her head. "One moment." She left the cell and returned with the sack. "Here are clothes—please have them on when I return tomorrow to free you. It will make our escape easier."

He took the bag from her hesitantly, frowning all the while, eyes darting to the open door. She must be quick, before he changed his mind.

"Kneel, please."

He became very still.

"You're too tall. Kneel so I may cut a lock of your hair."

He did as she bade, never taking his eyes from her face. She approached him, fear and resolve warring in her heart. She reached out and gently touched his hair, sifting through it for a lock that wasn't filthy. Beneath, near his nape, the hair was the color of golden sunlight. Mona cut it cleanly and slipped it into a pouch at her waist.

She held her hand out. He cocked a brow, looking from her hand to her face.

"Your hand, sir, so I may trim your nails."

He rubbed his hand self-consciously on his filthy breeches before placing it in hers. His hand swallowed hers, broad and muscular, the palm rough with calluses. She gently examined the nails. Dirty, but not unkempt. He'd apparently attempted to groom himself. She trimmed his nails and released his hand. When she gestured for his other hand, he frowned.

"How many do you need?"

"I have what I need, I just thought it would make you feel better."

He put his hands behind his back and rose to his feet, stepping away from her as if she were the dangerous one. He eyed her warily. "Why me?"

Mona placed the nails in her pouch and went to the door, shutting it behind her. She replaced the chain and the padlock. When she was finished, he was at the barred window, watching her.

"Because you are a great knight. Because you have honor. And . . . I trust you."

He stared at her incredulously. "Have ye gone soft in the head?"

She smiled, pleased all had gone well. "Perhaps."

He didn't return her smile.

"Until tomorrow, Sir Patrick," she said, and left him alone in the dungeons.

Mona sat cross-legged on her bed in her nightshift, bed curtains drawn and door locked. A single taper sat in its holder beside her. The curling lock of hair lay on the blanket before her, tied with a piece of string. She'd carefully washed it in the basin earlier and spent an absurd amount of time admiring the golden color in the fading sunlight. The nail parings had also been cleaned. She removed one of the beads from the iuchair, the string of beads passed on to her from Arlana. Though they did constitute a map to the Clachan Fala, they had other uses as well.

She held the items in her palm and asked for an answer to her dilemma. Could she survive without a protector? And was Sir Patrick Maxwell the one? It was such an important decision, not to be made lightly or without aid. How she wished for Arlana's counsel, though she knew they would only argue. According to the old witch, no man was to be trusted. She would advise Mona to do this alone. And yet Ridley's behavior toward her was proof she was not safe alone. He'd destroyed the herb garden today out of spite. She must have a man, however distasteful the prospect.

Mona put the objects in the pouch, held it tightly between her palms, and asked, *Is Sir Patrick a match for Ridley?* His reputation preceded him and was the reason Ridley had held him for so long. He was a great warrior. He'd served the French and Austrian kings. He'd fought the Turks and the Spanish. He'd even served in the king of France's personal guard. And on his infrequent returns to Scotland, he rode with the Annan Maxwells in many highly successful raids. In fact, when word was out that Sir Patrick was in the country, the Maxwells' enemies began madly fortifying their homes against attack, usually to little effect.

Such skill would be essential to stop Ridley. But was it enough? Ridley was cunning, moved in ways that were not clear. He was acquiring much land on the West March and arranging marriages for himself and his sisters. Mona knew this had to do with the war King Henry threatened to bring down on the Scots, that Ridley felt these things would help him accomplish something, but she didn't understand what.

More importantly, Ridley believed in the power of the Clachan Fala—that it would protect him from all harm. Seduced by the legends, he was determined to have it at any cost. The uneasiness returned at the thought of the Bloodstone. Always it had been something distant, unattainable. Only one Keeper had ever been charged with fetching it, and she had almost immediately returned it to hiding. How could such an instrument not overcome even the purest heart?

And that brought Mona to her last question. When the Bloodstone was finally in her hands, what would Sir Patrick do? Would he be seduced by its power? Or could he be trusted to help her deliver it to his brother, Robert Maxwell, Lord Annan? *A love match betwixt a Graham of the Eden grayne and a Maxwell of the Annan grayne will bring it from hiding.* The iuchair had told her Caroline found love with Lord Annan. The time had come.

Mona blew out the candle and crawled beneath the blanket, sliding the pouch beneath her pillow. She lay her head upon the pillow and asked for her dreams to reveal her path.

Patrick spent the night alternately berating himself for being a softhearted fool and trying to convince himself the woman was sincere. He might be free now! She was insane—or worse, evil. And he had let the opportunity to escape slip through his fingers.

Of course, if he'd attempted to escape, he might also be dead. He knew the dungeons were guarded at all times and that the men-at-arms were well trained and armed to the teeth. Though he'd done his best to keep his body exercised and ready for anything, the months in the dungeon had taken their toll. Some mornings the cold seeped into his knees and elbows, the now mended bones aching and stiff. Old wounds, long healed, were causing him discomfort. But he would be ready for anything if—no, *when*—she returned. He spent endless hours pacing his cell and pulling his body up on the bars until his arms trembled with fatigue. Tonight he worked himself to near collapse. It had been too long since he'd been with a woman, and the scent of Lady Graham, the silken feel of her thigh, had captured his imagination. Useless thoughts for a solitary prisoner.

When he finally fell asleep, the dreams came. It was the battle of Mohacs tonight.

The Hungarian king charged across the marshy bank of the Danube, splashing into its overflowing waters, lords and knights following. Patrick was certain taking warhorses onto boggy ground was a bad idea, but the melee confused him, having previously only fought in border skirmishes. Fighting the Turks turned out to be a different matter entirely and so, when his commander had fallen, he followed King Louis into the river.

The water was shocking, the current nearly sweeping him off his mount. The horse balked, trying to retreat back to the bank, but hands grasped at Patrick's legs, his saddle, pulling him off, into the rushing river. His armor was too heavy, dragging him under. He sunk to the bottom like a boulder, fear straining his lungs. He struggled to remove his mail shirt and swam for the surface.

Sunlight penetrated the water in shafts, but all Patrick could see was the churning of legs: horse hocks and booted, greaved legs, blocking his way to the surface. To air. To life. He fought his way upward, lungs close to bursting, but the hooves and feet kicked him back down. He saw the face of Isaac float by, bloated and blue, grabbing at him, forcing him down in the watery grave.

Patrick fought to wake himself. *A dream! A dream!* He was sitting up in the cold cell, bare-chested. The fat candle Lady Graham had brought him still burned. He'd shredded his doublet and flung it across the room in his sleep. His chest heaved, the bread and water he'd consumed hours ago threatening to make a reappearance.

Isaac. Bloody hell! He fought to put his old friend from his mind. Patrick couldn't think of Isaac without deep sadness and such feelings were pointless. They weakened him. He'd once had many friends, Scotsmen who'd come with him to fight the Good War against the Turks. But they were all dead. Trampled and drowned with King Louis in the Danube. He'd soon learned that was the way of things. It had been years since he'd had a friend.

He forced his mind away from Mohacs—away from battle. He called forth the face of Rosemarie, the soft blond curls, the wide blue eyes, the smile like sunshine, and his heart calmed. It had been more than a year since he'd seen her, and yet his longing had grown. In his memory, she was all that was good and warm in the world. He must get out of here, if only to look upon her again.

He stood, reaching for the shirt the dowager Lady Graham had brought him, and shrugged into it. He went to his cell door and stared out into the dark corridor, praying the beautiful widow would not abandon him.

2

Patrick no longer had any concept of night and day. He assumed day was when he received his meals. It seemed an eternity since the boy had passed gruel, bread, and ale to him through the bars of his cell door. He'd flipped through the book Lady Graham had brought him, uninterested. A treatise on warfare. He'd read it years ago—it was useless, written by a sniveling boob who'd never bloodied his hands in battle. He ripped several pages out and wadded them up, then used the candle she'd brought to light the pile. He held his hands over it, but it provided little warmth and soon petered out.

Patrick sighed deeply, elbows on knees, head resting on his crossed forearms, and thought about his spark of hope: the beautiful Graham widow, rumored to have bewitched Old Man Graham into wedding her. Patrick doubted witchcraft had been involved. It was probably nothing more than base lust and the desire to possess such a stunning woman. He'd heard, when he was still held in guest quarters, that Hugh didn't allow his wife to leave the castle grounds without him and even then accompanied by a heavily armed escort. There were some that said she'd been the death of the old laird. And when Hugh was gone, they whispered about the widow and her stepson, that they lived in sin, that she bewitched the son just like the father.

However, Lady Graham's *affaires d'amour* didn't concern Patrick. What did concern him was the interest she'd taken in him. That in itself wasn't so unusual. This wasn't the first time he'd been locked in a dungeon, and it wasn't likely to be the last. It was, however, his longest confinement. He'd escaped all his previous prisons with the help of a woman. They always seemed intrigued by Scots warriors. But they were also predictable. In the end they all wanted the same thing.

In this respect, Patrick sensed Lady Graham was different. She wanted to use him as surely as the rest, but he did not understand what she wanted to use him for. Once she freed him, she would expect repayment—some sort of service. That was what left the heavy lump of misgiving in Patrick's gut. He wanted it to be simple so he could be on his way. Unfortunately, nothing about the dowager lady appeared simple. She was vastly troubling, more so than any other lass he'd encountered.

She was a rare beauty, and he wouldn't be adverse to a bit of dalliance if she'd a mind for it, but there was something about her that reeked of danger if he stuck around too long. Patrick didn't like dangerous women. His idea of the perfect woman was one already wed to a rich old man—all she wanted was a bit of a tumble and then a quick farewell. He thought of Rosemarie and knew that even women like that could be dangerous.

The door at the top of the stairs creaked open. Patrick's muscles tensed, but he didn't rise as he usually did, for the sound wasn't followed by the slam and click of the lock reengaging. He strained his ears but didn't hear the shuffling step of the boy who usually fed him.

His heart was racing when the husky whisper drifted to him.

"Sir Patrick?"

He closed his eyes, sending up a silent prayer of thanks, and went to his rescuer.

"You came." He stared down at her through the bars in his door.

She wore a hooded cloak, so he could barely see the fine lines of her face, her large dark eyes. She unlocked the padlock and carefully laid the lock and chain on the floor so as not to make any noise. She started to open the door, but Patrick pushed it wide. She stepped back quickly.

"You came!" he said in a loud whisper, advancing on her, his heart nearly bursting with excitement and relief.

She continued backing away from him, slowly at first, until she realized he meant to grab her. She stumbled trying to escape him, but he caught her around the waist, determined to show her how pleased he was. The hood of her cloak fell back, briefly showing him the panic in her eyes before he lifted her and kissed her soundly on the mouth. It was a brief kiss, though hearty enough, but she didn't respond at all.

She blinked dazedly, gripping his shoulders. "Put me down."

He set her on her feet, grinning down at her. "Just wanted to thank ye, my lady."

"Well." She ran a hand over the silky black hair, in a thick plait that disappeared into her cloak. "You're quite welcome—but you may thank me later." She started to turn, then faced him again. "*Not* like that, however."

Patrick nodded dutifully, waiting for her instructions. She'd come for him! He couldn't believe it. Though he'd tried to convince himself she might help him, he hadn't truly believed it.

She returned to his cell door to fetch a sack she'd brought with her. "There's a cloak in here, as well as boots and a dirk. Please put them on."

Patrick complied, glad to have the weight of a weapon in his hand. He covered his head with the hood.

She viewed him critically, fine black brows arched. Her skin was the color of cream and looked soft as silk. He couldn't discern the color of her eyes in the dim torchlight, but they appeared velvety black, with a thick sweep of sooty lashes framing them. Jesus God, she was a sight for a man deprived of feminine comfort. It had been a very long time since he'd had a woman—longer than he'd been the Grahams' prisoner. They all thought he'd seduced the steward's wife. He'd certainly tried, hoping to gain an ally who would help him escape. He'd nearly been successful, but not quite, damn it all. But Lady Graham was making up for that failure.

"This would be simpler if you weren't so tall."

"I canna do aught about that, though you're the first to complain."

"Oh, I'm not complaining," she said hastily. Her voice was rough, husky, and low pitched. It sent the strangest shivers over him every time he heard it. Though she didn't speak as coarsely as a commoner, her speech nonetheless lacked the edge of refinement. "Your height will do nicely for my purposes," she continued. "But you draw attention to yourself being so . . . so . . . enormous." Her eyes traveled over him again, wide with disbelief. "Your poor mother . . . did she live through your birth?"

"Oh, aye—and both my brothers as well. They're taller than I am."

Lady Graham shook her head and turned away, obviously thinking hard. Finally, she shrugged. "It cannot be helped. Come."

Patrick followed her up the stairs. The door stood open

at the top. The guard was slumped against the wall, a cup on its side beside his outstretched hand. When Patrick hesitated, wondering if Lady Graham had poisoned the man, she sought his hand in the folds of his cloak, pulling him along after her.

They passed into narrow, musty corridors. Cobwebs heavy with dust fell from the walls and ceiling. Lady Graham held the candle high but didn't seem to need the light to find her way. Her slender hand remained firmly in his, leading him down stairs and finally outside, into the fresh air.

She paused outside the door they exited to survey the area. Patrick was glad for the respite. The effect of freedom nearly overwhelmed him.

It was night. Stars shone in the black sky. The moon was full. Cold air blew over his face, cleaning months of filth and stink from his lungs. He closed his eyes, breathing in, his knees growing weak, his eyes burning. He resisted the urge to fall to the ground and kiss it, to spread his arms wide and bellow with pleasure. He had to remind himself that he was not yet free.

"Come," Lady Graham's husky voice urged, and she tugged his hand.

The back of the castle was strangely deserted. Even at this hour there should have been some activity. He caught a whiff of fresh bread from the bakehouse, but there were no signs of life.

He discerned a glimmer of silver on the battlements and pulled Lady Graham against the bakehouse wall. She was silent, watching him as he waited for the man-at-arms to complete his circuit and disappear.

"All right," he whispered.

She smiled as if she were immensely pleased with him and led him swiftly across the courtyard. They followed the wall that surrounded the castle until they came to a deeply recessed postern door. It was barred with a heavy slab of wood and locked. Beside the door rested two large sacks. She released his hand to shove a sack at him. Patrick was amazed at its weight, but said nothing. What was inside? He tried to assess the lumps within.

Lady Graham reached into her bodice and pulled out a key. "You first."

Patrick moved past her and hauled the bar from its slots, setting it quietly aside. He went back to the entryway and scanned the courtyard while she unlocked the door. He frowned into the deserted darkness. Where was everyone? He knew Ridley Graham to be diligent, so why was the guard currently so lax?

"Sir Patrick?" Lady Graham called softly.

He turned to find her beckoning him in the open doorway. There was something sinister about her cloaked figure that filled him with foreboding. Patrick felt foolish for hesitating. He could think of no reason she would deceive him in this. This was freedom! He would be a fool and a coward to let a woman spook him.

He went to her and gathered the bags. There was another wall and another door they had to pass through, but Lady Graham had the keys to the castle. At the back of the castle there was a pool of rancid water, which they skirted around before hurrying across open ground, making for a bit of brush in the distance.

They collapsed behind the bushes. Lady Graham was breathing hard, her hand pressed to her chest. The hood had fallen from her head and her cheeks were flushed, her eyes wide. Ebony curls escaped from her plait to curl about her face. Patrick peered through the bushes but saw no sign of pursuit. Torches lit the battlements. Two men-at-arms paced the west wall.

Patrick gazed up at the moon and the cloudless sky.

They hadn't even the benefit of the ubiquitous fog to cloak them, and still not a Graham had detected their escape.

"Did you poison everyone? Or place a spell on the castle?"

She laughed softly. "Nothing so fanciful. Only a bit of my Bittersweet Buckthorn wine. My own special recipe."

"Remind me not to drink any." He knew buckthorn was a powerful purgative, but he was unaware of bittersweet's properties. He was sure the combination was highly unpleasant. "We should keep moving," he said, still frowning at the castle.

Lady Graham nodded and got to her feet. Patrick started moving north when she caught his cloak.

"No, this way." She pointed to the west.

"But my home is this way."

Her hold on his cloak was tenacious and she yanked at it, bringing him back to her side. "You will go with me now. We must talk—but not here!" Though her voice was low and husky, there was a thread of steel in it.

Patrick didn't like her tone or being ordered about. But he did owe her a great deal—for more than this escape. He owed her for the comforts she'd brought him for more than a month now. It rankled to be so beholden, but he relented, scowling irritably.

The smile once again graced her mouth, small and satisfied. She tugged him along, and he followed, like a dog on a tether. The more he thought about the analogy, the more annoyed he became. He liked it not. Great lords and kings had tried to cleave him to their sides and failed. This little witch didn't stand a chance of success.

But damn it all, he owed her.

They walked for hours in silence, until the sun began to rise. Lady Graham stopped, staring at the empty land behind them.

"Can we talk now?" Patrick asked.

Her delicate brows pulled together, lining the fine skin of her forehead. She really was a beauty, and he felt a deep stirring in his lower body. Small white teeth sank into her plump bottom lip as she apparently thought hard on whether they should stop.

"No one is following us, my lady. I'm sure of it. Besides," he slid his hand over her back, turning her back to the west, "you can tell me why you helped me escape while we walk, aye?"

"Very well," she said. "But I won't feel safe until we reach the forest."

"Is that it?" he asked as they walked swiftly. "Am I to see you safely somewhere?" That could be simple enough. Then again, what if she wanted to go to Wales or Ireland?

"That's exactly what I want, Sir Patrick."

"Where am I to take you?"

"I can't tell you that."

Patrick stopped.

Lady Graham continued on a few paces before turning to face him. "This is why I wanted to wait." She came back to him and grasped his arm. "Prithee, Sir Patrick, we must keep moving!"

Patrick refused to budge. "I'm not moving until I know where I'm going."

"Must you be stubborn? Can you not trust me?"

He shook his head incredulously. "No, I dinna even know you, except that you're a witch."

"Oh, stupid man! Ridley will not rest; he will come after me! We cannot just stand here!" She kept looking behind them frantically.

Patrick made a rude sound. "Bitterbuck wine or not, he let us go. That was no escape."

Her eyes grew wide with shock. Staring into them he

saw their true color. A deep brown, almost black. He'd never seen such large, dark eyes.

"What mean you?"

"Lord Graham is no fool, my lady. Our escape was too easy, even if your wine sent them squatting on the privies all night. He let us go . . . well, you at least. Perhaps he didn't count on my being with you."

She blinked, as if unable to comprehend his words.

Exasperated, Patrick said, "Why would he keep you prisoner? You're his stepmother. A widow and a free woman."

She shook her head at him as if he were a simpleton. "If what you say is true, I need you more than ever. Tell me, in all your military experience, did you ever have to hide from someone?" Before he could answer, she rushed on. "Because that's what I think we must do—hide. For maybe a sennight, or a month. I don't know, long enough to make him think he lost us and go home. Yes, that's—"

"Oh no," Patrick said, shaking his head vigorously and holding his hands out in front of him, as if to ward her off. "Hide for a month? I canna. I have somewhere I need to be."

"What?" Her hands were planted on her hips, her mouth set in an uncompromising line. "What commitments are you making while rotting in a dungeon, sir? And if I hadn't released you, how did you expect to ever meet them?"

Patrick tried a placating smile. "And I thank ye, my lady. You've done me a fine service and I owe ye a great debt. I'd be happy to see you to safety, so long as it takes less than a fortnight."

She stared at him as if he'd grown another head.

He reached out and touched an ebony ringlet that curled against her cheek, then brushed the backs of his fingers against her skin. She was soft and warm and so very lovely. Mayhap it was the effects of his confinement, but he thought perhaps she was the most beautiful woman he'd ever seen. "We can work something else out, if you'd rather."

She was utterly still, eyes locked on his. She pulled her head back, her expression cold. "You will not touch me, Sir Patrick."

His fingers were still suspended between them. He closed his hand in a fist and let it drop.

"There is nothing else to work out," she said, taking a step away from him. "But I will discuss nothing here."

Patrick glared down at her, anger at her stubborn finality warring with the need to get away. Already he felt as if a trap were closing on him again. "Fine. Let's go to this forest."

She nodded, her expression enigmatic. "Once there, I'll tell you everything you need to know."

He caught the subtlety of her words. *Everything you need to know.* The urge to abandon her was strong. He didn't want this—he didn't even want her anymore, not since she'd made it clear she didn't welcome his touch. When he still stood there, she took his elbow and coaxed him forward.

"Come, sir. You'll feel much better when you're clean and fed. I'm sure it will seem perfectly reasonable then."

"Very well," Patrick said, suspicious and filled with discontent, but he let her lead him west.

Gilford gathered up the shattered glass littering the floor. Lord Ridley Graham swept by again in his rage, and Gilford cringed, fearful the next object to shatter would be his head. But Gilford had done nothing to displease his master. It was the captain of the guard who would bear the brunt of Lord Graham's rage.

There was a brief knock, and Lord Graham stopped his pacing, pivoting toward the door, broken glass crunching underfoot. "Enter," Lord Graham called, his voice so calm and controlled that Gilford jerked and cut his finger.

The servant popped his finger in his mouth, peering up at Lord Graham uncertainly. He still could not accustom himself to his master's mercurial mood changes. Hugh had been so different, so predictable. Gilford had known just what pleased the old laird, as well as what angered him, and he'd acted accordingly. With Ridley Graham no one knew . . . except the dowager, and now she was gone.

The door creaked open and Brodie Armstrong entered. A Scotsman, but one who had served Hugh Graham faithfully for more than a decade. He faced the son of his old master with pale, clammy skin. Gilford felt sorry for the man, for he suspected what was coming.

It was well known in Graham Keep that Lord Graham harbored an immoral lust for his stepmother. It had been common knowledge before the old laird died. Hugh had known it, and though he had confided in few people, he'd done so in Gilford. He'd known what would happen when he was gone—had known and had let it occur. Ridley had sold off his sisters, deprived his brother of the beasts and capital Hugh had bequeathed him, and now lusted openly for his widow. But Hugh had also known Ridley would succeed where he had failed. That the Eden Graham line would not die out but grow strong and powerful because of Ridley's greed. *He'll stop at nothing to get the stone. Nothing. I have my limits, Gilford. Ridley . . . he has nothing to lose.*

Gilford cleaned up the rest of the glass, his deceased master's words still ringing through his mind. *He has nothing to lose.* Gilford hadn't understood at the time. To a common man like Gilford Graham it seemed Ridley had a great deal to lose. But now that he served Ridley, Hugh's meaning was clear. Ridley's heart was blackened and bitter with envy. He felt all that he already possessed was worthless, never enough. It was nothing to him.

"The prisoner has escaped," Ridley said to Brodie, his voice pleasant, conversational.

Gilford stood quickly and retreated to the back of the room, his cloth full of clinking glass shards.

Brodie's eye twitched. "Aye, my lord."

Ridley spread his hands. "Help me understand how this could happen."

Brodie swallowed. "My lord, ye said to let Lady Graham escape. I couldna stop him withoot stopping her."

"You could have hewn him down with an arrow or a well-placed lance."

Brodie's eyes seemed to bulge. A fine sheen of sweat broke out over his nose. "But . . . my lord . . . Lady Graham never would hiv left him there to die. She might hiv been hurt." The captain seemed to bolster himself and said in a firm voice, "My lord, the lady needs protection, she canna roam the countryside alone. Sir Patrick will see to this, surely—"

"Protect her?" Ridley said, his voice rising. "Protect her? I will protect her! Do you think I would let her roam alone? Do you think that?"

Brodie opened his mouth, confused, and finally shook his head.

No one knew Ridley's mind, though Gilford assumed he'd set a new spy on her tail, to watch her. Brodie was slowly coming to this realization as well, his eyes widening, his skin going a shade paler.

"Do you think she is safe with that fool? He will brutalize her!"

"I will go after them and kill him, my lord."

"And then just leave her to go on her way?" Ridley smiled sardonically. "Oh, she'll not be wise to me then, will she?"

Brodie stepped forward, resolved now in his decision.

"No, my lord, she wilna. I vow it. She is a good, kind woman . . . I will pretend to be smitten with her. She has helped me afore, so I do owe her—"

When Ridley stepped back, surprised and incredulous, Brodie hurried on. "I owe a much greater debt to you, my lord. I will slay Sir Patrick, and when she begs me to let her go, I will grant her wish."

Lord Graham seemed to consider this. The rigid lines of his face slowly relaxed, and he inhaled deeply. He was pleased, though Brodie would never know it. Gilford had served Ridley long enough to recognize the subtleties.

"I have a better idea," Ridley said.

"My lord?" The Scotsman stepped forward eagerly.

"You will follow them and wait for Sir Patrick to accost her—and he will, he's a Scotsman, after all."

Brodie winced at the insult but continued to nod.

"You will then kill Sir Patrick. She released the prisoner for a reason. She feels she needs protection on her quest. A good protector is not an easy find. She knows you, and if she feels you are beholden to her, she will try to engage your services. Do not be easy, but eventually, relent."

"I will leave immediately, my lord!"

When Brodie was gone, Ridley didn't move. He stared at the closed door, hands fisted at his side. Gilford hesitated, wondering if he should offer him refreshment or just keep his mouth shut. When blood began dripping from his master's clenched fists, Gilford set the broken glass aside and went to him.

3

The forest was dark and familiar, comforting to Mona. She was still far from her true home, as the largest concentration of Musgraves lived farther south, but this reminded her very much of the dense wood where she had once made a home with Arlana.

Her knight was still in a foul humor, though he remained silent and cooperative. She did not enjoy his delicate temperament or having to appease it. She also feared his honor wouldn't extend to all aspects of his life. The way he looked at her, with such heated intensity, was disconcerting. When he looked at her like that she recalled the feel of his fingers trailing along her thighs when he'd disarmed her in the dark cold of his cell.

"There is a stream near where you can wash."

The cerulean eyes stared at her, devoid of even the gratitude she'd become accustomed to. He looked at her as if she were a distracting insect.

Soon the bubbling of the stream could be heard and his step quickened, passing her. When the water was in sight he shed his garments, leaving a trail behind him. By the time he stepped into the water he was completely naked.

He was the biggest man she'd ever seen. Heavy chested, with round, bulging muscles on his arms and back. His thighs were heavy and thick, his waist narrow and his belly flat and lined with muscle. His skin was not as pale as many prisoners who'd been deprived of sunlight; it had a natural dusky hue. His broad chest was furred with golden blond hair, as were his arms and legs. He was also covered with a distressing amount of twisted scars. They covered him, many of them jagged and painful to look upon. He had been poorly tended after his battles. Odd, crescent-shaped marks covered his back.

He looked over his shoulder at her. When he saw that she stared at his back, his mouth flattened. "Never seen a man who's been trampled by warhorses before?"

Mona shook her head mutely. She should look away. It was unseemly to stare at his body with such interest. He was still filthy, the water he splashed over his body doing little to remove months of grime. Mona opened her sack and brought forth a ball of soap.

"Sir Patrick! Look what I brought."

When he saw the soap, his frown disappeared and he flashed her a smile. She tossed him the soap and he caught it easily, turning away from her.

While he washed, she laid out the other things she'd brought for him, clothes and weapons she'd bought or stolen from Ridley's men-at-arms. She was well pleased with her knight. The iuchair had advised her well. *The iuchair.* She must consult it to determine their next move. She glanced at him again and had to tear her gaze away from his back, beautiful in its strength. In the cover of the trees she could barely hear the sounds of his bathing. She knelt and removed the beaded necklace, holding it in her hands.

"Show me," she whispered, eyes closed.

A bird called above her and then she was soaring, high above the trees. The wind chilled her as she glided, weightless. The forest went on forever it seemed, miles and miles of thick foliage. She dove into the trees and saw a cottage and a young girl running about, carrying a wooden horse. Nearby was an ancient oak with markings carved deeply in its trunk, worn and smooth from weather and time.

"Lady Graham!" Sir Patrick called, irritation clear in his voice.

Abruptly Mona was sucked back into her body. It took a moment to orient herself.

When she returned to the clearing beside the stream she found him standing over the garments she'd gotten for him, rubbing his hair vigorously with a bath linen.

"Linens, too?" he said sarcastically.

Mona shrugged. It would be a long and difficult journey; there was no reason she couldn't travel in relative comfort.

Mona tried not to stare at his body. She'd seen many naked men before; he shouldn't be any different. Unfortunately, it was clear that something about him *was* different. Her cheeks flushed, and her breathing came so short she felt light-headed. What was wrong with her?

"You couldn't get your hands on my armor?" he asked.

When she chanced a look at him, she was relieved he'd put on the breeches she'd brought him. The bath linen was draped around his neck, covering much of his upper body, though she could see the ridged muscles of his abdomen.

"What about horses? Are we to walk the whole way . . . wherever it is we're going?"

Mona was disappointed he wasn't pleased with the jack and sword. "I don't know what Ridley did with your armor.

This was the best I could do, and I thought it wise to be inconspicuous—this is what all borderers wear."

He flashed her a look reminding her that he was a borderer and knew that.

"It was most difficult to find a jack that would accommodate your bulk. I bought this off a very fat man."

The look he gave her was withering.

Mona cleared her throat nervously, wishing for some way to please him. It had all seemed so simple just yesterday. He was a great knight. He would be so grateful to her for rescuing him. He would insist on giving his life to serve her. He would be courtly and kind, admiring her from a distance. It was true that she'd never met a man that remotely fit that description. Most of the knights and borderers she knew cared for nothing more than plunder and rape. But Patrick was supposed to be different. He'd fought on the continent under the king of France. She tried not to let her disappointment in him show.

"Get dressed and I will shave you and cut your hair. Then we'll talk."

He rubbed the linen over his curly beard, eyeing her suspiciously before finally nodding.

Mona dug a wood box from one of the sacks and went to the water's edge to await him. Soap from his washing clung to the stones in the stream. A squirrel crept down from a tree to investigate the opposite bank. Mona wandered along the stream, searching out any interesting plants. It was late in the season, but she always looked.

She felt a presence behind her and turned. Sir Patrick stood behind her, the collar of his white linen shirt open. He eyed her with boredom. He didn't want to be here with her, that much was clear. Mona didn't understand. She had rescued him, shouldn't he be eager to repay her?

"Prithee, kneel," Mona said, fetching her shears.

Sir Patrick glowered at her. "Did you bring the whole damn castle wi' ye?" When she didn't respond, he muttered, "I'm not carrying all that rubbish."

Mona gritted her teeth and ignored his grousing. It was hardly rubbish. It would serve them well where they had to go. She removed her cloak as he finally got onto his knees, grimacing like an old man.

"What ails you?"

"My leg."

When she frowned with concern he shrugged dismissively. "It's naught—it broke about five years past. It still aches when it rains."

Mona looked up at the canopy of branches. The sunlight filtered through, and it looked to be a clear day. When she looked back at him quizzically, he grinned, and she noticed that his teeth were very straight and surprisingly white.

"Och, fash not, lass, it'll rain. Mark me."

Mona said nothing and grabbed a handful of damp beard, shearing it off close to his face. He stared at her breasts. She could almost feel the heat from his eyes. Her cheeks and neck burned, and her mouth went dry. When she had shortened his beard considerably, she moved behind him with some relief, to tend his hair. It was a challenge to hide her disturbance—her hands trembled. This was absurd! Ridley had been leering at her for years and she'd been able to ignore it—why should Sir Patrick be any different?

She hated to cut the long, golden waves, but he was a warrior and they would only hamper him, so she chopped them off and trimmed the soft blond locks close to his head. She ran her fingers through his hair to check the length, enjoying the sensation of clean, damp hair against her fingers, until she felt more knobby scars along his scalp. She parted the hair to look closer. One of the wretched hoof marks was barely visible.

"Do you not wear a helm when going into battle!" She circled him and stopped before him, hands on hips. She caught her breath. Though he still needed a shave, he was devastatingly handsome. Like an angel, his face was. His jaw was wide and square, his brows well formed, his wide mouth turned up at the corners in a natural smile. His nose was a bit large and crooked, as if it had been broken several times. It was a face one trusted and depended on. It was a face few people could say no to.

And he was speaking to her.

"I'm sorry," Mona said, shaking her head as heat crept up her neck. What was wrong with her? She'd never been so affected by a man's countenance before. It must be the contrast between dirty prisoner and shining knight. He was a thing of dreams now.

"What were you saying?" she asked, her voice weak.

"Aye, I wear a helm going in, but whether it stays on my head or not isna always up to me."

Mona fetched the razor from her wooden box and turned to him.

He looked from the razor to her, then held out his hand. "I'll do it."

"You don't trust me?"

His smile was humorless. "I don't trust anyone."

"I would not hurt you."

His gaze darted to the razor, eyebrows raised. "Give me the razor or I stay bearded."

"You *can* trust me, Sir Patrick," she said, but she handed him the razor, unhappy that he was so suspicious. She grabbed her sack and climbed the bank. It was midday. They would eat and then continue deeper into the wood. They must keep moving until they reached the cottage the iuchair had shown her. It would be a good place to hide from Ridley. She rummaged through the bags. She'd packed dried meat, cheese, fruit, bread, and skins of ale and water.

When Sir Patrick finally joined her, she had a meal arranged on a handkerchief for him. He handed her the wooden box and sat on the log, studying the meal. His face was ruddy from shaving, and blood trickled down his jaw beside his ear. Mona wet a kerchief in water and went to him, dabbing the blood away.

Predictably, his brows lowered in irritation. He jerked his head back.

She gripped his chin firmly, turning his head so she could continue her ministrations. "Even the smallest cut can fester, Sir Patrick. It is neither brave nor manly to be so foolish."

He expelled a breath but held himself still, jaw clenched, body rigid with tension.

"Why do you behave so?" she asked, inspecting the cut critically. It was fairly deep but small. She didn't think stitches would be necessary. "Surely you aren't unaccustomed to the touch of a woman?"

One blond brow quirked imperceptibly, and before she knew what was happening a large arm slid around her waist, pulling her closer.

"Well, if I'd known ye had something else in mind, I'd let ye touch me as much as ye like." His voice was low, his heated gaze burning a trail from her breasts to her face.

She shuddered, something warm coiling deep in her belly. Fear? She was reminded of the men in her past and their demands on her body. This was what Arlana had warned her about, why she'd felt Mona must do this alone. But Mona had been dealing with this sort of behavior for years. She could certainly manage Sir Patrick.

She braced her hands on his shoulders and pushed away. "That is not what I had in mind."

He let her put some space between them, but his hands

remained on her hips, kneading. He regarded her as if he didn't believe her, his gaze finally coming to rest on her mouth.

Mona's heart sped, her skin prickled warmly. "I-I'll buy you a whore if you wish."

His hands dropped away immediately and he sat back on the log, staring at her with wide, disbelieving eyes. "Ye'll buy me a whore?"

Mona almost slapped her hand over her mouth, unable to believe she'd said such a thing. Finally, she nodded. Of course she would! If it would save her from his unwanted attentions and keep him happy, it was worth it. The last thing she wanted was another Ridley pawing at her constantly. She just had to keep him at arm's length until they reached a village.

He still stared at her. He opened his mouth as if to speak, then closed it in consternation. She backed away from him, letting out a deep sigh of relief. She'd never met a man who so unsettled her with his nearness. A quick inventory of her person told her she'd broken a sweat—even Ridley wasn't troublesome enough to make her overwarm. A small part of her was annoyed her offer had so effectively subdued him. It was clear it wasn't she who interested him—any female would suffice. Why should she care? She didn't, she assured herself—it was vanity that made her belly turn with an odd queasiness.

Arlana's voice whispered in the back of her mind. *He's the devil. He'll be your undoing, lass.*

"He is not the devil," Mona muttered under her breath.

True, that's giving him too much credit.

Mona chuckled.

Patrick looked around the forest, then back at her. "Are you talking to me?"

Mona's cheeks burned. "No, of course not."

"Then who, pray, were you speaking to?"

"No one . . . just an old friend. She's dead now, but we were very close, and, well . . . sometimes I hear her voice."

He stood. "Ye hear voices?"

"No! I know she's dead. It's me . . . speaking for her. Please sit down and eat, Sir Patrick."

He looked extremely unsettled, but he sat. He took a bite of the meat, never taking his eyes off her. "What did she say about the devil?"

Mona smiled blandly. "Nothing at all."

"You're lying. It was amusing—you laughed." When Mona didn't respond, he scowled and said, "Here we are. I'm clean and shaved. Out with it. I want to hear it all. Why did you free me? What do you want with me? Why west?"

Mona sighed and sat near him—but out of his reach—and began to eat. She'd known she'd have to address this and had been putting it off. She knew now that if he didn't like what she said he would not help her. She broke her cheese into pieces while she framed her thoughts, trying to determine the best way to present the story to him.

He rubbed at a scar on his chin, watching her.

"Eat, sir. You must keep your strength up."

He took a hearty bite of bread, staring at her expectantly. "We can sit here all day. I'm not moving until you tell me everything."

Mona fixed him with a grave stare. "I need you, Sir Patrick. Please consider all I have to say very carefully, for it impacts not only you and me, but your family and all of Scotland."

He frowned in mock seriousness. "Indeed."

"You think I jest." When he opened his mouth to protest, a slight smile deepening the corners of his mouth, she said, "Or that I'm just a foolish woman. But you're wrong."

"Then tell me."

She held his gaze for a long time, until he raised his brows and prompted her, "Aye?"

"You have heard of the Clachan Fala?"

Sir Patrick groaned and dropped his head into his hands.

"I see you have. I also see you doubt its existence."

"I suppose you'll tell me it's real and that you're the Keeper, aye?"

"That is exactly what I'm telling you. Hugh Graham took me from my home and married me against my will to learn the secret. His son held me for the same reason. But Ridley is far more ruthless. He was willing to marry his sister off to his sworn enemy, something Hugh refused to do. Your brother, Robert Maxwell, Lord Annan has been wed to Caroline Graham, Ridley's sister."

"And now you must fetch the stone?" Sir Patrick continued eating, showing more interest in the food than Mona's story.

"Yes. However, it was never as simple as Ridley thought, for the marriage must be a love match, not an arrangement."

"So, Rob and Lord Graham's sister are a love match?"

"Exactly."

"And how would you know? They canna have been wed but a few weeks."

Mona reached into the neck of her shift and drew out the iuchair, cradling the beads in her palm. It was as if a cool breeze blew over her; she felt Arlana's presence and all the Keepers before her, guiding her. "I consulted the iuchair. It revealed the truth to me."

"Oh, well then," he said. "That explains everything."

She did not rise to his bait, staring back at him with complete calm and confidence. It was important for him to sense her conviction, it would give him courage and purpose, help him believe in her and her cause. She very much needed him to espouse it with his whole heart.

He wiped his mouth and took a drink. "Why me?"

"Ridley wants the Bloodstone more than anything—"

"Why?"

Mona paused, wondering how much to tell him. Most stories transformed the stone into a weapon unparalleled, but it was not a weapon. If used properly, it was an instrument of peace. Though Mona had her doubts that anyone's heart was pure enough to use it properly, it was not for her to decide. She was only the Keeper. She wondered which would coerce the knight—the truth or the legend? But Arlana had forced her to promise. *You must tell no man.*

"You've heard the legends of King Arthur? You know that the scabbard for his sword, Excalibur, protected him from harm in battle?"

Sir Patrick shrugged.

"The scabbard was stolen, never to be seen again. But before it disappeared forever, one of your ancestors, an Annan Maxwell, tried to recover it. He was only able to bring back a single ruby. This Arthur presented to him on his wedding day. His bride was of the grayne that would one day become the Eden Grahams. But the bride's family was a greedy lot and wanted the stone for themselves. They massacred the Maxwells and stole the stone. Arthur's magician, Merlin, charged the Musgrave women with keeping and protecting the stone. And so, they entered Graham lands and stole the Clachan Fala. They have kept it hidden ever since . . . only one Musgrave Keeper has ever had cause to remove the stone from its hiding place."

"That was sixty years ago."

"Yes. Malcolm Maxwell and Elizabeth Graham—a love match. But once again the Grahams' greed ruined all, and the stone was returned to its resting place."

He had finished his meal and was inspecting the palms of his hands.

"Sir Patrick, would you let the Grahams succeed again?"

He looked up at her, surprised. "Me? I'm not the Keeper, what have I to do with it?"

"But I am. And I cannot do this alone. It's dangerous for a woman alone on the border. And if you're right and Ridley let me go, then things are worse than I thought. He has probably set a spy to follow me, believing I will lead him to the Bloodstone."

When he only stared at her helplessly, she gave him her most appealing look. "I need you, Sir Patrick. Your brother and sister-in-law need you. Their unborn child needs you."

Sir Patrick stood abruptly and circled the small clearing where they ate, rubbing the back of his neck. He came to stand behind the log he'd vacated. "How long?"

"For someone who's been imprisoned nearly a year, you're certainly short on time."

"I have commitments that are long overdue."

"What will another few months matter?"

"Months?" He shook his head, pacing away from her. "It matters to me."

Mona clenched her fists, desperate now. She must have him—there was no one else. The dreams the iuchair sent her were clear. It must be him. *No! No men,* Arlana argued. *He will ruin everything.* Mona ignored her.

"Tell me, Sir Patrick, what you want. What can I give you?"

He crossed his arms over his heavy chest, staring at the

ground, brow furrowed, as if it were a truly weighty decision. "That's not it. You've done enough."

She stood and went to him. "There must be something you want."

"What I want you can't give me."

Perhaps he wanted comfort. Most people were that way, though they didn't realize it. Men especially couldn't distinguish between wanting someone to understand them and rutting. Her husbands had taken her body involuntarily many times; she knew how to detach herself from the act. The Clachan Fala was more important than the physical body that contained her. It was more important than her life. Arlana had given her entire life for it; Mona could surely give her body.

She touched his arm gently until he looked at her. "Maybe there *is* something I have that you want."

"No, really, you canna help me."

"Sir Patrick," Mona said urgently, running her hand up to his shoulder. "Are you certain?"

His head turned slightly, a blond brow arched speculatively. "Oh, I see . . ." His heated gaze roamed over her from head to toe, lingering on her breasts, but he made no move to touch her.

"Well?" she whispered. Her heart beat painfully in her chest, her skin tingling with anticipation. Perhaps it wouldn't be so awful with him. He was so very handsome, and something about him drew her.

"That's . . . uh . . . a verra fine offer, but uhmm, no. My thanks."

Heat rushed to Mona's face, but she didn't look away. Her fingers curled into his leather jack. "A moment ago you were ready to tumble me."

"That was afore ye offered me a whore."

Mona dropped her hand and stepped back, her face burning like a fire in full blaze. "You'd rather have a whore?"

"What I'd rather have is a willing woman." He took a step toward her, towering above her. Mona fought the urge to retreat. "You, lass, canna even fake it."

"Fine." Her face felt brittle, like a mask that would shatter. "I'll buy you a dozen whores if it pleases you." When he was silent, she said in a harsh tone, "Does it please you?"

Sir Patrick sighed. "No, my lady, it does not. You think very little of me, aye? That I'm a stag in rut? I canna control my urges—so long as ye let me work it off I'll be docile and good?"

"What? Of course not." Mona tried to sound indignant, as if she'd thought no such thing, but he gave her a reproachful look.

"I have brothers. They're verra honorable men. They'll take care of you, I vow it. They're good at such things. Come with me to Annancreag." He winked. "And I promise they're not stags in rut, like me."

Sweat trickled between her breasts from her complete mortification. How had she managed to botch this? *Stag in rut?* She'd apparently even insulted him. She spread her hands before her, pleading. "You, too, are honorable, Sir Patrick. I've misjudged you. Please forgive me. I must have your help—*it must be you.*"

"My lady—"

"Prithee—I am Mona to you."

"Mona, I'll take you to safety if you wish, but I canna spend months chasing after a magical stone."

Mona dropped her hands to her sides, defeated. She turned away, back to the canvas sacks. "Go then. I'll do it myself."

As you should have all along! Look what a waste of time he was!

"He was not a waste of time."

Sir Patrick came over to stand in front of her, looking around the trees. "You're not talking to me, are ye?"

Mona ignored him and began stuffing her things back into the sacks.

"I can't leave you. I must see you to safety."

Mona faced him. "No, you mustn't do anything, as you have made abundantly clear. Please, tend to yourself, don't let me divert your thoughts another moment. I don't want to burden you."

He had the gall to look annoyed. "Come now, you're acting like a bairn. Do you always get your way?"

Mona thought she might explode. Never had anyone frustrated her so completely. "This is not *my* way! This is bigger than both of us. But you can't see past your own selfish needs. Go away!"

He didn't budge. He looked miserable and just as frustrated as she was. Good, she hoped he stewed in misery.

Mona bent back to her packing. "I don't want you anymore. Arlana was right, you're a waste of my time."

"Who's Arlana?"

When her sacks were packed, Mona swung her cloak over her shoulders, trying very hard to ignore the man glowering resentfully at her. She gathered up the sacks, dismayed at how heavy they were, and trudged off through the forest.

She didn't hear his footfalls behind her, and her heart sank. But she kept on. It didn't matter. She had to do this, with or without him. She tried to convince herself it would be easier without him. As she walked, her throat grew thick and her eyes burned. He was supposed to be the one. She had believed in him. Tears of disappointment blurred her vision. She hoisted the sacks higher over her shoulders, sniffing loudly, when suddenly their weight was lifted.

She stared in amazement at Sir Patrick's sour countenance as he settled the sacks over his shoulder.

Her smile grew as she stared up at him, unable to hide her joy. His honor had won out. He was a good man. He was the one.

He looked away, his expression hard and unyielding. He jerked his head to the west and started walking. "Let's go."

4

They traveled several days through the forest. Lady Graham was polite and uncomplaining, though Patrick drove her hard. He did it on purpose, walking fast and stopping for little rest. He hoped she would come to the conclusion they were not well suited for this partnership. If she was having such thoughts, she kept them entirely to herself. But then again, he did not encourage conversation. He avoided looking at her and answered her in monosyllables. Thus far, she appeared not to notice. She talked to herself more than she talked to him.

The nights were the worst. He slept little, afraid he would cry out in his sleep from a nightmare. Though he was eager to prove what a poor choice he was, he was not looking to unman himself. After all, she was still a lass, and a beautiful one at that. She'd made it clear she did not welcome his advances, and so he'd made an effort to detach that part of himself. But it was most difficult. He couldn't stop thinking about her thighs. Her skin was the softest he'd ever touched and probably the most beautiful—if only he could catch a glimpse.

It was nearly full dark when they finally encountered a cottage. It sat in a small clearing, surrounded by thick forest. Patrick had suspected on several occasions that they were lost, but Lady Graham had assured him repeatedly she knew exactly where they were headed. He also suspected she was much more afraid of him than she let on. She constantly fingered the beads about her neck, a nervous habit surely.

The cottage was closed up tight against the chill. Mona rapped sharply on the door. A dog barked hysterically.

"Who's there?" a woman shouted.

"Mona Musgrave."

The door opened immediately, revealing two women, one young, struggling to hold back the snarling beast, and one old. "My lady . . ." The old woman trailed off, pinning Patrick with a hostile stare. Both women were bulky from their layered clothing. Caps fit close on their heads, hiding their hair.

Mona stepped forward and took the old woman's gloved hands. "Gayle, it's been so long. I've missed you."

The old woman—Gayle—tore her gaze away from Patrick and gripped Mona's hands back, her lined face folding in on itself. "Oh, lady—how we've missed ye!"

They embraced warmly. Mona's hand snaked out to include the younger woman, who watched with tear-filled eyes. The three embraced for an eternity. Patrick tried to be patient, but just watching all this hugging made him uncomfortable. The dog had calmed and now crept forward, nosing Patrick cautiously. He held out his palm for it to sniff. It was a mound of black shag—even its eyes were covered with hair.

Mona stepped back, wiping tears from her cheeks. "Where is Jilly?"

"I'm here." A tiny girl stepped from behind the older women's skirts. She looked up at Mona shyly.

Mona crouched before the child. "My, how you've grown. Are you happy here with Gayle and Hazel?"

Jilly's chin bobbed, her gaze traveling up to stare at Patrick. Apparently, she didn't belong to either woman. He nodded at the child, his heart squeezing painfully. Seeing the child brought back memories of Rosemarie, commitments he'd made to himself that he was not honoring. He didn't want to be here. The need to escape the noose Lady Graham choked him with descended with sudden and painful clarity. She was his gaoler as surely as Ridley Graham had been.

Mona looked up at Patrick, smiling. "This is my friend, Sir Patrick Maxwell. He travels with me and protects me."

They were not friends. She knew nothing about him— that was clear by her proclaiming him "honorable." He did not want to be her friend. He did not want to protect or travel with her, and the last thing he wanted to do was spend the night in this henhouse.

"Sir Patrick," Mona was saying, "these are my friends, Gayle, Hazel, and little Jilly."

Patrick mumbled a greeting as the women stepped aside, ushering them into the warmth of the cottage. He set Mona's bags of junk near the door and flexed his hands and shoulders. The jack she'd acquired for him was big in all the wrong places and too tight through the shoulders. He left the top unhooked so he had a normal range of movement.

The women soon had them seated before the fire with bowls of barley stew and fresh bread. Patrick was ravenous. Mona had provided well for them and always made sure he had plenty to eat, but he was sick of hard bread and dried meat. He blocked the women's chatter out, focusing on his meal and the fire's warmth.

"Before Hugh found me he thought Gayle was the Keeper." Mona's small soft touch on his forearm alerted him that she was speaking to him. It was gone immediately.

"Aye?"

Mona nodded, forcing him to make eye contact with her. It was obvious she was trying to draw him into the conversation. Normally, he would have preempted her attempt with stony silence, but there was something about her eyes. She was not afraid of him here, in this place. There was a warmth to her that she'd kept from him these past few days, and it gave him pause, made something ache deep inside him.

"Yes. He kidnapped her. He kept her much as he did me, though he didn't wed her."

"Lady Graham saved me," Gayle said, gazing at Mona with adoration. "When Lord Graham realized his mistake, he turned me out with nothing. I couldn't go back to my family, but Lady Graham gave me money and clothes, and sent me here to live." Gayle reached out to grab Hazel's hand. "And then she sent me companions."

Jilly popped up from the floor. "I'm a companion."

Patrick nodded as if this were quite profound. "Aye, that ye are."

"You'll stay with us?" Gayle asked, turning to Mona and grasping her hands.

"Yes. I was hoping we could stay for a sennight or—"

"Tonight," Patrick said, wiping his mouth. "We leave in the morning." He looked around the cottage. "I dinna suppose you have some horses ye'd care to part with?"

The old woman shook her head, eyeing him with distaste. Mona's displeasure was also clear. He could almost feel her withdraw from him, and he clenched his jaw, annoyed that he even noticed, let alone felt a pang of disappointment. Let her be angry—perhaps she would send him away. He doubted that would be the outcome. No, she'd want to discuss it with him later. Rather than annoying him, a spark of anticipation ignited in his belly. He returned her look with studied boredom before looking away. That was sure to irritate her.

"What brings you this way?" Hazel asked, her curious gaze straying frequently to Patrick. Her face was comely enough. Patrick guessed her to be Mona's age—mid-twenties, perhaps.

"I cannot tell you," Mona said. "But I have a favor to ask."

"Anything, my lady," Gayle said.

Mona smiled gratefully, and Patrick noticed she hadn't touched her food.

"If anyone comes looking for us after we've gone—"

"I won't tell a soul I saw you," Gayle vowed.

Mona shook her head. "No, please do—tell them we stayed with you. But when they ask in which direction we are headed, tell them south."

"South?" Gayle repeated.

Mona nodded.

This led to a discussion on the proper footwear for long journeys. The women chattered nonstop, Mona only picking at her meal. Patrick resisted the urge to remind his companion she needed food to give her strength. What did he care if she ate or not? He wasn't responsible for her.

The little girl, Jilly, edged closer to him through it all, watching him with wide eyes. He found her charming, which was troubling.

When Patrick finished eating, he left the cottage. Though he appreciated the warmth of the home, he'd begun to feel stifled, closed in. He walked to the edge of the clearing and leaned against a tree, breathing deeply of the cold night air. How had he gotten into this mess? Women were trouble—and this one especially. And now he was bound to her indefinitely. Why hadn't he just walked away? Bloody Christ—she'd sent him away! But damned if he hadn't felt like the worst sort of knave. He'd vowed, as he sat in Ridley Graham's prison rotting, that when he got out, he would be a better man—for Rosemarie. But he couldn't go to her knowing he'd abandoned the woman he owed his escape— and perhaps his very life—to. He was trapped. Resentment simmered.

Patrick looked up at the sky, imagining it was the same sky Rosemarie saw from her window in the Chateau Aigues. These thoughts weighed him down with loneliness, reminding him of all he'd given up, of all that he could reclaim if he could just get away from Mona.

The hair prickled on Patrick's arms. He wasn't alone. Hand on sword hilt, he stiffened, turning. He scanned the clearing and the wood behind him and was about to turn when something tugged on his breeks. He looked down to find wee Jilly staring up at him. She held a wooden horse.

"What are you doing out here? It's cold."

"You're a great knight."

Patrick sighed. "No, I'm not."

"But the lady said you are and she's always right."

"Is she? Well, not about this."

"You're a great knight."

To change the subject, Patrick pointed to the horse. "Is that a stallion or a mare?"

She looked down at her toy. The dun hood she wore fit closely to her head and came to a point on top. "He's a warhorse, but he's lame." She held it out to him. Her cheeks were ruddy from the cold, and her breath came out in white puffs.

Patrick took the horse and saw the front leg was broken off. "I have a horse in France named Gorgon. He was fierce in battle. But he was wounded. Everyone told me to put him out of his misery, but I could not." Patrick squatted on the ground and searched out a sturdy stick. He broke it in half. "I tended his leg and it healed, but he limped terrible and could never go into battle again."

"What happened to him?"

"He still lives on my estate, free to roam and get fat and comfortable until he dies." Patrick cut a string from his shirt and tied the stick to the stump of the horse's broken leg. "He was a champion and deserves to be honored as such."

He held the horse out to Jilly. She took it and inspected the leg critically.

"Does your horse have a name?" he asked.

She met his eyes and said, "Gorgon."

Patrick grinned. "Go on inside, lassie. It's too cold out here."

Jilly took his hand. "You come, too, Sir Patrick. If it's too cold for me, then it is for you as well."

Patrick stood and reluctantly let her lead him back to the cottage. The women were bunched around the fire. They all turned to stare at him when he entered. He noticed a light of interest in the young woman's eyes when she looked on him. Hazel, her name was. Patrick ignored her, refusing to meet her gaze. She was not the kind of woman he dallied with. She would become attached, even after one night. Patrick steered clear of such associations. He didn't like messy situations. He preferred restless young wives married to decrepit old men unable to perform their conjugal duties, or lonely widows not interested in entanglements, only a moment of pleasure.

His gaze fell on Mona. She spoke to Jilly, exclaiming over the mended horse Jilly presented. She seemed wan and exhausted. He regretted his insistence they leave in the morning and decided that after irritating her a bit, he'd let her have her way.

Mona whispered something to the women and rose,

gliding across the room to where he hovered near the door. "Sir Patrick, we must talk."

He just stared at her.

"I think we should stay here at least a sennight. No one knows about this cottage—most people cannot even find their way through the forest. We're safe here."

"Not if we've been followed."

"How could someone follow without us knowing? This is a forest, not open countryside."

He snorted. "I grew up in a forest. It can be done."

She exhaled and set her jaw as she forced her face into a pleasant expression. He stifled a grin. She was hard to ruffle, but he so enjoyed doing it, one of his few pleasures in life these days.

"You are a great warrior—surely you'd know if someone followed us."

His mood darkened. "Stop saying that. You know nothing about me. I am not a great warrior."

When she looked up at him with that stubborn little chin set to defy him, he leaned close and added, "I'm not your friend either."

He detected a slight quiver in her lips. Regret pinched at him but he ignored it. He didn't want her for a friend or anything else for that matter. He just wanted her to let him go.

She looked as if she were trying to speak and finally said, "We'll talk again in the morning."

He watched her walk away, a black mood taking full possession of him. He would not let her manipulate him with her soft heart. He settled down near the door, refusing to feel guilty for rejecting her overtures of kindness. He was doing as she wished, accompanying her on this absurd quest. That was all that was required of him. Besides, even if he'd wanted to—which he did not—he had nothing to give.

* * *

Mona was sleeping soundly, cocooned between Gayle and Jilly, when screams ripped through her slumber. She came awake with a start. The fire had died to glowing embers, and the cottage was dark. There was a scuffling sound near the door. Sir Patrick swore violently. A crash—a loud *thump!*

Suddenly there was light. Gayle stood in the center of the room, holding a taper high above her head. It was still poor illumination, but it was enough to make out Sir Patrick and Hazel.

He had shed his jack and his shirt was gaping, a fine sheen of sweat covering his chest and face. He crouched in a stance of readiness, dirk in hand, back against the wall. He was breathing hard, his eyes disoriented and confused. Hazel cowered on the floor, sobbing, hands clutching her throat.

Cold fear coiled in Mona's belly, snaking up to encircle her heart. What had he done? Had he stabbed Hazel? Cut her? And that bewildered look in his eyes . . . it was familiar—too familiar.

Gayle went to Hazel's side, kneeling beside her. Jilly was awake and hid her face in the dog's thick coat, frightened.

After determining that Hazel was not mortally wounded, Mona stood and went to Sir Patrick. "What happened?"

He sheathed the dirk and ran a hand through his hair. His hands shook. "I-I dinna ken. I was asleep, dreaming . . ." He darted her a guarded look, swallowing hard. "And then she was screaming and I—I had her . . ."

"You *had* her?"

His skin had grown unnaturally pale and he looked away, his eyes moving rapidly, as if trying to recall something.

Mona pressed her fingertips to her lips, uncertain of

what to do, nearly choking on her horror. *No, no! Not like Edwin!* She prayed he was different, but she could almost hear Arlana cackling in the back of her mind.

Hazel had finally found her voice and cried, "He tried to kill me!"

Patrick stood, grabbing his jack and boots, and left the cottage, slamming the door behind him.

Mona had not felt such fear since her first husband had been alive. She tried to shake it off, to be there for Hazel. She knelt beside the woman, gently pulling her fingers away from her throat. A faint pink mark lined her skin. He hadn't hurt her badly—only frightened her.

"Hazel," Mona said gently, "prithee, tell me what happened here."

Hazel looked at Gayle, new tears welling in her eyes. "I . . . I desired to lay with him . . ."

Gayle made a sound of disgust and Hazel hung her head, cheeks flaming.

"Tell me," Mona urged.

Hazel wiped her nose loudly on her sleeve. She had removed the hood from her head, and dark brown hair spilled over her shoulders. "I went to him when everyone was asleep. His own sleep was disturbed and I tried to wake him . . . he grabbed me then."

"Did he choke you? Hit you? Try to stab you?"

Hazel shook her head. "I know not . . . it happened so fast . . . I think he pressed his arm against my throat, but when I screamed he shoved me on the ground."

"God's wounds, you foolish woman!" Gayle all but shrieked. "Count yourself lucky you're even alive! He's a mercenary—never touch them when they sleep."

Hazel shook her head, uncomprehending.

Mona touched Gayle's arm. "What do you mean? You don't touch them when they sleep?"

"You know I had a man once? He was a warrior—though not a great one like Sir Patrick. He relived every battle in his sleep, so if you disturbed him in the throes of a dream, you might meet an ugly fate." Gayle shook her head sadly. "I could not even sleep with him—he always left me after we lay together, afraid he would hurt me."

Hazel began to sob again. Mona stood, facing the door, trying to fight down her fear. Edwin had done odd, bizarre things, then later claimed to not remember doing them. Sometimes he'd accused her of plotting to kill him, or of poisoning his food—irrational things. When she didn't conceive a child, he'd become convinced she was a witch and that she was killing his babies and eating the corpses. She'd always met his accusations with fervent protestations of innocence and tears. She'd been a good wife, or at least she'd tried, until it became too much and her own life was in danger. Then she'd done what she had to. She did not relish traveling with a man such as Edwin, from whom she must always be on guard.

Mona gathered her courage about her and donned her cloak. She stood outside the door, scanning the clearing for some sign of Sir Patrick. When she didn't see him she began to panic. She hurried into the trees.

"Sir Patrick!" she called, circling the cottage. "Sir Patrick, please!"

She finally stopped at the back of the cottage, hidden in the trees. She was breathing hard, her breath pluming white in front of her. What if he'd left her? *So what if he did? He'll be the death of you, lassie.*

"I'm not convinced he's dangerous," Mona muttered.

What will it take to convince you? A knife in the gullet?

"He won't hurt me."

"Are ye sure of that?" The voice came from behind her and she whirled, heart in throat.

Sir Patrick stood behind her, leaning against a tree. "Ye'd never know what hit you, if I'd a mind to."

Mona's hand was on her breast, heaving from the surprise. He had composed himself since he'd run from the cottage. His jack was on, as were his boots. He eyed her up and down dispassionately.

"How is the woman?"

"You only frightened her."

His shoulders seemed to relax the slightest bit.

"Are you leaving me?"

"Should I?"

Mona inhaled deeply, willing calm to befall her. Maybe she should let him go. She might be in more danger from him than she'd ever been from Ridley. She fingered the beads about her neck. "No."

"Aren't you afraid of me?" His eyes glittered in the dark.

She was terrified, but part of her knew the fear to be irrational, out of proportion with reality. Sir Patrick was not Edwin Musgrave. There had been something wrong with Edwin's mind—that was clear to all who'd known him. His malady had affected him at all times, awake or asleep. Patrick appeared to be in possession of his mind when he was awake.

"No."

He snorted and shook his head, pushing away from the tree. He circled her, looking down on her with contempt. "You're a fool then."

Mona resisted the urge to turn when he was behind her. The skin on her neck tingled with awareness, but she faced forward, waiting until he was before her again. There was little light to see him, a quarter moon spilling a silvery glow through the branches.

"I'm no fool."

He stood before her, arms crossed over his chest. "Oh, aye?"

"Hugh Graham was not my first husband."

He raised an eyebrow, as if he didn't particularly care but was being polite.

Mona gathered her courage and took a step closer, maintaining eye contact. "Yes. *Edwin* was dangerous."

He was interested now. "Was he?"

"Yes. I feared him."

"And? What happened?"

"I killed him."

His eyes narrowed. "You jest."

"No, I do not. My life was in danger and so I took action. And if I begin to suspect my life is again in danger, I will not sit idly by."

He considered her for a long moment. "You haven't got the bullocks."

"You don't know what I've got, sir." She turned on her heel without waiting for his rejoinder. Her bravado had not been a complete act. She would do whatever it took to protect herself and the Clachan Fala—even from him. But she'd not enjoyed challenging him. At least with Edwin she could often momentarily appease him. Sir Patrick was remote, unreachable.

She returned to the cottage to find the women before the fire again, wide awake.

"Is he still here?" Gayle asked.

Mona nodded. She sat on the hearth, waiting for him to return. The others eventually fell back asleep. When nearly an hour passed without any sign of Sir Patrick, she left the cottage again. She didn't have to go far. He sat against the cottage wall, inspecting the blade of his sword. He didn't look up.

"Come inside. It's cold."

"I'm fine."

She wrapped her cloak tightly around her and knelt beside him. "Please come inside. You'll make yourself ill."

"I'm fine." There was a warning edge to his voice, sharp as a blade.

Mona hesitated. "Hazel has promised not to touch you again . . . you're safe from—"

He looked at her finally, his blue eyes blazing with anger. "You think I'm worried about myself?"

She shook her head.

"I could have killed her. I wouldn't have even known it." He thrust the tip of his sword into the ground between his thighs, burying it nearly halfway with the force of his anger. He folded his hands over the hilt and propped his chin on it, staring stonily into the dark.

Mona didn't know what to say. What he said was frightening, and yet part of her felt he was being too hard on himself. He didn't mean to cause any harm. She settled down beside him and cleared her throat.

"Perhaps if you told me about the dream—"

"Go away," he said through clenched teeth.

Her words and her compassion froze in her throat. She didn't leave, though; she stared at him, at his rigid posture, his eyes, shut tightly, his jaw clenched. She could almost feel the self-disgust coming off him in waves. But what could she do? He seemed to hate her. The hopelessness of their situation made her want to cry. She needed him and he hated her for it.

After a moment he said, his voice softer, calmer, "You should get some sleep."

She nodded, though he couldn't see her, his eyes were still closed. They would be leaving in the morning. She wouldn't fight him on it. Wouldn't make him face Hazel and Gayle when he felt such shame.

She stood and reached for the door to push it open.

"I'll keep watch at night," he said. "And sleep during the day, aye? Then you can all just steer clear of me. We'll stay here a sennight."

His eyes were open now, staring ahead of him. A statue in the moonlight, a battered knight, fighting to make some sense of his life. Tenderness wormed its way into her heart, unwelcome. She swallowed the lump in her throat and whispered her thanks, leaving him to his watch.

5

The week that followed went by quickly. Patrick slept during the day and stayed up all night. The women busied themselves outdoors in the morning, giving him the cottage all to himself. As far as Mona knew he had no more nightmares, but it was impossible to tell by looking at him. He was always awake by early afternoon, busying himself chopping wood, hauling water, or going into the woods to hack at trees with his sword. Training.

He declined taking meals with them, instead eating outside near the trees. Mona made some halfhearted attempts to draw him out but found she couldn't bear his cool disinterest. It troubled her, this distance he forced between them. She didn't know if she could, or should, attempt to breach it. But he was her protector and therefore he should feel some type of loyalty or friendship to her—otherwise how much could he care?

The evening before they were to leave Gayle and Hazel, the dinner hour came and went with no sign of Patrick. Mona took his bowl of stew and went into the forest, following the faint trail he'd worn into the fallen leaves and needles. She'd come out here many times in the past week, unknown to him. To watch him. It began with her fear that he would desert her. Her hold on him was fragile. But then she'd seen him, shirtless, wielding his sword, and all that had been forgotten.

He'd been hacking at a tree, graceless, and yet it was a beautiful thing to behold. It was clear this was an exercise to build power and precision. He hacked and hacked and hacked. Muscles bulging and rippling, sweat rolling down his back. Transfixed, she stood behind a tree and watched him, her body oblivious to the cold and damp. But she'd never revealed herself—until tonight.

Now as she followed the path through the wood her heart pounded, her palms damp around the wooden bowl. But the usual echo of him hacking at a tree did not lead her to him. When she came to the tiny clearing, he was sitting on the ground, watching her emerge from the trees.

"I brought you some dinner," she said, dismayed at the wavering of her voice.

He seemed to be hiding something, but when she came to stand before him he'd covered it with an old sack. He held his dirk in his other hand.

"My thanks," he said, accepting the bowl from her.

She didn't want to leave, not without trying again to make some connection with him. She knelt beside him. He refused to look at her.

"Tomorrow, we will head northwest—to a village not far from the forest. It will take a few days."

He nodded.

"Then, I thought we could head south for a while, before turning back. To throw Ridley off our trail."

He set the spoon in the bowl and stared at her. His eyes were the color of forget-me-nots in the fading light, such a startling contrast to the dark masculine lines of his face. He had been shaving and his face was smooth, only the shadow of a beard. She thought he would argue or protest, but after a moment he began to eat again, shutting her out.

She stood, depressed he was so detached. Tomorrow they would be alone again, the two of them traveling through the wood. She would make him talk to her then. For now, she had Gayle, Hazel, and Jilly. She would not let him ruin her last night with them.

She turned at the edge of the trees. He'd set aside the bowl and retrieved something from beneath the sack at his side, taking up his dirk again. It was a horse. A wooden horse.

Mona turned quickly and kept walking, her chest tight with emotion. She didn't even realize she was back at the cottage until she stood before it, staring blindly at the shuttered windows.

She would know this man who growled at the world and yet secretly carved children's toys. He might fight it, but what could he do but leave her? With powerful certainty, she knew that if she didn't find a way to bind him to her, she would soon be alone.

Patrick followed Mona through the forest, hoping they would soon leave the trees and darkness behind. Little sun leaked through the treetops, and the fog drifted about them in thick waves. She believed they were somehow hiding, but he felt as if eyes were on them always, watching in the shadows.

He was glad to finally leave the cottage behind. He was a coward, unable to face young Hazel and be polite. And he was angry with her for bringing on his violence. He'd never done anything like that before. But he was angrier with himself for being unable to control it.

He tried not to think about it. But it festered and filled him with self-loathing. The dreams had always been hell, but they were *his* hell. They were like a deep well he couldn't escape from, but once there had been the sunlight above him. Now it was closed off and would be forever night.

Christ God, he'd attacked a woman in his sleep. He could not be trusted with anything or anybody. *Rosemarie . . .*

His gaze settled on the woman walking ahead of him, black plait swinging down her cloaked back. She'd been chattering at him all morning, since they'd left her friends. And he'd been rude. She had finally given up—which had been his objective all along, but now she looked so dejected he took pity on her and asked the question that had been pricking him for a week now.

"You killed your husband, aye?"

Mona glanced at him over her shoulder. "Yes, I did."

"Why?"

The thick black rope of her braid transfixed him. What he wouldn't give to wrap that gleaming plait around his wrist and . . .

"Well, you're the first man who's ever asked." Her low-pitched voice took on a thoughtful tone. "He tried to murder me three times before I finally took matters into my own hands. I'd complained to the sheriff, who informed me marital discord fell within the realm of the church. So I went to the priest for help. He said it was my husband's God-given right to discipline me as he saw fit. Somehow I felt God never intended for Edwin to hold me under the water until I stopped moving."

Unbidden, Patrick's own experiences with near drowning flashed through his mind—the images too clear, too real. The white, bloated faces, the churning hooves. He shut his eyes, willing them away.

"Sir Patrick?"

He opened his eyes to find Mona standing before him,

concern etched on her face. She reached for him, to touch his arm. He backed away so fast he nearly tripped.

She withdrew her hand immediately, alarmed. "What is it?"

Patrick shook himself, dismayed at the growing frequency of the dreams and memories, at the terror that still gripped him. "Your husband . . . why did he hold you under the water?"

She averted her eyes, staring down at her hands. "I don't know . . . he wanted a child—so did I, of course . . . but I'm barren, I cannot conceive. He wouldn't believe this. He thought I was killing our unborn children."

Patrick gaped at her, but she wouldn't look up at him. "You mean? . . ."

She nodded, still looking downward. "Yes, in my womb . . . I don't understand what I did to make him think this. I did everything I could to conceive, tried every method, every philter I knew of. I longed for a child. Why would I do such a . . . a . . ." She shook her head, her brow creased. ". . . such a horrible thing? That he thought such things of me sometimes hurt more than his desire to see me dead."

Patrick was inexplicably distressed—angry, even—and so he started walking again, passing her. He was sickened, chilled. He'd met men like her first husband, not right in the head. He soon heard her hurried footsteps as she caught up to him, trying to fall in step beside him.

"You didn't have to tell me that," he said, not looking at her. "Such things cannot be easy to dredge up after so long."

"I have no secrets."

He grunted in disbelief. "Then where are we going?"

"It is a secret, but not mine."

"It's certainly not mine."

"In time, Sir Patrick, all will be revealed."

"Splendid."

They walked in silence for several moments, Patrick turning her revelation over and over again in his mind. Life with her first husband must have been that of predator and prey. A miserable existence. He finally asked, "So how did you kill him?"

"I poisoned him." At his wary glance she shrugged. "I couldn't bear to see him suffer, in spite of it all, and so I gave him a large quantity of poppy juice and hemlock. He went to sleep and never woke."

"Why not just leave him?"

She shook her head. "Tried that. He watched me constantly. He was a blacksmith, but once he decided I was a baby-killing witch, he stopped working, just so he could follow me and watch me. He was certain I was cuckolding him with the devil."

A blacksmith. A big man, and strong. Patrick glanced down at her with some admiration. Any woman of his past acquaintance would not have survived such an ordeal. He'd known such cruel men, men who abused their wives, children, servants, and beasts. The recipients either took the beatings in silence or struck back—usually to their detriment. The women never struck back.

"Good job, lass."

She looked up at him in surprise.

He smiled. Her cheeks turned an appealing shade of pink, but she didn't look away. He could get lost in the darkness of her eyes. He resettled the sacks on his shoulders and scowled at the trees in front of him.

"Can we not get some horses?"

"What have you against walking?"

"We'd make better time, and I wouldn't have to carry yer bedchamber aboot on my back."

"I told you I'd carry one—or both for that matter if it would stop your whining."

He swung the sacks off his shoulders and thrust them at her. She barely had time to put her arms out and catch them. She staggered backwards under their weight, the look of alarm on her face immensely satisfying.

"Think ye can manage, my lady?"

She repositioned them, her face set with grim determination. "Of course."

Patrick snorted and started walking again. He gave her a mile—not even that.

She jogged to keep up. "Sir Patrick?"

"Aye?"

"Why have you never married?"

"Because I like peace—women ask too many questions."

"Come! I answered your questions about Edwin."

He sighed and decided to try diversion. "Why did you wed again after your first marriage was such a disaster?"

"I had no choice."

"Surely you had some choice. Your first husband was a blacksmith. You're a commoner, not a noblewoman or even an heiress." He slanted a look at her, then said, "Ah, the Bloodstone . . . Hugh Graham meant to have it out of ye, eh?"

"Yes, but that's not what I asked. I asked about you. Why have you never married?" She took two steps to every one of his. She was red-faced and panting from lugging the sacks and trying to keep up. She'd soon insist on horses.

"Too busy."

Mona grunted dramatically, trying, to little effect, to reposition the sacks. Patrick pretended not to notice.

"I've never met a man too busy to sire heirs," she wheezed. "It takes little of your precious time to rut on a woman. And a wife cares for the home and children. So again, why?"

"Why does this matter?"

She managed to jog several feet ahead of him. Black

curls clung to her forehead, damp with sweat. "It does matter. No one should be alone. You should have a wife to comfort you, children to make you smile." She looked over her shoulder at him. "You really should smile more often."

"I don't want your pity." The look in her eyes, mysterious, alluring, sent heat straight to his loins. He stepped up the pace, leaving her behind again. "And I can get comfort whenever I need it."

She was a tenacious thing; soon she was trotting along beside him again, sacks and all. She didn't speak, however; she just kept glancing up at him periodically. Her cheeks had grown a furious shade of red from the exercise, and her black eyes were bright.

"What about you?" he asked, annoyed that nothing more than a look from her left him fully aroused. "Where's your husband and children? You could surely find another husband, comely as you are."

"I told you, I'm barren and have found the marriage bed unfulfilling. I have stepchildren who have filled my heart."

"Ridley?"

"Well . . . he is the exception." She stopped suddenly.

Patrick kept walking, but when she didn't catch up he turned around. She'd dropped the sacks and was bent over, clutching her sides and wheezing.

"You win!" she said between pants.

He returned to her side, grinning. "I always do."

She glared at him. "We'll stop in the next village and purchase horses."

Patrick reclaimed the sacks, swinging them easily over his shoulder. "I'm a gracious winner. I'll not rub your face in it. Come, why don't we rest a bit."

He went to a felled tree and looked back. She followed, clutching her side and grimacing. He dug out the water skin and presented it to her. She gave him a narrow look, but sat and took a long drink.

He sat near her, rubbing the cold from his fingers. He watched her from beneath his lashes. "One of your stepdaughters married my brother?"

Mona nodded.

"She couldn't have been much younger than you. How old is she?"

"Four and twenty." At his speculative look, she added, "Four years younger than me."

Eight and twenty. She was older than he'd thought. "Tell me about her."

She stopped drinking and pinned him with a hard look. "You expect me to answer your questions, but you refuse to answer mine."

"You have no secrets, remember?"

She scowled. "If I tell you about Caroline, will you promise to answer one question?"

Patrick considered her request. "Mayhap."

Mona shook her head. "No. You must promise."

"Very well. One question." He wasn't promising to tell the truth, after all, only to answer.

They set off again while Mona told him all about his new sister-in-law. According to Mona she was beautiful, intelligent, well-lettered, and incredibly talented. After listening to her various virtues Patrick finally conceded it was no wonder it had been a love match.

"I wasn't always in Graham Keep's dungeon. How is it I never saw this goddess?" He'd certainly noticed Mona. He'd been well guarded when Hugh was alive, but he'd been kept in well-appointed chambers, had amenities such as good food, clean clothing, servants to bring him baths and such. He'd been given a limited amount of exercise on the castle grounds. He'd even been allowed to hawk on occasion. It was during his exercise that he'd seen Mona—always from afar, and always commanding the attention of everyone in the vicinity. He'd been captivated by her. She'd seemed at once mysterious and fresh—comforting.

"Your reputation was well known, and not just on the battlefield. Hugh did not intend for his daughters to be spoiled by a Scots prisoner. He didn't want them to even look upon you, as if your countenance alone could seduce them." She chuckled at this, as if it were absurd.

He glowered. "What of his wife? I caught many glimpses of you."

"Hugh never trusted me in anything. But I made it my business to watch you. I had . . . a feeling about you from the first . . . and when he died and Ridley forced Caroline to marry your brother, it soon became clear."

She'd watched him . . . had a feeling about him . . . how he wished she weren't talking about sorcery and the dark arts. That's why she'd taken his hair and nails. Patrick wondered about her marriage with Hugh. Had she killed the old man, too? He'd heard Hugh had sickened and died. Perhaps the old laird'd had reason to distrust her. Patrick knew that if he displeased her, he'd not want to eat anything served by her hand.

"What about your other stepchildren? Hugh had four children, aye?"

"I would be happy to tell you all about Wesley and Fayth, but first you promised to answer a question."

Patrick had hoped she'd forgotten. "Very well."

She placed a hand on his arm, halting him. She stared up at him, blinking solemnly. "What did you dream the night you attacked Hazel?"

Patrick shrugged her hand off and began walking again. He hadn't realized until that moment he'd been opening himself to her, enjoying her company. What foolishness. "Nothing."

"Nothing? You were dreaming of something."

"I don't remember."

She darted in front of him and stopped directly before him. He halted impatiently.

"Dreams are windows to the soul. If you tell me your dream, perhaps I can help you stop it. Besides . . . you promised."

A twig snapped behind them. Patrick turned his head away from her, listening. Thunder rumbled overhead. He hated this forest. He'd traveled through many forests in his life, in Scotland and all over the continent. Had fought battles among mighty oaks, but none had felt so sinister. And never had he been so thoroughly distracted. His companions were always ugly, filthy soldiers, not soft, beautiful women.

"Sir Patrick," she said insistently.

"Hush." He held up his hand for silence, frowning. "I hear something."

He started to turn, but she grabbed his arm.

"I don't think—"

He dropped the sacks and clapped a hand over her mouth, pulling her around so her back was pressed against his chest. She made an indignant sound and squirmed, but when his arm tightened across her breasts, she grew still. Though he strained his ears he heard nothing else. The dark clouds churned above them, and the sky continued its low grumbling. Patrick slowly became aware of the soft body pressed against him. It had been so long since he'd held a woman. He was painfully aware of soft curves and a round bottom rubbing against his groin. He imagined what it would be like to taste her skin, the satin skin of her thighs. He lowered his head and breathed deeply of her scent. She smelled of herbs, fresh and green. Her hair was like a bed of rose petals. He removed his hand from her mouth.

Her breathing had become labored, the rise and fall of her breasts pressing against his arm. She gently extricated herself from his grip and turned to face him, her expression cautious. "Perhaps it's just an animal?"

He'd momentarily forgotten the sound, so intent was he on the woman. She wanted to be his friend, not his lover. She'd rather buy him whores than lie with him herself. She was afraid of him. He reminded himself of all these things, willing his body to behave itself.

She murmured something, turning away. He started to question her, then realized she wasn't looking at him but had that inward look he was growing accustomed to. She was talking to the ghost again. A chill traveled over him, effectively extinguishing any thoughts of seduction. That was another excellent reason why he should never touch her. She was insane.

He grabbed up the sacks and walked past her. "Your friend feeling talkative again?"

She didn't respond, but hurried after him. The woods—dark even on a bright day—had grown cold and gloomy from the gathering clouds. Patrick's knee had been aching all day, and he knew it wouldn't be long before the sky opened up. He'd been searching for shelter all afternoon but had spied nothing but trees. It was evening when the rain finally fell. Unfortunately they were still in the forest, and he didn't see the end in sight.

He pulled Mona beneath a tree. They were still getting wet, but it sheltered them from the worst of the downpour.

She took one of the sacks from him. After digging about in it she produced a large piece of oiled canvas and set off into the trees. Patrick knew what she had in mind. When she found a likely spot—a fallen log and several large stones—he helped her drape and anchor the material. They both crawled beneath it. Patrick grabbed several sturdy branches, which he drove into the ground and used to prop up their roof.

Little light came in through their exit hole, but soon Mona had a candle lit. They sat cross-legged, facing each other. He gave her an admiring smile. Her face was wet with rain, her hair sticking to the sides of her face. The shift beneath her bodice was sodden, clinging to the plump curves of her breasts.

"Are you still angry about carrying the bags, Sir Patrick?"

"You've thought of everything, aye?"

She shrugged, smug.

He gathered up stones to make a circle around their makeshift shelter, to keep the rainwater from washing in. Mona spread a blanket beneath them and set out a meal.

After they'd eaten, Patrick stretched out as best he could, leaning on his side, head propped on his hand. Mona unbraided her hair. There was nothing provocative in her behavior, nothing more than a woman tidying herself up. But by the time the ebony waves cascaded over her shoulders, his mouth had gone dry and there was a strange buzzing in his head.

Bloody Christ, he wanted her. He was rock hard and having trouble thinking straight. He could smell her hair, rosewater. He watched, entranced, as she combed her fingers through it, arching her neck.

As if feeling his heated gaze, she turned her velvety eyes on him. She returned his look for a full minute. "Sir Patrick, we are staying here out of necessity, nothing more. Remove any wicked thoughts from your head."

Annoyed, Patrick looked away. His neck was hot with embarrassment and unleashed desire. He hated this. Hated that he couldn't seem to stop lusting after her, even with no encouragement. Her rejection mattered little to his body; it still believed she could be coerced. "What know you of wicked thoughts?"

She ran her fingers through locks of black silk. "Oh, I know."

Patrick captured an ebony tress and curled it about his fingers. She stopped combing and looked down at his hand.

"You cannot possibly imagine what I'm thinking, my lady. If you did, you wouldn't be so cold."

She did not try to remove her hair from his fingers. "I've been widowed twice. There is no violation you could imagine that could possibly shock me."

Patrick wrapped her hair around his wrist, pulling her down toward him. His blood throbbed through his veins in anticipation. "I wasn't thinking about violating anyone . . . only keeping warm . . ."

He saw the shiver run through her, felt her resist his gentle tugging. She was not so unmoved as she pretended. He twisted his wrist again, wrapping more hair around it and bringing her closer still. All the reasons why he should not touch her fled. He'd imagined this, burying his hands in her hair, feeling the cool silk against his heated skin.

"I have no objections to laying close to you for warmth, but I fear you have something else entirely in mind." She was trying very hard to sound stern and superior, but her husky voice had dropped an octave, wavering slightly.

"You've never been kissed, have you?" He reeled her in closer. The candlelight played over her creamy skin; soft as a petal it would be, if only he could touch it.

A small frown marred her brow, and her lips parted. "How absurd! Of course I've been kissed." She was at his level now, had braced her elbow on the blanket to keep herself from falling on him.

"Not in any way that matters."

"Sir Patrick." A note of panic crept into her voice, breaking her calm mask. Her eyes widened. But he sensed a curiosity there, too, beneath the apprehension. Or perhaps that was only wishful thinking . . . he couldn't tell the difference anymore.

"Just a kiss," he coaxed. "I promise that's all I'll steal."

Her mouth trembled and the thick fringe of her lashes lowered, fanning against her cheeks. Her head jerked in a small nod. "Just one," she whispered.

Keeping his firm grip on her hair, he slid his other hand around the back of her neck and pulled her mouth to his. She tried to recoil at his sudden show of force, but he held her fast. Her mouth was soft and every bit as sweet as he'd anticipated. He tasted her gently, softly, until the tension drained from her neck and shoulders and a sigh whispered between her lips.

Her hand came to rest on his shoulder as he explored every inch of her mouth. When his tongue touched her bottom lip, her mouth opened readily to him. At the slow stroke of his tongue, her hand fisted at his shoulder, and he feared she would push him away even as her body loosened, her head falling back so he could rise above her and have access to her body.

Her fist opened, and her hand slid up his neck and into his hair. A violent shudder seized him at her touch and he lifted his head, looking down on her. Her lips were red and swollen, her breath coming in pants. She slowly opened her eyes. This close to her he could see the faint ring of mahogany circling enormous black pupils. The eyes that gazed at him were dazed, dreamy.

He kissed the corner of her mouth, traced the fine black line of her brow with his thumb, buried his hand in her hair. She didn't speak, only searched his face as if looking for some answer there, her hand toying with the hair at his nape.

"Well?" he asked. "Have you ever been kissed?"

She shook her head slowly. "Not like that."

When he kissed her again, she met his mouth eagerly, her tongue sparring with his, her breasts large and round pressing into his chest, until he thought he would go mad from wanting. She tasted so good, felt so right. But the moment he covered her breast with his hand, she turned her face away, breaking off their kiss. Patrick continued to trail kisses across her cheek, to her earlobes, his thumb rubbing over the hardened nipple he could feel even through the wool of her bodice.

"Stop, Patrick," she said, her voice hoarse, her hand pushing at his shoulder.

He rose above her, planting his palms on either side of her head. "Why?"

Her face was flushed, scraped red from his whiskers in places. She was so beautiful and soft and eager—she had been! He'd felt it. Even now, her hand curled into a fist, balling the linen of his shirt in it.

"Because I don't know if I want this . . . I . . . I need to think about it first."

Patrick sighed and rolled onto his back, draping his forearm over his eyes. Great. She was going to *think* about it. Nothing good could come of that.

He sensed her moving about next to him and lowered his arm. She leaned on one arm, looking down at him. Her hair fell in a curtain to pool on the ground.

"This meant nothing to you, did it?"

"Well . . . nothing is a strong word."

"Pray tell why you wish to lay with me?"

Patrick raised a hand, cupping her face. She was every bit as soft as he'd imagined. Softer. *Why?* He didn't know, except the normal reasons. She was beautiful, desirable. He could still feel her thigh beneath his hand, even when he tried to make the sensation go away. The scent of her skin, her hair, enchanted him so that he could recall them when she wasn't near, stirring him.

"Must there be a reason, besides the call of the body?"

She seemed distressed, her hand twisting the fabric of her kirtle.

He dropped his hand. "It was just a kiss. A bit of diversion, nothing more."

"A diversion?" she murmured, sitting up and crossing her legs beneath her.

"What do you want from me?" he asked warily.

"You can let your hackles down, Sir Patrick," she said, composure falling firmly in place. "The last thing I want is another husband."

He rolled onto his back and glared at the canvas ceiling. "Good. It's certain I dinna need a wife."

He could feel her staring at him but refused to acknowledge her. He needed to put the distance back between them—difficult, when his arm practically brushed her thigh.

Finally she said, "Well then. It worked out just fine. Disaster averted."

He moved his arm to fold beneath his head and inadvertently rubbed her thigh. His belly clenched. These close quarters wouldn't do. What if he had a nightmare and attacked her? He sat bolt upright, determined to stay awake.

"You should get some sleep," he said.

He wished she would stop looking at him. He avoided making eye contact with her. It had been a mistake to become friendly with her—he'd have to remedy that soon.

"Good night," she said and lay down on her side, her back to him. Rain tapped against the canvas, the chill seeping into his bones. He longed for a fire, for shelter, for a bed. He longed to wrap himself around her warm body and go to sleep. But he would not sleep—not beside her. He would not be able to live with himself if she came to harm because of him.

And so he sat through the long night, guarding Lady Graham from himself.

6

The sonorous bong of a bell tolled in the distance. The village was near. Patrick was walking too fast again. Mona puffed with the effort to keep up. They definitely needed horses. They had left the forest behind yesterday and now cut around fields and pastures. Farmers and their families stopped their work to watch them pass, raising a hand in greeting. Mona returned the gesture, but Patrick barely acknowledged them with a brief nod.

His continued silence grated on Mona's nerves. He'd barely spoken to her the past two days, ever since he'd kissed her. He never seemed to sleep, either. His face showed no signs of his sleepless nights, though the sun glinted off the golden stubble covering his unshaven cheeks. He'd refused her offer of the razor this morning. He walked strong and swift, as if full of life. Was he angry? And if so, what had she done? She didn't think it was the kiss. That meant nothing to him. A diversion. Mona was trying very hard to adopt the same attitude. Meaningless. Just a kiss . . . but oh, what a kiss! It brought a flush to her cheeks just to think of it.

She'd tried to distract herself from these thoughts by engaging him in conversation, with little luck. Her attempts were met with monosyllables or stony silences. A few days ago she'd thought they were finally forming a tentative friendship, but the fragile bond had vanished.

Mona was exhausted and not just from the pace Patrick set. Since leaving the cottage, she wasn't getting much sleep. The ground was hard, even with folded blankets beneath her. Though she had tried not to, she had grown somewhat pampered as Hugh's wife. Not that the life of Keeper was a shabby one. Far from it. She'd had Arlana's house, livestock, many dresses, and a constant flow of customers desiring love philters, beauty creams, and herbal remedies. Hugh had allowed her to take as much of it as she wished, but Mona had always felt she would one day return to the cozy home. She wondered now if the house was still unused, sitting lonely and forgotten, or if someone had made it their home.

"Sir Patrick, prithee, slow down!"

Sir Patrick obliged, glancing at her. "The village is near." His voice was urgent.

"Yes, and it will still be there if we walk slower."

Mona walked beside him, watching him. She couldn't look at him without imagining the magic his mouth had wrought. She'd been kissed many times by several men, and none had ever set her blood afire. Now, she was both curious and wary. She wanted to kiss him again, and perhaps more than kiss, but she was confused. His dismissive attitude offended her. More than offended—it hurt. These thoughts were deeply disturbing. She'd been married—possessed—by men, subject to their cruel whims. She would never be owned again. So . . . *what did she want?* The question nagged at her, but it was clear from the flutter of her heart every time he looked at her that she wanted something more than protection from him.

"Why do you keep looking at me?" he asked, not sparing her a glance.

"Because I wonder about you."

His eyebrow twitched, but he made no response.

"Don't you wonder what I'm wondering?"

"No." He began to walk fast again.

Mona jogged to catch up with him. "I pray you, let me rest a moment."

"We can rest in the village." But he stopped, looking down at her, his light blue eyes guarded. Mona believed you could see the soul in someone's eyes, but either Patrick had no soul, or he guarded it fiercely. She thought the latter was true. There was a kindness to him, a softness. Though he didn't realize she knew, she'd seen him slide the horse he'd carved into Jilly's blanket, beside the broken one, just before they'd left the cottage. He'd thought no one was looking, and indeed, the others had been oblivious.

She sat in the shade of a tree while he paced a circle around it. She was tired just watching him.

"Please, rest. You hardly sleep, you must be weary."

"I get all the sleep I require," he said, his eyes searching the open countryside. Always alert, always watchful. Mona wished she could thrive on so little sleep. She felt wilted and sore.

"Sir Patrick? Do you have a home?"

"I have a home . . . many homes."

"Which is your favorite?"

He stopped his pacing, folding his arms across his chest and staring into the distance. The sun reflected off his hair like burnished gold. A scar marred the dusky skin of his chin, a white twisting river, but it didn't detract from his fine features. "France. The banks of the Aigues. There's a castle there . . . and someone I . . ."

Mona watched his face as his words trailed off, a fist

tightening about her heart. There was someone. A woman? His eyes were sad, wistful. He looked down at the ground and sighed.

"Do you miss her very much?"

He looked at her sharply, eyes narrowed.

She forced herself to smile. "I sometimes . . . know things, or understand them."

"Because you're a witch?"

Mona shook her head, trying hard to concentrate on his words and not the odd ache in her chest. He was speaking to her again. This was important. "No, because I pay attention."

He nodded as if this made good sense.

"What's her name?" Mona was surprised by the strange catch in her voice.

"Rosemarie."

"Does she know where you are?"

He looked away again, his mouth a grim line, and shook his head.

He loved Rosemarie, ached for her, that was clear. His unhappiness was so genuine that she became confused and a bit annoyed that his kiss had been so ardent. He'd been so intense, as if she were the only woman in the world. She'd wanted to believe the way his eyes had burned was special, only for *her.* She'd known it even then for a fool's wish, but that didn't make it go away. Apparently he burned more brightly for Rosemarie. And if Rosemarie was so wonderful, why bother trying to rut with the witch?

Faithless, all men are, Arlana's voice whispered through her mind.

In the ways of love, perhaps.

If this is how he conducts the matters of the heart, how can you trust him with anything else?

Love for men takes place below the belt. They don't understand commitment and loyalty.

Exactly.

Mona hated it when Arlana was right. She stood abruptly. "I'm rested."

Patrick blinked, coming out of the depths of his thoughts, and grabbed her sacks. Mona rushed past him, walking fast now, not wanting to look at him. She didn't understand why she felt so foolish and jealous. It was sheer stupidity. She'd never wanted him for more than a protector. She'd never wanted him to kiss her, and she certainly didn't want him to have any hold over her. So why did she suddenly hate the name Rosemarie? She was probably blond and blue-eyed, a real lady with the bloodlines to prove it. Not a common, black-haired witch who was only good for a tumble, who was 'my lady'-ed only because she'd married above herself. It was likely that he wished to wed his Rosemarie. He only waited for her to be old enough—she was probably fifteen years old, ripe for the marriage bed, a virgin. Not an eight-and-twenty-year-old, twice-widowed hag! That was why he was so eager to get away from her—he wanted his youthful beauty. Mona was nothing more than a *diversion.*

By the time they reached the village, Mona was glad she'd discovered his Rosemarie. She'd wasted too much time fretting about a silly kiss. He'd become a distraction. Fetching the Clachan Fala was all that mattered, and his only function was to protect Mona and eventually the stone. Nothing more.

It was a small village, but bustling with activity. Patrick clamped a firm hand on her elbow and led her straight to an inn. After securing a room, he ordered a meal, then turned to ask her if she had the coin to pay for it all.

"Of course."

He took her upstairs to their room.

"One room?" she asked, looking around the sparsely furnished cell. The bed was a straw-stuffed sack set on a wooden bed frame and wedged into the corner, no doubt

crawling with fleas and lice. There was a table and two
stools, a basin and ewer, and a chamber pot that had been
dumped but not cleaned.

"We're traveling as husband and wife." When she started
to protest, he silenced her with a look. "Do you wish to
draw attention? A lady traveling with a protector? Everyone
will remember that, but a husband and wife? No one cares."

Though his ruse made sense, he was not a man people
would forget. "They will all remember you," she pointed out.

He shook his head, digging through her sacks. "No they
won't. Look at me. I'm dressed as a commoner. You, however, should always go about cloaked and hooded."

"Me?" she scoffed. "I'm just an old wife."

He cast her an incredulous glance. "Hardly. You turn
every head in a room. They all envy me." He shook his
head, returning to his search in the sacks.

Her cheeks flushed with pleasure at his words, and her
heart tripped over itself.

He laughed suddenly, harshly. "They would not if they
knew I was merely your mule!" He pulled out a multicol-
ored silk scarf. "What is this? Do we need this?"

Mona snatched the scarf from his hand and wrapped it
around her head. "Yes. I like to cover my hair with them."
She pulled it off and tied it around her braid, making a
large bow.

He watched her the whole time, strangely tense. When
she waggled her braid at him from over her shoulder,
adorned with the scarf bow, he turned back to the sacks.
"You do not leave the room with that on." He went back to
digging through the sacks, muttering all the while.

"What are you looking for, Sir Patrick?"

He turned on her, finger pointed in her face. "It's
Patrick. Dinna 'sir' me here—we're commoners, remember? Address me as Patrick, or Husband." He dropped his

hand, though he still seemed highly agitated. "I'm looking for your coin."

"I don't keep it in there." She reached into her bodice and found the string to her wee silk purse. He watched with fascination as she drew the purse from where she'd hid it between her breasts. "It's the only safe place." Her voice sounded strange to her own ears. He didn't respond, and she held it out to him. "Use whatever you need."

"Oh, I plan to." He looked down at the bright red purse, a strange light in his eyes, caressing the silk between his strong fingers. The sight of him caressing something that had so recently been against her skin sent a shiver through her.

"Stay here," he said. "I'll be back soon."

Mona set about putting their room to rights. It was filthy and stunk, but luckily she had anticipated the need to clean and had the appropriate supplies—limewash and fleabane. It was dark by the time she finished. She had washed the coarse ticking and managed to secure fresh hay from the innkeeper. She covered it with her own sheets and blankets, scrubbed the table, floors, basin, ewer, and chamber pot. She sat at the table now, candles lit and shutters thrown wide. The meal Patrick had ordered had been brought up and was now laid out on the table, waiting for his return. Street sounds had kept her company through the afternoon, and they only grew more boisterous with the coming night. She hoped Patrick had luck purchasing horses. As she stared at the window, stars twinkling in the dark sky, an ugly thought wiggled its way into her mind. How long did it take to buy horses anyway? And though he would certainly need to groom and board them, this was a very small village; there couldn't possibly be many choices.

She had promised him a whore . . . She hurried to the window and scanned the street, looking for a tavern or alehouse. Perhaps the innkeeper of this very establishment pandered flesh. A sickness coiled in her belly. Why did she care? She'd made the offer. At least he could have informed her he would not be back because he was whoring. She left the window and sat on the stool again, filled with a strange, restless unhappiness. The now cold meal was suddenly unappealing.

What if her silly assumptions were wrong? What if it was even worse than all that? What if he were hurt or in trouble? They were in England, after all, and he was a Scotsman. What if he'd run into some of the Maxwells' ancient enemies and, like all borderers, couldn't pass up a chance for revenge? Even now he could be lying broken and bleeding in some dark alley. . . .

She threw on her cloak and hurried out the door and down the stairs. After inquiring with the innkeeper, she discovered Patrick had last been seen in the inn stables. Mona hurried out the back and into the chill air. She entered the stable cautiously. Two fat candles set in candleholders bolted to the wall dimly illuminated the stable. Few horses lodged here tonight.

Mona searched the stalls for the familiar blond head, her heart racing. Her limbs went weak with relief. Patrick was in a far stall, his back to her, brushing a large, dark brown horse. A bearded man tended his mount across from him, and two boys slept in the hay.

She walked along the stalls until she was at the empty stall behind Patrick. He had removed his jack and rolled up his sleeves. His scarred forearms were thick and muscular, the sinew sliding and bunching as he brushed the horse's side. Mona glanced at the man across from them, but he was on the other side of his horse now and no more than a dim shadow.

Mona was oddly reluctant to disturb him. She enjoyed

watching him work. The back of his neck was hard and muscular and yet the skin was so soft, completely unblemished and covered with a down of pale blond hair that gleamed in the candlelight. She wondered what his neck tasted like.

Her lascivious thoughts were cut short when he straightened and turned toward her. Unsurprised to find her standing there staring at him, he stepped back and nodded to the horse. "What think you?"

"He's . . . nice." Mona wasn't much of a horsewoman, though she could ride if necessary. "He's very handsome."

"He's yours. His name is Dragon." He indicated a horse further down, an enormous bay munching contentedly on oats. "That's Laddy."

Laddy was a fine horse—much finer than Dragon. She turned back to Patrick. "Have we any coin left?"

He tossed her the red purse and she caught it, weighing it in her hand. Considerably lighter. She stuffed it back into her bodice. He leaned against the stall, watching her, his expression lazy, one hand still on Dragon's withers. He was far more relaxed than he'd been when he left her. It was as if the horses had soothed him. She noted how he stroked Dragon affectionately.

"Come here," he said. "Meet your new friend."

The stall door was unlatched, so Mona pulled it open and stepped inside. Dragon nuzzled her neck, sniffing loudly in her ear. Mona laughed, rubbing the velvety nose. Patrick reached around behind her and yanked at the red and yellow scarf still tied to her braid.

"I thought I told you not to wear this outside the room."

Mona bristled at his tone. She'd forgotten about the scarf and would have apologized had he been more polite. Instead she ignored him, focusing on Dragon. She'd always considered herself a patient person, but for some reason Patrick strained her patience. And that irritated her even more.

He moved behind her and tugged on her braid, forcing her head back. He leaned over her, wintery blue eyes locking on hers. "Don't ignore me."

"Release my hair." Her voice shook—not with fear but with anger and something else, something that strummed through her blood at the scent of him.

His eyes narrowed. "You thought I'd run off with your money, didn't ye?" He leaned in closer and whispered, his breath warming her forehead, "Or bought myself a whore."

"Let go."

He stared at her a moment before complying.

She turned immediately, facing him. He was uncomfortably close. "How do you know what I thought?" she challenged. How *did* he know?

He shrugged. "People always think the worst. I knew I'd been gone too long, and rather than realize my task took longer than I'd anticipated, you assumed I'd done something ugly."

Mona couldn't think of a thing to say. He was absolutely right, and it was bitter going down. She crossed her arms under her breasts. "I *did* promise you a whore, so if you—"

He swore and pushed past her to the stall door. Mona had never felt so awkward before. She always said the wrong thing to him. She caught his arm before he was out of the stall.

"Wait, Sir Patrick, I—"

"I told you to drop the 'sir.'" He glanced over at the stall across from them, but the man was gone. He turned, looking at her hand on his arm. "We're married, remember?" His gaze swept her from head to toe. He took a step closer. Dragon moved away from them to the back of his stall.

"What kind of husband would I be, if I left such a

woman in search of whores?" He raised a blond brow. "Such behavior would be noted."

Heat flashed up her neck, and she closed her eyes. "I seem thoughtless in these matters." She released his arm. "I'm not very good at this."

His finger was under her chin, softly, pushing it up. She opened her eyes to find he'd moved so close their bodies almost touched. "That's what I'm here for, aye?"

Would he kiss her again? Breathless with anticipation, her gaze moved to his mouth, wide and sensual and smiling the slightest bit. The scent of hay and horse was thick, a fine mist of dust hung suspended in the air. Her limbs were sluggish, heavy. She heard his little intake of breath and quickly met his eyes.

"Ye canna look at me like that, Wife, and expect me to be good."

Before she marshaled the words together to ask what he meant, he lowered his head. The kiss was a bold one, tasting her lips once before his hand slid behind her neck to draw her up on her toes, then plunging inside. Her knees buckled, and she had to grab his shoulders to keep from sagging to the ground. She burned from the inside out, thought dissolving into sensation.

She hadn't realized they were moving until she felt the wood of the stall bite into her back. He'd pushed her backwards, pressing her between the wood and his body, freeing his hands to roam. She slid her arms over his shoulders, around his neck, and sighed into his mouth. Let him do what he would. She didn't care so long as he kept kissing her.

His tongue stroked against hers, plundering the insides of her mouth. Her mouth tingled with awareness. She couldn't seem to get enough. His hand was beneath her skirts, hot against her thigh. He groaned into her mouth.

She shuddered at the violent clenching in her belly, a moan tearing free from her throat. She slid down the wall, boneless, clinging to his powerful shoulders.

And then he jerked away from her, and she sagged against the wood, blinking dazedly into the dim, dusty light. There was a crash and a thump. Her heart raced, and the blood roared in her ears so she did not immediately hear the struggle. When she realized Patrick hadn't left her of his own choice, she staggered through the stall door and almost tripped over him and another man rolling about in the dirt.

"Patrick!" She grabbed the other man, trying to pull him off. She caught his leather jack, only to be thrown back when they rolled away.

"Damn it, Mona! Get away!" Patrick yelled.

When he was looking at her, the other man punched him. His bottom lip split, and blood splattered across Mona's skirts. Patrick's lips drew back from his teeth as he slammed his fist into the man's head. The man froze, stunned, and fell back. Mona was finally able to see his face.

"Brodie Armstrong!" she cried.

He twitched several times, then went slack. Patrick was on him again, pulling his dirk from his boot.

"No!" Mona grabbed Patrick's arm. "You can't kill him!"

Patrick yanked his arm free, but Mona only latched onto it again.

"Please, Patrick!"

He pushed back onto his knees, his chest heaving, and stared at her incredulously. "He tried to kill me and certainly had ugly things in mind for you."

She shook her head. "No—he's Ridley's man. He's only following orders."

"And you think he will disobey, now that you stopped me?"

Mona nodded emphatically.

Patrick made a disgusted sound and got to his feet. "Your head is full of feathers, woman. He will stab me in the back and then take you to Ridley. Don't be a fool. Let me finish him—let it be a warning to Ridley."

His words angered Mona as nothing had. "You will not harm him, Patrick. Do you understand?"

He refused to meet her eyes, staring stubbornly at Brodie's inert form. Finally he said, "Well, mayhap I wilna have to."

Mona dropped to her knees beside Brodie, her fingers seeking under his beard, finding a weak pulse in his neck. She turned his head. A deep gash marred his temple. It already swelled.

Mona looked up at Patrick. She'd never seen a man who could hit so hard with his fists. It was possible Brodie would die—from a single punch. "Carry him to our room, so I might tend him."

Patrick snorted. "Are you witless? I'll not sleep in the same room as him."

"Then sleep elsewhere."

His nostrils flared, his mouth thinning angrily. "Ye're not making this job easy."

Mona stood and went to him. "All we do in this world, be it good or evil, comes back to us tenfold. Let us do this good and see what returns."

He rolled his eyes and muttered, "Jesus God."

They stared at each other angrily. His mouth was flat, his eyes fierce. Blood ran in a thin line from his lip. He thrust a hand through his fair hair so it stood on end.

"Very well," he said through clenched teeth.

He heaved Brodie over his shoulder and strode out of the stable, Mona close on his heels.

7

After dumping Brodie Armstrong onto the narrow bed, Patrick left the room, his temper still simmering. He returned to the stables to gather the things he'd left behind. Folding his arms over the top of Laddy's stall, he stared blindly at the horse.

His blood still surged from the kiss and the fight, and he couldn't seem to calm himself. He didn't like this barely restrained violence, though it had always served him well in battle. He rested his chin on his hands, breathing deeply, and closed his eyes. Hay rustled as Laddy moved nearer. Warm horse breath snorted in his ear, and the big bay lipped at his hair. He reached up to stroke the horse and it came closer, hanging its head over the stall door. Patrick pressed his face against Laddy's neck, stroking the horse, and waves of calm finally flowed over him, restoring him.

He straightened, looking in the horse's big, dark eyes. "One too many blows to my head, methinks."

The horse snorted.

"I dinna know whether to strangle her or kiss her."

And that was the problem. Just being near her was

slowly driving him mad with want. And it had become more complicated than all that, for he'd lied to her. He *had* considered purchasing a whore—after all, she'd promised him one. He never should have kissed Mona; now he thought endlessly of doing far more than that. He had to work it out of his system somehow. There was an alehouse at the end of the street, and he'd gone there to view the selection. He'd not even bothered asking, for after a dram and an inspection of all the women within—whore or not—he'd been unmoved. When he thought of lying with a woman, only one came to mind.

How had such a thing occurred? It couldn't last. Even if she were a witch and had bewitched him, surely it would fade. There was some comfort in that thought—that he wasn't responsible for his feelings and urges.

But why would she bewitch him when she didn't want him in that way? She'd seemed willing enough before Brodie Armstrong had attacked him—so willing he'd become oblivious to aught but the taste of her mouth and the feel of her body melting against his. But that was lust. In her mind, she did not want him. He was just a tool to her. A protector. As it should be, he reminded himself firmly. He didn't want her getting attached. What they felt was lust, completely natural under the circumstances. Nothing more to it. He had other commitments to fulfill when he finished with Mona. He would not let anything else come between him and Rosemarie.

He squeezed his eyes shut, unable to think of her now without grief. This diversion was beginning to feel permanent—as if he'd never return to France and see her sweet face.

He gave Laddy's nose a final rub before returning to their room in the inn. Mona fussed over her patient, still unconscious. Patrick had hit him hard—had meant to—

and knew Brodie might never wake up. He went to the
table and sat down, inspecting the cold meal. He started to
pick at the chicken, but Mona rushed over and slapped his
hand.

He sat back, folding his arms over his chest, annoyed.
What now?

"Don't eat that!" She grabbed it off the table and threw
it out the window.

"What—"

"You must never eat meat that has been sitting out for
hours. That's why it's important to either salt it, or eat it
soon after it's cooked. It will make you ill otherwise."

Patrick clenched his jaw. "There have been times when
I've had little choice but eat rancid meat or die. And here
I am."

Mona shook her head, eyeing him from head to foot.
"You are not a normal man."

Patrick frowned, wondering if that was an insult or a
compliment. She had removed her cloak and bodice. Only
her kirtle over her embroidered shift remained. It was unfortunate they had company, for her current state of un-
dress and dishevelment was stimulating.

He gestured to the rest of the meal. "May I eat the bread
and cheese? Drink the ale?"

Mona nodded.

He began eating, but soon she was beside him.

"Turn please."

She had a rag and a flask. He knew by now it was simpler to comply and so thrust his chin out with a sigh. She
dabbed at the cut on his lip, scrubbed at the dried blood on
his chin. Her breasts were practically in his face, and her
scent, sweet and herbal, engulfed him. He wanted to bury
his face in the curve of her neck and breathe her in. The
mellow scent of whiskey reached his nose. He took the

flask from her hand. Her fingers, now free, went to his jaw to steady him.

The feel of her fingers, soft and cool against his skin, was painfully arousing. He swallowed hard, wishing he didn't want this woman. Too complicated. Too much trouble.

To distract himself, he said, "What you said, about goodness coming back to you . . . do you really believe that?"

She stepped back, removing the rag from his skin but still holding his face. She looked deeply into his eyes, and his blood was churning again, his belly clenched tight. Her eyes were so large and soft and lovely.

"Yes, I do."

"I've only seen you do what you thought was good and right . . . so how did you end up with your first husband? Or with Hugh Graham? Why were you kept prisoner by Ridley? You do naught but good. When will it come back to you?"

She moved away from him, sitting on the stool opposite. His skin still tingled warmly where her hand had been. She rested her chin thoughtfully on her fist.

"I suppose it depends on what you believe was wrong with Edwin. I once believed he'd been possessed by a demon, so my killing him would have been a good thing, right? So why did I nearly hang? Why did Hugh take me and keep me like a prisoner?"

"And now?"

Mona sighed deeply, looking away from him to the floorboards. "Arlana taught me much about healing and the body. She didn't believe demons went about possessing people . . . she didn't even believe there were such things. She said Edwin possessed an imbalance of humors that made him melancholy. He imagined plots and evil where there were none. So when I killed him, as a healer, I did him an injustice. Perhaps Hugh was my punishment."

Patrick blinked at her. "So you should have just let him murder you?"

"I should have tried harder to understand and help. As a healer and a wife, it was my duty."

"Did Arlana tell you this?"

Mona shook her head. "No, she thought he was better off dead, since his life was a misery of suspicion."

"I tend to agree. You were protecting yourself. If you didn't kill him, sooner or later he would have succeeded."

"That is the warrior speaking."

"No, it's good sense."

Mona shrugged. "Perhaps it should trouble me more, but it doesn't. I did what I felt I had to at the time. And a lot depends on how you look at things. I have many rewards in my life. Arlana, my stepchildren. And now you. Many of these things came to me because of Hugh, so perhaps he was a reward, too."

Patrick had just taken a bite of bread when his mouth went dry. He drank from the flask of whiskey he'd taken from her, washing the bread down and warming his throat. She considered him a reward? His head buzzed with the thought—alarmed and pleased.

"Dinna expect too much from me, else you'll be disappointed."

She broke off a piece of cheese and met his gaze. "Why? You have proven yourself naught but honorable."

Patrick placed his palm on the table and leaned toward her, narrowing his eyes. "If your friend hadn't pulled me off you in the stable, I'd have had you up against the stable wall without a thought. Is that honorable?"

As he watched, her color rose, flooding her cheeks. She licked her lips, and his groin tightened in response.

"If I'd asked you to stop, you would have." Her husky voice was low, a soft purr.

He shook his head slowly. "I canna remember thinking of anything but being inside of you—else I would have heard Brodie afore he attacked."

She swallowed, her eyes never leaving his. "That doesn't matter. You would have stopped."

He'd grown powerfully aroused, watching her unexpected reaction to his words—or perhaps the memory of what had occurred in the stable. "Come around here and we'll give it another go—we'll see who's right."

She only stared at him, her lips parted, her eyes wide. Her breasts rose and fell beneath the fine linen of her shift. She didn't say no. He stood to come around the table and grab her.

Brodie moaned from the bed, and her head whipped around, the hazy look in her eyes disappearing. She hurried to the bed. He wanted to curse and hit something, but he only watched her, hands planted on his hips. *What the hell was he doing?* He acted like a slavering dog when she was near, eager for any crumb tossed his way.

Obviously Brodie Armstrong wasn't going to be gotten rid of so easily. Patrick wandered to the foot of the bed and stared down at their new friend. Mona wiped his forehead with a damp rag, speaking softly. She had cleaned and sutured his cut. He opened his eyes, and a huge, hammy hand rose slowly to finger the cut. Brow furrowed, his eyes finally focused on Mona. Patrick tensed.

"My lady . . . ," Brodie rasped. "Me head . . . Jesus wept, I can hardly see." He groaned, rubbing restlessly at his forehead.

Mona held a cup. "Here, drink this—it will help. Can you sit up a bit?"

Brodie struggled to push himself up on his elbow and froze, blinking at Patrick, as if he couldn't quite make him out. And likely he couldn't. Patrick had taken more than a few blows to the head and knew they were hard to shake off.

Brodie's hand flailed out until he grasped Mona's wrist, startling her so she spilled her concoction. Patrick reacted immediately, leaping over the corner of the bed. One hand gripped Brodie's throat, the other crushed his wrist. "Let her go."

Brodie's hand sprang open, releasing Mona.

"Patrick, please don't—he didn't hurt me."

Brodie gasped, his eyes bulging, a trickle of blood seeping from the cut at his temple.

"Why are you following us?"

Mona touched his arm. "Patrick, I pray you."

Patrick ignored her, holding Brodie's gaze. He loosened his hold on Brodie's throat so the man could speak. Brodie only shook his head, shooting Mona a pleading look.

Mona tried to pry Patrick's fingers off Brodie's wrist. "Let him go. He will not hurt us—will you, Brodie?"

Brodie shook his head.

"Why should I believe him? He tried to kill me."

Sweat plastered Brodie's hair to his head. "I had to."

"Lord Graham sent you? To kill Sir Patrick and bring me home?" Mona asked, still trying to free Brodie's wrist. Patrick only squeezed tighter.

"Patrick!" Mona slapped his shoulder, hard.

He released Brodie, surprised, and stepped back to stare at Mona. "You hit me!" He rubbed at his shoulder.

She fawned all over Brodie. "You're being unreasonable. He is in a great deal of pain and of no threat to anyone—especially not with you hulking over him like some crazed beast."

"Fine."

Mona waved him away as if he were an irritating moth.

He sulked back to the foot of the bed, crossed his arms over his chest, and glared at Brodie.

Mona mixed together another witch's brew and proffered it to her patient. He took it cautiously and, after sniffing at it, drank it down. He lay back on the bolster and closed his eyes.

"My thanks, my lady. Ye always did hiv a gentle touch."

"Just rest now . . . you'll feel better when you wake."

"Good enough to slit my throat and rape you?" Patrick sneered.

One of Brodie's eyes opened. "I'd never harm Lady Graham. I thought ye were accosting her in the stable." He closed his eye again. "Had I kent she was willing, I'd hiv stayed away."

"Oh?" Patrick asked, annoyed to see how mortified Mona appeared. So Brodie knew she was willing—was that so awful? Apparently so, by her fiery cheeks. "Is that why you were skulking about the stables, watching me?"

Brodie sighed. "I was sent to fetch Lady Graham back home . . . but I knew she didna want to come, and I couldna blame her. So I only sought to be certain she was safe wi' ye, afore I returned to Graham Keep."

Mona blinked, her hand covering her mouth and her eyes filling with tears.

Patrick rolled his eyes. "He's lying. He doesn't care about you."

Mona stood and went to Patrick, her eyes still misty. "Finish your meal and let him be. I believe him."

"I do not," Patrick hissed, taking her arm and pulling her to the window. "You are softhearted, and that's fine for a woman. But when it comes to the matters of men, your pudding heart has no place. Let me handle this—isn't that what I'm here for?"

"My *pudding heart?*"

"Aye—as soon as he said he was looking after your

safety, you got all teary. Dinna ye think he knows that? He's only playing the cards he knows are winners."

Mona gave him a reproachful look. "This is not a card game, and I do not have a pudding heart. I know Brodie—he's been master of the guard since I married Hugh. He's never treated me with anything but kindness and consideration." She lowered her voice. "He could be of great use to us—feeding Ridley false intelligence and setting him on the wrong trail."

"And you think he'll do this just because you ask prettily?"

"No . . ." She glanced back at the bed where Brodie appeared to be sleeping. "I have done him many favors."

"I see. He owes you." Patrick still didn't like it. "But what about Lord Graham? Doesn't Brodie owe him for his livelihood?"

"Yes, he does. But he will do what's right."

Patrick scoffed at her naivete. It was hard to believe a woman who seemed so intelligent could have such stupid ideas.

Mona held up a hand. "Perhaps not immediately, but he will come around." She left him and returned to her patient.

Patrick didn't like it, not one bit. He stared out at the empty street. She moved around behind him, her humming smoothing over the ragged edges of his temper. He wished he knew more about their adversary. All Patrick remembered of the Eden Grahams was Hugh—a fierce foe, but a borderer and therefore predictable. He'd always meant to ransom Patrick. But then he'd fallen ill and died. Then Ridley became Lord Graham and all that changed. Patrick had soon realized that Ridley'd never intended to ransom him, perhaps had even meant to let him die in his dungeon. He'd been a more diligent gaoler than any who'd ever tried to keep Patrick.

Unfortunately Ridley had never shown much interest in his prisoner, and so Patrick had exchanged nary a word with him. Brodie could provide Patrick with the answers he sought. But Brodie could also set him free. As soon as the thought occurred, his mind snatched it up. If he could assure himself that Brodie did indeed care about Mona's welfare, then he could take over as her protector. Patrick would be free to return to France without any niggling feelings of guilt for having abandoned her. And since she'd known Brodie for so long, surely she would feel much more comfortable with him than with Patrick.

But first, he reminded himself, he must determine if Brodie was trustworthy. He was so deep in thought that he didn't realize Mona stood beside him, looking out the window.

"How's Brodie?" he asked.

"Asleep. But he will recover."

"Good. You might be right about him. Perhaps he means no harm."

He felt her silent gaze and looked down to find her staring up at him with wary disbelief.

"What?"

She shook her head slowly. "Just when I think you're incapable of seeing the world with anything but suspicion, you surprise me."

He shrugged, looking away from the softness in her eyes. Her words made him pleased, warm—and shamed him. She was wrong about him. He was only grabbing at the first possible opportunity to escape the noose she'd tightened around his neck. He was starting to care about what happened to her. And he knew from experience that such fond feelings were always a mistake. The last thing he wanted was to add Mona to the faces that haunted his nightmares.

*   *   *

A groan in the darkness snapped Mona to full wakefulness. She'd laid her pallet at the foot of the bed so she could tend to Brodie should he need it. As she reached for the candle, she heard the groan again and realized it did not come from the bed but from the door, where Patrick had lain down to sleep.

Her hand froze in the act of striking the flint. His nightmares. His violence. She struck the flint again with new urgency, fumbling in fear. She did not want to be in the dark with him. When the candle was finally lit, she held it high, looking toward the door.

Patrick was huddled on the floor, blanket gone, hands over his head as if protecting himself. She looked toward the bed, but Brodie still slept soundly. She hadn't expected any different—the philter she'd administered rendered him senseless.

Mona looked back at Patrick and saw him jerk as if struck. Her heart hammered in her throat, unable to look away. Instinct warred with terror. She wanted to go to him, to wake him. No one should suffer like that, every night. And yet, memories of his attack on Hazel—and deeper memories, of Edwin—held her back.

It was the night, the darkness, that made her feel so vulnerable. The moon shone through the open window, and Mona could almost imagine it was twelve years ago and she was a maid of sixteen, her entire world gutted by a man. The flame flickered and jumped from the trembling of her hand.

He was having a dream. It was nothing more. Gayle had warned her not to touch him, and so she lay back down, candle beside her, watching the shadowy lump across the small room. Why did he cover his head? She recalled the hoof marks on his head and back. Was he trampled in his dream? An unending barrage of hooves, beating him senseless? She closed her eyes, fighting against the urge to wake him.

He gasped and writhed as if in pain. She couldn't just lay here and watch. She reached into her bodice and removed the small silk purse. She picked a coin from it, took aim, and threw. It hit him in the shoulder.

He jerked awake, rolling over, dirk in hand. His eyes scanned the dark room, finally settling on Mona. He sheathed the knife and searched the ground until he found her missile. He stared down at the coin in his hand for a long moment.

"You were dreaming," she whispered. Her fear had dissolved now that he was awake.

He swallowed hard and nodded.

"Will you answer my question now? What were you dreaming?"

He curled his fingers over the coin and lay back on the pallet, closed fist on his chest. He didn't speak.

Mona sighed. He would never tell her anything. He would never let her help him. She spied his blanket, wadded in the far corner. She fetched it and brought it to him. When he still wouldn't look at her, his face turned to the door, she draped the blanket over him.

He turned his head to her then, and she saw the pain in his eyes, a deep, heart-wrenching anguish.

Mona went to her knees beside him. "Please tell me."

He studied her for a long moment, then closed his eyes tightly, as if collecting his thoughts. "It's . . . not the same dream."

Mona's breath caught in surprise, and a strange, swelling happiness filled her chest. He'd chosen to confide in her. "You had a different dream tonight?" she prompted.

He shook his head. "No . . . they're always the same . . . but there's four—no, five—different ones."

"Tell me about the one you had tonight."

He swallowed hard, his jaw rigid. "Ye dinna want to hear about it . . ."

Mona touched his forearm where it rested on his chest. "I do. I want to understand."

He sighed deeply, exhaling long and slow, then said, "I dreamed tonight about invading Naples. It was some . . . fifteen years past, I was but eighteen years old. King Francis sent an expedition to Naples—it was a complete disaster, but the reason I dream of it . . ." He trailed off. Deep lines bracketed his mouth and again he swallowed, as if forcing down strong emotion.

"Why do you dream of Naples?"

"Because of Julian."

His frequent silences told Mona he was unaccustomed to talking about himself—and was uncertain of revealing this part of himself. That he still tried touched Mona deeply, and she decided then that she would not be satisfied until he was no longer plagued by nightmares.

"Who is Julian?"

"A . . . friend. Though I sold myself out as a mercenary, I had no reputation and was not even a knight. I'd not made a good squire, and well, word got around, so I wasna favored by the French lords and knights. They considered me difficult."

"I can't imagine."

He shot her a narrow look. "It was also well known I had survived Mohacs, when many had perished, including the King of Hungary. Some said it was because I'd run." He shook his head, moving as if to sit up. "I dinna ken why I'm telling you this. It makes no difference now."

Mona stayed him with her hand. "It matters to me—and you're telling me because I asked you to."

"Very well." He seemed to relax, staring into the dark above him. "Julian was squire to Odet de Foix, the Marshal

Lautrec. He defended my name against the other squires—
and even some of the knights—who called me coward. He
didn't insult my French, which has always been poor . . .
and well, he knew some verra bonny lassies."

The side of his mouth curved in a small smile, and he
glanced at her. Mona smiled back, nodding for him to continue.

His smile faded and he took a deep breath. "As I said,
the campaign was a disaster. During the retreat, Julian fell
from his horse. I couldn't tell if he'd been wounded. So I
fought my way back through the flood of horses . . . my
mount wanted naught to do with my plan and threw
me . . . I tried to crawl through the stampeding horses to
Julian, but . . . I kept getting trampled. I would get up on
my hands and knees and try to crawl to him, only to be
trampled again." He met her eyes. "It wasn't so much the
French—they didna mean to trample us. It was the Italians—when they saw us there, on the ground, they made
their horses stomp us."

Mona's hand was over her mouth, her throat tight and
strained.

He saw the look on her face and laughed softly. "It's a
common practice, Mona, I assure you. Gorgon—my old
warhorse—has beat many an enemy senseless with his
hooves."

"It's still horrible."

Patrick shrugged. "Aye. I finally fainted. When I woke,
I could hardly move—I had some broken ribs, and my
head buzzed like a beehive. I found Julian . . . I was only
able to identify him by his tunic . . . we'd already been
robbed by the Italians' camp followers . . . I couldna even
take his rosary back to his mother."

"You dream about this . . . a lot?"

He nodded, then shrugged. "Aye—though that's not the

one that troubles me the most." He glanced at her, then away. "But I dinna want to talk about that one."

And Mona didn't want to hear about it. Not right now, at least. In time, she hoped to hear all his dreams. She stretched out on the floor beside Patrick, pillowing her head on folded hands. "Why do you think you dream of Julian?"

He shook his head again, slowly, thoughtfully. After a moment, he turned on his side to face her. "Here, the floor is hard." He scooted back so she could lie on his pallet. She hesitated, not certain she wanted to be that close to him, especially if they happened to fall asleep, but she decided it would be rude to refuse his kind offer. She didn't want to offend him right now, not when she was making such progress.

When she was comfortable again, she asked, "In the other dreams . . . are they also about someone important to you dying?"

His nod was short and hard, his mouth a grim line. He leaned on his elbow, head in hand. "Do you dream about Edwin? What he did to you?"

"Sometimes, but not like you. And it's always about when he tried to drown me . . . but I don't have the dreams very often anymore."

"How did you make them stop?"

"I didn't . . . they just went away. What Edwin did doesn't hurt me anymore. Maybe you still dream because you're hurt—you miss your friends."

"That won't just go away."

"No," she said sadly, thinking of Arlana. "But it will become easier to bear if you make new friends."

Mona's hands weren't very comfortable under her head, and she fidgeted about. Patrick moved his arm from under his head and straightened it. "Here, lay your head."

His voice was warm, like fine whiskey. She froze, staring into his eyes, azure as the sky on a summer day. He seemed calm now, relaxed. Perhaps she had helped him, just a little bit, and that heated her to her toes. She lifted her head and let him stretch his arm out beneath it. He scooted a bit closer, but still she didn't object, though Arlana was crowing like a fishwife in her head. Mona tucked her away, not wanting to listen. Not now, when she caught the faint scent of hay and horse from him. Even in the dark she could see how fine and smooth his skin was. The blond of his whiskers caught the candlelight and glimmered like gold dust.

Two hand lengths separated their faces. His leather jack was rolled up beneath his head and he stared at her now, into her eyes. All she could think about was the stable. *If your friend hadn't pulled me off you, I'd have had you up against the stable wall without a thought.* The very memory of his words and the look in his eyes when he'd said them— all liquid heat—sent waves of longing through her, centering deep in her belly. She must think of something else.

"Do you have any friends, Patrick?"

"Hmm? . . ." He roused himself from his thoughts. "No. Not really."

"What about your brothers?"

"Well, brothers are brothers."

Mona frowned. "I have neither brothers nor sisters, so I don't understand that."

"What I mean is that they're not friends. A friend wouldn't nag me as Robert does. I'm barely home before he's harping about how long it took me to get there."

Mona smiled, for there was great affection in his voice. "What about Alexander?"

"Ah, Alex . . . Alex was always in trouble. Too much work to keep track of him . . . and when I'm there I spend all my time mediating Alex and Rob's arguments. Besides, Mother and Father always loved Alex best . . . and well, that's hard to forget, especially when your face was rubbed in it as often as mine was."

"But in spite of it all? . . ." Mona said, eyebrows raised.

Patrick rolled his eyes dramatically. "Aye, in spite of all their many, many shortcomings, I do miss them. They are the only people who truly matter to me, besides . . ."

"Besides Rosemarie," she finished for him. The pain in her chest stole her breath, but she refused to reveal how it affected her. It would be humiliating. And more than that, irresponsible. The most important thing in the world to her was the Clachan Fala. She must never lose sight of that. Patrick was only a tool. She should not care that she didn't number among those who mattered to him. *She should not.*

So why did it hurt?

He looked away from her, and the muscles beneath her head contracted.

"You don't like to talk about Rosemarie. Why?"

"It's the only thing about her that is mine alone—my knowledge of her."

Mona's brow furrowed, trying to make sense of his words. "Your knowledge of her?"

Patrick met her gaze again, his eyes infinitely sad. "Aye. Rosemarie is my daughter."

8

Patrick watched Mona's face register shock, understanding, and finally sympathy. But she didn't understand, not really, and he was angry with himself for telling her anything. He'd never spoken of Rosemarie to anyone, ever. Why did he suddenly want to tell her everything? Talk about Rosemarie? It burned in his chest, the need to re-create his daughter, share how precious she was so he could feel it fresh and new, but he reined it in. He'd said too much already.

"You have a daughter?"

"Aye."

"How old is she?"

"Five."

She blinked, dark eyes round. "Where is she?"

Why was he still blathering? No more. He'd never told anyone so much about himself. He was uncomfortable now. Rosemarie's current situation shamed him. He could not tell her about that. He shouldn't have mentioned it at all. But Mona looked up at him with such interest, such concern, it made him oddly warm, comforted almost. Her skin was silk in the candlelight, the thick black plait that lay across her neck was a satin rope. She wore only her shift, and he could see the shape of slim hip and thigh, narrow waist and full breasts.

He touched the curling ends of her plait. She'd wrapped a string about it, to secure it, but the ends were thick and smooth. He let it curl about his finger, caressing it with his thumb. When he met her eyes, she wore that look again—the one that made him rock hard and mindless with lust. Her thick sooty lashes were half lowered, her lips parted, as if focusing on some sensation within, and yet her gaze never left his face.

She licked her lips and swallowed, her gaze darting to his mouth before quickly lowering to watch his hand on her braid. "Your daughter. Where is she?"

He'd given her too much already. "I don't want to talk about Rosemarie."

She met his gaze and held it, searching. "Then I should go back to my pallet."

She probably should. But he didn't say so. He took the weight of her braid in his hand, fingered the silky locks. "I like the braid, but you should wear it down. I've never seen hair so beautiful."

"It wouldn't become a widow—or a wife—to go about with my hair down like a maid. It would certainly draw attention to us."

"Then you should do it for me."

"That would not be wise."

He let his hand travel to her face, tracing the fine arch of her brows, black as raven's wings. Her eyes drifted shut, and she released a shuddering breath. He knew she wanted him, perhaps not as desperately as he wanted her, but she was not immune. Her cheek was warm where it pressed against his arm. His fingers went to her ear.

"Such a tiny ear," he mused, gently tracing the delicate lobe. "Like a seashell."

"Patrick," she whispered, her voice low and rough. "I pray you, stop." How could he, when she spoke? Her voice never failed to send waves of heat through him.

And she didn't want him to stop, not really. Her body showed all the signs of arousal. Her color was high, her breathing shallow. Her words came back to him. *If I'd asked you to stop, you would have. You have proven yourself naught but honorable.* Maybe he should take this opportunity to prove her wrong. Then she would be happy to see him go. Thrilled to have Brodie protect her, instead of Patrick.

He trailed his fingers down the line of her jaw. Her skin was the color of cream, so fine he could see a vein in her temple, pale and delicate.

"Patrick . . ."

Her words trailed off when he ran his thumb over her lips. Her mouth was soft, pliant, the bottom lip full and pink. She inhaled sharply but didn't move. A pulse throbbed in her neck. His mind buzzed, as if he'd been knocked in the head. Touching her was like that—like someone had knocked him senseless, rendered him incapable of coherent thought. It was all sensation and heat.

His body thrummed with anticipation. He curled the arm that her head rested on, bringing her in close. Her hands came up to ward him off, but he caught one, enfolded it in his, and brought it to his mouth.

"Ye dinna really want me to stop," he whispered against her palm. He planted a soft kiss in the center, then another, finally tasting her with the tip of his tongue. She gasped, trying to pull her hand away. She'd brought her legs up, clenching her knees together tightly.

He released her hand, and it immediately went to her breast, where she clasped it. He moved closer, cradling her head in the crook of his arm and leaning over her. He skimmed his other hand over her shoulder and arm. Barely an inch separated their bodies.

She gazed up at him, unblinking.

He slid his hand over her hip and up to her ribs. "If you really wanted me to stop, ye'd get up and walk away. I'm not holding you down." He prayed she would not. He wanted to have her naked and soft beneath him. He could forget with her—he sensed it somehow, that in her arms his heart and mind could be free of burdens, if only for a short while.

She blinked at him as his words sunk in. Her throat worked as she swallowed. "I like how it feels. But we should not do this."

Despite her words, her resistance melted away. He felt the tension leave her and her body flow toward his. He put his arm around her, his hand smoothing over her hair, pulling her braid over her shoulder. Her breasts pressed to his chest, setting his body alite, her thigh nudged between his legs.

He lowered his head to kiss her. A moment before their lips met, their breath mingling sweetly, she asked, "What about Brodie?"

He didn't particularly care about the man on the bed, but he did recall being attacked the last time he attempted to have his way with Mona. He looked up at the bed, at the motionless lump. The lump he meant to abandon Mona to—after he ravished her. His fist clenched around the silk of her braid, and he looked down into her face, so beautiful, so trusting.

What would she say if she knew that even now he plotted to rid himself of this obligation—of her? And would he be able to walk away from her free of guilt if he took her to his bed?

Damnation.

Her hand was on his face, stroking. "What is it?" Her husky voice, rich with desire, sent a shudder through him.

He wanted to lean into her hand and close his eyes, put these thoughts from his mind. But he could not let himself care.

"Go." He rolled onto his back, laying his arm flat so she could move away from him.

She did nothing at first, the weight of her pressing on his arm. Her hand trailed over his chest, caught his chin and gently tried to turn his face. He held himself rigid. If he looked at her, he'd lose his resolve, his strength. She was becoming a weakness for him. He feared it was too late already—he *must* leave.

"You were right," he said. "This is unwise. Go back to your pallet and leave me alone."

Her head was gone from his arm. He watched the shadows rise and fall against the wall as she took the candle and crossed the room. His body ached with unsatisfied lust. He rolled onto his stomach, burying his face into his arms, forcing himself to formulate a means of discovering Brodie's trustworthiness. He had to get away from here— away from her.

There was little change in Brodie. Mona continued to sleep at the end of his bed, increasingly worried about the man. At times his speech was slurred, and his memory spotty; at others his memory and speech were intact. But the dizziness and vomiting hung on. He could barely stand without swooning.

Patrick had become impatient with the entire situation. He tried to question Brodie, but Mona refused to let him upset her patient. She'd made a great deal of progress with Brodie. He swore he meant them no harm and would do all he could to see her to safety. Now Mona just had to heal him so he could do her bidding. She just wished she could make Patrick understand.

She'd had little opportunity to probe Patrick further about his nightmares. He made himself scarce, and Brodie seemed to demand all of her attention when Patrick was present. There was no repeat of their night of intimacy and shared confidences. Patrick slept little, and if the nightmares visited him, Mona slept through them.

A week had passed this way when one night she was roused from a light sleep. She knew immediately it wasn't Patrick that woke her but sounds from the open window. It was full night, but there was a great deal of activity on the street below. She rolled over to find Patrick at the window, hands braced on the sill, staring out.

Mona rose and joined him, pulling her blanket around her shoulders. "What is it?"

He moved aside so she could see out the window. Men filled the street, most on horseback, some on foot, all wearing jacks or mail. They held torches aloft and were armed. They appeared to be gathering, waiting. More men rode in from the end of the street, but still they waited. They talked, but it was not boisterous, it was quiet conversation. Serious.

"A raid," Mona said.

"Aye. There've been no raids nearby, so they're instigating it." His body turned toward her, but she could not look at him. Not in the dark and standing so close. Never had a man so confused her, never had anyone tried her patience so sorely.

"My lady," he said, to capture her attention.

She forced herself to look up at him and wished she hadn't. He wore only shirt and breeches, the shirt open at the throat. Blond hairs peeked out of the V, glinting in the faint light from the torches below. His neck was thick and muscular, his jaw dusted with blond whiskers. The cerulean eyes fixed on her were very serious. She forced herself to attend to what he was saying.

"We cannot stay here. There will surely be a counter raid—if not tonight, then in the coming days."

"Brodie is not well—"

"To hell with Brodie!" He thrust away from the window, running an agitated hand through his hair.

"I can't just leave him."

He turned toward her, palm extended. "What of the Clachan Fala? I thought that was the most important thing to you? Bigger than both of us, you said."

"It is," she whispered, not wanting to wake Brodie. "That is why I'm doing this."

"No." He grasped her arms. She could do nothing, as she was holding the blanket closed. "He will never help us, my lady. You're a fool to think different."

My lady. He'd returned to formalities the morning after his revelations.

"That's not so. He promised to help me."

He released her arms. "You're too trusting. That's the healer in you, wanting all to be right with the world. But the world isn't fair or good. You are also the Keeper. You cannot let one interfere with the other. The healer is thwarting the Keeper."

"Is that what you do? Separate the friend from the warrior?"

His eyes narrowed, and he turned back to the window. "I'm friend to no one."

"I thought we were friends."

"I have a duty to you, that is all."

That wasn't all. She knew it, had felt it from him. But he had rebuilt his wall higher and thicker to keep her out. Mona was no longer tired, but she couldn't stand here, at the window, beside him and not touch him. His back was to her, the shoulders broad and heavy. A bulwark against emotion. She longed to run her hands down them, to circle his waist and press her face to the columns of strength.

Where had such thoughts come from? She returned to her pallet and lay down, facing him. Sleep didn't come, not while he stood there, tension flowing off him in waves. She lay there for hours it seemed, watching him, thinking about him. Her thoughts were circular. He was moody, dangerous. And yet at times she glimpsed kindness, humor. It was the nightmares that plagued him. That and the mystery of his daughter. There was something more that he refused to tell her. Something about Rosemarie. Why would he not speak of her? And why had she not heard of this daughter? She'd made it her business to learn all she could about him. It was not difficult to discover if a man was married, had children. Even bastards were uncovered easily enough— unless someone went to great lengths to hide them. But why? It didn't make sense.

She so wanted to help him, if only he would let her. She was drawn to him, as she'd never been to a man.

That is lust.

For the first time in a very long time, Mona didn't welcome Arlana's memory into her head. Perhaps it was lust, but what was so wrong with that? She'd never felt anything so powerful and exciting.

He can use it—use you.

He wouldn't.

It didn't matter. She closed her eyes tightly, blocking him from her sight. He didn't want her anymore. He never tried to touch her, hardly spoke to her, and had stopped even looking at her unless it was necessary. He was just doing his job.

She woke sometime later, surprised she had fallen asleep at all. The room was freezing—they only had a brazier to keep them warm. A shiver wracked her body, and a moment later something heavy fell across her. Footfalls moved away from her. She cracked her eyes to see Patrick squatting in front of the brazier, adding coals. Had he not slept at all? His blanket and his jack were both draped over her. He must have been beside her, for she'd heard no approach before he'd covered her.

She pulled his blanket and jack closer, inhaling deeply the scent of him, a sense of comfort and security descending on her. Her fingers sought the iuchair, the beads warm from her skin. All would be well, so long as Patrick was near.

The raiding party returned to the village at dawn, laden with plunder and herding hundreds of kine and sheep. Those who didn't return to their homes dispersed to the various drinking establishments. Patrick took advantage of the celebratory mood to engage in some games of chance and managed to win back most of Mona's money. The villagers were in a rare lather, drinking to the king of England's health, as well as the local warden, Lord Wharton.

Their raid had been successful, ransacking a Scots town on the border. Not an unusual occurrence in itself, but what had them so excited was a different raid or battle—at Hadden Rigg. Patrick was reluctant to show his ignorance and so waited for someone to reveal the significance of this battle. But other than spitting out the name like rotten meat, they revealed nothing. It was frustrating. He'd lost nearly a year in Graham Keep and didn't know the state of the border. Lawless and violent, always—that was not news. But war?

Brodie Armstrong. He could tell Patrick all he wanted to know, but every time Patrick interrogated him he threw up or started screaming. Then Mona would scold Patrick. He'd given up his plan to abandon Mona to Brodie days ago. He would never trust such a gutless knave with

Mona's safety. The longer they stayed in the village with Lord Graham's henchman, the more uneasy Patrick became. Unfortunately, Mona refused to believe Brodie was useless—and quite possibly a danger to them.

The anger suffused him again, commonplace now, and he pushed away from the table. She must always have her way. What was the use of having him? He was her pleaseman, a prisoner to her whims. If he wasn't lusting after her he was furious with her. It had become an unpleasant existence. He left the alehouse and strode across the street to the innyard, determined to have the truth from Brodie or kill him, Mona be damned. She was wrong about Brodie Armstrong—he wouldn't help them. They had to leave here. They had to get out of England. Though he'd been unable to glean any specifics without attracting unwanted attention, it was clear something was brewing on the borders, more than a simple raid.

Patrick climbed the stairs to their room. He was nearly to the head of the stairs when the door to their room opened inward. Someone was leaving. *Mona.* Patrick hurried back down the stairs. He would hide until she was gone, then go up and question Brodie without her hovering over him. See if he was so confused without Mona present.

The person descending the stairs was not Mona. It was a boy. He mounted a pony in the innyard and rode out of the village. Patrick climbed the stairs as quietly as he could and crept to the door, pausing outside to listen carefully. No sound of Mona's humming, though there was much scraping and banging.

He pushed the door open. Brodie stood beside the table, digging through Mona's sacks. He was alone. He whirled, eyes wide. Patrick closed the door behind him. Brodie looked to the window.

"Where's Lady Graham?" Patrick asked.

Brodie clutched his belly and began to groan, limping toward the bed. "I dinna know. I was just looking for the brew she gives me to soothe me stomach complaint."

Patrick went to the sack and inspected the contents, but nothing seemed to be missing. Brodie fell on the bed, moaning.

Patrick walked to the bed. "You had a visitor."

"I'm goin' to bock," Brodie said, gasping and retching.

"Aye, well, get it over wi'. And ye'll clean it up, too, else I'll rub yer nose in it."

Brodie didn't bock, but he continued rolling around in the narrow bed, his face averted.

"Answer me. Who was your visitor?"

Brodie continued acting as though he were oblivious to Patrick's questions until Patrick's temper snapped. He pulled the man up by his beard.

"When I hit you this time, you wilna wake." He leaned in close. "I'll make certain of it."

Brodie swallowed hard. "The lad was from Lord Graham."

Patrick thrust Brodie away and paced the room, hands on hips. "So he knows exactly where we are."

"Aye," Brodie said, remarkably healed of his stomach complaint. He sat up on the bed, watching Patrick uneasily.

"What happened at Hadden Rigg?"

"A battle. The East March warden, Sir Robert Bowes, with the Douglases, set out to raze Teviotdale."

Patrick turned, frowning. "Why? Was it a reprisal or a hot trod?"

Brodie shook his head. "Nay . . . the king wished it."

The English king? Patrick rubbed at his chin. "Why?"

"Last year, the Scots King was to meet with King Henry in York. Your king didn't come. King Henry was furious. Shortly after, he beheaded his . . ." Brodie frowned, counting on his fingers. "His fifth queen. The king has been crazed ever since. He claims ancient sovereignty over Scotland. He is planning an invasion and has set the wardens the task of weakening the Scots in preparation."

"Hadden Rigg?" The Douglases had been out of favor for some time. No doubt they were hoping King Henry would invade Scotland so they might win back their lands and titles.

"We were routed by the Scots under Huntly."

Patrick was torn. He must get Mona to safety—deeper north into Scotland. And then he must answer the call to arms that would surely be issued by King James. He wondered how Mona would take this news and decided not to tell her. He would take her to his brother, Alex. He had a fortress on the western coast, safe from invasion. She could stay there until the danger was over. And then Alex would help her. Alex couldn't resist a good deed or a bonny lass.

Decision made, Patrick felt better, as if a weight had been lifted from his shoulders. He trusted Alex with his life. And Mona couldn't protest; Alex was a skilled warrior. He would make a good protector.

The door opened, and Mona entered. She pushed the hood of her cloak back. Rose bloomed on her cheeks. She carried a basket piled with plants. She paused, looking between the two men suspiciously as she shut the door.

"Look at him," Patrick said. "There's nothing wrong with him. And he's been receiving visitors while you were out."

Mona removed her cloak and crossed to the bed, frowning down at Brodie. "What visitors?"

Brodie stood, eyes darting wildly about the room—to the door, to Mona, to Patrick and back.

A frisson of dread passed through Patrick. He stepped forward. "My lady, stay back—"

But it was too late. Brodie grabbed her and pressed a dirk to her throat. Mona gripped his wrist, struggling until

Brodie twisted her arm behind her back. Her cry of pain and surprise ripped through Patrick. He'd already drawn his sword and was circling them.

Brodie's breath hissed through his teeth, his face greasy with sweat. "If ye want her to live, ye'll let me go." Brodie edged toward the door, dragging Mona along.

Patrick knew Brodie didn't want to hurt her—Lord Graham would kill him if he did, as would Patrick. But he also had to know that his life was already forfeit once he released her. Patrick wouldn't allow him to live after using her so.

Patrick blocked his exit. "If you kill her, you're a dead man. If I don't hew you down, Lord Graham will."

Brodie's gaze darted around the room, looking for escape. "Let me out," he growled, teeth barred, "or I'll break her arm!" He yanked her arm up higher. Mona keened, back arching, tears leaking down her cheeks. A film of red fell over Patrick's vision. His palms gripped his sword, longing to cut Brodie down, but not wanting to cause Mona any more pain.

With her free hand, Mona gripped Brodie's wrist. The knife didn't waver, still pressed against the soft underside of her jaw. Mona lowered her chin, pushing her head back, and sunk her teeth into the side of his hand. Brodie didn't drop the knife, but he yelled and tried to yank his hand free of her teeth. Patrick attacked, grabbing the arm Mona had bitten, and jerking it away. He pushed Mona aside and thrust his sword into Brodie's belly. It was over quickly. Brodie lay on the floor, clutching his stomach in earnest now as blood pooled around him.

Patrick went to Mona. She sprawled on the floor where he'd shoved her, blood smeared across her mouth and cheek, staring at Brodie.

Patrick knelt beside her. "Did he hurt you?"

Her skin was unnaturally pale, the blood a stark contrast. "You killed him?"

Patrick used the edge of her kirtle to wipe at her face, relieved to see unblemished skin beneath all the blood. He sat back on his heels. "If he's not already dead, he will be soon."

She covered her mouth with both hands, tears welling in her eyes. "What have you done?"

Patrick grabbed her shoulders and gave her a hard shake. Her eyes finally left Brodie's body and rested on him.

"He was betraying you. He had a visitor, a boy, from Lord Graham today. Ridley knows just where we are."

She blinked, uncomprehending.

"He's following us, don't you see? Letting us do the work for him. And then he will take the Bloodstone from you and kill us both."

She still seemed too stunned for his words to be sinking in. Patrick stood and, after wiping down his sword, began gathering her things, stuffing them into the sacks. When he was done, he grabbed her cloak and pulled her to her feet. She was utterly compliant as he clasped her cloak at the neck and pulled the hood over her head. Perhaps she finally realized he was more experienced in these matters and that they should be left to him.

She followed him out the door and down to the stables. If someone discovered Brodie's body, he didn't know what would happen, but it wouldn't be good. They rode out of the village with no more than a few curious looks. Patrick drove the horses hard, not stopping until dusk. They were both silent, urgent. The moor provided little cover, a few rocks and some scrub, but they wouldn't be stopping for long.

Mona wandered about in the gloaming, picking up dry leaves and twigs.

"No fire," Patrick said.

"We'll freeze."

"If we light a fire they'll see us from a mile away." He stared out across the desolate moor, wondering if Brodie's body had been discovered yet. There had been no sign of pursuit. Once they crossed into Scotland, they'd be safe from Brodie's murder.

Mona sat behind him, tucking her feet beneath her. Patrick squatted beside her and examined her critically. Her face was drawn, and there were dark smudges beneath her eyes. He hadn't done a good job wiping Brodie's blood away. Rusty smears still marred her skin.

"Something is amiss with you."

"I don't understand how this happened. I've been working on Brodie all week. He was going to help us. *He was.*"

"No, he wasn't. He played you false." He sat down near her and began digging through one of the sacks for food. "I told you not to trust him."

"Yes, you did."

He gave her cheese and bread and then had to urge her to eat it. She did eventually. Her withdrawal troubled him. He wasn't accustomed to her silence.

"We'll head for the firth at first light," he said.

"The firth?"

"Aye—we'll cross into Scotland there."

The dazed look faded from her eyes. "No. I told you, we'll go south and hide. We must throw Ridley off our trail."

"No. We can't stay on the border. A war is coming."

She made a rude noise. "A war is always coming."

"Well, it's really coming now. The borders aren't safe. We must keep north. Isn't that the direction the Bloodstone lies?"

She nodded absently, then narrowed her eyes at him.

He grinned at her and took a drink of her whiskey. "Is it in the Highlands? Or an island?"

She pursed her lips tightly. "So you know it's north. You'll learn nothing else from me until it's necessary."

"Ye dinna think you can trust me? I saved you back there."

Mona shook her head and turned her face away.

Patrick stopped mid-drink and lowered the flask. "What's this? You believe not the danger you faced?"

She looked at him pointedly. "I wasn't finished with him, Patrick. He could have been a great asset if you hadn't killed him."

Patrick stared at her incredulously. "Asset? He tried to twist yer arm off."

Her fists clenched on her lap. "He was frightened. You nearly killed him in the stables."

"I should have killed him in the stables."

"No," she said, angry now. "You don't have to kill everyone. That's not what I wanted."

"Then what do ye want? Bloody hell! I protected you. Isn't that what I'm supposed to do?"

"Why does that have to mean killing? Now we have no one to set Ridley on the wrong trail and a new problem. If the villagers aren't already after us, they'll report it to the warden. Then we'll be put to the horn."

Patrick was angry now. The ungrateful little witch. He'd protected her back there, and now she railed at him as if he were an unruly bairn. He stood, taking a deep swallow of whiskey, letting it warm his belly.

She glared up at him. "And you have to drink all my whiskey, too? I didn't bring it for you—it's for cleansing wounds."

Patrick capped the flask and dropped it in her lap. "Forgive, my lady," he ground out. "You won't have to suffer my presence much longer."

He started to walk away, but she was up and after him. She grabbed his arm. "What does that mean? Are you abandoning me?" Her cheeks were flushed, ebony locks escaping her plait to fly around her face in the breeze.

"You dinna need me. I'm just mucking up your grand plan." He yanked his arm away and went to the horses. He was sore tempted to ride away and give her a good scare.

"If you would just listen to me, that wouldn't happen."

"No, you listen to me. I'm not going to die for your foolish Bloodstone and I'm not going to die for you. You don't know what you're playing at. I said I would help you, but not when you're behaving like a child."

Her face flushed crimson and she opened her mouth, but he cut her off.

"It's become clear to me that I'm not the man for the job. I'm taking you to my brother, Alex. He'll keep you safe until this war business is over. Then he can see you to your fairy stone. He's just the kind of man you're looking for."

"You will not abandon me, Sir Patrick Maxwell!" She trembled, fist clenched so her knuckles were white. Patrick had never seen her so furious. "Do you hear me?"

Patrick ignored her, leading the horses forward and gesturing to her to mount up.

"Is that what you did to Rosemarie? Abandoned her so you could get on with more important matters? Is that why you won't speak of it?"

He froze, a black cloud of shame churning in his belly, which quickly transformed into bitter anger. She didn't know. She was guessing, probing for a wound that would bring him back. And she'd found a raw one.

She stood there defiantly, cloak billowing out around her, chin held high. He dropped the reins and retraced his steps until he stood before her. She showed no signs of fear, meeting his eyes boldly.

"Do not speak of my daughter," he said in a freezing

tone. "I don't want to hear her name fall from your lips ever again. Do you understand?"

By degrees, the defiance left her stance. Her shoulders sagged, her face softened, the corners of her mouth turned down. "Patrick . . . I was angry . . ."

"I should beware then and drink nothing served by your hand, eh? Else I'll be joining your husbands."

The disbelief and hurt in her eyes quickly froze to contempt, and she nearly sneered at him. "I don't need you anymore." She went past him and mounted her horse.

Patrick was still angry, but at himself now, too. He shouldn't have said that, but then, she had no right to assume things about Rosemarie. "You can't ride alone. It's nearly dark. You'll get lost."

She tapped Dragon's sides and rode away from him.

Patrick paced. *She'll be back. She left her bags of junk.* He continued pacing, watching her grow smaller until the dusk swallowed her. He stared at her sacks and the discarded flask. *Damn it.* Did she leave them on purpose? Knowing he'd follow?

Fog rose from the moors, swirling about his knees. Soon he would be unable to find her. She'd be lost and alone. Why did he care? He ground his teeth in frustration. He did care and he didn't want to. He was free now. He could go to Annancreag and see his brothers. Join the king's army and fight the English. And then he could return to France and Rosemarie. He'd stop this eternal fighting and settle down on his estate, eventually marry Rosemarie's mother. And then what? Have another child? And just maybe, sometime in the night, he would assault his wife and children when they tried to rouse him from a nightmare.

He shut his eyes, disgusted with himself. He couldn't abandon Mona. What if the villagers came after them for

Brodie's murder? What if they found Mona? She would be helpless. Worse than that, Ridley surely had more men than Brodie following her. The image of Brodie's hands on her, his dirk pressed against the pale skin of her neck, rose in his mind, driving Patrick to his horse, following her into the mist.

9

Mona entered the village on the shores of the Solway Firth alone. She'd forgotten her sacks in her anger and was filthy, hungry, and sore from sleeping on the hard ground without even a blanket. She'd hardly eaten since the bread and cheese she'd shared with Patrick. But she still had some coin tucked into her bodice.

Wood and thatch buildings sat far from water's edge. It was a clear day, and Mona could see Scotland across the firth. The tide was low, and she could even make out a sandbank in the distance. She wanted to spur Dragon forward and ford the firth now, put England behind her. She could never come back.

But it was a deception. She would be stranded on a sandbank or drowned if she tried to cross. She must find a fisherman to take her across when the tide was high. As this was a fishing village, that shouldn't be difficult. Already she mourned parting with Dragon. He couldn't come with her.

She found an inn and was able to arrange for the sale of Dragon. She ordered a meal in the common room. There was an empty table near the window, so she claimed it.

She'd been alone for three days now. She'd spent the first day wandering the moor, trying to find the place she'd stopped with Patrick, hoping to at least locate her sacks, if not the man himself. By the second day she'd admitted to herself she was lost. She'd consulted the iuchair and it led her to this coastal village. She shouldn't have left Patrick. It had been foolish, but it couldn't be helped now. She shouldn't have said that about his daughter. She didn't blame him for striking back.

She stared at the activity outside the window. Men, women, and children hurried about their work, racing the setting sun. Mona spied a young couple in a doorway. A plump lass, clutching a basket of bread to her middle. The lad leaned in close, as if trying to steal a kiss.

A wave of longing rose in Mona. She'd never felt so alone. She even missed Patrick's sullen silences. Just his presence had been a comfort. More, she missed the times when he'd talked to her and those even rarer occasions when he'd lit the world with his smile.

Her meal was set before her, and she resolved to put Patrick from her mind. He'd managed to fracture her focus. The most important thing was recovering the Clachan Fala and delivering it to Caroline and Lord Annan. She was better off without Patrick. She'd begun to have the most unthinkable ideas when she was with him. Things that could never be, that he would never want.

As she ate, she noticed a man pass by the window repeatedly. She tried to convince herself it meant nothing; she merely sat where he chose to sell his fish. But it comforted her little. Patrick had been right about Brodie, he'd been playing her false. She might not like how he had dispatched the threat, but the truth was, he'd only done what she asked him to do. Protect her.

The fishmonger stopped in front of the window and slid

her an oily look, quickly averting his eyes when he discovered Mona staring back. Mona's appetite shriveled. Was the fishmonger one of Ridley's minions, keeping watch over her? Would she ever be able to escape him?

She looked out over the common room and noticed two men playing cards and drinking. The one facing her had shaggy black hair and a twisted scar across his cheek. He was watching her. Seeing he caught her eye, he winked and gestured for her to join him. Did he think her a whore? Or easy prey, being a woman alone? Mona ignored him, looking back out the window. The fishmonger was still there.

Panic gripped her, and she wished desperately for Patrick. Why had she spoken such harsh words to him? Why had she left him? Pride and anger would be her undoing.

Mona took her loaf of bread and went up to the room she'd rented. There was no way to bar the door. Bar the door from what? Ridley wouldn't touch her until she had the Bloodstone. Mona washed with cold, smelly water, wishing she'd taken at least one of her sacks so she could use soap. The bed linens were reasonably clean. She crawled under the blanket, determined to enjoy sleeping in a bed this night. It might be the last bed she slept in for some time.

Her sleep was troubled, filled with images of horses trampling her as she tried to reach Patrick. At dawn, she collected the money for the sale of Dragon and bid him farewell. She pressed her face against his warm neck as tears pricked her eyes. Arlana had warned her the life of the Keeper was a lonely one, and yet Mona had never been alone as Arlana had, not until now.

She left the stables and went to the docks, looking for someone who might give her passage to Scotland. The tide was high now, and the expanse of white sand had disappeared. Water lapped against the wood of the dock. The scent of fish was heavy in the air, and the firth was already dotted with dozens of fishing boats.

She scanned the fishermen still on the dock, readying their boats, and noted the scarred man from yesterday evening. She paused, staring uncertainly at him. He straightened, seeing her eyes on him, and nodded, a smile breaking across his face. It seemed doubtful he was associated with Ridley. He was too eager to attract her attention.

Deciding he was safe, Mona smiled back and approached him. She passed a cloaked man who turned away from her to finger some nets. Was it the fishmonger from yesterday? She tried to get a better look, but he continued to turn away from her, his face hidden.

The scarred man ran a hand over his shaggy black hair, as if that could set it to rights. He was her age, or perhaps younger, and not unattractive, but he was in dire need of a bath and a comb.

"I must join my husband across the firth," Mona said. "I was looking for passage."

His smile disappeared. "To Scotland, eh? And you're married?"

She nodded. "I can pay you."

"It'll take me all day to get you there and back . . . I'll lose a day's business."

"I can compensate you."

When he still stared at her uncertainly, Mona pulled her sack of coins from her bodice. The scarred man's eyes glittered as he watched her, a strange smile curving his lips. She'd seen that look on Patrick's face before—it had set her blood afire. This man made her want to run.

She removed two shillings from the sack and held them out to him. "Will this be enough?"

He grinned. "My name's 'artwood, but everyone calls me 'art." He took her money and tucked it away in his tunic. He led her down the dock to a long boat bobbing in the water. It was filled with cages and nets. He cleared a plank for her to sit on and gestured to a group of men farther down the dock. When the men joined them, Hart explained that he was taking Mona to Scotland. After a round of cursing, three men hopped into the boat with them to help row.

Hart had not been exaggerating. The trip took the entire morning. Mona had brought her bread, and Hart shared his ale with her. He chatted with her amicably, asking many questions about her husband that she found difficult to dodge. She suspected he knew she was lying by the time they pulled the boat up on the sandy beach.

Mona climbed out of the boat and turned to thank Hart, but he was beside her.

"I need to go to the village." He gestured to the others to wait with the boat. "I'll take you to your husband."

Mona smiled vaguely, not meeting his eyes.

"If you were my wife, I'd not let you cross the firth alone."

"The smith keeps my husband busy." Edwin had been a blacksmith and though not as large as Patrick, his arms had been substantial. He'd managed to offend many with his erratic behavior, but few had challenged him for fear of feeling his fists. She hoped that would be a sufficient inducement for Hart to leave her outside the smithy.

Mona looked back out over the firth. Another fishing boat approached. Though it was still some distance away, she was certain she spied a cloaked man—the same one from the docks. Mona's heart slammed against her ribs.

"Is aught amiss?" Hart asked, studying her expression.

Mona started to say no, then realized Hart's attraction might be useful. She pointed to the approaching boat. "I think that man is following me."

Hart peered at the approaching vessel. "The big one—with the brown cloak?"

"Yes."

"Wait 'ere." Hart went back to his boat and conversed with his friends, pointing to the cloaked man. When he returned, he smiled. He took her arm, directing her toward the path that led to the village. "Don't worry, 'e won't follow you anymore."

Mona looked over her shoulder, slightly alarmed. What if she'd been mistaken? Hart's friends were now standing at the water's edge, waiting for the craft to beach. What would they do to the cloaked man? What if he was just some poor old man who happened to be in the wrong place at the wrong time? She forced herself to put these thoughts from her mind. She would have to be ruthless to outwit Ridley. She remembered Patrick's words to her about Brodie—she couldn't let a pudding heart jeopardize everything.

She turned back to Hart, determined to put the cloaked man from her thoughts. She had Hart to worry about now. He would soon enough discover she was a woman alone and that she'd lied to him. She couldn't anticipate what he might do. There was a time when she'd thought herself a good judge of character, but that was before Brodie. Patrick had been right about him all along. At the thought of Patrick her heart sank lower. Would she ever see him again? He'd wanted to go to Annancreag to see his brother. Perhaps he would still be there when she delivered the stone to Lord Annan. Would he even speak to her?

When they arrived at the village, Hart insisted on sharing a meal with her. Mona was anxious to purchase a horse and be gone, but she did need to eat first. She picked at the salmon, trying not to seem impatient. She couldn't stay here with all these eyes on her. She was about to thank Hart and say good-bye when a familiar figure entered the tavern.

The fishmonger. And he wasn't wearing a brown cloak. In fact, now that she looked at him, it was clear the man in the cloak could not have been the fishmonger. Though he'd been bent with age, he'd stood at least a head taller and had been thrice as broad as the narrow fishmonger.

Panic throbbed through her. She'd committed an innocent man to a beating and she hadn't eluded Ridley's spy. The fishmonger's close-set eyes rested on her briefly before he turned his back and disappeared into the gloom of the tavern.

Mona pushed away from the table. "I must be on my way. My thanks, Hart, for everything."

"Wait!" Hart tried to follow her, but the room was closely packed, and he couldn't get through the crush fast enough. Mona darted out the door. She must find a place to hide. She raced along the street, pulling her hood up to cover her face and weaving through the villagers milling about. She ducked into a narrow alley between two buildings.

Air burned in her lungs. What was she doing, racing through the streets like a thief? She didn't know what to do anymore! She didn't know whom she could trust, who could help her. If only she hadn't left Patrick! She couldn't stop berating herself for that folly. He was the only one she could trust, the only one who could protect her. Why had she been such a damned fool? Even if she somehow found him, he'd probably refuse to help her.

Her breathing began to calm, and she hoped she'd escaped both Hart and the fishmonger. She peeked out of the alley and found herself confronted with the cloaked figure. He pushed her back into the alley, an enormous hand closing over her wrist. A panicked scream caught in her throat, and she looked up, trying to jerk her wrist away.

She cried the only name she knew in this village. "Hart!"

Her captor yanked his hood back, revealing gleaming blond hair and angry cerulean eyes. "Is that his name? Hart?"

The fear drained from Mona, replaced by happiness. "Patrick? *You're* following me?"

He gripped her shoulders and shook her. "Who is this Hart? You were verra familiar with him." He scowled down at her but didn't give her a chance to answer. "I'm verra easy to replace, aye? I thought it *had* to be me."

Mona wanted to laugh hysterically. He thought he'd been replaced. "How long have you been following me?"

"Since ye rode off like a lackwit into the fog three days past."

She let out a surprised breath. "Why didn't you show yourself?"

"You said you didn't need me anymore."

"Fool! I went back to find you. If you were following me you'd know that."

The scowl faded as he considered her. "I thought you went back for your bags of rubbish . . . I thought about riding ahead and leaving them somewhere you'd find them, but you didna seem to know where you were going and I couldn't risk losing you."

Mona shook her head and looked up at him imploringly. "Patrick, I made a mistake. I'm—"

Hart grabbed Patrick's shoulder and swung him around. "Leave her alone." His three friends stood behind him, fingering their dirks. They were all bloodied and bruised—one's arm hung at an awkward angle.

"Hart, no—I was—"

"Get your hand off me," Patrick said, his voice low with warning, eyes locked on Hart.

"Patrick, please—"

Patrick rounded on her. "Please? Spare your new friend? Ye think I'd kill him, too?"

Hart and his friends exchanged uneasy glances.

"No," Mona said, becoming exasperated. Before she

could say another word, Hart shoved Patrick and punched him. Patrick's head snapped back, and then he was on Hart, grabbing handfuls of his tunic and tossing him down the alleyway.

He started after Hart.

"Patrick no!" Mona cried, grabbing his arm. "There's someone else—one of Ridley's men, following me. We must go!"

Patrick stared at Hart, who was slowly getting to his feet, then nodded. He took her hand. They turned to find the three men blocking their way.

"Move!" Patrick growled, and after a moment's hesitation they made a hole for Patrick and Mona to pass through. Mona hung onto his hand, letting him drag her where he would, joy nearly bursting her heart. He'd not abandoned her. He'd been protecting her all along. She was safe now. He would take care of everything.

He led her to an inn. She pulled on his hand just inside, stopping him. The feel of his warm hand engulfing hers was pure bliss, like a shield against danger. "Should we stay in the village tonight? We need to lose Ridley's spy."

"Just shut up and give me the money."

Mona fished out her red purse and placed it in his open hand. He got them a room and led her up the stairs. Once the door was shut behind them, he turned to her, his face thunderous.

"What were you doing with that man?"

"He took me across the firth."

"He did more than take you across the firth. He walked ye to the village and you shared a meal with him."

"I didn't know how to make him go away. I was afraid he would be angry when he found out I lied to him." Was Patrick jealous? He was overreacting just a bit. A thrill went through her.

"You certainly seemed to enjoy his company," he muttered and went to the window to stare down at the street. He'd removed his cloak, and she wondered how she'd failed to recognize the broadest shoulders in all of England and Scotland—even cloaked and hunched.

Mona went to him. "Forgive me for what I said about Rosemarie." Her voice was a whisper, a prayer almost, that he'd accept her apology.

He nodded without looking at her. "I . . ." His voice cracked, and he cleared his throat. "I shouldn't have said that . . . about you poisoning me."

"You were angry . . . as I was." She touched his arm hesitantly. He looked down at her hand, though he didn't meet her eyes. Cords of muscle stood out on his neck, his jaw was tight.

"You were right about Brodie. You did what you had to. I'll not question you anymore."

He nodded thoughtfully, still staring at her hand. She removed it nervously, wondering if he didn't want her touching him. He returned his gaze to the street below. "We canna fight Ridley if we are fighting, aye? We must be as one in thought and deed."

"Yes," Mona whispered.

"So someone must be in charge."

Mona tried not to bristle at what he implied. He was a warrior, a knight. He lived by the rules of combat.

When she didn't respond, he said, "We'll do this my way, or I'm going home."

Mona bit her lip, staring down at her hands. She needed him desperately. She didn't want to do this without him. "Very well."

He straightened, the tension and anger gone from his face. "Good. Where are we going, then?"

Mona moved away from him, drifting toward the bed.

He wasn't going to like her answer. Would he think her a liar? Would he leave her then? Fearfully, she said, "I . . . I know not."

"You know not?"

Mona sat on the bed. "The iuchair reveals the way to me . . . but it only does it a little at a time. I do know where the Bloodstone is, but I don't know place names."

"Then tell me what you know."

She pulled the iuchair over her head and gestured for him to join her on the bed. She was doing now what she'd vowed to Arlana she'd never do—share the secrets of the Keeper. With a man.

Patrick sat beside her, grimacing in pain.

"Are you hurt?" She touched his chin lightly, examining him for wounds.

"No . . . it's my knee. Rain comes."

There was a bruise on his cheekbone, but otherwise his skin was unblemished. Her fingers lingered too long on his whiskered chin. He looked down at her, his eyes darkening. Her body pulsed with awareness. She dropped her hand hastily and held the iuchair out to him.

He took it from her, turning it over in his hands, fingers caressing the oddly shaped beads. "It's a map," he whispered, his voice wondering.

Mona nodded. "I've never left the West March before, so I can't tell you exactly where it is we're going. The iuchair keeps telling me north and west. And I see an island . . . but Scotland has many islands, so I won't know which one until we're closer."

"These are landmarks." Patrick fingered each bead. "I know some of them . . . but some I've never seen before."

"Arlana made me memorize the order in which the beads are found." Mona picked out three stones. "We've already passed these."

He frowned. "I dinna recall . . ."

"This one was in the forest . . ." Mona touched a long narrow bead—the ancient tree. Their fingers brushed and she shivered. "I only saw it in a vision. The others I know were there, but since we were doing things your way, we didn't see them."

He looked at her. His expression was tight, contemplative. "If we are to do this right, we should see each landmark." He sighed. "Verra well. You lead the way—but in everything else, listen to me. I canna keep you safe otherwise."

Mona nodded, unable to look away from his face. His hair seemed lighter, streaked with strands so pale they were nearly white. As he returned to examining the necklace, she gazed at his profile. His lashes were dark gold, tipped with silvery blond. His sandy whiskers were heavy, hugging a strong, square jaw. No hair grew on the twisted scar that marred his chin. He was a warrior angel with his sword. Her Michael.

As if he felt her staring, he turned his head slightly, blue eyes meeting hers quizzically.

Mona looked away, her neck burning. What were these things she felt? Since he'd found her in the alley, she'd been nearly overwhelmed with emotion, and all for him. Even before, her heart had been heavy with his absence. And now she was giddy from his presence, drunk on his nearness and the knowledge he'd been with her all along.

"You haven't shaved . . . did you leave my sacks?"

He snorted. "Nay—I've been dragging them around for days. Yer *friends* threw them in the firth when they attacked me."

"Oh."

Thunder rumbled in the distance. Patrick returned her beads and went to the window. "What did I tell ye? Rain."

Mona fingered the beads, frowning. One was missing.

Her heart leapt as she went back to the beginning and fingered each bead in sequence. She halted where the missing one should be, the air leaving her. The bead she'd used for the dreams of Patrick. She'd left it behind, back at Graham Keep. Would its absence affect her visions? She bit the inside of her lip, queasy.

"Let's hope yon fishmonger gets a soaking and sickens."

Mona went swiftly to the window. "Where?"

Patrick pointed. The fishmonger stood outside the tavern across the street, yelling, "Fresh fish!" and staring up at the quickly darkening sky. He darted a look at their window and turned away, wandering farther down the street.

"He was waiting for ye across the firth," Patrick said.

"But how did he know where I'd be?"

Patrick shrugged. "He'll not follow us out of this village, nor be able to tell a soul he saw us here."

Mona looked up at Patrick, eyes wide. The protest rose, but she shut her lips against it. They must be ruthless.

Patrick had turned to her, leaning a hip against the wall, arms folded across his chest. Waiting.

"Do what you must," Mona murmured.

"I'm not asking you to watch."

"I said, do what you must," Mona repeated, a strained edge to her voice. "I don't want to know about it."

He walked past her and lay on the bed. "I'll sleep now, while it's day. Wake me at dusk and the bed is yours."

The bed was narrow but could hold two. She almost suggested they share it, but remembered his nightmares. He was protecting her from himself. She wanted to tell him she wasn't afraid. That she trusted him, even in his sleep. But that would be a lie.

She nodded and returned to the window, watching for the fishmonger. Over the next hour he passed beneath their window several times. And then the rain came and he entered the tavern. She stared out at the driving rain, shivering. She extended her hand into the downpour, enjoying the cold splash against her skin. She leaned forward, and rain washed over her upturned face.

There was a thud behind her. She whirled around, wiping the rain from her lashes.

The room was gloomy except for the candle that burned on the table near her. The thud sounded again and Mona realized it was Patrick having another nightmare. She took a hesitant step forward, wanting to go to him but remembering all too well what had befallen Hazel. Still, she was drawn to him. He had come for her, protected her. Why should he face these demons alone?

She took the candle and stepped quietly across the room, setting it on the floor beside the bed. She stood over him, afraid to touch him. He huddled on the bed, his great shoulders jerking from whatever horrors haunted him in sleep.

"Patrick?" she whispered. "Wake—it's but a dream."

He didn't respond. He groaned, thrashing about, kicking the wall again.

Mona gathered her courage. He hadn't really hurt Hazel—he'd awakened before he'd done her any harm. She sat on the bed and touched his shoulder.

"Patrick? Please wake."

His short blond hair was damp at the temples. She touched it, her fingers trembling. His torment wrapped a fist around her heart, made her long to comfort him in some substantial way. She stroked his hair, amazed he allowed her to touch him. She combed through the soft locks, her fingers tingling.

The frown between his brows eased. Something fluttered deep in Mona's belly, and she moved closer to him, her other hand stroking the broad muscular back through the damp linen of his shirt. His breathing grew easier.

He was calm now. She'd banished his demons, at least for the moment. She looked to the window and then scanned the dark, empty room. She wanted to lay beside him and sleep. She was so tired. It was for warmth and comfort, she told herself, and to prove to him that she trusted him.

She pushed her shoes off and lay beside him. After a moment of nearly paralyzing embarrassment, she let her body relax against him, sliding her arm around his waist. Her cheek was pressed against his back, and she could feel the erratic beat of his heart. She waited for his heart to slow as normal sleep overtook him, but to her distress it continued to pound. It took her a moment to recognize his utter stillness.

He was awake.

Her own heart tumbled over itself, fear and mortification burning her cheeks. She waited for him to thrust her away, but he did not. His hand, rough and warm, covered hers. Mona closed her eyes, the tightness in her chest painful. His fingers slid between hers, curling over her palm. He sighed, deep and heartfelt. His heart began to slow.

But Mona could hardly breathe, overwhelmed that he had accepted the comfort she offered, overwhelmed by the sensations coursing through her body. She had banished his nightmares and he'd welcomed her. In that moment she understood the wild emotions that had seized her. Patrick had captured her heart.

10

It was still raining outside when Patrick woke. It was morning, judging by the gray light. There would be no travel today, and so Patrick felt no need to get out of the warm bed just yet. Mona's arm was still around him, her breasts pressed against his back, her thighs against his. He couldn't remember the last time he'd slept with a woman—didn't think he'd ever actually *slept* with one. He was pretty sure this was the first time. Sometime during the night one of them had dragged the blanket over them, and though his nose was cold, the rest of his body was comfortable and lethargic.

He was in trouble. He'd grown hard, just lying here, thinking about her behind him. He wanted to roll over and make love to her before she was awake enough to tell him no. He fought the urge down, but the thoughts would not disappear. She moved against him, stretching, her hand slipping lower to rest against his abdomen. He bit back a tortured groan as lust washed over him afresh, coiling and knotting in his belly. He could feel her soft breath through the linen of his shirt.

He should just get out of the bed. They might not be able to leave today, but he could still make preparations.

Sighing and already miserable at his unfulfilled lust, he eased away from her, rolling to his side so he could climb over her. But once he faced her, he stopped. Her skin seemed to glow in the faint light, so pale and fine, translucent. They'd been together a month now and he'd grown accustomed to her . . . comfortable, even. Who else but Mona would crawl into bed with him while he was in the grip of a nightmare? She had not been afraid. She would cure the world if given the chance. Little fool. He was afraid for her, and that was not supposed to happen. He didn't want to care, but he knew it was too late. He'd never forgive himself if anything happened to her. He tried to tell himself it was because she was his new sister-in-law's stepmother, but he knew that wasn't why.

She was stronger than he was, cleaner, in some elemental way he couldn't understand. She'd suffered horribly at the hands of her first husband, had been kept a prisoner by her second, and yet none of these things soiled her; she'd come out of these ordeals ready to take on the world. All the ugliness Patrick had seen seemed to cling to him like filth, claiming his dreams, even his life. He was drawn to her, feeling somehow she could make him fresh again.

Her hair was unbound, flowing over the blanket. He touched it with his fingertips, moving it away from her temple. She shivered at his touch and scooted closer, so she was pressed against his chest. He closed his eyes, savoring this, knowing it would never be enough. He stroked her hair, putting his face into the silken curtain. She smelled of rainwater and herbs. He knew the moment she woke. She stiffened and drew her body away from him. He lifted his face and his hand from her hair and waited for her to leave him.

Slowly, she raised her head, dark eyes meeting his in the shadows. There was fear in her eyes, apprehension. His disappointment was bitter. She did not trust him—she was merely courageous, paying the debt she felt she owed him. He wished she'd woken him as he'd asked, rather than forcing herself to comfort him.

"What are you afraid of, Mona?" he asked, his voice hard. The deep twisting in his chest was as unwelcome as it was painful.

"You're angry."

"I'm not. Surprised to find a woman in bed with me, but not angry."

She frowned, examining his face.

"You shouldn't have done that," he said, never looking away from her. He could have strangled her or stabbed her last night. She *should* be afraid. But he hated that she was.

"You *are* angry."

He let out a loud breath and kicked the blanket away. "I'm not." No, not angry. Unsatisfied, frustrated, wanting. He had to get away from her, to clear the fog of lust from his head. He'd go after their fishmonger.

"Patrick," she said, laying her hand on his arm. Her voice wavered. "Don't leave. . . ." Her hand, small and perfect, touched the front of his shirt, pulling slowly on a tie until it dangled.

Aching need pulsed through him at her words. He wanted to push her back on the bed and spend himself in her. He wanted to explore every inch of her body until she had no secrets. He slid his hand over her hair and gripped the satin tresses at her nape, forcing her head back so she stared into his eyes.

"Why?" he asked. Did she seek to reward him for returning to her? Or did she pity him?

Sooty lashes swept down to hide her eyes. She had not undressed, but the white length of her throat arched before him, urging him to drop this line of questioning and plant his mouth on it.

"Do you not want me?" she asked.

What was wrong with him? What did it matter why she wanted to lie with him? *It didn't.* He couldn't see straight from the throbbing in his loins. She offered him what he yearned for. He lowered his head and kissed the soft column of her neck. Her pulse throbbed beneath his lips. He breathed in the clean scent of her skin. She wound her arms around his neck, her fingers threading in his hair.

He took her mouth, pressing her back into the mattress. Her kiss was nectar, food of the gods, and he gorged himself, like a starving man. She arched against him, moaning deep in her throat. He pushed her skirts up and her woolen hose down, sliding his hand over silken thigh to the curve of her bottom. Her pressed her hard against him, temporarily assuaging the sharp ache. She gasped in his mouth and slid her hands inside his shirt.

She wore a simple bodice with hooks on the side. He made short work of them and tossed it aside. Her breasts were round and heavy, filling his hand through the linen of her shift, her nipples hard beneath his stroking thumb. She moved restlessly beneath him, raking her nails across his chest and back, pushing his shirt off.

He undid the tie holding her shift closed and dragged it off her shoulders. She struggled to remove her arms from the sleeves and he helped her, pushing the shift down around her waist. She lay back on the bed, ebony hair pooled around alabaster shoulders. She ran her hands over his arms as he gazed down at her. She was more beautiful than his imaginings. A marble statue, polished to perfection. Her skin was flawless, luminous like a pearl.

"Patrick." His whispered name fell from her lips, uncertain. Her eyes were wide, fearful—but not of him.

He stretched out beside her, remembering all she'd told

him. She'd never found the marriage bed fulfilling. Her first husband had been crazy and cruel. And Hugh had wanted her for nothing more than the Clachan Fala. He would wipe those memories away and replace them with something she wanted to recall.

His hand skimmed over her ribs to cup her breast, pink-tipped and lovely. Her lips parted as she gazed up at him, eyes cloudy with desire. The air seemed thick, charged. He watched his hand caress her, so rough and dark against her ivory skin. He leaned over and laved her nipple, lost in the burning pleasure of her taste, her quivering body that filled his arms.

His mind grew fevered as he touched her and kissed her. He didn't think he could wait. He feared he would burst into flames if he didn't plunge into her. Her hands fisted in his hair when he slid his hand between her thighs, rubbing against the damp curls. She was ready for him, her body already shuddering and clenching with her pleasure.

He yanked at the laces of his breeks. Her hands were there, pushing them off his hips. He drove into her, teeth gritted against the nearly painful pleasure of her body gripping him, hot and tight. Her arms were around him and she kissed him, her tongue mating with his. There was a wildness to her that snapped his tenuous control, and he plowed into her, crushing her to him. She welcomed him, urging with hands and hips for him to thrust deeper. Her breath panted in his ear; whimpering cries were wrung from her lips. The pleasure rose in his chest, expanding, piercing through him. When he finally spilled his seed into her he thought his heart would shatter from the intensity of it. He cried out, hugging her to him, his face pressed to the damp skin of her neck.

She was limp in his arms, boneless. Afraid he'd injured

her, he rolled away. She lay there, eyes closed, head lolling to the side.

"Mona," he whispered, berating himself for the coarse way he'd attempted to wipe her poor memories away.

Her heavy lashes rose and she met his worried gaze, her eyes black pools of warmth. Her mouth curved into a smile, sated and languid. "We should have done that a long time ago."

Mona stretched in the tiny bed, her naked body touching Patrick's. He had pulled the blanket back over them after they made love, but Mona didn't need it. Everywhere their bodies touched she burned. His body generated heat like a bonfire, consuming her.

He'd grown quiet and thoughtful, staring into the gloom. One arm still encircled her, holding her against him. His fingers traced patterns on the small of her back. She watched him think, seduced by the power of his body. She wove her fingers through the crisp blond hair on his chest. He caught her hand in his, held it against him.

The startling blue of his eyes settled on her. "Where is your . . . iuchair?"

Mona was surprised to realize she'd not put the beads back on after showing them to Patrick. She hadn't even noticed the absence of its familiar weight on her throat.

"On the table."

He rose from the bed. She watched the layers of muscles shift and bunch under taut skin as he fetched the necklace. He slid back into bed, pushing her up against the wall. He shivered from the damp cold. It still rained. Mona had forgotten to close the shutters, and a puddle had formed on the floor beaneath the window.

He fingered the beads, frowning. Mona fought down the urge to snatch them away. Arlana's voice had become but a whisper to her, and though she'd loved the woman, Mona now understood that Arlana's path was not the one for her. Hadn't the iuchair given her Patrick?

"Which is the last landmark?" he asked.

She touched the last four beads. "These go together. A group of standing stones on an island."

"And the Bloodstone is somewhere in the circle of standing stones?"

Mona shook her head. "It's in a church."

"Has Ridley seen these?"

"Yes. But he doesn't know what they are. He thinks they're witches' baubles."

His hand closed around the necklace, and he turned his head to look at her. "Are you sure?"

"If he knew what it was, wouldn't he have taken it from me long ago and fetched the stone himself?"

He sighed but seemed unconvinced. "I wish I knew what island it was, then we could bypass this nonsense and sail there."

Mona took the iuchair from him. "This 'nonsense' has protected the Bloodstone for hundreds of years."

"What if we arrive at the church, only to find the Clachan Fala long gone? Some priest dug it up by accident when tilling his garden?"

"Who said it was buried in the ground?"

A blond brow arched. "Where is it?"

A shadow of unease weighed on her. Patrick's questions reminded her too much of Ridley, interrogating her. "The iuchair will show me when we get there," she lied.

He accepted her falsehood and asked no more questions, his attention now riveted on her hair. He filled his hand with it and let it slide through his fingers like water.

"We are slothful today," he mused, his other hand sliding over her hip.

"It rains. What else can we do?"

He said nothing, intent on her, his hand stroking a fire in her belly. "You were married to Hugh a long time."

"Nearly seven years."

"Did he mistreat you?"

"No. He did when he forced me to wed him—but after, he did try to be a good husband—the only way he knew how. He had a nasty temper, though, and often raged at me when I refused to tell him anything about the Bloodstone."

His hand moved up to her ribs, his thumb rubbing the underside of her breast. Liquid heat pooled between her legs. Her breasts tightened, the coarse blanket abrading her sensitive nipples. The powerful hunger rose in her again, stronger than before.

She slid her hand down the ridges of his belly, following the narrow trail of silky blond hair, and touched him. He hissed through his teeth, his eyes burning. He was hard, ready. A thrill of anticipation shivered through her as he leaned over her, his mouth capturing hers.

They spent the day in bed, getting up only to eat and check on the fishmonger. When night fell, Mona slept, Patrick's arm heavy about her waist. She woke some time in the night. Patrick's breathing was deep and even against her back. It was not his nightmares that woke her. Warmth bloomed in her chest. She'd once thought she loved Edwin Musgrave, but if that sentiment had ever been real, it had died long before he had.

No, what she felt for Patrick was deeper, more primitive than anything she'd felt before. It was more an instinct, a fierce protectiveness that was strong yet tender. She snuggled deeper in his arms, puzzling at what had wrenched her from sleep. As she drifted off again, she realized it was the silence that had woke her. The rain had stopped.

*   *   *

Ridley stared at the man being led across the hall to him. He took his meal alone, at the long table in his newest acquisition, Gealach, a tower on the Rhins of Galloway. He didn't like living among the Scots, even surrounded by his men as he was. But there was no help for it. Mona was headed this way, and so he must stay put.

"Fitzjames, my lord," Gilford said, gesturing at the filthy man before him. He still stunk of rotten fish.

"Can he speak now?"

Fitzjames was one of the many scum Ridley had employed to follow Mona. He was the second spy Sir Patrick had discovered. He'd killed Brodie Armstrong—a complete waste. But something might be salvaged from Fitzjames. Ridley needed to know why Brodie's attempt to kill Sir Patrick had failed. Fitzjames had come to Ridley a fortnight ago, his neck nearly crushed, unable to speak. He couldn't write either, so Ridley had been waiting to finally communicate with him.

"Aye, my lord," Fitzjames rasped.

Ridley turned to him and saw the look of revulsion in his face. Fitzjames quickly averted his eyes. The expression was rapidly becoming familiar. Anger welled in Ridley, choking him. It was his face that disgusted everyone. He who had once been so fair was now too hideous to look upon. His own sister had done this to him. His lips pulled down in his rage, and he shuddered at the searing pain it caused. It had been four days since his sister, Fayth, had shoved a candelabra in his face—twice—burning him and flinging hot wax across his face. Though the pain had lessened—no thanks to the incompetent healers who merely smeared foul-smelling concoctions over his ruined skin—it still felt as if his skin was scorching. He couldn't get the stink of burning flesh and hair from his nostrils. The only way to contain the pain was to keep his face expressionless, and in light of all that had occurred over the past week, that was impossible.

"Well? What news?"

"The other man still trails them. Sir Patrick only saw me. They are still heading northwest." His voice was a scratching hiss, ruined forever by a Maxwell.

Ridley already knew this. He had other eyes and ears. Had seen her for himself just a sennight ago, though she had been completely oblivious. She only had eyes for that Scottish boarhound.

"How is it that Sir Patrick came to assault you?"

"They knew someone followed them, though I didn't realize they'd marked me until Sir Patrick came after me."

"Were you able to discern anything at all about their destination?"

Fitzjames shook his head. "I paid the innkeeper to listen at their door—they were in there an entire day alone together. All she heard was rutting."

"What?" Ridley said, the blood freezing in his veins. His face, a tight mask of burns and scabs, grew even tighter.

Fitzjames hesitated. "Rutting, my lord . . . all day."

Hate knotted Ridley's belly. He'd spent years wooing Mona, and that great ox had her on her back in a month. Perhaps it hadn't even taken that long. He'd discovered after he'd let her escape Graham Keep that she'd been visiting the prisoner for some time. Had it begun then? She preferred filthy, uncivilized Scotsmen to Ridley, a man of breeding and wealth. *He'd loved her.* It sickened him that he still did.

Her betrayal clawed at his heart. Gilford sent Fitzjames away as Ridley stared blankly at the food before him. He was a monster now. Mona would be repulsed by him. More important than Mona was the Clachan Fala, and for the first time Ridley acknowledged that Sir Patrick Maxwell might be more than an inconvenience. He'd not only stolen

Ridley's woman but he might actually keep Ridley from the Bloodstone.

Brodie had failed to kill Sir Patrick. Ridley mentally inventoried his men-at-arms, selecting the three largest and most skilled. It was time to send more effective assassins.

Ridley tried to smile and winced. The hot wax had melted part of his lips, so that they stretched uncomfortably when he tried to smile. Fayth had ruined him. It was small satisfaction that he sat in her lover's tower, ate his food, and spent his riches. He wanted both Fayth and Alexander Maxwell dead for what they'd done to his face. *Maxwells.* The bane of his existence.

He pushed away from the table, restless from the rage smoldering in his heart. How could he just sit here and wait while his family turned on him like a pack of ravenous wolves? There was one person he could make pay right now, and Ridley had kept him alive for just that purpose. He went through the kitchens, into the larder, and down through a hole in the floor. Gealach sat on a cliff riddled with tunnels and natural catacombs, some filled with treasure. The rooms just beneath the larder, however, could be used as holding cells.

The area below the ladder was ablaze with torches. Ridley came down here frequently and didn't like the damp darkness. The man chained to the wall stirred, blinking blearily at Ridley.

"Good day, Wesley!" Ridley greeted his brother. "I trust you're well rested?"

Wesley was naked except for his breeches, his arms spread above him like wings. He'd been so four days now, ever since he'd helped Fayth and Alexander Maxwell escape after they'd melted his face. Ridley had fed him little and flogged him several times.

"Water?" Wesley croaked.

"Which is it? Water? Or news of your wife? I'll grant you one request."

Wesley's eyes widened, and he stumbled to his feet, chains clanking.

Ridley smiled inside. Wesley hadn't bothered to mention his other betrayal—stealing Ridley's betrothed. Ridley had sent him to the earl of Dornock's daughter to marry her by proxy and fetch her back so the marriage could be consummated. Instead, the worm had married the girl himself—and with the earl's blessing! Yes, Wesley had been busy cozening him. Of all those who strove to hurt Ridley, Wesley's betrayal had been the most shocking. He'd not thought his little brother capable of such perfidy.

"Yes." Ridley nodded. "I know all about the wedding. Lord Dornock wrote me. So . . . which shall it be? Anne? Or water?"

Wesley closed his eyes wearily and whispered, "Anne."

His answer infuriated Ridley. All Wesley cared about was that stinking Scottish pig. And she'd never been meant for Wesley. By right she belonged to Ridley. The betrothal had been broken, and Ridley would see Dornock and his fat daughter pay for it.

"You really thought you could get away with such a scheme?"

"What does it matter?" Wesley said, his face set in stubborn anger. "You didn't even like her."

"I pray you—if you tell me you love her I shall be ill." *Love.* He was heartily sick of the word. Fayth had ruined his face for her lover and now Wesley.

"Then I won't tell you," Wesley said, his eyes narrowed.

Ridley rolled his eyes. His stomach *was* becoming queasy from the rage boiling in his gut. "Apparently Lady Anne does not return the sentiment."

Wesley's bearded jaw tightened, his fevered eyes lighting hungrily. Ridley wanted to kick him like the dog he was—and he planned to, later. For now he laid the blow he hoped would shatter Wesley's soul.

"She has agreed to annul the marriage and honor her betrothal with me."

That was a lie—the bitch had written him a cold missive, inquiring about the whereabouts of her husband and intimating that if anything evil befell him, her father would retaliate. And Dornock himself had requested Wesley be allowed to return "home." Ridley had shredded both letters and burned them. There wouldn't be enough left of Wesley for his widow to bury when Ridley was finished with him.

Wesley's lips curled, his shackled hands gripping the chains that had been driven into the stone wall with spikes. Ridley recognized the signs and stepped back as Wesley kicked out at him with a guttural roar. Ridley waited until his brother had expended his fury and was sagging against the wall again.

Wesley glowered up at him, his chest heaving from the exercise.

Ridley shook his head, clucking sadly. "All for naught, Wesley. You betrayed me for naught."

Wesley's breath hissed through his teeth. If he were free he'd kill Ridley or die trying.

"I still get my lady wife, and Fayth and Alexander have been caught. Red Alex has been executed, and Fayth is already on her way to her new husband's arms." Another lie, but it didn't matter. All these things would come to pass, but Wesley wouldn't be alive for them. Ridley wanted Wesley to die knowing his betrayal had come to nothing. That he had failed and Ridley had succeeded.

"New husband?" Wesley rasped, frowning. "Who?"

Fayth's betrothed, Lord Ashton Carlisle, had been killed by Fayth's lover.

"Yes. Carlisle might be dead, but he did have a son and heir. And he has graciously agreed to wed the hellion—and tame her." That much was true. With an English invasion looming, Carlisle's eldest son was eager to keep the alliance.

Wesley shook his head slowly, his eyes never leaving Ridley. "I don't believe you. Anne hates you, and her father will never force her to marry a monster. And you are no match for Red Alex—for any Maxwell. You lie."

Ridley's face throbbed and burned. The fact he knew Ridley bluffed was galling enough—but to call him a monster? Wesley was one to talk, himself sporting an enormous scar on his cheek. But he saw himself as better now. Ridley's lips pulled back from his teeth, the pain excruciating. Healing wounds broke open, and wetness dripped down his face.

Wesley looked away, revolted.

He didn't believe him? Well, perhaps Ridley would let him live long enough to see it all come to pass. He kicked Wesley in the ribs, a thrill whipping through him at the crunch of ribs and Wesley's groan of pain. Yes, give him a life—one of pain and loneliness. He would watch Ridley sire children on Lady Anne while all along the pig would think Wesley dead. He would see his sisters' and their lovers' broken bodies, he would see Ridley possess the Clachan Fala and Mona join him in his prison, for Ridley to keep for all time.

And then, perhaps, he would be merciful and let him die.

11

They had left the coast behind, though they continued traveling north. Patrick was still irritated Mona had refused to make a detour to the Rhins to see his brother Alex. He'd promised her he would not abandon her there, but she apparently hadn't believed him. They'd hardly seen a soul in a sennight except their tracker. Patrick had noticed another man following them a few days ago. This one was smarter than the fishmonger. Rather than follow, he tracked them, trying to stay out of sight, but he wasn't always successful. Yesterday Patrick had lain in wait for him and chased him several miles. They'd not seen him since.

Patrick stopped at a burn to water their horses. As Mona washed herself and filled their waterskin, Patrick wandered to the top of a rise, scanning the landscape for their tracker. They'd made poor time. It had rained frequently, turning the ground to a muddy stew, and his futile pursuit of the tracker had wasted an entire day.

Seeing nothing, Patrick started back to the burn, intent on Mona. She'd unbraided her hair and combed through it with wet fingers. The sight of her never failed to rouse him.

It had been a fortnight since that night at the inn when she'd crawled into bed with him. He'd not had a nightmare since. He'd fallen into an odd sort of friendship with her. He found himself telling her about some of his dreams—and sometimes he just talked about his brothers, which she seemed to enjoy. And she told him more about Arlana and her stepchildren. They talked a great deal, more than he'd ever done with anyone else—even his brothers. It was so very odd . . . and yet he enjoyed it. He couldn't remember the last time he'd been so content, despite the conditions of their travel.

He worried about what she would do when this was over. She'd said that after she delivered the stone to Robert and Caroline she must stay until a son was born. Even then she must make certain he lived and instruct him on how to use the Bloodstone.

It sounded like a lot of foolishness to Patrick—magic stones and an unborn nephew destined for greatness. But Mona believed in it, and so he would see this through—for her. Perhaps they wouldn't find the stone and she would give up this folly, or if they did find it, she would discover it was nothing more than a valuable gemstone, containing no secret powers. But that didn't comfort him or ease the guilt that grew in him each day. He'd begun to understand Mona and knew that if the Clachan Fala was not real, then she would feel she had no purpose. She *needed* it to be real.

He stopped beside her, gazing down at her gleaming crown of black hair. Lord knew he tried to keep his hands to himself, but he lost the battle every night—and sometimes during the day. He'd planted his seed in her belly so often over the past two weeks that if she were not barren, as she believed, she must surely be carrying his child. He couldn't understand himself anymore, what drove him. It was madness to continue on this way, and yet he was helpless to stop. He loved Rosemarie, but it seemed he was intent on either never seeing her again or destroying Mona.

She glanced up at him.

"We'll rest here. I think we can make the next landmark by nightfall."

Mona shook her head. "There's no cover there. It's just a circle of standing stones." He didn't ask how she knew this. He'd seen her sit and rock with the beads in her grasp, then afterwards clearly describe a landmark. When they arrived it was always just as she'd said.

"The standing stones will provide some cover."

She blinked at him. "We can't sleep in a stone circle. We'll be taken to the fairy kingdom to sleep for hundreds of years."

Patrick shrugged. "Then none of this will matter, aye?"

"Patrick, we cannot make light of such things."

He lowered himself to the ground beside her. "You don't really believe that rubbish?"

"It's not rubbish. Those stones are ancient."

"So?"

She gave him a reproving look. "Many say they are a meeting place of the dead. Others believe they are the ancient magicians turned to stone."

"Well, I say they're a bunch of rocks."

He was picking at her on purpose and she knew it. She would get her way. She always did. She made a face at him.

"Are you hungry?" she asked, tying her hair back with a leather thong. "There's still some bread and dried meat left."

He pulled at the thong, sending her hair cascading over her shoulders. She wore it down for him sometimes, when he was insistent. He would be insistent today.

She scowled at him and tried to snatch back the thong.

"I want to look at it," he said, holding the thong out of her reach.

She sighed and pulled their small leather bag to her, searching for the food. He toyed with the curling ends of her hair, thinking about making love to her beside the stream.

She straightened. "Patrick." Her single word was infused with so much fear and disbelief that he didn't even look at her expression but twisted around to look behind him. Three men on horseback rode toward them, still some distance away, but coming fast.

Patrick was on his feet, hauling Mona up with him as she hastily threw on her cloak and gathered up their meager belongings.

"Maybe they're not after us," she said.

"I'm not taking any chances. Let's go."

They mounted and splashed across the burn, pushing the horses to a run. They raced across the heather, but it was soon clear they'd made no mistake, the men were after them. There was nowhere to hide—hill after hill of heather and gorse and not a tree in sight. Even the jagged gray rocks jutting out of the ground were not big enough to conceal two horses. Though they drove the horses hard, they couldn't keep the pace up much longer. Their horses were fatigued and not of the same caliber as their pursuers' mounts. A cottage lay ahead. No smoke rose from the thatched roof, and the yard was deserted.

An unfamiliar fear had fallen over Patrick. It had been a very long time since he'd been truly afraid before engaging in combat. This new concern was for Mona, not himself. He'd lived through a great many battles—but he'd always failed to protect those he cared about. And so he'd stopped caring—it was easier that way, since the loss was inevitable.

At the cottage, he dismounted. "Get inside and bar the door."

"What about the horses?"

"Forget the horses!" Their mounts already wandered

away, toward a patch of green behind the cottage. "They'll not go far."

Mona stared at the approaching men. "I can't just leave you out here."

He forced her toward the door. "Go, damnit! I canna protect ye when ye're out here in the open."

She clung to his hand. "Don't die," she said fiercely, her mouth set in an uncompromising line.

"Aye, my lady." He pushed her inside and pulled the door closed. He was relieved to hear her block the door. "Check for any other ways in and block those, too," he yelled.

He turned as their pursuers slowed, realizing they'd cornered their prey. Patrick drew his sword. They remained on horseback, circling him. "Good day, Sir Patrick," the biggest one said. He tapped his sword hilt with gloved fingers. He had a bushy brown beard and a scar that slashed from cheek to eyebrow.

The second one had a narrow face and long blond hair. His teeth were as long and yellow as his hair. He edged close to the cottage, as if trying to wedge his way between Patrick and the door.

Patrick stood fast, leveling his sword to the horse's hock. "I'll lame him if ye dinna back away."

Yellowteeth yanked on the reins, backing away several paces. The third man merely watched the proceedings from the broken fence. He was powerfully built, with a close-cropped graying beard and a full helm, the nose guard blocking his features. The other two would be easy to take—Graybeard he would have to watch.

The scarred man smiled. "Why don't you come with us? Make it easier for the lassie. It's you we came for."

It was as he suspected. They'd come to kill him, just as Brodie had. If he went with them, Mona would be safe. For now. Until she found the Bloodstone, then Ridley would be all over her. Patrick wasn't about to just walk away and leave her defenseless, but he couldn't let them use her against him. If things had gone just a wee bit different with Brodie, Mona might have ended up with a broken arm or a slit throat.

He decided to play along, to lure them away from Mona.

"Let me get my horse."

"No horse," the blond man said.

Patrick did a quick inventory of their weaponry. Swords, daggers, crossbows, Graybeard even had a dag—a long-barreled wheel-lock handgun. All Patrick had was a sword, and not a good one at that. He didn't like the length, the steel was of poor quality and would likely snap at a strong blow, and it was poorly weighted. It would have to do until he disarmed one of them.

"This will be fair, aye? Throw down your crossbows and that dag," Patrick demanded.

The men exchanged a wary look, then complied. They rode forward, one by one, dropping their weapons in front of him. With three-to-one odds they obviously thought he would be dispatched easily enough. Let them think what they would. He would not take an arrow or lead in the back.

"Sir Patrick? Now you will come?" Graybeard asked, speaking for the first time.

Patrick started forward, passing warily among the horses. They followed, surrounding him. They hadn't gone far when Patrick heard the door to the cottage open. He turned, angry, praying the little fool wasn't trying to follow him, when Yellowteeth kicked him in the head.

He went down hard, losing his sword. He groped for it, his vision blurred. The horse shrieked above him, and for a paralyzing moment he was back on the battlefield, struggling to reach Julian while hooves hammered relentlessly at him. He rolled away as the horse came down hard, pummeling the ground with its hooves.

He was on his feet just as Mona threw herself in front of him, arms spread wide. Her hair blew across his face.

"Leave him!" she cried.

"Bloody hell!" Patrick grabbed her shoulders and swung her around. "What are you doing?"

"I recognize all of them—they're Ridley's men. They won't hurt me. Ridley would kill them."

The men exchanged uneasy glances. Scarface said, "My lady . . . prithee stand aside. We wish no 'arm to you."

She gave Patrick a knowing look and turned back around. "No! I'll not leave him—you'll have to kill me first."

Patrick leaned down, mouth pressed to her ear. "They'll just keep following us, trying to get me alone. They won't go back to Ridley without my head."

"Listen to the man," Yellowteeth said, grinning. "Go on back to the cottage."

Graybeard dismounted and came forward. "It'll be a clean fight, my lady. You have my word."

Mona looked him up and down. "You're an assassin. Why should I believe you?"

Graybeard went to Yellowteeth and took his sword. A broad, two-handed sword. He came forward, offering it to Patrick hilt first.

Patrick tried to move her aside and take the proffered sword, but Mona latched onto his arm.

"I won't let you do this." Her black eyes were wide, frightened.

He placed his hands firmly on her shoulders. "Even if they let us go, it's not over. They'll be smarter next time, ambush us. I might not be prepared—at least now I know what I face."

Her expression was tight with strain as she searched his

eyes. After a moment she turned, facing the others. "When he wins, you two will leave us?"

Scarface and Yellowteeth looked at each other, but Graybeard answered. "Yes."

Yellowteeth started to protest, but Graybeard held up a silencing hand. "You will."

Mona grabbed the front of Patrick's jack, pulling him down to her mouth. She kissed him hard and whispered against his mouth, "Don't you dare die." Then she backed away.

Patrick took the sword and Graybeard backed away, drawing his own. Patrick liked the way this sword felt in his hand. He could do some damage with it. They circled each other. Graybeard's eyes were as steely as his beard, the color of a storm. Patrick did a cursory inspection of his opponent's defenses. He wore chain mail and a leather jack. He did not remove his helm, and though he wore leather gloves and breeks, neither were reinforced. A cut to the wrist, lower body, or just beneath the chin would take him out.

Patrick attacked, driving his opponent back with a series of powerful blows that sent sparks showering between them. Graybeard blocked them all and even managed a few counterattacks. He was good. But Patrick's best defense had always been a strong offense and so he kept the blows coming, preventing Graybeard from taking the initiative.

Graybeard stumbled. In the periphery of his vision Patrick caught Scarface's approach. Attention fragmented, Patrick swung around. Graybeard's blade caught him in the arm, cutting through his jack. Scarface struck at him and Mona screamed, but the sound was immediately muffled.

Panic gripped Patrick as he blocked Scarface's blow and backed away in time to avoid another slice from Graybeard. Patrick scanned the area wildly and saw that Yellowteeth held Mona, a hand clamped over her mouth. She struggled vainly against him. Patrick swore and faced his opponents again. He'd not expected honor from any of them, but was still angry Graybeard had deceived him.

They separated, one on either side of him. Scarface wore a steel bonnet and no gloves. Patrick slid his dirk from his boot and went for Scarface. They both converged on him and Patrick feinted, ducking under Scarface's arcing blow and meeting Graybeard's. Scarface had swung with such force that Patrick's feint unbalanced him. Patrick drove his dirk into Scarface's throat. His sword clattered to the ground and Patrick snatched it up, facing Graybeard now with two broadswords.

Patrick smiled, advancing on Graybeard, who was finally beginning to look nervous. Patrick struck, not giving Graybeard any time to formulate a plan on how to defend himself against two broadswords. Patrick brought the blades down inelegantly, concerned more with force than finesse. His wound burned, weakening him, and he still had another adversary to dispatch when he finished Graybeard.

Graybeard was strong and skilled, able to keep up with Patrick's assault. Patrick formed a rhythm with his blows, waiting for Graybeard to fall into it. He delivered the expected blow with his right, and as Graybeard parried, already readying himself to counter Patrick's next strike, Patrick swung around behind him, slamming his other sword across Graybeard's hamstrings.

Graybeard went down in a gush of blood and screams. Patrick turned toward Yellowteeth, but he'd abandoned Mona and was scrabbling onto his horse. Patrick ran for the cottage, where they'd left their crossbows, but by the time he'd loaded a quarrel, Yellowteeth was out of range.

Patrick lowered the weapon and looked at his arm.

Blood dripped from his fingertips, slicking his hand. Good thing he hadn't noticed that before.

Mona was in front of him, unhooking the jack.

Patrick grabbed her wrists. "Not now. There may be others he runs to warn—or worse, bring them back to try again. We'll take their horses. Go catch them."

Mona looked torn, but he urged her on with a gentle push.

He gathered up the crossbows, quarrels, and the dag, weighing the last in his hand. He'd used a few, just to try them out, and found them inaccurate, but it still might prove useful.

He went to where Mona held the horses for him. Graybeard dragged himself through the dirt, toward the lifeless body of Scarface. Mona watched him, her face creased with sympathetic pain.

"His friend will be back this way. He might live, though he'll be crippled."

She swallowed hard and nodded.

Patrick secured the weapons to their saddles and gave her a leg up on the sorrel. These horses were much bigger than the last ones. They seemed neither shy nor nervous, so he hoped they would serve them well on the remainder of their journey. He mounted his, a white stallion with gray mane and tail, and they sped north, horses flying across the heather.

It was full dark when they reached the standing stones. Patrick had pushed them, determined to put as much distance between them and Ridley's men as possible.

"There," she said, pointing.

Patrick squinted, peering through the swirl of fog. The stones slowly became visible. He gave her a curious look, wondering if she'd actually seen them, or simply knew they were there. They dismounted, leading the horses up the hill the stones sat upon. Mona stumbled, her fatigue making her clumsy. Patrick grabbed her hand, dragging her toward the stones. There was a desperation to him. He had to get her somewhere safe, where he could protect her. The stones seemed a good place for tonight.

She dug in her heels, shaking her head vigorously. "No, we cannot go there—it's not safe."

Patrick continued onward, relentless. "Why?" he asked, though he knew what her answer would be.

"They're magical—the fairies."

"Fairies," he scoffed.

She threw her weight backward so she was nearly sitting, forcing him to stop or drag her bodily through the heather and stones. The horses had proven tolerant and gentle, and Mona's mare took this behavior in stride, stopping and taking a step back.

"Mona," he said, hauling her to her feet. "Think about it—they will be as frightened as you are. They'll not follow us here tonight. We can sleep and be safe."

She grew still, wide black eyes fixed on his. Her breath came out a white puff, and his stomach clenched at how cold she was, at how poorly he was caring for her. After a moment, she nodded, her body relaxing.

"Good." He took her hand firmly and pulled her up the hill. They entered the ring of monoliths, Mona pressed against his side, holding his hand tightly. He chose a large stone that would shelter them from view and tethered the horses nearby. He collected brush to make a fire. The landscape was devoid of trees, so the fire would be pathetic and difficult to keep burning, but he must try to warm her. Her nose was red with cold and her teeth chattered.

Once the fire was fighting for life in the ring of rocks she'd prepared, they leaned against the stone. Patrick put his arm around her and pulled her close against his side.

"Let me see your hands," he said.

She pulled them from the folds of her cloak. Her fingers were red and stiff, but he saw no damage. He rubbed them briskly between his and said, "Tomorrow, I will find us someplace warm to sleep. And get us food and drink."

She smiled at the thought but didn't speak. He wanted to say it again, to promise it until she acknowledged that she believed him, but he didn't. His heart was twisted with fear that she would freeze or starve—that he would be the death of her.

"Your arm," she said, pulling away from him.

He'd forgotten about it. It had grown numb, but now that she reminded him, a dull throbbing started up. He shrugged out of his jack. They had nothing to stitch it with, but Mona cleaned it with the water and ripped a strip off her shift to dress the wound.

They finally fell asleep, wrapped in Mona's cloak.

It was Mohacs again. He plowed into the Danube, pursuing not the King of Hungary but Mona. She was foolish and reckless; he had to stop her. He wasn't alone in his pursuit—there was another man. Edwin. Patrick had never seen her husband before, but his dream gave him the face of a devil, red eyes and dripping fangs. They both splashed into the river, but Edwin was ahead of him, gaining on Mona as Patrick fell behind, hampered by the current and a testy horse.

He saw Mona's horse sink. She fought to stay above the water. Edwin's horse stayed afloat, carrying him swiftly to her. Patrick dove off his horse and sunk like a rock. He fought to shed chain mail, spurs, boots, sword, but they dragged him down. He kicked his way to the surface. He could see her legs thrashing frantically above him. Edwin held her

under, and she fought at him. Patrick couldn't swim
fast enough, couldn't reach her.

He woke with a gasp. Fog hung thick and wet in the air,
but it was morning. They were still bundled under Mona's
cloak, his arms wrapped tightly around her. He lifted his
head and found her gazing back at him, her eyes enormous
and velvety soft. A sickness crept into his heart—he could
have killed her in his sleep and not even known it. What had
he been thinking? That the nightmares would just go away
because he slept with a woman? He was a danger to her.

As if she knew his thoughts, she whispered, "You didn't
hurt me."

He was breathing hard from the dream. His throat was
too tight to speak. He could only stare down at her in horrified wonder that she could be so calm.

Her arms were around his waist. She squeezed him.
"I'm not afraid."

Emotions simmering deep inside boiled to the surface,
wild and raw from the dream and fear. His mouth descended on hers with nearly brutal force, pressing her head
into the ground. He didn't want to hurt her, he didn't want
to frighten her, but he ached for her. His groin throbbed
from spending the night with her in his arms. The smell of
her surrounded him.

She did not fight him. Her body surged up, her hands
clutching at his back as her mouth opened beneath his,
welcoming his tongue inside. The kiss only inflamed him
further, made him frantic to be inside her. He raised himself over her, his hands pulling at her bodice. Her lips were
swollen from his kiss, her face flushed with passion.

"Oh God, Patrick," she said, her voice deep, husky. She
tried to help him unhook her bodice, but her fingers were
clumsy. He brushed her hands aside and yanked at the of-

fending garment, lifting her off the ground in his eagerness to see and taste more of her flesh. She gripped his shoulders and came off the ground, her mouth hot on his neck, sucking. It sent a bolt of nearly painful lust straight to his groin, and he feared he'd spill himself right there, in his breeks.

Finally, her bodice was open. Her breasts strained against her shift. He pushed it off her shoulders and down, following it with his mouth. She hissed, her back arching, hands on his head. He took a nipple in his mouth, sweet as nectar, and sucked. Her hips writhed, her hands holding his head to her breast.

He fought at the folds of her kirtle, bunching it up at her waist. His hands trailed over wool stockings until he reached the silken skin of her inner thighs. He nearly sobbed when he slid his fingers between her legs and found her slick and ready. He managed to rip his breeks open and grabbed handfuls of her soft round bottom.

"Oh, please, Patrick, now," she moaned, her hands pulling at him.

He sunk himself into her hot tightness, his blood singing, heart slamming against his ribs. He leaned over her, sliding his hands beneath her head and kissing her. She bucked against him, and he pumped into her again and again. She gasped into his mouth. Her body shuddered and spasmed around him. He couldn't hold back another second and drove hard and fast into her, finally spending himself.

The blood still roared through his head, even as the tension drained from his body. Coherent thought descended on him as he lay there, his face buried in her fragrant neck. What was the matter with him? He'd taken her like an animal. He'd never wanted a woman with such ferocity.

Her fingers threaded idly through his hair, her thighs,

which had tightly gripped his hips, going slack. He felt as if the strength had been sapped from him. He lifted his head to gaze down at her. She was so beautiful, the thick fringe of her lashes sweeping down over dark eyes as she examined his expression. Before she could speak, he kissed her, long and deep.

"I'm sorry," he whispered against her lips. "I was a beast."

"I'm not complaining."

He pressed his forehead against hers. "It was the dream . . . and the fighting yesterday."

"Is that all?"

He raised his head and gazed at her with narrowed eyes. What did she mean? She looked up at him uncertainly. When he didn't respond, she looked away, moving as if she wanted him off her. He sat up and watched her adjust her clothes. *Is that all?* What did she mean? He wanted to ask but was afraid of her answer.

"What did you dream?" she asked.

He shook his head, standing and relacing his breeks. "We should go."

She caught his arm. "Tell me . . . you were wild when you woke, frightened." When he shook his head again, she asked, "Was it about Rosemarie?"

Patrick closed his eyes. "No." He'd been trying not to think of his daughter. Every day he spent with Mona he became more conflicted. Once his only care had been Rosemarie. He now felt a similar longing for Mona, to somehow have more in his life. But it was impossible.

"Tell me about your daughter."

He sighed, giving in to the desire to speak of her. He leaned against a stone twice his size. Mist swirled around them, obscuring all but the nearest standing stones. "She has my hair and my eyes . . . but she's verra bonny and such a wee thing. She has a dog and a pony—I think she must love animals."

Mona frowned. "You think?"

Patrick looked down at his hands, regret and unhappiness clawing at him. "She doesna ken I'm her father." He didn't look at Mona but sought a way to fill the heavy silence. "I have an estate not far from her home. I oft visit the man she believes is her father. I . . . I seldom speak to her, though I bring her things and give them to her mother to pass on. I don't know if she does."

He finally forced himself to look at her, afraid of what he'd see in her eyes. Disappointment? He was a poor father, he knew, and a coward at that. He never should have let Nadine manipulate him, use him like a stud. He'd been relieved at first when she'd wanted nothing more from him than his seed. But over the years, as he watched his daughter grow, that had changed, and he wanted more.

Mona was beside him, her hand on his arm. Her eyes were round, misty with emotion. "You must go to her and tell her, claim her as your own."

Patrick pushed away from the stone. "I canna . . . you don't understand. Her father is a good man who loves her. But he's old . . . so I wait."

"For him to die? Then what?" Her voice was small, as if she already knew.

"To be her father."

"But you're her father now."

"No. Gaspar de Aigues is her father. He's the only father she's ever known and she loves him. It would break her heart to learn it was all a lie . . . and it would be wrong to his memory. It's not his fault this happened. So . . . I'll step in, after, as many men do."

"Step in?" Her echoing spoke of disbelief and hurt.

Patrick hadn't known how she would react to this, had

never planned to tell her. He'd never planned any of this, but it just kept happening. He braced himself and said, "I'll marry his widow, if she'll have me."

"I see."

"I dinna think you do—"

"Why wait?" she asked.

He turned. Her jaw was clenched, and her nostrils pinched with fury. Her mouth twisted into a smile, but there was no softness in it. "I'm good with poisons. Let me mix you something to take back to him. Then you can get on with your life." Her shoulders slumped suddenly and she laughed, a brittle, unpleasant sound. "I finally understand why you were in such a rush to get back to France. You're afraid he's already dead and your lover might have taken another husband." She shook her head, going to her horse and trying to mount. "I can see how that would make a man impatient."

"Mona . . ." He tried to help her onto her horse.

She jerked around, ripping her arm from his grasp. "Don't touch me!" Her face was bloodless, stark with pain.

He shouldn't have told her. This was his worst mistake yet, and he'd made a damn lot of them in his life. He never should have touched her or told her about Rosemarie or anything else. He didn't know why he'd expected her to understand. Fool!

She managed to mount her horse by leading it to a stone and using it as a step. Patrick drew his horse alongside hers, wishing he could take his words back.

"Where to now?" he asked hopefully.

"You can go back to France," she said, tapping her horse's sides and cantering down the hill.

Patrick sighed and followed, suspecting the rest of their journey would be a cold one.

12

Ridley held up the polished silver mirror, staring at the ruin of his face. The searing pain had subsided. Now there was only a tightness to his skin. It felt as if his face would rip if he smiled. The skin was pink and shiny . . . except where it rippled and blobbed like the wax that had melted his skin. He still had lips on the right side of his face, but the left was a flat, gaping hole.

Ridley set aside the mirror, unable to look at his own countenance for long periods. Despair, bitter as bile, roiled in his belly. Mona would never have him now. With Fayth's cruel, thoughtless act, she'd ruined his chances of ever winning Mona's love.

The Bloodstone was all that was left for him. It would bring him power, titles, the king's favor, and whether or not she ever loved to look upon him, it would bind Mona to him forever.

The sun was setting, and fog floated through his window. It was time to visit with Wesley. His brother still rotted in Gealach's cellar. Ridley had clothed him warmly and fed him just enough to keep him alive. He'd received another letter from Wesley's bride today. She was on her way to Gealach to join her husband. Ridley hadn't expected her to be so cooperative. When she arrived he would inform her of Wesley's demise and then wed and bed her. Let her father protest, perhaps even retaliate. Ridley would cut him down, too.

Very soon Ridley would have the Clachan Fala and would add his men to the duke of Norfolk's host. Ridley meant to take many prisoners in the invasion of Scotland— it was the border way, after all. But he did not intend to ransom them afterward, as was common practice. Once the Scots were defeated and Scotland annexed, Ridley's prisoners would meet with unfortunate accidents, their lands forfeit to the king, who would surely bestow them on Ridley for his exemplary military service in the coming conflict, thanks to the Bloodstone.

He would be one of the most powerful lords in the kingdom, perhaps even be made an earl.

He smiled, and the left side of his mouth pulled tightly. He was frightening when he smiled, a monster. Lands and titles couldn't give him his face back. But those who caused him his disfigurement could be punished.

Someone scratched at his door. He threw it open and found Gilford outside, his face a mask of apprehension.

"My lord, Stroud has returned."

Ridley stared at his servant. "The news is not good?"

Gilford shook his head. "Only two return. Penton is dead and Wycliff crippled."

Ridley pushed past Gilford, his vision fogging with rage. Patrick Maxwell still lived? Why would he not die?

In the hall, Stroud stood nervously before the fireplace, twisting his gloves in his hands. When he spotted Ridley's approach, he lowered his eyes.

"You failed."

"Yes, my lord. He is a superior warrior. We have no one to rival him . . . except perhaps you, my lord."

"Perhaps?"

Stroud hesitated, then said, "He's very good . . . and he's enormous."

"Where are they?"

"The Highlands, traveling northwest. They were last seen in Strathclyde."

Ridley looked the man up and down. "How is it you came back whole and unharmed?"

Stroud paled. "He took on Wycliff and Penton at the same time—I'm no match for either of them alone. I didn't stand a chance. I thought it best to report back so a new strategy could be devised."

Ridley had already devised a new strategy. It was clear he would have to dispatch Patrick Maxwell personally.

"Since you're so reluctant to engage in combat, you will take twoscore men and escort my brother across the border to Graham Keep."

Stroud's jaw clenched at the insult, but he nodded. "Yes, my lord."

"The Scots are readying for a war, so go by sea, avoid all contact with the Scots. If Wesley isn't there when I return I will hold you responsible."

After sending Stroud away, he gave orders to the small host of men staying behind to man Gealach. Lady Anne was to be escorted to England the moment she arrived—by force, if promises of seeing Wesley didn't work.

The tower was suddenly a flurry of activity as most of the men-at-arms prepared to leave with either Ridley or Stroud. Glad to finally be leaving this hovel, Ridley barked orders as his armor was strapped on and his horse readied. He'd chosen a new helm—this one covered most of his face, and when he wore it he felt almost normal.

He was mounted in the courtyard when Stroud dragged Wesley from the cellar.

"Where are you taking me?" Wesley demanded as his hands were bound behind his back.

"You're going home, Brother. You, too, will be a casualty of the coming war."

Wesley was shoved onto a horse. "You can't get away with this." His face distorted with pain. He had several broken or cracked ribs.

"Really?" Ridley swung onto his horse. "I've managed to get away with a great deal thus far."

"And God has punished you. He shows all the world how grotesque you are by putting your ruined soul on your face for all to see."

A vein ticked in Ridley's temple as he rode beside his brother's horse. "You suggest your sister is an instrument of God?"

"Yes." Wesley glared at him, righteous in his mistreatment. "And it was only a warning."

Ridley struck him, sending him tumbling from his horse. He landed awkwardly on the ground and couldn't right himself. He hissed, his face pressed into the dirt.

"It is you who will be punished for betraying me!"

Stroud yanked Wesley to his feet and forced him back onto the horse.

Blood trickled from Wesley's nose into his mustache. "You left me no choice. You've been betraying me since Father died."

That he spoke the truth mattered little to Ridley. Of all those who served Ridley, he'd trusted none so much as Wesley. And Wesley had taken that away. Now there was no one.

"Get him out of my sight," Ridley muttered and rode out the gates to claim his destiny.

* * *

They entered a hamlet on the western coast near noon. They were close. Mona fingered the beads about her neck. She'd come to the missing bead and the gap in the map. However, her memory of the bead was clear. She might not be able to use it to locate the landmark, but at least she would know it when she saw it.

Though it had been days since Patrick's revelation that he planned to wed Rosemarie's mother, Mona still couldn't look at him without her heart breaking all over again. He'd never promised her marriage or made any commitments, and his lust for her had been clear from the beginning. If their liaison left her brokenhearted, that was her own fault. She'd known better than to fall in love. Arlana had warned that all men were the same, and Mona's husbands had proven that Arlana knew of what she spoke. Mona also well knew that when a man lay with a woman it held no more meaning than any other physical urge they experienced. Making love was no different than taking a piss. An ache they must relieve.

It wasn't as if Mona hadn't been aware of all these things. Yet somehow, in the time she'd spent with Patrick, she'd come to believe he was different. He was the exception.

Arlana had returned loud and clear, cackling in her mind. Why had she ignored her old friend? Set her memory aside to lie with a man?

Because he is the devil's spawn, sent to deter you from your purpose.

He is not the devil's spawn.

Still you defend him!

Mona grit her teeth. Yes, she still defended him. Love didn't just die. And she loved him, with all her heart. His nightmares had returned, and she suffered as he thrashed about, but her pride would not let her go to him though she knew he'd find solace in her arms.

Once he'd even tried to apologize for misleading her,

but it had only made her angrier. He *hadn't* misled her! She'd misled herself. She'd allowed herself to dream of a life with Patrick, of being mother to his daughter. Her barren womb ached with the loss of that dream.

The hamlet was nothing more than a cluster of cottages. As they rode down the single lane, it appeared there wasn't even a place to buy a meal or drink.

Patrick stopped beside a cottage from which the mouth-watering fragrance of baking bread and simmering stew wafted. He leaned down to knock on the open shutter.

A woman appeared in the window. Her long black hair was braided and coiled around her head. "Aye?" she said, sharp blue eyes inspecting them critically.

"Share a meal?" Patrick asked. "We have coin."

"Good for you I've made plenty. Ye're the second couple to come begging this way."

Patrick dismounted and helped Mona down from her horse. Good manners kept her from rejecting him. She was supposed to be his wife, after all, she thought bitterly.

"If ye take yer horses around back, my husband will gi' them some oats."

"My thanks," Patrick said and left Mona alone with the woman.

Mona sat on the wooden bench outside the cottage and waited. When the woman brought food Mona would ask if there were any standing stones in the area. She didn't want to do it with Patrick present since she hadn't told him a bead was missing.

"Here ye are, lass." The woman handed her a wooden bowl with a spoon and a thick slice of bread. "And one for yer bonny man." She set the other bowl on the bench beside Mona.

Mona thanked her and asked about the standing stones. The woman gave her an odd look. "Why, what's so interesting aboot them stones? The other couple I mentioned, that's just what they was looking for."

A chill went through Mona. *The bead she'd left behind.* Had Ridley found it and discerned its purpose? Had he sent people to retrieve it?

"A couple?" Mona asked. "What did they look like?"

"Och, they were fair like you and yer man. Nobles, methinks, though they denied it—I've heard of them going aboot like common folk, don't ye ken. Our king has been known to mix among the commoners. Why, me own sister . . ."

Mona sat patiently through the woman's tale. Patrick returned and joined her on the bench, listening politely as their benefactor regaled them with the story of how her sister rubbed shoulders with royalty, hinting that she might've shared more than pottage with the king.

When she finished, Mona prompted, "The couple was fair?"

"Och, aye. He a long lad—like this one here," she gestured to Patrick, "a bit taller though. And she was a wee thing. Said their names was Maxwell."

Patrick jerked. "Maxwell?"

"Aye . . . Alex, he said."

Patrick's hand fell on Mona's knee and squeezed hard. "When were they here?"

"Not but a few hours ago. They were asking aboot the stones, just like yer wife. That's where they are now."

"Where are the stones?" Patrick asked, already on his feet.

The woman gave them directions, then said, "But they'll come back this way. They left their horses and their friends." She pointed to a cottage across the way. "There's a mute and a few others playing dice and drinking all of Alice's ale."

Patrick thanked her profusely and paid her too much.

His excitement was palpable. He believed this Alex Maxwell to be his brother, though he said nothing to Mona. They rode in silence as they almost always did now. It hurt that he didn't at least try to return to their old rapport. But why would he? He'd never really cared about her at all. Just doing his duty.

The stones were soon in sight, sitting at the top of a rise. They heard the barking of a dog moments before the couple came into view. Patrick reined in his horse, staring.

Mona's gaze went first to the tall man. His long, reddish-brown hair was pulled back and secured at his nape. He wore no hat or helm. He was taller than Patrick, and though he was sizable he wasn't as broad, but there was no mistaking this man was kin to Patrick.

Then her gaze fell on the woman. Mona screamed and almost fell from her horse in her frenzy to dismount.

"Fayth! Fayth!"

The couple had been so intent on each other they hadn't noticed Patrick and Mona. They stopped at Mona's scream, staring at them for a long moment before they both broke into a run.

Fayth flew ahead of the man and flung herself at Mona. "I've been searching for you—Ridley, he's been following you—he knows where you are." Fayth's excited words ran together. She stopped to take a breath, then burst out, "I've missed you so much!"

"And I you. But tell me—how come you to be with a Maxwell?"

Fayth loathed the Maxwells. The last time Mona saw her stepdaughter she'd been plotting ways to rescue her sister, Caroline, from her new Maxwell husband.

Fayth's face flushed. "Alex is my husband. I'm a Maxwell now."

Mona gaped. *"You* married Red Alex?"

Fayth nodded, her tawny eyes bright. She was as lovely
as ever—more so, even as bruised as she was. Her reddish-
brown hair was pulled back in a short plait, her small face
animated with happiness. It even appeared she'd put on
some weight—something the lass sorely needed.

Mona squeezed her stepdaughter's hands, her heart
swelling with joy that Fayth had evidently found love. "Let
me meet your husband, and then you must tell me everything."

Arms hooked, they returned to the horses, where Alex
and Patrick stood together, talking. A wolflike dog with
linens wrapped tightly about its ribs and foreleg lay on the
ground at Alex's feet, tongue lolling.

Alex turned at their approach, his eyes falling on his wife.
The softness and affection reflected there touched Mona.
Fayth had found love in her marriage. It was all Mona had
hoped for her stepchildren. The iuchair had told her Caroline
had found love, and Mona was anxious for the time she
would meet Lord Annan. But of Wesley and Fayth Mona had
worried. They were both so angry, so misguided. She'd
feared they would never open their hearts to another. It had
been their father's fault, feeding this hatred of Maxwells
until it became so twisted up with their love for Hugh that to
not hate a Maxwell seemed a betrayal of their father's memory. But Fayth had overcome that. In spite of a myriad of
cuts and bruises on her face, she glowed. If only Mona could
see Wesley so happy, her heart would be complete.

As she looked at Patrick and saw how he had with-
drawn, stepping back from their little group, she knew her
heart would never be complete. Not now.

Alex's arm slid around Fayth, bringing her flush against
his side, and turned to his brother. "This is my wife, Fayth."

Patrick smiled and nodded, murmuring a greeting.

Then Alex turned to Mona, a charming smile curving

his lips. He was very handsome. His eyes were midnight blue, and though he had an alarming scar at his temple, it didn't detract from his fine features.

"And you must be my new mother-in-law?" He looked Mona over from head to toe, brows raised in disbelief. "I canna call her Mum—she's younger than I am!" He slanted his brother a stern look. "I hope you've been taking good care of her—she's kin to me now."

The smile faded from Patrick's face, and he averted his gaze. Alex's eyes narrowed on his brother.

To fill the awkward silence, Mona took Fayth's hand and said, "So how did this happen?"

Fayth glanced up at her husband, a world of meaning in their exchanged look. "It's a long story."

"I must see the standing stones. Why don't you tell me everything while Patrick speaks to his brother."

Patrick stared after the women climbing the hill. "Married?"

Alex nodded. "Aye. A sennight ago in Ireland." He stared hard at his brother. "How did you escape Ridley? Did Lady Graham release you? You don't look bewitched."

Patrick sent his brother a sharp look. "Who said I was bewitched?"

"Well . . . 'tis what everyone says, that she's a witch."

"She's not a witch."

Alex scratched his head, inspecting Patrick with narrowed eyes. "Then what are you doing with her?"

"She helped me escape. I owe her my life."

Alex looked unconvinced. "And?"

Patrick scowled. "Is that not enough?"

"For most men, aye. But not for you."

"Good it is to ken ye think so highly of me. No wonder I rotted in Ridley's dungeon nigh on a year."

Alex laughed and slapped Patrick on the back. "You know you'd have been free long ago if I had the kind of coin Ridley asked for your release."

Patrick knew that but was still irritated his brother thought so little of him. Never mind that he *had* been most reluctant to repay his debt to Mona. Was it so obvious to everyone that he possessed such a poor sense of gratitude?

"What are you doing this far north?" Patrick asked. "Last I heard war was brewing on the borders."

"Aye. The king has summoned you to advise Huntly."

Patrick straightened at this news. "So this is more than an idle threat?"

"Aye. I'm taking Fayth to Annancreag and then I must join Robert and his men in Edinburgh. You will come? We should deliver Lady Graham as well, she'll be safe with Caroline."

"I think my business with Mona will soon be finished. I'll join you then."

"Is this the business of the Clachan Fala?"

Patrick gave him a sharp look. "How did you know?"

"I've been looking for you since we learned of your escape." A moment of raw emotion passed over Alex's face, and he gripped Patrick's shoulder. "God, it's good to see you, man."

Patrick squeezed his brother's arm. "Aye. I've missed you."

"You'll not run away to France this time? You'll stay and become friends with your new sisters?"

Patrick sighed, dropping his hand away and stepping back. "I'll stay and fight, but I must return to France afterwards."

Alex's gaze probed him. "Do you still have the nightmares?"

Patrick bit down on the caustic remark threatening to

emerge, feeling chagrined he would not have held back if it had been Mona. His brother only knew of the nightmares because they had drunk themselves insensible and passed out together on several occasions. Unfortunately, consuming prodigious amounts of whiskey tended to enhance the dreams rather than extinguish them—a fact that caused him to imbibe infrequently.

"No," Patrick said.

From Alex's look he well knew Patrick lied.

"So how did you find me?" Patrick asked, to change the subject before it became uncomfortable.

"A bead . . . in the shape of one of the standing stones at the top of yon hill. I found it at Graham Keep in Lady Graham's chambers, along with a lock of your hair and nail pairings. I recognized it as a landmark and hoped one had to do with the other."

"Ah," Patrick breathed, smiling slightly. "She consulted the iuchair on me."

Alex raised a brow. "The what?"

Patrick shook his head. "Now you've found me."

Alex nodded. "Aye, I have. And now I must ask what ye've gotten yourself into?"

Patrick snorted. "I might ask you the same question, little brother. Marrying Ridley's wee sister? Mona tells me she was meant for some old man—Carlisle? What are ye thinking, man?"

"Mona, is it? Not Lady Graham?"

"Ye didna answer my question."

Alex rolled his eyes and sighed. "Fine. I love her—I made her my wife though I've nothing to offer but my protection."

Alex's impassioned sentiments gave Patrick pause. He'd never known his little brother to be passionate about anything but feud and land. He looked hard at Alex, seeing now that the angry lad was gone, replaced by a man with responsibilities. And he carried them much better than Patrick.

"You have nothing? What of Gealach?"

Alex shook his head slowly. "Ridley holds it."

"Christ."

"Aye. He's grown powerful, Patrick, and his reach is far. Even Robert doesn't dare strike at him."

"And he thinks this Bloodstone will aid him."

Alex shrugged, eyebrows raised to show what he thought of that bit of folly. "It makes him seem more cracked than dangerous, but dinna underestimate him. He's consumed with this obsession. He'll kill you to get to the Bloodstone."

"He'll have to. But I wouldn't wager on him winning."

Alex grinned. "My wagers are always on you, Brother."

"Do you love him?" Mona asked as they climbed the hill arm in arm.

"Oh, yes. He's nothing like Papa said. He's not evil and cruel . . . and he didn't kill Jack."

Mona smiled to herself. She'd felt all along that accusation had taken on a life of its own. Fayth's betrothed, Jack Graham, had been taken prisoner in a raid nearly a year ago. When Wesley had gathered the money to ransom him, Red Alex had sent word that Jack was dead. And returned the money. Wesley had been enraged, and Fayth's despair had quickly transformed into seething hate. Both were convinced Red Alex had murdered Jack cruelly. Though such a thing was not uncommon, the murderers generally did not return the ransom money. But Fayth and Wesley had refused to assign any significance to that detail. Mona had always suspected they misjudged the notorious red reiver.

"And he loves you?"

Fayth turned to her at the top of the hill and clasped her arm tightly. "He gave up his home for me. Ridley tried to force me to marry Lord Carlisle, but Alex came for *me*— not Gealach." Her small face was hard, her eyes somewhere distant. "But we'll get it back. I'll not let Ridley take our home away."

Mona had seen that look before and was distressed.

Fayth focused on Mona again. "The tower is beautiful, you should see it—and you will, of course. You should see Alex's face when he speaks of it. If it's the last thing I do—"

Mona shook her, hard. "It *will* be the last thing you do! Don't throw everything away, Fayth. Gealach is a thing! You have a man who loves you. Make babies and be happy, forget about *things,* they won't make you happy."

"Then why do you live for the Clachan Fala? It's a thing."

Mona dropped her hands and went to the oblong standing stone with a hole in it. "I have nothing else. You do."

"You have me. And Caroline and Wesley."

Mona smiled at her. "My lad and lassies, yes. Of course, you're right. But this must be done. I cannot allow Ridley to possess the Clachan Fala. Besides, it is for Caroline and her new husband."

"He knows where you are . . . I was in Luce Bay, I saw you. I almost called out to you, but Ridley was there. He grabbed me. He was watching you."

Mona could only stare at Fayth. She'd thought nothing could surprise her anymore, but she'd been wrong. Ridley followed her personally and she'd never suspected. Queasy fear clutched at her. How could they win against such a man?

"He . . . has sent assassins, twice, to murder Patrick," Mona said. "The last time he sent three men." She blinked at Fayth. *"Three men against one.* He has no honor . . . I never suspected he was so . . . such a . . ."

"Demon? Spawn of Satan? Pile of shite?"

Mona nodded.

"It's worse than all that," Fayth said, her elfin face grave. "I burned him . . . his face. It's quite bad, I think. If he ever gets his hands on me, Mona, I'll not live through it."

Mona sighed. "Then your man must take you to safety." She turned to the stone and looked it up and down. It wasn't a bead but perhaps it was enchanted. She placed her palms against the stone and stared through the hole in the center.

Tell me which way.

Nothing happened. Mona closed her eyes and concentrated. *Show me.* But she did not take flight, her arms did not become wings. Her feet were very much on the ground. She straightened. This would take some thought. The iuchair had told her nothing. The map was broken. She'd tried everything she knew to see her way these last few days. They were so close—too close to lose their way now.

The men were climbing the hill, their conversation serious.

"It's war they discuss," Fayth said, her voice low as she watched her husband. "He must join King James while I wait." She looked up at Mona, frightened. "I don't know how . . . and I'm so afraid of losing him."

Mona embraced her stepdaughter tightly. "The Maxwell men are strong and smart, they will return. You must believe that."

The men stopped talking when they were in hearing distance.

"So, where now?" Patrick asked.

Mona toyed with the iuchair, avoiding his gaze. "I'm not certain."

There was a long silence, then, "You're not certain?"

Mona sighed. "A bead is missing . . . this is the landmark . . . but this stone is not enchanted. It tells me nothing of the way."

Patrick just stared at her.

Mona removed the iuchair and took it to him. "The next landmarks are on an island . . . but I don't know which one."

"Splendid." His eyes were blue ice. "There are hundreds of islands clustered about the west coast. Most probably have standing stones. How are we to determine which one without your magic beads?"

Mona looked away from him, swallowing hard, and shook her head. She didn't know. She was ashamed she'd brought him all this way and it might come to naught.

Alex held out his hand. "May I see?"

Reluctantly Mona placed the iuchair in his outstretched hand. He turned it over, fingering each bead.

"These are all tiny landmarks, just like mine."

"Just like yours?" Mona asked.

"Aye," Patrick answered. "He found one of your beads. Fancy that. Ye didna bother to tell me one was missing."

Mona arched both eyebrows. "You are angry that I withheld important information from you?"

His eyes narrowed, then he shrugged. "Makes no difference to me."

Fayth looked between them curiously, but Alex didn't seem to notice, too intent on the iuchair. "I recognize a lot of these stones. I've been all over Scotland."

Mona's heart leapt, and she hurried to his side. "These four, they're a group of standing stones on an island. Do you recognize them?"

Alex frowned at them a long moment, rearranging the beads on his palm in a variety of ways. Mona said nothing, as she'd held those beads and had seen them clearly from the air, though without the missing bead she had no way of knowing exactly where they were.

A smile broke over his face. "Aye—I know this place. When I was a novice Father Gilbert took me there on a pilgrimage. There's a small church—"

"Yes!" Mona cried. She whirled around, grasping Patrick's arm. "We found it."

His smile was forced, and Mona dropped her hands, embarrassed.

"Well," Patrick said, stepping away from her. "What are we waiting for? Let's get this over with."

13

Patrick rowed across the choppy gray water. He faced
Mona, his gaze fixed on the mainland, his arms straining
under powerful strokes. He couldn't look at her. Her anger
mounted as she stared at him. He couldn't wait to be finished with her. And now he would no longer have to suffer
her presence alone.

Alex and Fayth stayed behind in the village to watch for
any of Ridley's spies. Alex had led them a day's journey
west, to a small coastal village. The island where the
Clachan Fala was hidden was visible from the beach. This
morning, before she and Patrick left, she'd tried to send
Fayth and Alex away, worried that they were involving
themselves in something that would cost them their new-
found happiness, perhaps even their lives, but both insisted
on waiting in the village. And so Patrick and Mona had
rented a small boat and set off for the island alone.

But a hundred people might as well separate them as
much attention as Patrick paid her. She couldn't understand how he could sever their relationship so cleanly—her
own wounds were still raw and aching.

He's a coward, Arlana whispered in her head. *There's naught else to understand.*

"In matters of the heart he is," Mona muttered under her breath.

Patrick looked at her sharply, pulling the oars in so the boat wallowed, riding the waves.

"Why are you stopping?" Mona asked. "Aren't you in a rush to get this over with? To be finished with me so . . ." She trailed off, clamping her lips tightly shut. She hadn't meant to be such a shrew, wearing her hurt and jealousy so blatantly, but every day it grew more difficult to be with him and not touch him, to not share her thoughts with him and talk about whatever came to mind. It was a strain to maintain her anger. And yet her pride demanded he make some amend before she forgave.

"What?" he said.

She turned on him. "So you can hurry back to your woman? So you can get on with your life!"

Patrick began rowing again. "Oh aye, I canna wait until I no longer have to suffer through your muttering and cursing my name every time you look at me."

Angry at her own behavior and yet somehow unable to stop, she said, "If you had just told me—"

Patrick thrust down the oars again. His pale blue eyes darkened to an icy gray. "As you told me you were missing an important part of the map? I thought you had no secrets?"

"You never wanted to help me! I couldn't tell you that! You'd have left me."

"Now that's a fine thing to say. I haven't left you yet, have I? And you've given me plenty of reason."

She gasped indignantly. *"I've* given *you* plenty of reason? You used me like a whore!"

"I'm not a monk. When a beautiful woman crawls in

bed with me and begs me not to leave, I'm not going to argue."

"So this is my fault?"

He shrugged and picked up the oars, rowing again.

So much for forgiving him! He was not about to make any amends, the bastard. Mona slowly stewed as they approached the island. It was over. They would never talk now, never work this out. His brother was with them, and he would use Alex like a shield to keep her at a distance. And that was just fine with him. He didn't care. The thought made her angrier, until she could hardly stand to look at him.

When they neared the beach, Patrick dropped the oars in the bottom of the boat and hopped into the surf, dragging the boat ashore.

Wind blasted over the rocky, treeless island. Mona stood on the pale sand of the beach, gazing out at the sea.

"Where is this church?"

"We must go to the stones first." Mona fingered the iuchair, eyes closed until she saw them from above. Four gray monoliths jutting out of a knoll, standing sentinel over the island. She circled round, finding the figures standing on the beach. A woman, her black braid whipping about in the wind, and a man, his incredibly broad shoulders hunched against the cold, short blond hair damp from sea spray. He watched her, intent. A lock of hair whipped across her face and he reached out, gently, as if to push it away.

Mona's eyes snapped open. Patrick was staring down at her, hand lifted. He dropped it abruptly, turning to look out over the island. A seagull cried overhead, and Mona's gaze turned upward. She raised her hand in greeting.

"This way," she said, leading him to a faint trail worn in the long brown grass. It was a small island, craggy with rocks jutting from the sandy ground. They climbed upward until they reached a series of thatch-roofed cottages. Children came out to watch them. Women laundering stopped their work to stare, but no one said a word. Mona smiled and waved, but their return greetings were cautious.

Patrick called out, "Where's the kirk?"

A woman pointed in the direction opposite where they were headed. Patrick shot Mona a triumphant look before following the woman's directions.

Mona sighed.

The trail wended among rocky outcroppings and tufts of flowing grass. Sheep dotted the hillside, bleating into the wind. A stone building came into view. Small and squat with a thatched roof. They halted before it. A wooden cross was mounted above the doorway.

This was not right. The doorway before them was a typical door frame. There was no arch. In fact, this did not look anything like the church Arlana had described to her in such detail, then forced her to memorize.

"What's wrong?" Patrick asked.

Mona shook her head. "This isn't it . . . this isn't the church." She started back the way they'd come. "I must go to the standing stones."

Patrick caught her arm. "Why? You said the iuchair would tell you where in the kirk it was hidden. Well? Consult it."

Mona shook her head, trying to pull her arm away. "No—that's not the church."

"If there was another kirk on this wee island, why did the woman not ask us which one we wanted? Or tell us where both are?"

Mona couldn't dispute his logic, but was becoming desperate. "But there's no arch."

"So? Arches dinna make kirks."

A man stepped out of the doorway and waved to them. His green robes identified him as a priest.

Patrick gestured for Mona to wait right there and went to the man. They conversed briefly in the Scots tongue. The priest nodded with seeming wisdom and pointed to the south. Patrick waved Mona over.

"Father Duncan says there was another kirk on this island, but it's been falling into ruin for many years. They built this to replace it more than a decade ago. The ruins of the old kirk are south of here."

Excitement welled in Mona. "That must be it! Let's go."

Patrick thanked the man and followed her along the faint trail. It was a small island, maybe a few miles across, and it wasn't long before they approached the ruins. Little was left of the church but an arch and the base of a few crumbling walls, bright green with the fuzz of moss. Mona went directly to the arch, inspecting it critically. A solid structure, still standing strong when the rest had not survived. The locals had scavenged the ruins for stone to build their cottages, but they'd left the arch intact. Starting at the base, Mona counted nine stones up and four stones over. She found a jagged rock and tried to chisel away at the mortar between the stones. When that didn't work she tried scratching away the mortar, putting her weight behind it.

"What are you doing?" Patrick asked.

Her grip slipped and her knuckles slammed into the arch, scraping the back of her hand along the rough edges. Mona hissed and shook her hand, then scratched an X into the surface of the chosen stone.

She straightened, sucking on her bloodied knuckles. "It's here. We must remove this stone." But when she turned to Patrick, he looked neither jubilant nor pleased, nor even cynical.

His eyes were stormy, the cerulean dangerously dark.

"Is something amiss? We're here! Help me . . . we must find something to dislodge the stone."

Wounds forgotten, she searched the ground, refusing to humor one of his sulky moods. Finally, she would be the one to take the Clachan Fala from its resting place and deliver it to its worthy new owners. And soon—*very soon,* she prayed daily—she would be able to shed the mantle of Keeper and lead a normal life. And really, with his own freedom so close he should be able to taste it, he shouldn't look so damn grumpy. Her misgivings returned, dampening her excitement. The stone was too dangerous, too powerful for *anyone,* even Patrick's brother. Perhaps even too dangerous for her. She forced the dark thoughts away. It was not her place to decide such things. She was only the Keeper, and her task now was to recover the stone. Nothing else.

Unfortunately, this island was devoid of trees, so a sturdy tree limb was not to be had. At a scraping sound she turned to find Patrick chipping away at the mortar between the stones with his dirk. Mona went to his side, her hands clasped tightly together.

"Good!" she said, encouraging him.

The tight set of his jaw didn't soften, nor did he look at her, so intent was he on his task.

Mona wrung her hands until the raw skin of her knuckles burned, watching as slowly he knocked away the mortar. He set aside his dirk and pried at the stone with his fingertips. Still stubbornly stuck, he went at it again with the dirk.

Mona could hardly stand the suspense. New fear blossomed in her. This was some horrible jest. There was no Clachan Fala. Arlana had been a madwoman, setting Mona on the path to madness. Her heart throbbed in her chest as the certainty grew within her. Patrick would remove the stone and there would be nothing. Her whole life reduced to nothing. She *would* go mad.

Patrick set his dirk aside again and pried at the stone. This time it wiggled. Mona's breath caught, her hands curled into fists, nails digging into her palms. With excruciating care he worked the stone free.

Mona held her breath as he set it aside. They both peered into the small cavity. Something was there, wrapped in stained and rotting linen. Patrick removed it, slowly unwrapping the cloth. Beneath was a leather pouch. He unfastened it only to remove yet another pouch, this one red velvet.

It's real. It wasn't all for naught. It shivered through her, a relieved giddiness as she stared fixedly at the fine material.

When this one lay in the palm of his hand he looked up at Mona, an odd frown of consternation marring his brow. "You didn't know . . . all this time you were afraid it wasn't real."

"Well, I'd never seen it before . . . sometimes I did doubt."

He returned his attention to the pouch, working the drawstring and slipping his fingers inside. He drew out a ruby, bloodred and cut in a half-sphere. It was set in gold, a twisting, knotting pattern, circling it like a nest.

Mona was afraid to touch it. It was so beautiful, so precious. And yet it was just a stone. It didn't glow or sing. The earth didn't move with its reemergence. It was a simple gem. She frowned at it, disappointed.

Patrick looked up at her. His face was nearly bloodless, deep lines bracketed his mouth. "It's not."

Mona started, becoming aware it was the second time he'd responded to something she'd not said aloud.

He stood, staring down at her, the Bloodstone clutched now in his fist. "You lied to me. The iuchair didn't tell you where it was. You always knew it was in the arch."

Mona gazed at him, wide-eyed. "The Clachan Fala has told you that?" she whispered. So it was all true, all Arlana had told her. The *knowing*. Then the *sight* must also be true. And the *unseen*. All of it. And what of the rumored properties? The ones not even the Keepers were certain existed? Healing, fortune, more . . .

Patrick scowled. "It's been obvious for some time. I didn't want to believe it . . . but I know it's true . . . now."

Mona didn't know what to say. She *had* lied to him. There were no excuses, he held the Clachan Fala and so saw into others' hearts and minds. Fear distilled over her. He was seduced by the power already. He would take it now and use it for evil.

"Give it to me, Patrick." She held out her hand.

He approached her, his eyes narrowed. She met his gaze, trying to show a resolve she didn't feel. He grasped her wrist and placed it in her hand, grinding it in her palm, clasping his own hand around hers. And like a jolt she felt his anger, a violent churning of emotions that nearly made her ill. When he released her hand, she jerked back as if burned, and the Clachan Fala fell to the ground between them.

They both stared at it, as if it were a living thing and dangerous.

"Put it away," she whispered, shaken by what seethed inside him. He was hurt, he was angry at her lies and at her lack of trust.

"Someone has to touch it," he said. "You're the Keeper." And he turned away, following the path back to the beach.

Patrick sat in the boat, working hard to exorcise all thoughts from his head, to keep his feelings carefully neutral. He didn't like the Bloodstone. It was wrong that one should know another's thoughts or feelings without their consent. Nothing good could come from such knowledge. It was a curse. He didn't wish it on his brother or his unborn nephew. And it must never fall into Ridley's hands. His belly clenched at the thought of the destruction such a tool could wreak. To discern another's intentions, to know how an enemy planned to act before they made a move. It was omniscience. Such power made man as close to a god as possible. Did it bestow other powers? Eternal life? So you could watch all you love grow old and die around you? Second sight? So you could foresee their deaths? It was bad enough to know Mona had not trusted him, had feared he would take the stone from her and use it for his own purposes. He knew she was hurt—he felt that, too, a deep pain that he'd caused. Though she may not trust him as a man, he'd been certain she trusted him as a protector. He sat in the boat, waiting, and came to the conclusion she was mistaken. The stone should not be given to anyone. It should be destroyed.

Sometime later she came down through the stones to the beach, carrying a basket. Patrick fought down the feelings that welled in his heart. Sadness, desire, hopelessness, anger. He would not have her know about him what he did not yet understand. He cleared his mind.

She stopped before the boat and stared at him. "We can't go back at night. The islanders say the sea is dark and dangerous. We could end up in Ireland . . . or worse, smashed against the rocks of some island."

Patrick gazed upward at the darkening sky. A chill breeze rushed over them, parting her cloak and plastering her skirts about her thighs. He still wanted her, couldn't look at her without thinking of the times they'd made love. He looked away.

"Come. Eibhlin offered us dinner and shelter."

She waited patiently as he secured the boat to some stones.

"Does the basket help?" he asked.

She shrugged. "A bit."

Stay out of my head.

She made no indication she heard his thoughts, strolling serenely back up the path. They returned to the group of cottages. A woman waited outside for them, the scents of pottage and mulled ale greeting them.

Eibhlin gestured for them to follow her inside. To Patrick's relief, Mona set her basket in a corner, sliding onto the bench beside him. Eibhlin's husband soon joined them, along with two lads.

Mona introduced him as her husband, Patrick, and explained that he brought her here to search for red clover. She'd heard it was plentiful on this island. The woman agreed that it was, and they talked for some time about the best places to find it.

A pallet was laid before the fire and a blanket provided. The cottage was a single room, so they were forced to follow through with the marriage farce.

Patrick lay on the pallet watching as Mona stalled as long as she could, helping Eibhlin clean the wooden bowls and wipe down the table and benches. Eibhlin finally shooed her away, and Mona reluctantly slid under the blanket beside him. He understood her reluctance, for he shared it. It was hard enough not touching her, but each day the wall he'd built between them grew thicker. To be so close to her with the wall intact would be painful—but worse would be tearing it down.

"Come here, Wife."

She held herself stiff in his arms, and he felt inexplicably angry. He couldn't blame her for any of it, really. She shouldn't trust anyone with the Bloodstone, least of all someone with as few scruples as he possessed. And by omitting his plan to wed Rosemarie's mother and reaping the pleasures of her body, he'd led her astray. A woman such as Mona would see commitment, perhaps even love, in such behavior. He wished he had such things to give her, but his heart seemed full of nothing but violence and anger, emptiness, sadness. For a short while, he had been happy despite their danger. But that had been a dream, transient.

It was some time before he finally fell asleep. Her body grew soft and warm long before his. When sleep finally came, it brought dreams.

He was tied to a stake driven into the ground. The Turks laughed at him and kicked him. They'd been torturing him for hours: flogging, near drowning, trying to learn the movements of King Ferdinand's army. The leader circled him, his black eyes cold. Patrick wanted to rip that rag from his head and strangle him with it. They would have to kill Patrick— they couldn't make him talk.

They dragged Kristof out of a tent. He was yelling at Patrick in his broken English, telling him not to talk—no matter what. Patrick struggled against the ropes binding him, panicking as they bound Kristof to a stake opposite him. The Turks circled them, pressing in. The leader came forward.

"You tell me?" he said, brandishing a long, thin blade, wickedly sharp.

"I know nothing."

The Turk smiled and began to flay the skin off Kristof's face. Kristof screamed but could not move or fight, so tightly was he bound. Patrick cursed them and fought to free himself. He turned his face away, but they grabbed it, forcing his eyes open, forcing him to watch as they peeled Kristof's skin from his body—

"Patrick, wake."

The voice brought him instantly awake, staring into Mona's dark eyes. Her skin glowed in the dying fire.

He was hot, sweating, though the air around him was cold. He'd thrown off the blanket and was huddled near the hearth. Mona leaned over him, a small hand on his shoulder. His stomach still roiled from the dream. It was the worst—he hated it. Sometimes he vomited afterward, and he fought now to keep his dinner down.

"You were dreaming," she whispered, pulling the blanket over him.

Patrick lay back, covering his eyes. "Why won't they go away? Ten years since Kristof died, and still I dream about it—worse now than after it happened."

"What happened?"

Patrick shuddered and put his back to her. The images of Kristof's skin being peeled away were branded behind his eyelids, would not go away. He stared blindly into the dark. She touched his shoulder, tentative at first, then stroked her hand over him.

"Since you told me about Julian, have you dreamed of him?"

Patrick thought back. He hadn't, but that was not unusual. There was no pattern to the dreams; they haunted him at random.

"No."

"Then tell me this one. Let's make it go away."

Patrick snorted. "Forgive, but you did not make any dreams go away. It will be back, mark me."

Her hand slid away, and he instantly regretted his remark. He turned to her. She lay on her back, eyes closed, mouth flattened.

"I'm sorry," he whispered. "About . . . everything." When she made no reply, he said, "I canna go to Rosemarie like this, a man possessed. She needs a real father . . . a good man, who wilna hurt her if she wakes him . . . who doesn't see murder every time he closes his eyes." He sighed. "I'm no good to her. And I'm not good for you, either."

The more he thought on the coming conflict with England, the more anxious he was to join the king. It seemed wrong that he continued to live when so many men he'd served with had died. So many friends who'd trusted him to watch their backs. He was a fool to think he could ever be a good father or husband. Mona deserved better than him.

Her head rolled to the side, and she fixed him with a frown. "Patrick, having bad dreams has nothing to do with whether or not you're a good man. And you've woke from nightmares thrice now, with me lying beside you, and never hurt me. You didn't hurt Hazel. Have your nightmares ever hurt anyone?"

He shook his head but was not convinced. "That doesn't matter—maybe once it would have, but not anymore."

Mona's frown deepened, and she turned on her side to fully face him. "That just doesn't make any sense. What has changed?"

He shook his head again, jaw clenched. He didn't want to talk about this. He was confused, upset . . . angry even, that he could no longer force the images away when he was awake. They came at him now: Julian's trampled body, a bloody lump, barely recognizable; Isaac, bloated and white, floating away from him; Kristof, screaming as the skin was flayed from his body . . .

Patrick pressed his fists against his closed eyelids. Mona's hand slid around his wrist, trying to pull his hands away.

"Do you know? Can you see it all now that you have the stone?" He couldn't bear it if she knew what he had seen, that he had been powerless to stop any of it. No one should have to see such things—especially Mona, whom he wanted to protect from ugliness and evil.

"No . . . but I can still feel things . . . it's like a residue . . . slowly wearing off. I can feel that you're hurt . . . angry . . . and revolted?" She said the last questioningly, as if she didn't quite trust what she felt from him. "And it seems like these feelings are directed at yourself, instead of at others."

He let her pull his wrists away, but wouldn't look at her.

"Why?"

"Because it's my fault."

"Julian's death could not have been your fault."

Patrick shook his head grimly. "I should've had his back."

"Patrick," Mona said, a worried frown creasing her brow. "You're but one man, and at the time a very young one. Julian knew the danger he faced. He didn't expect you to protect him. If it had been you who died, would you want Julian torturing himself over it?"

"You don't understand."

"Mayhap not—but I feel the anger and it's useless to you—"

Patrick turned to her, suddenly, fiercely. "I don't want you to *feel* my anger. That Bloodstone—it must be destroyed. I dinna want my brother to have it. I don't want anyone to have it—it's bad . . . verra bad."

Mona returned his gaze, troubled. "I'm afraid Patrick . . . I don't know what to do."

Patrick wished he had the stone right then so he would know what she was thinking—which confirmed his feelings that it was wrong. It was seductive, to have all revealed to you, whether that person wished you to know or not.

"What do you mean?" he asked.

She worried her bottom lip, plump and soft and so sweet it made him ache. "Arlana saved my life . . . I was to be hanged for murdering Edwin, but she used her influence to have me freed and took me under her tutelage, gave me a new life, a better life. She gave me purpose. For ten years, the Clachan Fala has been my whole life . . . I was one of the chosen ones. And now I doubt all that I am. I doubt Arlana . . . though I cannot blame her. She was only doing as she was taught. I don't know what to do next."

Patrick understood these feelings, had them often enough himself. He also realized this was her decision—one he could not make for her. Which meant he must accept it if she chose to give the Bloodstone to Robert and Caroline.

She looked so troubled, her dark eyes wide, looking inward. He reached for her, tracing the line of her black brows, the straight sweep of her nose. Her eyes focused on him, widening. He smoothed his hand over her temple and into her hair. Her mouth trembled, heavy black lashes swept down to hide her eyes.

She was so beautiful, so strong. He wanted to hold her and protect her. With his fingers curved around the delicate curve of her skull, he brought her closer. "Arlana never held the stone. She didn't know."

"I know. I've thought of that."

He pressed his lips against her forehead, smooth and warm. He wanted to stay like this forever. She made him happy, even if it was fleeting. He kissed her. Her mouth moved beneath his, warm, responsive. She moaned, a small, tortured sound, and turned her head away.

"No, Patrick. I can't do this . . . not anymore." She tried to pull away, but he held her tight. He could sense her distress, felt the aching pain in her chest, and wondered if the effects of holding the stone still lingered in him, then realized it was only his own pain.

He shushed her, still holding her against him, but tucking her head beneath his chin so she was curled against his chest.

She started to protest, and he pressed his mouth against her ear. "We're married, remember?"

She sighed, relaxing. He was glad she finally gave in. He'd feared he would have to tell her the truth—that he needed her to keep the nightmares at bay.

14

Wesley sat on a rock, waiting to cross the firth. He worked at the rope binding his wrists. Back and forth he wiggled them, up and down, small movements meant to loosen. The weather had turned chill and wet. A cloak had been draped over his shoulders, hiding his wrists. Stroud had only been able to secure two longboats. They refused to enter any villages—a good plan, since of late the Scots were hostile toward any strangers they suspected were English.

So after killing a small group of fishermen, Stroud decided to row them over in two groups. Wesley was to be part of the second group.

The fog had lifted, and he could already see the boats returning with lone rowers. He struggled against his bonds in earnest, but all it did was send pain ripping through his ribs. He gritted his teeth, bearing the pain, working at the rope until he felt blood slicking his fingers. He had to get away soon. Once they imprisoned him in the bowels of Graham Keep he'd never see the sunlight—or his wife's face—again. That thought gave him strength, and he kept at it, even as the pain made him light-headed. He fell over once, and a guard pushed him back onto the stone.

Even now they didn't forget he was Ridley's brother. He might be a prisoner, but he would not be mistreated. Ridley was too unpredictable. They all feared he might change his mind about Wesley, and then they'd pay for harming him. Wesley knew better. Ridley would not rest until everyone was as miserable as he was.

Stroud paced the shoreline impatiently. He couldn't wait to be back in England. England was the last place Wesley wanted to be. He had a Scots wife, a Scots earl for a father-in-law, and a fine estate in the north—in all but blood he was a Scotsman now, and it had happened in a few weeks. He'd gone from having nothing and being Ridley's toady to having every dream fulfilled. He would not give that up.

He would not give Anne up. The land, beasts, and capital he would grudgingly part with, but not his bride. There had been nothing before her—emptiness. She'd filled his life.

Several men ran out into the water when the boats were close and dragged them onto the beach. Stroud helped Wesley to his feet. The tall blond man had been solicitous and polite since this began. He'd always been Ridley's man, but Wesley had been friendly with him. He hoped that friendship might be useful now.

"He's bleeding," one of the men said in a low voice as they led him to the boat.

Stroud pushed Wesley's cloak aside and examined his hands. He said nothing about the wounds, pointing to a plank, and then settling in next to Wesley. He signaled for them to shove off. As they rowed into the firth, he said, "I wish I wasn't doing this."

Wesley stared straight ahead. "Then don't. Let me go."

Stroud shook his head. "Your brother . . . has changed.

He cannot be reasoned with. He will kill me if I lose you. I'm sorry."

Wesley kept working at the rope, though it did no good. The boat glided across the water, bringing him closer to England and farther from Anne. It occurred to him to throw himself into the water. He was a fair swimmer, even with his hands tied as they were. But the water was frigid, and they would easily recapture him.

"I saw your stepmother," Stroud said, not looking at him.

Wesley turned on the plank seat. It was the first news he'd heard of Mona in some time—Ridley talked of her frequently, but it was difficult to discern the truth from his fantasies.

"And is she well?"

Stroud nodded. "Sir Patrick takes good care of her."

Wesley continued to stare at the blond man. He must have been a spy or an assassin Ridley had set on Sir Patrick. Once Wesley had hated all Maxwells—particularly the Annan ones.

All that had changed. His wife was a Scot and both his sisters had chosen Maxwell men. And now Mona had chosen yet another Annan Maxwell. Wesley had been wrong—he understood that now. His father had been wrong, as had generations before him. There was only one way to set it all to rights. A plan had been forming since he learned he was to be moved from Gealach to Graham Keep—one worthy of Ridley's slick mind. If only he could gain his freedom.

"If Ridley is dead," Wesley said in a low voice, "I will be Lord Graham."

Stroud nodded again, still not looking at him. "I know."

"You're right—you cannot go back to Ridley if you lose me."

The blond man smiled slightly. "You see my dilemma."

"Then do not go back. Serve me. I have lands in Scotland and have need of good men. Ridley murdered mine, and the Scots don't yet trust me. One day—perhaps soon—Graham Keep will be mine and we can return to England."

Stroud finally turned his pale eyes on Wesley and said gravely, "What you said back at Gealach, about God punishing him . . . I believe that." He ran a trembling hand over his face. "And God will surely punish me as well, for helping him."

"Untie me," Wesley said, "and help me stop him." His heart hammered painfully against his cracked ribs as he prayed Stroud would join him. He wasn't lying when he said he needed men. The Scots might accept him as laird because Lord Dornock told them to, but they'd not rush to his banner in battle. Not yet.

After a moment of thought, Stroud removed his dagger and slit the rope.

Wesley grinned, flexing his hands in front of him. He grimaced at the raw skin of his wrists, scored deeply from the rope. The men in the boat all looked to him now.

"Turn around—let's go home."

They left the island early the next morning. Mona still carried the Clachan Fala in a basket, secure in all its wrappings. The feelings that had been rolling off everyone had ceased. Patrick was again inaccessible. The urge to hold the stone, just to know what went on in his head was strong—but this was quickly followed by a stronger urge to fling the cursed thing in the sea he rowed her across. This was what she'd spent her life protecting? This was what she'd sacrificed so much for? Patrick was right. There was something sinister about it . . . how could anyone do good with such an instrument? How could you ignore the ugly? Not seek to punish those who wished you ill? And the stone not only told you these things but also gave you the means to accomplish them.

And yet, should she be the one to make that decision? Shouldn't Lord Annan and Caroline be the ones? The stone was their destiny.

Her whole life she'd been so certain of her decisions. Even when she'd slipped poison into Edwin's mulled ale she'd felt no uncertainty. When a noose had been slipped over her neck she'd not been sorry. Sorry she'd gotten caught, sorry no one seemed to remember he was insane, sorry she'd not left the village in the middle of the night. But not sorry she'd escaped Edwin the only way she'd known how.

Patrick watched her, his eyes probing. "What do you fash on?"

"The same."

He drew in the oars, laying them across his knees. "Throw it in the sea. Now. No one will ever find it. It will be lost forever."

Mona eyed the basket, wanting to do just that. But she could not. What if she was wrong? What if Arlana and all before her were right? That the recipient of the stone was the only one who *could* control it. Then she would be a fool for throwing it away.

The pregnant silence drew out. Mona couldn't meet his gaze. She was a coward. After a moment the oars dipped into the water again.

"Why must it be a love match?" Patrick asked. "What if Robert didn't love Caroline?"

"I used to ask Arlana the same thing. I don't know if she really knew herself, but she told me only a deep abiding love could produce a man worthy of the stone."

Patrick nodded thoughtfully. "Aye, it would be in the way they raised him." His face darkened. "But ye dinna have to love a child's mother to love the child."

"I know." A small pain wrenched her heart as she thought of how impossible and selfish her feelings for Patrick were. He longed for his daughter. She knew that longing for a child. It was selfish to want Patrick and his child for herself.

"I ken ye know. I saw you with my brother's wife, Fayth. She loves you, that was clear."

Mona shrugged. "I suppose Hugh's children are more like siblings to me in many ways . . . except they needed a mother and accepted me in that role."

He began to row harder, his face granite as he stared at some spot on the horizon. She wanted to reach out to him, keep this tentative communication going, but she knew it was hopeless, and so she lapsed into silence with him, staring out at the water. She thought about his nightmare. Though he'd not hurt her, he'd seemed much worse after this dream than after the others. He'd been pale, clammy, ill. And he'd been deeply shaken.

"Who was Kristof?" Mona asked.

"He was a soldier . . . a Hungarian. He was but a lad . . . Christ. I should never have taken him."

"Was this in Austria?"

Patrick nodded, his oar strokes slowing. "Aye, 1532. I was fighting for Ferdinand then . . . by that time I had something of a reputation and he sought me out. We were sent to drive back the Turks invading lower Austria. I had a mixed group of mercenaries . . . One was Kristof. He was eighteen and reminded me so much of Alex . . ."

He fell silent, the oars plunging deeply again, the boat moving faster.

"But he wasn't Alex . . . he had no fighting experience. I thought to train him—perhaps make him my squire. I took him with me to scout out the Turks' encampments, and we were captured. I shouldn't have brought him . . . he was unskilled in such things." He sighed, his eyes regretful. "Their leader believed I knew something of Ferdinand's plans and tried to torture the information out of me. After a bit of that, they realized it was no use, I wouldn't talk. So they turned to Kristof."

"They thought he knew something?"

Patrick shook his head, his jaw rigid. "No . . . they suspected I might be able to bear my own pain, but not a friend's agony." His jaw bulged from how hard he clenched it. "And they were right." His voice was thick, hoarse. He'd stopped rowing altogether now, the oars trailing in the water as he stared into the bottom of the boat.

Mona's fingers were over her mouth, fearing he would go on, that he would tell her what they'd done to Kristof, while he'd watched. She didn't want to know. Judging by his revulsion last night it was gruesome.

He shut his eyes tightly, pulling in an oar so he could press his fingers hard against his eyelids. After a moment he began to row again, his face clear, calm, his blue eyes vivid against tanned skin.

"What happened, Patrick?" Mona whispered.

"I . . . uh . . . told them everything I knew. And they killed Kristof anyway. They meant to kill me, too, but they wanted to take me to their general, I think. I understood little of their tongue. After what I'd done, I couldn't let them live to tell anyone. I managed to escape and I killed the leaders—and anyone who might be privy to what I said—the interpreter as well. Then I tracked down the messenger and killed him."

When he smiled at her, it was ghastly, cold. His eyes were empty. "I was knighted for it. For watching my friend's skin flayed away, spilling my guts, then murdering anyone who bore witness to it."

Mona shivered, pulling her cloak closer around herself. "I'm sorry, Patrick. No one should have to see things like that . . . and to relive them in dreams." She wanted to ask him why he continued to be a mercenary, but it was clear why. He was good at it. It was profitable. And after a time, perhaps there was nothing else. He said he had no friends.

He had a daughter. But he didn't even know her. Mona felt his aloneness so keenly she wanted to weep.

He shrugged. "Perhaps it's punishment . . . a ring of hell here on earth I must endure."

"Why? Why should you be punished?" In spite of all that had passed between them she still believed he was an honorable man.

"For Rosemarie . . . that's when the dreams became frequent . . . and bad. After she was born."

A swift wind blew across them, sending up sea spray. Gulls screamed overhead.

"Do you love Rosemarie's mother?"

Patrick shook his head, mild humor curving his lips. "No." He met her questioning eyes and sighed. "I suppose I owe ye something of an explanation. I was serving the French king at that time . . . he'd awarded me lands on the Argens and many other things, so it was profitable. I was passing through Aigues, and Gaspar agreed to garrison my men for a few days." Patrick chewed the inside of his lip, as though he were uncomfortable with this subject. "Gaspar is very old . . . and his wife, Nadine . . . well, she was much younger."

Mona's cheeks burned, but she kept her face carefully neutral. She hated Nadine.

"Gaspar is a good man, and when Nadine crawled into bed with me that first night, I tried to send her away."

"You *tried?*" Mona said, annoyed at the caustic tone of her voice.

Patrick shrugged. "Perhaps I didn't try very hard. Anyway . . . this went on for a few nights . . . until I started feeling guilty. I like Gaspar verra much . . . so I told her to stop cuckolding her husband. That's when she informed me that if I'd managed to impregnate her, she'd have no more need of me . . . I was a stud, you see. Gaspar hadn't managed to get an heir on her—on any of his wives, for that matter—and Nadine feared losing everything to his brother when he died. Arnou had been circling like a vulture for years, waiting for Gaspar to die. She was desperate for an heir.

"I suppose I was something of a disappointment, giving her a girl. But I wasn't the last poor fool. When I left France a year ago she was with child again."

The mainland was finally in sight, though still some distance away. Mona stared at it, wondering what to make of Patrick's story. His daughter had changed his life, given it purpose. She couldn't compete with that, didn't want to. What she wanted was this Nadine person gone. She sounded dreadful. She probably wasn't even a good mother.

"You think I'm not fit to be her father . . . but that's not so. There will be no more fighting after I wed Nadine. I will do this right, I vow it."

"I don't think that," Mona said, her hands folded tightly in her lap. "I wish you happiness and I hope to one day meet your lovely daughter . . . and wife. I plan to stay with Caroline for some time . . ." *Forever.* There was nothing else for her. She wouldn't marry again—unless it was Patrick, and that could never be. "Surely you'll visit your brother."

"Aye." He wouldn't look at her, his golden lashes hid his eyes from her. She would never meet his daughter. She would never see him again. And now it was truly over. She could see people on the beach, waiting for them. Probably Alex and Fayth. She would not have another moment alone with Patrick. She wanted to tell him she loved him. But that was stupidity. What could it matter to him now? He would pity her, think her pathetic.

They drew closer to the shore. There were many people there . . . and most of them were doing nothing more than standing around, waiting. Mona looked around them, realizing for the first time they had the entire stretch of water to themselves. No fishermen. No ferries.

"I wish, . . ." Patrick began and stopped abruptly when he saw her face. "What is it?" He swung around, taking in the scene.

Mona squinted, trying to make out individual figures, but they were still too far away.

Patrick cursed under his breath. "Ridley's taken control of the village."

"What about Fayth and Alex?"

Patrick shook his head, intent on the coast. "Alex can take care of himself—and Fayth."

Mona wrung her hands, terrified for Fayth and Alex. She prayed Patrick was right.

"What can we do?" Mona asked.

Patrick ran a hand through his hair. "We canna just row ourselves to them, but neither can we go back to the island—they'll only follow and in better boats." The stretch of shoreline before them was long, perhaps a mile before it ran into cliffs and dangerous rocks.

"Wherever we try to land on the beach they've only to come and get us . . . our only chance is to head for the cliffs. Find a cove or a cave somewhere."

Mona stared at him, her stomach flipping queasily. The rocks were treacherous. They would be smashed upon them—and she couldn't swim. "B-but can't they just follow us there, as well?"

"They'll try—but we'll get farther on water than they will over that terrain."

"You can swim?"

He shot her an odd look. "Aye."

Mona bit back further protests. He was right. They were trapped. This was their only chance. He rowed southwest now, still moving toward the mainland, but farther down the coast. Mona saw the moment the people on the shore realized their plan. Half the men vacated the beach.

Mona's stomach sank further. She'd been hoping they were somehow mistaken, but it was clear that Ridley had found them. Had known where they were all along. This was why she'd needed Patrick. She glanced down at the basket nestled in the bottom of the boat amid Patrick's crossbow, quarrels, and swords. If they crashed into the rocks, the Bloodstone would be lost.

She snatched it from the basket and jiggled it from the leather pouch. Patrick watched her stuff the velvet bag into her bodice. It was bigger than her sack of coins and quite uncomfortable. She raised a brow at his grim stare, and he looked away. She was not going to throw it into the sea . . . not yet, at least. Perhaps it could even be of use to them.

She felt a heightened awareness and wondered if it came from Patrick or just the Bloodstone making her more sensitive. It had other properties, aside from knowing other's thoughts. Being . . . unseen, which Mona didn't really understand, and the sight, which she did. Arlana'd had the sight. Mona tried to remember how she'd called on it—what words she'd used. It had been fickle and unpredictable.

The beach was out of sight now, and they rowed along the cliffs. Mona gripped the edges of the boat as the surf caught them, forcing them closer to the rocks. Her gaze locked on the waves beating violently against black granite.

"You're too close!" Mona cried.

Patrick ignored her, maneuvering the boat as if he knew what he was doing. Mona tried not to panic, tried to trust him. The boat rose on a swell and then they were rushing down. Mona tried to sink down into the floorboards, her eyes jammed shut. Frigid water washed over her.

Mona blinked, sputtering and shaking her head.

"I see some caves," Patrick yelled over the roaring surf.

Mona chanced a look at the rapidly approaching wall of jagged rock and quickly shut her eyes again. The buffeting of the boat was making her ill, dizzy.

"What if the caves go nowhere? Just fill up with water when the tide comes in?" Mona shouted back.

"Then I guess we'll drown, eh?"

Mona cracked an eye to glare at him. He was grinning! His hair was wet from the water, and he was clearly straining under the force of wielding the oars in the angry water. But he seemed to be enjoying himself. Mona could see no humor in the situation. Rigid with fear, she whispered to the Bloodstone pressed against her heart, "Will we live? Show me."

Water rushed into her mouth, choking her. It closed over her head, pulling her under, pressing on her chest. Her body slammed against something.

Mona wrenched her eyes open, breathing hard. Their boat was close to the rocks now. Patrick was trying to maneuver it into the caves. But they wouldn't make it. The Clachan Fala had shown her.

"Patrick, no!" she cried, reaching for him. "We can't go there!"

He frowned at her but kept rowing. He was going to kill them. She grabbed his arm, trying to pull the oar away. He stared at her incredulously, shouting something that was lost in the surf. Mona held on, determined to stop him from making a fatal mistake.

He gave a hard yank, shoving Mona backward into the boat with his other hand. When Mona righted herself, gripping the plank seat desperately as the boat rose, she saw Patrick hanging out of the boat, reaching for something.

The oar—he'd lost it. It was too far. It rose on an enormous swell bearing down on them. He would fall in. Mona surged forward and grasped the leather of his jack, determined to either pull him in or go over with him. He twisted and clamped down on her arm a moment before the wave washed over them.

Water filled her mouth, choking her. She heard the sharp crack of wood, and then freezing water swallowed her. Mona reached for Patrick. He no longer held her arm. She flailed, her movements heavy and slow as she was pulled along. Her lungs strained for air. Her body slammed into something hard and sharp, and the world went dim.

She was grabbed under the arms, and then there was air. She sucked it in and coughed violently. Water splashed over her face. She was still nearly submerged. She began to struggle.

"Put yer feet beneath ye, damnit." It was Patrick, hauling her along.

Mona let her feet drift downward until she felt the sandy bottom. She clung to him, still afraid. The sea pulled at her, trying to drag her back out. They were sheltered in some rocks, but she saw no cave. They must have passed it. Patrick helped her until the water was to her thighs, then he peeled her off.

Her legs were wobbly, but she stumbled after him. A sheer cliff rose before them with a jumble of stones at its base. Patrick wended his way between them until he was on the dark, wet sand at the base of the cliff. Mona's eyes traveled up the cliff, following the barnacles crusting the black rock to nearly eye level.

It was low tide. Mona swallowed hard, shivering uncontrollably as the surf lapped at her sopping shoes. Patrick's back was still to her as he scanned the cliff and the rocks all around them. He had not one weapon, she noted. He'd even managed to lose the dirk he kept in his boot. A piece of wood from the boat washed up past Mona, resting in the sand near Patrick's boot. He looked down at it for a long moment. Then he kicked it violently.

"Bloody Christ! *What was that?* We were almost in the cave and you become hysterical!"

Mona quailed at the anger in his voice. "Patrick . . . I . . ." Her voice rasped in her throat, catching on a cough. "The Clachan Fala . . . it gave me a vision. I thought . . . I mean, I saw us smashed upon the rocks."

He turned to her and looked her over from head to toe. Then he shook his head, eyes closed, hands on hips.

Mona's stomach was bloated with swallowed seawater, and her eyes burned. She felt like such a fool. The vision had come true, but only because she'd made it so. And he was furious with her. She could have killed them—they might still die. She was confused and upset. And she could feel the frustrated anger coming off him in waves.

"I'm so sorry . . ."

He held up a hand in disgust. "Not now. Let's find our way out of this first."

She followed him as he picked his way through the rocks. He reached an impasse, and they had to climb. The wind tugged at her, trying to blow her onto the jagged rocks below. Patrick boosted himself up on a rocky shelf and held his hands out, hauling her up after him. The cliff was not as high as it had seemed at its base. They continued on this way until the tops of the rock were covered with a soft carpet of heather and Mona was able to clamber after Patrick with little difficulty.

Patrick walked along the edge of the cliff, looking down into the water. Mona watched him, shivering violently in her wet gown and cloak. The Bloodstone was a heavy weight between her breasts. She should throw it over the side of the cliff now. It was useless, worse than useless—misleading. But she didn't.

He finally turned to her, hands planted on hips. "That . . . *thing* sent you a vision? While we were in the boat?"

She nodded, biting her lower lip. "It was clearly wrong . . . it didn't come true until I tried to stop it."

He strode toward her, his face set. Mona was queasy from the wreck and the climbing and the cold. Sick with guilt that she'd almost killed them.

He extended his palm to her. "Give it to me."

Mona blinked, folding her hands protectively over her bosom. "Why?"

He pointed toward the sea with his other hand. "This is a good place to toss it, methinks."

Mona shook her head, backing away. He came after her and she turned. The backside of the cliff was a steep, rocky hill, cushioned with thick heather. It descended into a stretch of green upland before dropping off again. Mona stumbled down the hill, her head whirling in panic. She heard him behind her, sending a shower of rocks around her. She wasn't ready to just throw it away. She still had to think on it a great deal before she could act so rashly.

She knew he would catch her, though it happened sooner than she expected. He snagged the back of her sodden cloak and yanked her into his arms.

"No!" She tried to shove away from him. He was too strong and held her fast. She hit at him, but he caught her arms, pinning both her wrists in one of his.

"I'll not let that damned thing kill us!" He jammed his hand in her bodice, groping. She kneed him in the groin. When his hold slackened, she tried to twist away, but he kept hold of her wrist even as he fell to his knees, groaning.

She felt possessed, frenzied—she would not let him

take it from her. She tried to kick him while he was down, but he dragged her onto the ground beside him. He grasped her shoulders and gave her a hard shake, his eyes freezing her.

"Ye almost killed us! For that blasted Bloodstone!"

"It was my fault—not the stone's!"

He stared at her, squeezing her shoulders hard. "Do you hear yourself? It's doing this to you, isn't it?" One of his hands had crept to the side of her bodice, quickly and familiarly unhooking it. As soon as the stiffened material loosened, Mona felt the Bloodstone slip. His hand was at the top of her shift again. Mona caught it, despair rising in her throat.

"Don't do this, Patrick, please." His face blurred from the tears gathering in her eyes. He couldn't do this to her. If he took the Clachan Fala she would have nothing. No purpose to her existence.

His hand halted on her chest, his other arm hard around her waist.

Tears burned her cold face as they fell and she saw him above her, his face a tight mask of uncertainty. His hand slid up her chest to the back of her neck. He whispered her name, pulling her against him and pressing his lips to her forehead. She couldn't feel him through her own churning emotions, but didn't care. He held her and she was safe.

Her eyes drifted shut, reveling in the feel of his mouth on her skin, pressing hot kisses. Her hands, which had been fisted against his chest, pushing, flexed open to slide up and around his neck. She tilted her face up and his mouth covered hers. She thought her heart would explode from the emotions pulsing through her. She loved him so much it was an ache, tearing her apart.

He unhooked her cloak. The heavy weight fell from her shoulders. He buried his hand in her hair, pulling her head back so he could explore her neck. "So soft," he murmured against her skin. She shivered in his arms, his touch warming her. He pushed her bodice and shift down, pinning her arms to her sides.

He kissed her again, his hands on her breasts, and she murmured against his mouth, "I love you." And she felt him pluck the Bloodstone from its hiding place.

Her eyes sprang open, her body going cold.

His face was unreadable as he stared down at her, but he held his hand behind his back.

"You bastard," she said through clenched teeth, fury and humiliation suffusing her.

"Well, I've been called worse." He stood and backed away from her, back toward the cliff.

Mona struggled to her feet, not bothering to replace her bodice, letting it fall to the ground as she pulled her shift back over her shoulders.

"Where are you going?" The heat of rage replaced her cold, that his kiss had been nothing more than a cold calculation. And she had told him she loved him.

He was climbing the ridge, his back to her.

"Don't you dare throw it!" she yelled at his broad back. Almost at the top, he turned to look back at her. The wind whipped at his hair. He froze, staring down at her. His mouth opened, but the roar of the sea and the wind stole his words. His gaze was not on her—it was behind her and full of alarm.

A chill raced over her as she turned.

Ridley stood at the edge of the upland, his men filing up behind him.

15

Patrick started back down the ridge, but it was too late. The man was on her, his arm around her throat. She clawed at the gauntlet, staring back at Patrick with wild eyes. He didn't know the man, but he must be Lord Ridley Graham. He wore a breast and back plate, painted white, fancy silken and velvet breeks, high leather boots that folded over at the knee, and a plumed helm that completely obscured his face. Within minutes a score of men-at-arms swarmed up the hillside.

Patrick's gaze locked with Mona's again. She shook her head imperceptibly—but he understood. He held the cursed Bloodstone and she didn't want him to give it up, even if it meant her life. Little fool. As if it were worth that.

Patrick closed his eyes briefly, his mind racing with crazed plans before snagging onto the only one that had a chance. Barely. Not only was it sorry and doomed to failure but it involved her beloved Clachan Fala. When he opened his eyes all he could see was Mona, trapped in Ridley Graham's arms. His head was bent to her ear, whispering.

Patrick knew too much, and it made him sick with fury. Ridley's emotions were powerful and dark, lustful, ugly.

He wanted the stone but he wanted Mona, too, and in the same twisted and obsessed way.

Ridley raised his head. "She says she doesn't have the Clachan Fala." He ran his hands intimately over her body, even shoving one under her skirts. She gritted her teeth through it all, eyes locked on Patrick. His muscles tensed, ready to spring should Ridley harm her.

"It seems she speaks the truth," Ridley said. "Where is it?"

Mona's gaze bore into him. *It wasn't on the island.* That's what she wanted him to say. That there was no stone. They'd went where it was supposed to be and found nothing. But Patrick already knew that Ridley wouldn't believe them—and that he planned to kill Patrick no matter what. The loathing Ridley felt for him nearly blasted him, overwhelmed him. He fought to push it away but couldn't. Other thoughts and feelings bombarded him with distressing randomness—the men-at-arms. They thought Ridley a wizard. Some of them were bored, tired, hungry. One wanted to kill Patrick and Mona for the fun of it. Patrick didn't want to know these things, didn't want to feel them. They distracted him, made his head pound.

He backed farther up the ridge until he was at the top. The men-at-arms moved forward slightly, but Ridley stayed where he was, his arm locked around Mona's neck.

"I have it," Patrick said. He slid it from the velvet pouch and hefted it, tossing it and catching it, then turning it so the sun caught the deep blood red. Exposed, it seemed to hum, a vibration deep in his bones that startled him.

Patrick couldn't see Ridley's face, though the sun caught the gleam of his eyes, and Patrick knew he slavered in anticipation. Ridley's fingers curled into his prisoner's hair. Mona's shoulders sagged, and she turned her face away.

"But why would I give it to you?" Patrick yelled. "I hold omnipotence in my hand."

"Because I'll kill the woman if you don't. And I don't believe you can stop me." He placed his gloved hand beneath her chin and gripped it as if he meant to snap her neck. But he wouldn't. If Ridley had a weakness, it was Mona. It was the one thing Patrick had in common with the man. The only thing.

Patrick tossed the Bloodstone again. Ridley's eyes tracked it, greedy.

"Then kill her—what do I care?"

Ridley squeezed her neck and she gasped. He ripped a dagger from his waist and pressed it to her throat. "You think you know my thoughts, eh? Because you hold the Clachan Fala? Read me now, Knight. I *will* kill her."

If he was bluffing, he was damn good at it. The wind tore at Patrick, trying to rip him from the cliff. He squeezed the stone and felt nothing but hate from Ridley. He swallowed hard and raised his hand, ready to throw the stone into the sea. "Send the woman to me, or I throw it."

Ridley laughed. "Then you'd both die. You're not stupid."

Patrick gripped the cursed stone. Ridley was right. Without the stone he had nothing to bargain with.

"We both want the woman," Ridley said. "And we both want the Clachan Fala. Let us trade."

Patrick didn't give a damn about the bloody gem, but he certainly didn't want Ridley to have it. And he was right about Mona; Patrick wanted her as far away from here as possible.

"What say you?" Ridley called, lowering the knife to Mona's breasts.

"You'll kill me as soon as I give you the stone."

"Patrick, no!" Mona screamed.

Ridley clamped a hand over her mouth, wrenching her

head violently to the side. Patrick clenched his teeth, wanting to hew the bastard down. But he didn't have a single weapon on his person. His mind raced, trying to find a way out of this with Mona and the stone, but he could think of nothing. Their only chance was a trade.

"You have my word I'll harm neither of you. Until you're off the mountain, that is."

So he'd give them a head start. It was something Patrick could work with. "Very well—but I dinna like the odds. We'll do this my way."

Mona pried Ridley's fingers from her mouth. "No!" She fought his hold. He sheathed the knife, trying to hang onto her. She struck at his head, knocking his helm askew. He shouted something and two men came forward and grabbed her arms. He removed the helm.

Patrick drew in a breath at the sight of Ridley's face. One side was nearly normal, with a few slick pink burn scars, the other was a jumble of melted skin, hairless and raw.

Ridley turned to Mona.

She stared at him, wide-eyed. The wind sent her hair whipping about her. "Good Lord. Ridley . . . Fayth never meant to do this."

Ridley threw his helm down. "Your first words are for Fayth? What of me? Look what she did to me!"

Mona shook her head sadly.

"Hey," Patrick yelled, bringing Ridley's attention back to him. He didn't like how Ridley looked at her—all betrayal and hurt. Dangerous. If Patrick failed, her fate would be ugly. "Send your men back to the village. Leave two horses. Put Mona on the back of one. Then I'll give you the stone."

"You'll try to kill me."

"I'm unarmed."

Ridley considered him, eyes narrowed. "The Bloodstone . . . it gives the advantage. You can use it to hurt me."

Patrick wished he truly had such an advantage, but simply knowing what someone felt and the occasional thought was of little use to him in this situation. Particularly when Ridley meant everything he said. If the Bloodstone had other powers, Patrick knew not what they were. He wished suddenly and passionately for Ridley's demise, but nothing happened. The sky did not open and send down a bolt of lightning to strike Ridley down.

The wind gusted against Patrick. Gulls screamed. "Ye'll have to chance it, aye?"

Ridley gave orders to his men. All but the two holding Mona prisoner vacated the rise.

"Back up," Patrick said.

When they descended the hill, Patrick followed at a distance, uneasy now without the cliff at his back. The further he got from the sea the more empty his threat became. He had to hope Ridley truly feared the stone. He stopped while he was still close enough to race back and toss it into the sea if necessary.

"Bring the horses up here."

"It's difficult to coax them up a mountain—"

"Do it!"

Ridley signaled to his men below, then turned back to Patrick with a small bow.

"Send the dogs away."

Ridley reluctantly dismissed the men holding Mona, taking her in his arms again, dagger to her throat. He whispered something to her and Patrick could barely restrain himself from springing forward to knock his face away from her hair.

The minutes stretched by, and finally one horse was led over the rise and onto level ground.

"I said two horses," Patrick ground out.

"Yes, you did. But too many problems with that—especially if we let Mona mount first. She doesn't like your plan . . . I'm afraid she'll do something unfortunate. She doesn't want me to have the stone, you see. Troublesome, that."

Patrick only stared at him, gripping the stone so hard its setting cut into his palm.

"Here's how it will be. Get on the horse, Sir Patrick. Ride over here and offer me the Bloodstone. I'll take it and give you Mona."

Patrick swore. They wouldn't get far before their backs were bristling with arrows. It was a decent horse, but carrying two it would tire quickly. Patrick didn't believe Ridley meant to give them a head start. But what could Patrick do? This was their only chance.

The man holding the horse retreated. Patrick went to it and mounted. Mona wanted him to ride away and leave her. To deliver the Bloodstone to his brother.

He will not kill me.

No, but some things were worse than death.

She bared her teeth at him in frustration when he rode forward, her dark eyes flashing. If they lived, he'd get an earful.

He brought his horse alongside them. "Put the knife away."

Ridley hesitated, his pale blue eyes and long lashes odd in his ruined face, then he nodded and sheathed the dagger. His gaze was fixed on the Bloodstone, darting occasionally to Patrick's face.

Patrick stretched his hand out, palm open, the bloodred gemstone offered. Ridley reached for it, but Patrick drew back. "Release her."

Ridley licked his lipless mouth greedily. "Very well. We'll do it at the same time."

Patrick extended his hand again. Ridley's hand covered the stone, and he pushed Mona forward. Instead of coming to Patrick, she turned, throwing herself against Ridley's arm and sending the stone flying. Patrick watched it arc through the air, shimmering, as both Ridley and Mona raced after it. Patrick swore and spurred his horse forward.

Ridley was faster. He would get the stone and then have Mona, as well. His men were already returning, nocking their arrows. Patrick reached down, slid his arm around Mona, and dragged her over the saddle in front of him. She screeched her fury. Patrick yanked on the reins, turning the horse west, climbing back up the cliff. The horse's muscles strained, its hooves picking a path through the rugged hillside. Then Patrick turned it south. He would follow the coast as far as he could before heading east. The terrain was relatively flat here, but they were going too fast and Mona was already slipping. She was doing nothing to help him.

Ridley's men hadn't expected him to go back up the cliff, but they quickly raced after him. Arrows flew around them, one grazing his neck. Ridley's men had left their horses somewhere below, so Patrick was able to put some distance between them by the time the cliff began to descend. The way before them was dangerous, but behind it was fatal. He slowed the horse and helped Mona sit up and swing her leg over the saddle in front of him.

"Why—"

"Shut up," he hissed in her ear and started down through the rocks.

She sat stiffly in front of him but didn't say another word. They must keep moving, take advantage of their head start if they were to escape. Ridley would send men after them and also try to cut him off by riding south on safer roads. But they would likely stop for the night and so Patrick pushed, even in the dark, sticking to the valleys, where they would be easily spotted but could make good time.

Eventually Mona fell asleep against him, her head

lolling against his shoulder. They came to a stronghold the next evening and begged shelter. The steward sent them to the great hall, where they would sleep on rush mats with the other men-at-arms. This was fine with Patrick, but Mona shivered and needed a bath and a change of clothes. Patrick asked the steward to relay his name to the laird. When Artur Lamont learned of his guest, he gave them fine chambers, sent a bath and clothes, and invited them to break their fast with him in the morn.

Patrick let Mona bathe first. She dismissed the servants sent to aid her. He sat in a chair across the room, trying not to stare at her. She was so beautiful, and she loved him. She'd said so on the cliff, just before he'd taken the Bloodstone from her. Though he'd tried not to think of it, not when their situation had been so dire, it had been there, lurking at the back of his mind ever since. And now that they were safe and warm, it dominated his thoughts.

She loved him.

Had anyone but his mother ever said that to him? He could not recall. Perhaps there had been a lass or two, but he'd known they never meant it—not as Mona did. She accepted his nightmares, his violence, even his secrets. And it tore at him. He didn't know what to do about her.

She rose from the wooden tub, and he caught a tantalizing glimpse of her naked body streaming with water before she covered herself with a bath linen and stood before the fire. Her profile was solemn, so beautiful and strong. She gazed into the flames, deep in thought. Then she looked down, spreading one hand before her, turning it over, inspecting the palm, then back again. After a puzzled moment she gripped the towel with her other hand and repeated the ritual, finally fisting both hands in the sheet.

She thought of her Bloodstone. He didn't need the infernal thing in his hands to know that. The anger rose in

him again. She would have given her life for that unworthy
piece of rock.

He stood and removed his jack, tossing it on the chair.
He pulled his shirt from his breeks and pushed off his
boots. She turned to look at him. Seeing his intention, she
moved away, gathering up the clean shift Lady Lamont had
provided. Patrick caught her as she tried to move past.

"What's wrong with your hands?"

She shook her head, not meeting his gaze, a small frown
between her eyes. "Nothing at all . . ."

He wanted to shake her out of this mood. She'd barely
spoken to him since they'd escaped Ridley. He'd expected
her to rail at him, but thus far she'd maintained a sullen silence. He released her, and she disappeared behind the
screen.

He finished undressing and sunk down into the tub, still
warm and smelling of rose water. He thought of her behind
the screen, of her satiny skin, fragrant from the rose water,
and of sharing a bed with her. Of sleeping with a woman
who loved him. She reemerged as he washed and settled
onto the bed, running a comb through her long, wet hair.
He grew hard and hot just watching her, but when he rose
from the tub she didn't notice. She looked at the wall,
never stealing the smallest peek.

He joined her on the bed, linen wrapped around his
waist. After a long silence in which he watched her intently, hoping to make her so uncomfortable she would say
something, she spoke. "Why one bed? You didn't refer to
me as your wife."

"No . . . but they apparently assumed you are my lover."
Her cheeks flushed and her mouth flattened.

He reached out to toy with the hem of her shift. "Why
do you blush? It's true."

"It *was* true. I made a mistake."

"I make lots of mistakes. Constantly. Mayhap we could make another tonight?"

She glared at him.

"Ah . . . I didna think so." He sighed and lay back on the bed, hands folded behind his head.

She looked away. He watched her through his lashes as she raked the comb through her hair, tearing violently at knots. He winced as she yanked at a particularly nasty one, and he heard the hair breaking. He sat up and grabbed her wrist, plucking the comb from her fingers.

"What are you doing?" She tried to take the comb back.

He gripped her shoulders and turned her away. "You're angry with me—not your hair. It doesna deserve to be ripped out on my account."

"That's not necessary," she said, but let him run the comb through her hair, gently untangling the knots.

"You are vexed with me."

"Yes."

"Why? Because I managed to save our skins again, but ye dinna like how I went about it?"

"Nothing matters but the Clachan Fala. It would have been better to throw it over the cliff than to let Ridley have it."

The comb glided through her hair, free of tangles now, but he kept combing it, loving the feel of it in his hands, the clean floral scent. "Why did ye need me then? I was there to protect you."

"Protect me until I got the stone—then it was the stone you had to protect."

"You didna tell me that."

Mona sighed. "I thought you understood."

"Even if I did, it wouldn't have mattered. I would not let him have you."

"Why? Why should it matter to you?"

Patrick set the comb aside and placed his hands on her

shoulders, pressing his mouth to the wet hair over her ear. "It matters."

She shuddered and pulled away from him, sliding off the bed and crossing the room. "It shouldn't matter. You have your future all planned out, and I'm not part of it. It's wrong for you to make my decisions."

"He meant to kill me. I decided I wanted to live."

"Then you should have taken the stone to your brother, or given it to Ridley and left me with him. I would have found a way to get it back."

Patrick stared at her incredulously. "What he has planned for you, sweetheart, makes death look inviting. I couldna leave you to that."

She gazed back at him, black eyes huge and fathomless. "It doesn't matter."

Patrick pushed off the bed. "If you're so eager to be with your stupid Bloodstone, then go! I'll not stop ye. Go to him."

"I will."

Patrick couldn't believe he was hearing this. He covered his face with both hands and took a deep breath. When he dropped them, he pinned her with a hard stare. "Stop it, Mona. Your jests do not amuse me."

She turned away from him. "I do not jest. I have to go to him."

Anger swept through him and he crossed the room, grabbing her and swinging her around to face him. "I'll tie you to my bed, stupid little witch."

"Your wife might not like that."

"I'm not married yet."

"Yes, I know. You don't have time to keep me prisoner. You have a bride to catch."

He wanted to shake some sense into her—shake the poison from her tongue. It didn't matter that everything she said was true; he was tired of having it flung in his face. So he kissed her, wanting to stop the fool words falling from her lips.

She twisted her face away. "Why are you doing this?" she asked, her voice a whimper. She fought his embrace.

"You said you love me."

When she looked at him, her face was stricken, disbelieving. "So you seek to deepen the wound? To hurt me more?"

He wanted to tell her he loved her, too. Anything to wipe the hurt from her eyes. But he didn't want to love her. He couldn't have Mona *and* Rosemarie. He loved Rosemarie, wanted to be part of her life more than anything. And yet he could not let Mona go to Ridley.

He held her tight even as she struggled against him, his face buried in her hair. "Don't go to him, Mona," he whispered. "Don't leave me."

She stilled, her breath warm on his neck. "Why?"

His bath linen was slipping, but he didn't try to save it, didn't dare let her go. He didn't know why he felt this way, desperate, urgent. She was going nowhere tonight. But he needed to hear the words from her, needed her promise that she wouldn't give her life for that worthless rock.

"Don't go," he whispered forcefully.

She rested her forehead against his bare shoulder. "You say that because you feel guilty . . . you feel responsible for me. I release you of responsibility."

"You can't do that. And I feel more than guilt and responsibility."

It thrummed through him now, desire and longing. He wanted her safe and with him; even though he knew it couldn't be, it didn't stop the ache for it.

She whispered his name, her hands no longer pushing at him but spread wide on his chest. He felt wetness against his skin. He urged her chin up. Tears tracked her cheeks, clumped her thick black lashes together.

"Dinna cry," he whispered, pressing kisses to her eyelids. "Not because of me."

He kissed her, drowning in her mouth and soft body. His bath linen slipped all the way, but he didn't care. He lifted her in his arms and carried her to the bed.

Mona let him take her, knowing it was wrong, that she should not let him use her this way. But she couldn't say no to him. Her heart was greedy, wanting every moment, every taste and sensation. Soon it would be over and she'd have nothing but the memories.

They'd come together many times in the past weeks, but he'd never been like this. He was exceedingly gentle and slow—none of the urgency he usually possessed her with, as if he was trying to banish some demon with her body. His hands smoothed over her, seeking and giving pleasure. Mona returned his intimate caresses and kisses, doing things to him she'd never dreamed of doing to her husbands. And when he surged into her she thought she might die from the sweetness of it.

She lay awake in his arms while he slept soundly, his chest rising and falling beneath her head, and her happiness was bittersweet. She wished for the Bloodstone, to hold it and know what was in his heart. From the way he'd gazed down at her as he made love to her in the candlelight, his voice hoarse with emotion when he whispered her name, she could almost convince herself he loved her. But she wanted to know—needed to. Even if they could never be together.

And that was why she must retrieve the Bloodstone from Ridley. If she, who had devoted her whole life to ensuring that the Clachan Fala be used only for good, could be seduced into using it for her own selfish desires, then there was no telling what Ridley would do. And until tonight she'd not understood how dangerous it was for Ridley to have the stone.

She lifted her hand before her face again, staring hard at the knuckles. She'd scraped them on the arch when trying to chisel away the mortar. The scrapes had been raw, painful. They should be scabbed over now. But they weren't. They were simply gone. Not even a scar.

The Bloodstone could heal simply by holding it.

She slid her hand over Patrick's chest, feeling scars beneath her fingers. It hadn't healed his old wounds. But then he hadn't held it for very long.

She thought of him on the cliff, threatening to toss the Clachan Fala away if Ridley didn't free her. His genuine concern for her was a balm, healing some of the hurt he'd caused. He'd risked his life for her. And she would make do with that. He might not love her, but he did care for her. If she was meant to know more, he would tell her. It was wrong to take from him what he didn't want to give.

She slid her arm around his waist, holding him closer. She would stay with him and do as he wished for now. They were returning to Annancreag, where he said she would be safe. He believed Fayth and Alex had gone there when Ridley took the coastal village. Mona hoped he was right. Ridley had whispered many evil things to her—most about Wesley. That he had not mentioned Alex and Fayth gave her hope. Had he captured or killed them he would have been sure to tell her that. It made her heart sick to learn Wesley was Ridley's prisoner. He was another reason she must go to Ridley. She had to help her stepson. She could not allow Ridley to hurt him anymore, not when Wesley had finally broken free of his brother's hold.

Ridley still wanted her, still believed he loved her. She'd felt that from him, lingering effects of holding the stone so close to her heart. And she knew her family's only hope was for her to go to Ridley as a supplicant, give him what he wanted. Then kill him.

It would not be easy. He had the stone. He would know she was insincere. She must discover a way to block her feelings from him—to fake not just her behavior but her very emotions. It would take much thought. She had time. They still had several days of travel before they reached Annancreag. Once they arrived, Patrick and his brothers would go off to war, and she would leave to seek out Ridley.

16

Over the next few days they saw no sign of Ridley or his men. Mona worried what she would do if they encountered him. She knew what she *should* do—give herself up to him. Ingratiate herself to him any way she could. But these days with Patrick were like a dream, and she was not yet ready to wake.

The weather was cold and the terrain difficult. They had lost all of their coin either in the sea or on the cliff and so they couldn't purchase another mount. Patrick said he could have stolen one, but he didn't want the trouble if he got caught. Mona thought it more likely that he didn't trust her. Though they'd not spoken of the Bloodstone again, she suspected he knew what she planned and kept her close.

And so they continued unarmed, southward, scavenging or begging food. Sometimes they rode together, sometimes Patrick led her while she rode, and other times they both walked, leading the horse they'd named Sandy.

She should be miserable—cold, hungry, filthy, but for Mona it was bliss. During the long hours of travel, Patrick talked to her. He told her about his friends: Julian, Kristof,

Isaac, and others. He spoke of them at first with grief and regret, and later with laughter as he regaled her with tales of youthful pranks.

Mona suspected he'd not spoken of them in many, many years and was warmed that she was the one to crack through his defenses. He even spoke of Rosemarie sometimes, his eyes wistful. He'd only had one nightmare since they'd lost the Bloodstone, and though it had woke them both, he'd been fine afterward—relieved, even. It had been unpleasant for him but not terrifying. Mona prayed it meant the end was in sight for him, that his nightmares would diminish, and, though they might never go away completely, they'd not torment him so.

Yes, for now Mona was glad they'd not met up with Ridley or his men. She feared she could not do the right thing. She didn't possess the strength to leave Patrick. He would be the one to leave her, and as they neared the borders and his family's home, she knew that time drew near.

When Annancreag was finally in sight, a heavy silence descended on them both. They could not go on as they had, talking and touching with such intimacy. Sleeping in each other's arms. She couldn't let her stepchildren know she'd taken Patrick as a lover, and he surely wanted the secret kept from his brothers. This was the end for them. He would return to his life before her and she, to whatever the future held.

His hand, which had been heavy on her thigh, disappeared. Already he withdrew. "This is my home . . . one of them, at least. It's where I grew up."

It was large by Scots' standards, the keep rising high above the castle's gray walls. Men patrolled the battlements, their helms gleaming through the embrasures as they passed. They crossed a wood bridge to the gatehouse, flanked by two round towers. The gates were barred to them. Patrick dismounted and identified himself to the porter. The portcullis was raised.

A lump gathered in Mona's throat as excitement filled her. *Caroline.* Though it had only been a few months since she'd last seen her oldest stepdaughter, it seemed a lifetime. Caroline had never needed mothering, but she'd needed a friend, a confidante, and had graced Mona with that position. Most thought her a cold child, unapproachable and superior. Pious. They had not known her. She'd been lonely and uncertain.

Patrick led the horse into the courtyard, Mona still perched on the saddle. Mud from recent rains churned under Sandy's hooves. The great wooden doors of the keep opened, and an enormous man stepped out—taller than both Patrick and Alex. He was older as well, his dark hair silver at the temples. As soon as he lay eyes on them he broke into a smile, and Mona caught her breath. It was clear this was Robert Maxwell, Lord Annan, for he had the same beautiful smile as his brother.

He jogged across the courtyard to Patrick, chickens and geese making way for him with much honking, squawking, and flapping. Patrick hadn't yet smiled or greeted him, though the lines beside his eyes deepened in pleasure.

Lord Annan stopped before Patrick and gripped his brother's shoulders. "You look like hell."

Patrick grinned. "And you look old." They embraced.

A flash of color caught Mona's eye. Caroline stood in the open doorway, her hands over her mouth, staring at Mona.

Mona slid down from the horse and ran to her stepdaughter, her throat too thick to speak. And to Mona's surprise, Caroline didn't stand there in her dignity, as she was wont—always afraid of revealing emotions that others could ridicule. No, she lifted her skirts and ran, meeting Mona halfway and hugging her.

The embrace took Mona by such surprise that she was

rendered speechless. Caroline had never embraced her. Mona had forced affection on the woman, but it had never been openly returned. It wasn't that Caroline did not love her, it was just her way. She'd never been comfortable expressing her feelings openly.

Mona drew back and stared up at Caroline. She was a tall girl, always had been, towering over most men and intimidating them. She had been awkward when she was young. It had led to cruel nicknames and much hurt. And Ridley had been the worst. No man in Graham Keep had dared to approach Caroline, even those who found she'd flowered into an attractive woman. They would never risk Ridley's ridicule. And when she'd made it clear she meant to be a nun, that had only added to her separateness. She was different, above petty words and spite. But Mona had always known it was a mask the hurt child hid behind.

But Caroline was different now—radiant. Golden hair trailed down her back, her cheeks pink with health. She smiled at Mona, her eyes bright with tears. *Tears!*

Before Mona could choke out a word, Caroline gripped her hand and blurted, "I'm pregnant."

Mona did choke, coughing violently. Caroline was at her side, patting her back and apologizing for shocking her.

Lord Annan appeared beside his wife, his hand moving possessively to the small of her back.

"She couldn't wait to share the news, I see. I told her to let ye clean up and get some food down, but she's fashed and fashed for you since she heard you were missing, fearing she'd never see you again. And here ye are." He leaned close to Caroline and whispered, "I told you Patrick would see to her."

Mona hardly glanced at Caroline's husband. She couldn't tear her gaze from Caroline. She was so beautiful and happy—and *pregnant*. And this man clearly loved her.

And then behind Lord Annan she saw Fayth and Alex appear in the doorway—safe. Mona couldn't help herself; it was all too much. She burst into tears.

Patrick stood at the fireplace, sipping mulled ale and watching Mona with his new sisters-in-law. It still surprised him to see Alex so domesticated, but Robert had been born for it. Alex and Fayth had arrived shortly before them, dirty and travel worn, and Robert still hadn't gotten over the shock that Alex had married Fayth.

"Are you insane?" Robert said, his voice low as he cornered Alex beside the fireplace, eyes the color of storm clouds. "She tried to kill us."

Alex rolled his eyes and nodded. "I know—but she's my wife now."

Robert shoved Alex lightly. "Dinna roll yer eyes at me, man. Six men dead. Their wives widowed thanks to that piece of fluff. Dinna tell me she's not dangerous."

Patrick sent a speculative look at his diminutive sister-in-law and noted the guard hovering about behind her. Robert was clearly taking no chances.

From the rigid set of Alex's jaw, Patrick could tell he was beginning to get angry. "*You* wed a Graham."

"Aye, and Caroline has proven herself trustworthy—Fayth has not."

"She has to me."

Robert shook his head, mouth grim, and turned on Patrick. "And what of you? Where the hell have you been all this time?"

"Well, I was locked in a dungeon well nigh a year—"

"After that."

"I was, ah, helping your mother-in-law." And helping

myself to her. He chewed the inside of his lip. There'd been a tightness in his gut since they'd arrived, an anxiety he didn't understand and couldn't shake.

Robert sent an arched look at where Mona huddled with Caroline and Fayth. "Doing what?"

"Fetching your Clachan Fala."

"Mine, aye? Well, where is it?"

"Ridley has it now."

"Was it real?" Alex asked.

Patrick nodded. "Aye . . . too real."

Robert frowned, arms folded over his chest. "You're telling me that stone is magic?"

Patrick shrugged. "It's something."

Alex chuckled. "He hasn't changed, has he? Canna get him to stop blathering."

"Aye, well," Robert said, shooting Alex a wry look. "Mayhap he only speaks when he has something worth saying."

Patrick managed a grin for his brothers' sharp teasing. He'd always been the most reticent of the three until large amounts of whiskey were poured down his throat—then he became quite gregarious. It was only with Mona he couldn't seem to stop blathering.

"I've plenty worth saying," Alex said to Robert, "if you care to listen and stop making judgements."

"All right, lads, that's enough." Patrick grinned at them, falling into his old role as mediator of his brothers' many disagreements. "I've spent a bit of time with Fayth, and she's as sweet a lassie as I've ever met. Why would she marry Alex if she meant us harm?"

Alex grinned at Rob, brows raised knowingly.

Robert scowled, but Patrick could see him softening. "Mayhap you're right. I've been wondering how to tame Alex for years. Perhaps she is the answer. He's finally found a lass who can put him in his place. Did she tell you about when she shot him?" Robert chuckled, shaking his head.

Alex's face reddened. "I was unarmed."

"She stole his horse, too—and managed to hang onto it."

It was Patrick's turn to be amazed. "Bear? I didn't think Bear could be stolen." Alex had always had a way with animals. He could train them to do anything and somehow inspired amazing loyalty. He'd had Bear for years. The horse had been stolen several times but always managed to escape and return to his master. "Well, if Fayth was able to lure Bear from your side, she's most definitely the woman for you."

Patrick sighed, wishing he had what they did. They both stared across the room at their wives, smiling fondly. And soon Robert would be a father. The urge to speak of Rosemarie was strong. Somehow, being with Mona had made his tongue loose. But he wasn't ready yet. Soon, he would tell his brothers about their niece.

"What of the war?" Patrick asked, shaking off his dark thoughts. "Last I heard we routed the English at Hadden Rigg, but that was some time ago."

"Aye," Robert said. "That victory was short-lived. Last month the duke of Norfolk invaded. He burned Kelso and Roxburgh and hung a handful of Scots as spies. They retreated after only six days. King James mustered an army, and we gathered at Fala Muir, but we were unable to intercept Norfolk. The king wanted to pursue them across the border, but the weather had turned and supplies were short so the earls refused and scaled the army."

"And that's it?" Patrick asked, disappointed to have missed it all.

"You'll get your chance," Alex said. "It's just begun. King James has called for another conscription—here in the West March. He means to invade England from the west. He's at Lochmaben now with Lord Maxwell."

Robert said, "I was preparing to join him when Alex arrived. We only awaited your return. We need you, man. The king needs you."

Patrick finished his ale and set the pewter tankard aside. It was good to be needed in a way he understood. He missed being with his brothers, the easy comradery and acceptance. Perhaps he could even convince Nadine to visit Scotland often.

"When do we leave?"

Alex and Rob began talking about how many men they could raise and how long it would take them to reach the king's forces. Patrick listened but was more interested in what Mona was doing. She and Fayth did all the talking, while Caroline listened intently. They were an attractive roost of hens. Caroline, long and statuesque, Fayth, wee and pert as a flower, and Mona . . . perfect, in every way. To him, at least. He wondered what they were cooking up and hoped it had nothing to do with the Bloodstone. She'd not mentioned it since their argument—in fact, everything had been perfect since they'd left Laird Lamont's castle. He'd even let himself pretend they could go on after this was over. She'd pretended, too, he knew, but they'd not fooled themselves. He would still try to wed Nadine—for Rosemarie—and she would give her life for the Clachan Fala. Nothing had changed.

"What do you think?" Alex asked, punching Patrick in the arm.

Patrick returned his attention to his brothers. "Oh, aye—whatever you said."

Alex scowled and leaned around Robert to see what had captured Patrick's attention. Robert turned, too.

"Stay away from my wife," Robert said.

Patrick feigned shock. "She's my sister-in-law! How could ye think such a thing?"

Robert only stared at him, tankard of ale in his hand. "I know you, Sir Cuckold."

Patrick groaned.

"She must be the first lass of Rob's you haven't been at first," Alex said. "I'm sure he'd like to keep it that way."

"You both wound me. That is not so. I've never touched Celia." The raven-haired lass in question passed by, winking at Patrick. He nodded back.

When she was gone, Patrick leaned into Robert, grinning wickedly. "Your wife puts up with you keeping your mistress under her nose?"

Robert sighed wearily. "Celia has not been my mistress for a very long time—in fact, she's married now—but still, I cannot get her to leave. Caroline has become attached to her, God help me, and cares not about the past. Her husband, however, wants to go home, so I hope to be rid of her soon."

Patrick looked back at the women. "You've both done well. Bonny lassies, both of them." Patrick shook his head and shot a look at Robert. "Jesus God your sons will be huge."

"What of you?" Alex asked. "Fayth thinks you've debauched her stepmum. I hope not, else I'll have it from your hide."

When Patrick said nothing, Robert groaned. "What are ye thinking? Will you be leaving a bastard behind for me to raise?"

Patrick turned on him, cold with anger now. "I wouldna do that. I'll burden ye with no bastards, Brother, rest assured."

"Really?" Robert said, eyebrow raised. "Wait here."

Patrick's blood simmered. There were no bastards in his

past but Rosemarie—and after Rosemarie he'd made certain there would never be any more. If Mona had not been so certain she was barren he would have taken precautions with her, as well. It infuriated him that Robert would imply such things. Lord Holier-than-thou had never done anything without thinking it through meticulously. It was certain he drew up lists for and against each mistress he'd ever contemplated.

Patrick felt Alex's gaze on him. "What?"

Alex shook his head. "I dinna want to nag, but God's wounds! What were you thinking? She's my mother-in-law . . . in a manner of speaking."

"Christ Jesus—look at her! I'm not a monk like you."

Referring to Alex's days in the monastery had once been enough to not only change the subject but to send Alex on a vitriolic diatribe against the church—utter blasphemy. Patrick always found it highly amusing.

But Alex only shook his head, undeterred. "You could always marry her. Stay here in Scotland."

Would that I could. "I cannot."

Robert had returned, an open missive in his hand. "Aye, it seems he has business in France to settle first."

Patrick took the letter, frowning, and went to the fireplace.

Robert brought him a chair and said, "You'll need it."

Patrick lowered himself in the chair, suddenly afraid to read the letter. His brothers left him, joining the women. Patrick stared at the unfamiliar handwriting. It was addressed to Robert Maxell, Lord Annan, and brother of Patrick Maxwell, knight. He unfolded the paper. It was written in French.

It was from Nadine de Aigues, and she was looking for Patrick. It seemed she was now a widow.

* * *

"Will you be here with me? Through the pregnancy and midwife my baby?" Caroline asked, her pale green eyes hopeful.

Mona nodded, feeling like a liar. She wanted to be here for Caroline. She hoped she would be. But there were other matters to attend to first, and she couldn't speak of them now.

"What will you name the child?" Fayth asked, almost timidly. Her wavy, copper brown hair was pulled back in a plait, and she wore a bright yellow-and-green striped gown. It was fine to see her so feminine and pretty—she usually went about dressed like a lad.

Mona arched a brow at her. She'd been acting odd ever since Mona had arrived—as if she were afraid of Caroline. Very unusual, as Fayth was fearless. Unfortunately it generally wasn't raw courage that drove her but an impetuousness and sense of justice.

"We haven't really discussed it," Caroline said, the familiar cool tone to her voice. She didn't look at Fayth when she spoke and Fayth averted her eyes, her jaw tight. Something had happened between the sisters, though Fayth had not spoken of it when Mona had been with her previously.

It all came flooding back to Mona. She'd been so wrapped up in her feelings for Patrick, her worry about the Clachan Fala, that she had forgotten Ridley's plans for Fayth. He'd sent her to Caroline to wait for the Bloodstone and take it. But of course the stone had never arrived, and when Mona had met up with Fayth and Alex, all she'd heard about was the forced marriage to Carlisle and how Alex had rescued her.

"What has happened?"

Fayth looked down at her hands and Caroline asked, "What do you mean?"

"I mean something is wrong. I've never seen you and Fayth this way . . . you are angry with her."

"I have forgiven her."

"But she can't forget," Fayth said. "And she'll never trust me again."

Caroline's face was expressionless, serene and distant. A few months ago this wouldn't have troubled Mona, but in the hour since Mona had arrived, Caroline seemed like a different person. What had occurred to make her revert back to her old ways in the presence of Fayth?

Caroline didn't seem inclined to talk, so Mona turned to Fayth. "Tell me what happened."

"You know that Ridley sent me to Caroline to await the Bloodstone . . . well, I didn't believe it was real, but I had to take the chance. He vowed I would not have to wed Carlisle if I did as he wished. I also came for Caroline. You remember how it was before she left? Ridley was horrid to her. I *believed* Caroline when she said she wanted to be a nun. She talked about it all the time." Fayth's voice had taken on a pleading, questioning tone, asking for Mona's reassurance, as it was clear now that Caroline no longer had any interest in assuming the veil.

Mona nodded encouragingly. "Yes, she did try to make everyone believe that."

Caroline looked sharply at Mona, eyes narrowed, but remained silent.

"Well, she convinced *me*," Fayth said. "I never believed in the Clachan Fala. I thought only to rescue Caroline, even if it condemned me to Carlisle. And while I was here, she was so miserable. The marriage had not even been consummated. She was exiled to a remote tower."

Caroline's face reddened. "I was not exiled. I chose to live there."

"And," Fayth continued, "she cried! Lord Annan kept guards on her constantly, and one night he even barged into her room and began roaring at her like some beast! It was just awful how he treated her—I couldn't bear it."

Caroline spoke to Mona rather than her sister. "He was vexed because I had moved to the tower without discussing it with him."

"I didn't know!" Fayth protested.

"She didn't ask."

"Hmm . . ." Mona looked between the sisters. Both were flushed a deep red, though it was more pronounced on Caroline's paler skin.

"I've only been here a short while," Mona said carefully, "but it seems Lord Annan adores Caroline."

Fayth nodded, mouth tight. "Yes, it has been that way since Alex and I arrived . . . but I swear, he was not this way when I was here before."

Mona nodded thoughtfully, stealing a glance across the room to the fireplace, where the three men stood. Patrick drank ale and talked to his brothers, smiling, his brow clear. The way to loving him had not been an easy one.

"Do you love Alex?" Mona asked.

Fayth's head snapped up. "Yes."

"And he has always been gentle and kind? You never argued? Or perhaps angered him?"

Fayth opened her mouth to protest, then apparently thought better of it and just shrugged, frowning deeply.

"We often argue terribly with those we love," Mona said, touching Fayth's hand. "Silly, when we care about them above all else, but that is oft the way of it." Mona took Caroline's hand next and squeezed it. "Look you at this? You fight with your sister, whom I know you love."

Fayth sat forward suddenly, her eyes fierce. "No, *I'm* arguing. She just sits there like an ice queen. When has she ever argued with anyone? Even now, when I know she hates me, she will not argue!"

"I do not hate you," Caroline said, voice cool, face expressionless. This was how she'd driven Ridley into lathering fits of rage—and she was using it on Fayth now. Mona suspected Caroline was deeply angry and reconciliation would not come easy.

"I can see why Caroline's behavior alarmed you. I, too, was surprised by the change in her, though I think it becomes her."

Caroline smiled at Mona, her gaze warm.

"I do, too." Fayth glanced up at her sister hopefully.

Caroline looked down at her hands, sighing deeply, but said nothing.

"Then what happened?" Mona prompted, releasing their hands and sitting back on the bench.

Fayth looked away from Caroline with reluctance. "Then I . . . pretended to be a whore, incapacitated Alex, and let Wesley and his men in. They . . . killed some people but didn't manage to take much. Wesley forced Caroline to leave. She was hysterical. I began to suspect then that I'd done something wrong."

"A whore?" Mona squeaked, appalled.

Fayth rolled her eyes impatiently. "I didn't lay with him. I only kissed him, then smashed a jug of whiskey over his head."

"And he married you?"

Fayth scowled at her stepmother.

Mona was still stuck on the whore part and had to force herself to move forward with the story. "Listen to me, Caroline."

Caroline looked at Mona, a brow raised.

"Your sister had good intentions, but she obviously made a mess of things. She promises to never make decisions for you again. To always ask you how you feel and not assume. Isn't that right, Fayth?"

"I swear, Carrie."

Caroline's hands were clenched in her lap as she considered Mona's words. Her shoulders relaxed, and she looked at Fayth. "It's not really you I'm still upset with . . . it's Wesley. You've apologized many times already, but I've heard not a word from him. It's . . . it's as if he's disowned me because I chose Robert."

Mona hesitated, somehow reluctant to share what Ridley had whispered to her on the cliff but feeling the sisters needed to know. Wesley needed their prayers now, not their anger. "Wesley is no longer aiding Ridley. He defied Ridley—I don't know how, but Ridley is insane in his rage. He is keeping Wesley chained to a wall in his dungeon. And Wesley suffers . . . he is wounded and untended."

Caroline's pale eyes filled with tears.

Fayth's hands clamped hard over her mouth as she stared at Mona in disbelief. "It's because of me. Ridley's punishing him because he helped Alex and me escape."

Caroline turned to her sister, a tear spilling over her lashes to track her cheek. "He helped you? He helped Alexander?"

Caroline was clearly distraught. Her hand pressed her belly.

Robert appeared behind her, his hands on her shoulders, his brow creased with concern. "What is it? The bairn?"

Mona stood to leave Fayth and Caroline alone with their men. "I told her of Wesley and it has upset her. I'll make her an infusion that will calm her."

She started for the kitchens to inspect the dried herbs the cook kept, and paused when she caught sight of Patrick. He sat in a chair before the fire, reading a letter, deep in concentration. As she watched, the letter fell from his fingers, drifting to the ground. He stared blankly into space.

Alarmed, Mona went to him. She wanted to touch him, to stroke his hair, but could not in front of the others. "Patrick? What is it? What news?"

He snatched up the letter and folded it, shaking his head. He stood, distracted, rubbing his eyes. "It's nothing . . . I . . . nothing." He glanced behind her, at his brothers. "We're leaving in the morning, to join the king."

Mona nodded. She had suspected as much.

"I will come to you tonight," he whispered, still not looking at her. "There is something I must tell you." And then he walked away, leaving Mona twisted up with anticipation and dread.

17

After spending so much time alone with Patrick, Mona was amazed and annoyed at how difficult it was to get away from people. Everywhere she went she was accompanied by either servants, Caroline, or Fayth. And it seemed Patrick had it worse than she did—he couldn't shake his brothers.

She did have her own chambers, and so she waited for the evening to drag by. It was wonderful to be with her family again, and she was enjoying getting to know Alex and Robert, but the call to be with Patrick was stronger than all of that. She felt a twinge of resentment toward him for putting a damper on her evening, but more, she just wanted to know what he had to tell her. From his expression it was probably nothing she wanted to hear, and yet her heart fluttered with hope.

Caroline and Fayth made a tentative truce, and, after Alex silenced Fayth's wild plots to rescue Wesley, the sisters sat beside each other near the hearth, talking about their husbands. Mona swallowed the bitter jealousy that she could never speak of Patrick so freely. She wanted to be happy for her stepdaughters, not jealous because she didn't get *her* Maxwell brother. After a time she noticed that Patrick had managed to escape. A quick search of the hall did not reveal him. Unable to bear another moment of suspense, she stood and kissed Caroline and Fayth good night.

She hurried along the wall to the corridor that led to her chambers. The hall had several recessed window seats. Curtains had been hung to create private alcoves. A hand reached out of one as she passed and pulled her between the brocaded curtains.

A candelabra sat on the windowsill, backlighting Patrick, hiding his face in shadows.

"I thought you were coming to my chambers?"

"I didna think that wise."

Mona's heart sunk. It really was over. It struck her that this was the last time she would be alone with him. The last time they could speak freely. He did not touch her now but sat on the cushioned bench beside the window and looked down at his hands. Mona sat beside him.

He had bathed recently, the sandy ends of his hair, longer now, curled about his neck and ears. His hands, callused and scarred but cleaned, the nails tended, curled into loose fists. The candlelight caught the golden tips of his lashes. He wore a silk doublet of deep navy, silver buttons climbed from his waist to his neck, the white collar of his shirt peeping out, snowy against his tanned skin. The black breeches he wore were snug, outlining heavily muscled thighs. She'd never seen him so finely attired and thought him magnificent.

"What is it, Patrick?" Mona asked. She'd been so anxious for this, to be alone with him, and now she wanted the torture over. This was awful, to sit here with the wall back between them.

"Gaspar is dead."

Mona closed her eyes, the pain his words brought forth

excruciating. She'd believed his conviction that he meant to marry Rosemarie's mother, but somewhere deep inside she'd hoped Gaspar would live forever—or that Nadine had already remarried. Selfish, when he only wanted to be with his daughter.

"And Nadine is free?" she asked, keeping her voice neutral.

"I think. He died months ago . . . she has been looking for me. She wrote Rob, asking for his help. She has a son now, too."

Mona didn't know what to say, didn't know why he felt he needed to tell her this. He knew how she loved him; it was like twisting a knife in her heart.

"Why does she need your help? Didn't Gaspar provide for her?"

Patrick shrugged. "I know not. Something must have happened. I'll soon find out."

"Soon?"

There was a long silence, then he said, his voice almost a whisper, "Rob didna know what would become of me . . . if I was even alive . . . so he invited Nadine and Rosemarie to Scotland. He offered to care for Rosemarie, or both of them, if Nadine did not wish to leave her daughter."

"When was this?" Mona heard herself ask through the buzzing in her head.

"Six weeks ago. He has not heard back from her and suspects she accepted his offer—is on her way now."

Mona's stomach roiled. She feared she might actually be ill. Nadine and Rosemarie, *here?* Mona might even get to attend the wedding. She pushed away the urge to shriek, and then to laugh. If she did either she would dissolve into a pathetic puddle of tears.

"Do you wish me to leave . . . so it's not awkward for you?" Her voice was surprisingly steady, calm.

His fists were clenched, the knuckles white. "No. I just . . . thought you should know."

Mona stood. She would not cry in front of him. She would not allow him to see how this hurt her. "You will make a good father, Patrick. I wish you well."

He started to look up at her, but she turned, bursting through the alcove's curtains and racing through the castle to her chambers. She did not wish him well! She wished him misery in his marriage—to know the emptiness that she felt. She loathed Nadine, hoped her ship sunk when crossing the channel. But it was wrong. She locked the door to her chambers and leaned against it, her balled fists pressed to her eyes. She didn't wish that. She wanted him to find happiness with Rosemarie, just not with Nadine. It was wrong that she got Patrick—a woman who used her womb to bind men to her. She didn't want children for their sake; she wanted them to further her ambitions.

As Mona slid down to the floor, many puzzling questions presented themselves. Why Patrick? If Nadine looked to further herself, surely she could do better than a Scottish mercenary. Her deceased husband was a lord of some sort, why step down? Many men—French men, certainly—would be eager to stepfather a child-heir. Why did she bother with Patrick? Or was it because he didn't care about any of that? He only cared about his daughter. He would let Nadine do as she wished with the inheritance.

Mona wished she had asked, but it was too late now. After the way she'd run away, she couldn't go back. Besides, it was not her problem. It never had been. As she stared blindly into the dimly lit room, hands crossed on her knees, she knew she could not stay here and watch him reunited with Nadine.

She readied herself for bed, sliding beneath cool sheets and furs. After a good cry, she lay in the dark for hours, eyes wide, wondering if it would get easier to bear. She'd never loved a man until Patrick. Never felt such possessiveness.

Sounds from the courtyard drifted through her shuttered window. The clank of the portcullis chains. Raised voices. Normally she would be curious as to who was arriving, but she didn't want to get out of bed. She didn't care. She probably should offer to help Caroline. If it were important guests, chambers would need preparing.

But Mona just lay there, trying to think about Ridley and the Bloodstone. She should leave tomorrow, after the men did. But if there was a battle coming, perhaps she should wait for the outcome. Ridley might die or be taken prisoner. But he had the Clachan Fala. How might that affect his part in the battle—or even the battle itself? But he didn't know how to *use* it. Just like Patrick on the cliff—it had been practically useless to him. She rolled onto her stomach, indecisive.

There was a soft knock on her door, then the latch jiggled. Mona sat up and stared at the door, her heart pounding. Was it Patrick? Coming to her to say good-bye? Mona slid out of bed and went to the door just as the knock came again.

"Who's there?" she asked.

"It's me, Fayth," came the whisper.

Mona's shoulders slumped as she unlocked the door and threw it open. "Is aught amiss?"

"Caroline sent me to fetch you. We have guests . . . and one of them is ill—a child."

Mona went to the chest, where she had thrown her bodice and kirtle, and began dressing. "What ails the child?"

"She is unresponsive. Her mother says she's been vomiting."

"Are they from the village?" Dressed now, Mona began braiding her hair.

"No—that's the oddest thing. Did you know Patrick had a daughter?"

Mona's hair slipped from her fingers. She turned to Fayth, disbelieving. "They're here?"

"Yes—a French woman and two children. Alex is vexed. Patrick never said aught to him about a daughter."

Mona's hands shook so that she could not braid her hair. She decided to forgo the plait and tied it back. "Take me to them."

Patrick couldn't think. Everything was happening too fast. He sat in a chair near his daughter's bed. A little boy—Gaspar, she'd named him—banged a spoon violently against a wooden bowl. Nadine stood over Patrick, complaining in French. He stared alternately at Nadine, then back to the bed, where only Rosemarie's face was visible above the covers, pale and lifeless.

The room had not been ready for guests, but Caroline quickly remedied that. Clean sheets had been brought, and Alex held Rosemarie's limp body while Caroline and Celia changed them. Patrick could only watch. After setting the small child in the bed, Caroline brought cool water and a rag to wash her skin. Rob leaned against the doorjamb, arms folded across his chest, and Alex sat on the bed, speaking softly to Rosemarie. Fayth had disappeared.

"You listen not to me!" Nadine said, her voice rising, forcing Patrick's attention back to her. Wee Gaspar squealed at his mother's tone, pounding the bowl harder. "I have nothing, Patrick, nothing. Arnou told him everything." Arnou was Gaspar's brother and, as Patrick had just learned, Gaspar junior's father.

Patrick rubbed at his forehead. The room was hot and close. It felt as if wee Gaspar beat on his brain, not a bowl. He wanted to escape, but could not leave his daughter. "So . . . you cuckolded Gaspar with his own brother?"

Nadine's dark eyes and slashing brows drew together. "Are you not listening to me? Arnou set me up! He suspected all along you were Rosemarie's father—and so he seduced me with promises to wed me when Gaspar died. I would have gotten rid of the child, but I assumed Arnou would accept his own child as heir. Silly me! But I got nothing. He told Gaspar everything and now will not even acknowledge his own son!"

Patrick made a tent with his fingers, frowning at Nadine. "Isn't Arnou already married?"

Nadine rolled her eyes. "He told me he would get rid of her!"

Patrick's gaze darted amongst his family. Alex spoke French fluently—and he suspected Caroline did as well. Robert understood little, only enough to get him by at court. Nadine thought them all ignorant because they were Scots. She didn't realize she was telling them all what a little fool she was. They were thankfully silent, pretending to be oblivious of Patrick's mess. He did not want to marry Nadine he realized grimly. He'd forgotten what a selfish, self-centered shrew she was. She embarrassed him. He sighed heavily. What else was he to do? She had nothing— he couldn't turn Rosemarie's mother out.

"Gaspar loved Rosemarie. Are you telling me he left her nothing? He was not a cruel man, despite how you wronged him."

Her brown eyes hardened. "You wronged him, too. I didn't do it alone. And he left everything to Arnou, confident you would care for Rosemarie, and Arnou would see to Gaspar. But does Arnou care about his son? No! He claims Gaspar isn't even his, that I had many lovers!"

Patrick paused then asked, "You're certain Arnou is the father?"

Nadine's face turned crimson and she whirled away as if to leave, then saw Robert stationed in front of the door and whirled back, hands folded hard over her breasts. Wee Gaspar stared up at his mother uncertainly, his bottom lip trembling.

Well, her lack of response answered his question. Gaspar lost his spoon and was winding up for a big scream. Patrick leaned over and fetched it for him, slipping it into his chubby hand.

Mona swept into the room, sleeves rolled up and lovely face set with purpose. She looked as if she'd dressed hurriedly, her hair already escaping the tail at her neck to curl about her face. Relief that Mona was here to see to his daughter mixed with unease that she was in the same room as Nadine. He hoped she didn't understand French.

Alex rose from the bed so Mona could take his place. Patrick stood and brushed by Nadine, watching Mona examine the child. Rosemarie was unresponsive to her proddings. Mona lifted the child's lids to peer at her eyes. Patrick's heart squeezed in his chest. Rosemarie was finally here, within his grasp, and it looked as if she might die. And according to Nadine, she also knew Patrick was her real father, and now they might never speak. He might never tell her how he'd watched her play for hours on end and how he'd adored her and cherished every smile she'd blessed her ponies and dogs with, wishing they'd been for him.

Mona began removing Rosemarie's clothes. Her body was limp, boneless, like a dead hare. He couldn't look at her—it was too frightening—and so he paced away, rubbing his hands over his face.

Mona would save her. He repeated this to himself and it eased his heart some.

"How long has she been this way?" Mona asked.

Patrick turned to find her looking across Rosemarie's body at Nadine, who wasn't looking at her child at all but scowling at Patrick. How could she be so unmoved? Rosemarie looked dead, and she was still absorbed in her own problems.

Patrick relayed Mona's question in French.

Nadine turned to look at her daughter. "A few hours."

Patrick translated for Mona.

"When was the last time she threw up?" Mona asked.

"After her first fit," Nadine answered Patrick, then she sighed wearily. "It is the falling sickness. She always does this. She has a fit, vomits, has another fit, then sleeps. But she's never stayed asleep for so long."

Patrick stared at Nadine, a sickness seeping into his soul. The falling sickness. He'd heard of it, though he'd never known anyone affected. It caused a person's limbs to seize and shake as if possessed by demons.

"She is not asleep," Patrick said, his voice rising to a shout. He grabbed her chin and twisted her face toward the bed. "She cannot be woken—it is like she's dead! Do you not care?"

Nadine jerked free, rubbing her chin. But she stared at Rosemarie now, a small frown between her heavy brows.

When he looked to the bed he saw Mona staring at him with raised brows, waiting for him to relay Nadine's answer. Before he summoned the words, Caroline whispered, "She has the falling sickness."

Mona untied Rosemarie's shift and then paused, staring. After a moment she pulled the garment off. A freezing stone settled in Patrick's belly. The child's torso was covered with small, puckered burn marks. He felt a tingling sensation along the back of his neck, as if his mind were withdrawing, turning control over to another part of himself. He grabbed Nadine and yanked her around to face him. "What have you done?"

Robert was there, pushing between them, but Patrick felt crazed. Such things were not normal—there was no good reason for a child to be covered in burn marks. Gaspar began to scream. Alex walked over and scooped the child up, bobbling him, and left the room.

"The physician," Nadine cried, her eyes filled with tears. "He said the cold and moist humors must be removed—he said cauterizing would cure the falling sickness!"

Caroline translated Nadine's babblings to Mona, who stared at Patrick.

"We tried everything!" Nadine went on, hysterical. "The priest tried to drive the demons from her body . . . Gaspar spent a fortune on treacle—it is supposed to cure everything, to help the soul reject sin. But nothing worked. I confessed to the priest that she was a bastard born from adultery. He said it was punishment for our sins, Patrick—yours and mine. He said she cannot be cured. One day she will never wake. It is God's will, his judgement on us."

At Robert's urgings, Patrick released Nadine. His hands shook. Nadine was sobbing now, stroking the quilt draped over Rosemarie.

Mona whispered something to Caroline and left the room. Caroline began to wipe Rosemarie's face and body with the rag.

Patrick followed Mona to the kitchens, where she was giving Cook orders to brew a decoction, giving him a list of herbs. After gathering several more items, she finally turned to Patrick. Her face was a mask, revealing nothing but mild disapproval. She thought Nadine a poor mother. Patrick did, too.

"Will she live?"

"I don't know . . . probably. I have seen the falling sickness before, and usually the person wakes. But Rosemarie has been in a dead sleep for a long time, Patrick . . ."

He stared at the floor, his jaw tight, feeling as if this were somehow his fault. The priest had told Nadine it was because of their sins. He had many, many sins on his soul. Why should his daughter pay for them all? How was that right or fair or good? She was an innocent, a child. Or was it his punishment to watch, helpless?

"But I will do my best to help her," Mona said softly.

He looked up, and she gave him a small, encouraging smile and went to her patient.

Patrick trailed behind her but was blocked from entering the room by his two glowering brothers. Patrick sighed, knowing this was unavoidable. "Let's talk about this later. I need to be with Rosemarie now."

Robert's hand clamped onto Patrick's shoulder, turning him. "She's in good hands. Dinna fash on her."

In the great hall Robert released him. Patrick wandered to the fireplace, his back to his brothers, his mind filled with imagines of his daughter's body shaking with this ailment. He hadn't felt so near to weeping since he was a child.

"I canna believe you have a daughter and never told me," Alex said.

Patrick turned at his brother's wounded words. Alex loved children as much as he loved animals—and they loved him, too. He couldn't understand why Patrick had kept it a secret. Of course, Alex would never have been in such a situation.

"To what end?" Patrick asked. "I could not acknowledge her."

Robert came to stand beside Patrick, frowning. "What will you do? The child needs care. She's very ill."

Patrick nodded. "Aye. I will care for her. Now that Gaspar is dead, I will wed Nadine."

"What?" Alex cried. Even Robert appeared stunned.

"I cannot just snatch her from her mother. What if someone had ripped one of us from our mother when we were so young? It's wrong and I wilna do it."

"Our mother wasn't a whore who burned us with hot irons," Robert said.

"She's to be my wife, I'd appreciate it if you didn't call her a whore." He stared at his brothers' incredulous faces before muttering, "Even if she is one."

"Don't do this, Patrick," Alex said, coming to stand on his other side. "You don't love her. You don't even like her. I've seen you with Mona, the way you look at each other—"

"Rosemarie is my daughter, damnit!"

"Then take her," Robert said. "What can Nadine do? She's one woman. I'll not let her leave Annancreag with that child. Mark me."

Patrick closed his eyes. They were saying what he wanted to hear, but it wasn't that easy. "Rosemarie has just lost a beloved parent. I will not rip her from her mother and force her to live with strangers."

"Do you really think she'd be happier with that woman than here with us?" Alex asked.

Patrick didn't know. He'd like that. If he could have Rosemarie and still have his freedom. Freedom to choose his own bride. *Mona.* His pulse quickened at the thought.

"Pay her," Alex said.

When Patrick raised an inquiring brow, Alex nodded slowly.

"I heard everything she said. She's greedy. I can't believe she'd want to marry you anyway, now that I think about it. You're not even a lord, and a Scotsman at that. She doesn't seem verra motherly, either. Do you really think she wants to manage a child with the falling sickness? She'll likely take the money and run."

"My funds are in France."

Alex glanced at Robert. "Rob will lend you the money."

"Of course," Robert said. "Whatever you need. It's yours if I have it."

A tight fist of eagerness and anxiety formed in Patrick's gut. He wanted their plan to work. He wanted to believe them. But why else would Nadine come to him, like this, with her children?

"You heard what she said." Patrick sighed deeply. "She's penniless. She has nothing else. That's why she came to me. She wants me to take care of her. I can't turn out Rosemarie's mother."

"You wouldn't be!" Alex said, exasperated. "You'd be paying her off. She could live comfortably until she snagged a rich man and made his life hell."

"But what about the falling sickness?" Patrick asked. "I know nothing about such things."

"Mona," Robert said, brows raised. "She seems competent enough."

Patrick turned away from his brothers. Would she have him after he'd hurt her? Of course she would. She loved him. He smiled suddenly, hopeful as he'd not been in years.

"You're both right," he said.

"Of course we are," Robert said. "You should listen to us more often."

Alex let out a breath and closed his eyes. "Thank you. I dinna think I could bear that woman as a sister-in-law."

Patrick laughed, eager to return to his daughter. As soon as he was assured she was well, he would talk to Nadine. And then Mona . . .

Rosemarie eventually woke. She was groggy and frightened, but Mona spoke soothingly to her. When others tried to move in to see her, Mona sent them away and gave Patrick a hard look. He rose from the chair where he sat vigil and came slowly to the bed. It had been years since he'd spoken to Rosemarie, and then only with Gaspar present. He was afraid. Terrified of a little girl.

Blond curls framed her face like a halo. Wide blue eyes fixed on him.

"How do you feel?" he asked.

"My head hurts. Where's Mama? And my brother?"

Patrick didn't know and so he said, "They will be here soon. They wanted you to rest."

She sent Mona a sidelong look, then said to Patrick, "I can't understand what she says to me. What is her name?"

"Mona," Patrick said, smiling when Mona looked up at him questioningly. "She has been taking care of you. She speaks English."

Rosemarie studied him. "You are English?"

His heart sank a bit that she didn't remember him, but it was not unexpected.

"I am Scots, but yes, I speak her language. Would you like me to tell her something for you?"

"I'm thirsty."

Patrick asked Mona for water, and she handed him a cup. He raised the child's head, holding the cup for her. She sipped at it, studying him with sleepy eyes. When she settled back on the pillow, his fingers lingered, touching the soft golden curls that framed her face.

"You are the knight that visited my father . . . Mama says you are my real father."

Patrick's throat grew tight and he nodded. *She remembered him.*

"Will we stay here? In this place?"

"Would you like to?"

Her small face crumpled. "I miss Papa. I want to go home. Fritz is there, and Belle." Her pony and dog. Patrick knew all their names.

Patrick chewed the inside of his lip, trying not to feel

hurt. Gaspar was the only father she knew. From what Nadine had said, it might not be possible to get Rosemarie's pets back. But Patrick would try.

"I'm your Papa now . . . you can call me that, if you like."

She only stared at him, her brow troubled, blue eyes wide.

"I must leave in the morning, but I will be back, and then we'll be together always. Would you like that?"

She shrugged, averting her gaze. She was frightened. Patrick looked to Mona helplessly, then remembered she didn't understand French. She did, however, perceive by their expressions that the conversation wasn't going as he wished.

She smiled encouragingly. "You're doing fine. Give her time."

Nadine entered the room and began fawning all over Rosemarie. Strangely, the child did not seem relieved to see her mother. Her face creased with worry, and she said, "I'm sorry, Mama. I tried to stop it . . . but I could not."

Nadine soothed her, telling her not to worry, she was not angry. Mona gathered her things quietly and left the room. Patrick resisted the urge to go after her. He had to deal with Nadine first.

He stared at the Frenchwoman, noting how poorly she'd aged. White powder crusted in the lines beside her eyes and mouth, fake rose stained her cheeks. She was younger than Mona and yet looked well used. A life of greed and lies had done this to her. And that waspish tongue of hers—he shuddered at the thought of being yoked to such a shrew.

No, he did not like her at all. He'd been addled to even consider marrying her. He thanked the Lord his brothers had managed to talk sense into him. She was probably infested with pox and would cuckold him at the first opportunity. Besides all that, she could not care for Rosemarie. Her treatment for the falling sickness had been burning a small child's body. Patrick shuddered to think of it. Mona would love his daughter and care for her properly.

When Rosemarie finally drifted to sleep, Nadine said, "We don't have to sit with her." She'd been shifting restlessly for some time. "She doesn't have fits very often. And once she's over one, it is usually a long while—weeks, months sometimes—before another strikes."

Patrick stared down at his daughter, his heart sore from all that had passed. He wanted to pick her up and hold her, to protect her. But he didn't know how.

"Why did you come here?" Patrick asked.

"You are Rosemarie's father."

"I will take her—but I won't marry you, Nadine."

She looked shocked, then laughed, her hand to her chest. "I don't want to marry you! And I certainly don't want to live in that . . . hovel of yours on the Argens." She viewed Rosemarie's bedchamber, sniffing delicately. "Or here, either."

Patrick narrowed his eyes. "Then pray tell what you want?"

"I'm a lone woman. I haven't the means to care for two children—especially one as ill as Rosemarie." She tilted her head, looking away from him, down at sleeping Rosemarie. "I have . . . friends who will take me in and provide well for me. But I cannot go to them like this—penniless, in rags, with my bastard children."

She wanted money. Relief washed through Patrick. She didn't want him. It sounded as if she didn't even want Rosemarie. But he was disgusted, too. He'd been giving her money for years—she'd always claimed it was for Rosemarie, but Patrick knew better. His guilt had always opened his purse, though. Now, it was the desire to be rid of her that made him generous.

"How much do you need?"

"Enough to get me back to France. Once there, I will

need new clothes, rent for a place to stay—no filthy little inn, I know a nice place where I can rent a room."

"I thought you said there were people who would take you in?"

"They will, but not if they know I'm destitute. I must give the illusion I'm doing well."

"Very well. I can get the money for your passage to France—but you'll have to go to Argens for the rest. I'll write you a letter to give to my factor."

She smiled. "As soon as I'm settled, I'll send for the children."

A fist tightened in Patrick's chest. Here it was. The moment he'd been dreading. "No. I'll give you the money—but you must promise to leave Rosemarie and I alone—forever."

Her smile faltered. "But . . . she's my daughter."

Patrick said nothing, holding Nadine's gaze. He could see the wheels turning in her head, calculating, thinking she could take his money and still do whatever the hell she wanted. Let her try.

"I can't just give up my daughter."

"You will not leave Annancreag with Rosemarie. You can take the money or leave it, but Rosemarie stays with me."

One thick, dark eyebrow arched. "I'll need compensation for the loss."

His mouth thinned. "You'll be compensated."

"Very well. I must get back to France soon." Nadine looked around the room distastefully. "So I'll need the money for passage as soon as possible." But she didn't leave. She sidled close to Patrick and placed her palm on his chest. "About the baby . . . Arnou won't claim him . . . I can't feed him. . . ."

"I'll take the wean, too."

She smiled up at him, toying with the silver buttons on his doublet. Lip paint bled into the tiny lines feathering her mouth. "That's why I chose you, you know, to sire Gaspar's heir. Because you are the perfect knight."

He had no words for her. He was not the perfect knight, far from it, but he didn't care what she thought and so saw no reason to argue with her. She left, giving him an inviting look over her shoulder as she paused in the doorway.

He ignored her, pulling the chair beside the bed, staring at his daughter. Now he had two children—and no wife. He could almost cry with relief if his daughter weren't so ill. He didn't understand this falling sickness, but Mona did. She would be the perfect mother and probably thrilled to hear the boy was staying, too. She loved children. Hadn't she told him how sad it made her that she was barren? How she longed for children of her own? Well, Rosemarie was very young and Gaspar was still a wean—it was pretty damn close to having her own bairns, Patrick thought. This would bring her great joy. He imagined the look on her face when he proposed and told her of the children.

He waited for her, and finally she came. He stared at her while she examined Rosemarie.

"She seems fine," she whispered. "You should get some rest. You must leave in the morning to join the king." When he didn't move, she glanced up at him. "Why are you looking at me like that?"

"Marry me." Inelegant of him, he knew, but he couldn't help himself. He couldn't leave in the morning without knowing she'd be his wife and that she would be here caring for Rosemarie in his absence.

She stared at him, her mouth slightly agape. "What?"

Patrick rose and circled the bed, coming to stand before her. He took her hands and stared down into her velvety dark eyes. "Marry me."

She seemed flustered, her cheeks flushed. "Why? I don't understand—"

"Nadine doesn't want me—she only came to beg money and she's leaving the children with me."

She blinked at him, clearly not as overjoyed as he'd anticipated. After a moment, a small frown marred her brow. "So . . . she's abandoning *both* of her children . . . to you?"

Patrick nodded, smiling. "It's perfect, aye? You canna have children—and I have two that need a mother. And you canna deny we suit quite well."

Mona drew her hands away and looked down at the bed. "I cannot marry you. I am the Keeper, remember? I cannot make any commitments so long as Ridley has the stone."

"To hell with that cursed stone!" Patrick said, angry that it continued to insinuate itself into his life. "Do you not want me? I thought we got on well together."

Mona searched his eyes. "You don't want *me*. You want a mother for your children. A healer to care for Rosemarie."

"That is not so," Patrick protested. "You must know how I feel about you."

Mona's eyes grew misty, and she swallowed convulsively. "Tell me."

When he only stared down at her, the words lodged in his throat, she pushed past him and ran from the room. He started after her, cursing himself for mucking this up, when a soft cry came from the bed.

Patrick swung around to find his daughter fretting in her sleep. He sank down on the bed beside her, staring at the troubled frown that marred her sweet brow. What did she dream about that troubled her so? His hands hovered over her, uncertain what to do to soothe her.

He thought of Mona then, of how she touched him when he suffered with nightmares. He gently stroked his fingers over Rosemarie's hair. He wanted to clutch her to his chest, unable to bear that she did not sleep well. Was

that also his fault? Was she doomed to suffer nightmares
and falling sickness because he'd sinned with Nadine?

It was wrong and Patrick wouldn't have it. Not anymore. Everything was different because of this child. And
because of Mona. She had banished the shadows from his
life, and he knew she could do the same for Rosemarie.
Tonight, he would give Mona a chance to think about it.
And tomorrow he would ask her again.

And he would keep asking until he wore her down.

18

Ridley arrived at Graham Keep to discover his brother had never been delivered. Half of the men had returned to tell an interesting tale. They'd only been able to secure two boats to cross the firth. They'd been the first group that crossed, but they'd waited in vain on the English side for their leader, Stroud, and the prisoner to join them. Fearing an accident, they'd set out for the Scottish side. But when they'd arrived, all they found was two empty boats—one with a coil of cut rope in the bottom, stained with blood.

But it wasn't a total loss. Wesley's wife, Lady Anne Irvine, daughter of the earl of Dornock, had arrived at Gealach and been delivered to Graham Keep, as ordered. In the past, Ridley might have raged, might have destroyed something, or punished someone. But he was not the same person. He had the Clachan Fala. He could hear everyone's thoughts, feel everyone's feelings.

And they all hated him. But they also feared him. Some thought he was mad—possessed. Others were sickened by him. They were all horrified by what was happening to his face.

It hadn't been noticeable at first, and Ridley had thought he was imagining it. A slight softness to some of the slick burns, a fading in the redness. Just normal healing. But then a few days ago, when he'd woke, he'd realized his face no longer hurt when he smiled, the tightness was gone. When he'd consulted the looking glass, he'd seen a plumpness to his mouth—his lips were re-forming. He'd ordered a gold chain fashioned and wore the Clachan Fala next to his heart, praying to it daily to heal his face.

But no one was happy for him. No one cared. That angered him the most. They thought him a wizard now and whispered about him. Some wanted to go to the king and have him hanged. But Ridley did nothing—yet. This fear was useful.

There were many letters waiting for him. He didn't bother reading them, since he knew what they all said. Why had he not answered the king's summons to York? Why had he not been part of the pathetic invasion into Scotland? Ridley wasn't worried about falling out of favor. He had only to tell them of capturing Red Alex's tower in Scotland. They would all see he fought for the king's cause and had fared better than Norfolk. At least Ridley still held Gealach. Norfolk had come away with naught, doing nothing more than reducing a few villages to ash.

But the war . . . over? Ridley was vexed. He'd not meant to miss it all—but then he'd assumed it would last longer than six bloody days. And the Scots had not even been engaged! The English had merely retreated. Something about a scarcity of ale. He fingered the Bloodstone where it hung about his neck . . . it told him things. Not always things he wanted to know, but it answered questions, showed him men's hearts. He knew not what else it could do, but he meant to find out. He still regretted having to give up Mona. She could tell him all he needed to know and now, with the stone to aid him, he could force her to tell him everything. He would have her yet. The knowledge burned deep inside him. It must be the Bloodstone, telling him it would be so.

He went to see his guest. The men-at-arms guarding her room stepped aside so he could pass through the door. One of them feared that what marred his face was contagious. Fool. Ridley would show him how contagious it was later with a bit of hot wax.

He opened the door and found Lady Anne within, standing at the window. She was not so plump as she'd been the last time he'd seen her. A good thing.

She turned. "I was told . . ." She trailed off when she saw his face, her eyes widening, then she cleared her throat and went on. "I was told Wesley was here, but I've not been allowed to see him."

Ridley had been planning to rape her for some time, to get a child on her to hurt his brother, but had feared he wouldn't be able, fat as she was. Her worry for her husband had given her a new, slender form that he found appealing. In fact, her heavy bosom was reminiscent of Mona's.

Her face was no longer round and pudgy, but high cheekbones led to a narrow chin. She was actually quite attractive. Her yellow gown was disheveled and torn—that would have to be remedied.

"Have you been treated well?" he asked, approaching her.

She eyed him warily, pressing her back to the windowsill. She feared him but was not repulsed. Interesting.

"I want to see my husband."

"In time . . ."

When he stood before her, she studied his face. "What happened, my lord? Your face . . ."

Ridley said nothing, frowning at her. She meant well.

She cared. "My sister, Fayth, burned me. Your husband helped her."

She looked down at her hands. A breeze washed through the room from the open window, stirring the dull brown hair against her pale neck. She thought that if Wesley had done such a thing he must have been justified.

The bitch. His anger rose again and he grabbed her.

She inhaled sharply, her hands coming up to push at him.

"We had an agreement, you and I, a betrothal. You betrayed me."

Anne shook her head slowly. "No—we didn't suit. We would have been miserable. I love Wesley." She gasped again, tearing her eyes away from his face to look at her hands.

Ridley ignored her, running his hands over her back and buttocks, squeezing violently, willing himself to become aroused. But he felt nothing. He crushed his mouth against hers. She struggled, trying to twist away, and finally slapped him.

"Why are you doing this?" she cried, tears streaking her cheeks. "You cannot abide me!"

"That is not so," Ridley said, rubbing at her breasts, trying to imagine Mona's body. But it was no good. "I very much want to get a child on you."

She shook her head, pushing at his hand, her gaze focused on his chest again. "No . . . I felt how much you hate me."

Ridley released her, his hand curling around the Bloodstone suspended from the gold chain around his neck. She did know. What had she felt when she'd touched it? That had made her gasp? What had it told her about him? He would have to be careful, not allow others near it.

She watched him fondle the stone. "What is that?"

"A charm. To protect me from liars and cheats. It tells me when someone is false."

He felt her terror now, her horror. She thought him evil for having such charms—a wizard. He felt a stirring in his lower body. It was true. With the stone, he was more powerful than any wizard. Able to heal his own ailments, know other's thoughts. Who knew what else? He must determine how to use the damn thing, how to harness its power. He felt certain it could do more than what he'd seen thus far. He advanced on Anne, smiling. His grin was terrifying, he knew, and she looked away. He took pleasure in her revulsion at the thought of being raped by something so hideous. He no longer cared that he was a monster—for soon he would be restored.

"Come here, pretty," he said when she tried to slip away. He caught her arm. "Your husband has betrayed me many times over. I wonder how he'd like it if I planted a child in his wife's belly? I might even still marry you when he's dead, if you're good."

She fought at him, but he tore at her clothes, pushing her down on the bed. He became frenzied, power surged through him. The thought of Wesley's anguish fueled him, as did the anticipation of having his face back. He grew stiff thinking of it, and this drove him further. It had been years since a woman other than Mona had roused him. He'd lived like a monk because of her and now, finally, he was a man again.

Anne screamed, but no one would help her. She clawed at him. He captured her wrists in one hand, laughing at how weak and ineffectual she was. He bared her breasts, imagining she was Mona. His heart pounded, his groin aching and painful. He reached down to open his breeches, to bury himself into his brother's wife, ready to burst with raw lust, when the stone began to hum and vibrate between them.

She didn't notice, screaming and bucking hysterically. But Ridley backed away. His initial urge was to rip it from his neck, but he didn't. He moved away from the bed. Anne nearly fell off the other side trying to escape him. She grabbed the ewer, sloshing water all over herself as she held it like a weapon.

But Ridley's lust had fled, replaced with fear. The pulsing reverberated through his body, but it was not unpleasant. It was trying to tell him something. He felt it building like a climax he couldn't quite reach. A vision of his destiny? He gripped the stone in both hands and whispered, "Show me."

The scene burst before him. The light was bright and pale gray—an overcast day. He saw an enormous expanse of green, filled with men, artillery, and horses. The Scots were massing, knights, lords, common soldiers. Hundreds, thousands. And above it all flew the lion rampant of the royal house of Scotland.

The vision cleared like a mist and he found himself on the floor, staring at Anne's face. She crouched on the other side of the bed, watching him warily, ewer still clutched in her fist. His hair was damp, his palms slick where he clutched the Clachan Fala.

The war was not over. The Scots mounted a secret invasion in the west. Ridley was on his feet, nearly running from the room, Anne forgotten. No one thought the Scots would invade, though there was word of troops massing in the east. And so the English were guarding the eastern inroads, leaving the West March open and vulnerable to attack.

Ridley sent a rider to Lord Wharton, the West March warden, and shouted for his men to ready themselves to ride. The Bloodstone had given him the intelligence to accomplish all of his plans. He would be honored and rewarded for this service. And soon, he was certain, he would have his face back, and all would be as it should.

It was midafternoon when Mona returned to Annancreag. She'd had little luck in her search for herbs to treat Rosemarie's falling sickness. Lord Annan's cook had some that might prove useful: byrony, heart's ease, cinquefoil. But what Mona really needed was Paeony, dittany, or sow's ear. There was none to be had within or without the castle. Mona was not surprised, for it was late in the season, but she had to try. She couldn't leave without at least attempting to help Rosemarie.

A guard had been foisted on her when she'd left the castle, and he'd finally gone back to his duties once inside the castle walls. As soon as Mona trudged into the courtyard she felt the difference, the emptiness of the place. The men had left this morning to join King James's army. Mona had hid in a tower room and watched Patrick leave with his brothers. And when they were no longer in sight, she'd fled to the forest, unable to face anyone.

She closed her eyes briefly, bolstering herself. She'd done the right thing. She'd only done what she had to. She couldn't face him and maintain her resolve. The Bloodstone was all that mattered. And by the time he returned to Annancreag, she would be gone. When this was over, perhaps they could talk of marriage, but she wouldn't wed another man who didn't love her. It was not enough to simply suit. But what she feared the most was that Patrick would wear her down with his smiles and kisses, make her believe that was enough.

In the great hall, she found Caroline and Father Jasper, Caroline's priest, sitting on a bench with Rosemarie. Mona approached them.

"Good day," Rosemarie said to Mona when she approached.

Mona stopped, her mouth agape. The girl spoke English.

Rosemarie giggled at her expression and let loose a torrent of French that had both Caroline and the priest smiling.

"We're teaching her English," Caroline explained, "to surprise Patrick when he returns."

Mona smiled sadly. "That will give him great pleasure. Where is Gaspar?"

"With Fayth in the garden."

"And their mother? Nadine?"

Father Jasper's brows rose censoriously. "Still abed."

"Patrick said she wouldn't be staying long," Caroline added.

Mona nodded, her throat tight. She felt useless. She couldn't help Rosemarie—she couldn't even communicate with her. And Caroline and Fayth were perfectly capable of seeing to Patrick's children until he returned. *Children.* The thought still swamped her with hurt anger. Why hadn't he mentioned that Nadine's other child was his, too? When he'd asked her to marry him, she'd longed to say yes. But all he wanted was a nursemaid for his children while he went off to fight battles.

Mona returned to her chambers and began gathering her meager belongings together. She had to go to Graham Keep and take the stone back from Ridley. She couldn't think of Patrick now. *Impossible.* She thought endlessly of his words last night. *Marry me.* Then his inability to even lie to her when she'd practically begged for words of love. She must find a way to put him from her mind, or all would be lost. If Ridley sensed she thought of aught but him he would be furious.

She was shaking out her cloak when Caroline slipped into the room, tall and slender in a pale green gown. Her hair was pulled back into a golden braid. Her gaze darted to Mona's cloak. "Where are you going?"

Mona sighed. "I'm the Keeper. I have to take the Clachan Fala from Ridley."

"I can't let you go. I promised Patrick."

The mention of his name set Mona's teeth on edge, sent pain knifing through her chest. "Patrick cannot keep me prisoner."

"He only wants you safe."

"It's not his place to worry on my safety."

Caroline laughed shortly. "As he plans to marry you, I think it is."

Mona swung around, incredulous. "He said this to you?"

"He said it to everyone. He was most furious this morning. He searched everywhere for you—the men were late starting out because of him. He even refused to leave with Robert and Alex at first. I had to promise to keep you safe until he returned."

Angry tears pricked at Mona's eyes. Why was he doing this? "I cannot marry him, Caroline. I am the Keeper."

Caroline crossed the room, taking Mona's hands. "What difference does that make?"

"All the difference. These past months with Patrick . . . I've lost sight of what I am. I cannot be wife, mother, *and* Keeper. Methinks that's why God made me barren. I was never meant for such a life."

Caroline's hands tightened on hers. "How absurd! My mother was a stranger to me. You're the only mother I ever had. That Fayth and Wesley ever knew. How can you believe you were not meant to be a wife and mother?"

Mona smiled, tears welling in her eyes, and squeezed her stepdaughter's hands back. "You're so lovely, Caroline, but my duties were different then and your father left me no choice. As Keeper I was not supposed to wed but to guard my secret in silence, only sharing it with an apprentice. And I did guard the secret. But now that the stone is in the world, my duty is to it alone." She released Caroline's hands and took up her cloak. "I forgot that . . . for a time."

"You don't believe that," Caroline said softly.

"I *must* believe that. Arlana spent many years instilling these things into me. I cannot throw it all over for . . . *him*."

"I saw you look at him. You love him."

"He doesn't love me."

Caroline frowned. "Since when did love become a reason to marry?"

"I've been twice widowed—I have no need of another husband. Love is the only reason I'll tie that noose again."

"How do you know he doesn't love you? He was most distressed this morning. Why would he worry so for you if he doesn't love you?"

Mona averted her eyes, her shoulders slumping. "He only needs someone to take care of his children."

"If that's all he needs, why then is he so insistent that it must be you?"

Mona threw up her hands. "I don't know! Because he's surly as an old bear and doesn't want to trouble himself to search for a wife. He's used to me. He knows I'll put up with all his irritating habits."

Caroline laughed softly. "He *was* most bearlike this morning. But if he didn't want to trouble himself I doubt he would have taken Gaspar in. The lad isn't even his. He has a kindness to him that reminds me of you."

Mona could only stare blindly at the wooden floor. So Gaspar wasn't his son. He hadn't lied to her. But that didn't change anything. He still didn't love her, and she was still the Keeper.

That didn't stop the hope from blooming in her chest when she looked up at her stepdaughter. He'd taken that sweet baby in. How many men would do such a thing? "Was he really worried?"

"Oh yes," Caroline said. "He was beside himself. He didn't want to leave until he'd spoken to you."

Mona found herself laughing through her tears. He *did* care. She let herself bask in a moment of happiness before sighing. "I still have to go after the Bloodstone." She swung her cloak over her shoulders and started for the door.

Caroline grabbed Mona's hand, her face creased with worry. "Please wait. Just a few days. The borders are more dangerous than ever. You can't chance getting trapped between two armies. And if the English have caught wind of the invasion, Ridley won't even be at Graham Keep."

Mona hesitated, torn. Caroline was right, and yet Ridley'd had the stone too long already. But what was the use of going to Graham Keep if Ridley wasn't there?

"Robert said there will be no delay. The Scots king means to attack immediately. Wait for Robert to send word, Mona. I beg you."

When Mona still hesitated, Caroline said, "Rosemarie asked for you this morning." Seeing Mona weaken, she rushed on, "What would we do if the falling sickness strikes her and you weren't here?"

"Very well," Mona said, pulling off her cloak and tossing it aside. "One day."

Caroline smiled and linked her arm with Mona's. "Three—give Robert a chance to send word."

Mona shook her head. "Two and no more!"

"You never could say no to us."

Mona laughed, feeling happy as she had not for a very long time. "So tell me . . . what else did Patrick say this morning?"

Patrick was impressed with the size of the Scottish host now gathered a dozen miles from the border. He stood to the side, watching as the lords came forth, pledging their numbers to the king. In all, it was just shy of twenty thousand men. Another, smaller force had been sent to the east, to protect the capital, but also to mislead the English. Patrick wandered among the men, observing and listening. It was important to know the mood of the men—low spirits could jeopardize a battle. Most were eager to fight, still

angry at Norfolk's incursion on the East March. But some
of the gentlemen and lords spoke ill of the king's favorite,
Oliver Sinclair.

Patrick tried to keep his thoughts on the coming invasion
and away from Mona. He'd been terrified that she'd gone
off to find Ridley, but the guards at Annancreag had sworn
she'd never left the castle. Which meant she was hiding
from him. He knew why, too. She knew she couldn't keep
saying no to him. She knew he'd wear her down eventually.
It troubled him she was so determined to reject him. It hurt
that she put the Bloodstone before him. He didn't like being
second, not to a rock. And so he had to get that damn stone
and end this, so she was finally free of it forever.

Patrick paused by a cannon, his thoughts distracted by
an unsettlingly familiar young man. He was with the earl
of Dornock. Of average height and slightly built, he wore
the armor of the border: a reinforced leather jack and
breeks, and a steel bonnet held loosely under his arm. His
beard was short, cropped close to his face and the same
color as his curly brown hair. It didn't quite obscure a nasty
scar on his cheek.

Patrick came forward. "I know you."

The man straightened, his eyes registering recognition,
though he didn't seem surprised to see Patrick. The earl
turned at Patrick's voice. He was a short, round man, encased in armor.

"Sir Patrick Maxwell?" Dornock queried.

"Aye."

"I've heard much about you. Wesley told me you were
no longer Lord Graham's prisoner, but we all wondered
what had become of you! Good it is that you've joined us!"

"Wesley," Patrick said, not taking his eyes from the
young man. "Ridley's brother."

Wesley had not yet spoken, watching Patrick warily. He

finally said, "Do not confuse me with my brother. I'm here in Lord Dornock's service." And so it seemed he was. The cross of St. Andrew was pinned to his shoulder.

The earl finally seemed to note the tension in the air and clapped a hand on Wesley's back. "Oh, aye. Sir Patrick, meet my son-in-law. Wesley has wed my daughter, Anne. He can be trusted, though his brother cannot. Ridley agreed to break the betrothal with Anne, then kidnapped her after Wesley wed her. Scurrilous dog!" He squeezed Wesley's shoulder. "We'll get her back, lad, dinna fash."

Wesley gave a short nod, warmth in the look he directed at the earl.

Deciding Ridley's brother was no threat, Patrick turned to leave, but Wesley stopped him.

"My stepmother? She's safe?"

Patrick nodded, pain lancing through him at the thought of Mona.

Wesley glanced over to where Alex and Robert stood, heads together in conversation. "And my sisters?"

The lad looked so worried that Patrick relented. He placed a hand on Wesley's shoulder. "Dinna fash. They're in good hands."

Wesley nodded, swallowing hard, and turned back to the earl.

Patrick passed by the king's camp and watched him speaking with Oliver Sinclair. The king seemed distracted, not fawning over his favorite as gossip purported. Jealousy had likely caused such talk. The king was a hard man who favored few.

It had been years since Patrick had seen King James. He had changed. He was thin and pale, but he was here for his men, in full armor, a circlet of gold on his head. Though he was younger than Patrick, his chestnut hair held streaks of gray. He received all his lords, standing as though ready to fight, but all knew he would retire to a safe place before the battle. He had promised his queen that he would not lead the army personally as he had no heir yet, though the queen was heavily pregnant, and he could not risk leaving his kingdom without a leader. When Sinclair left the king, Patrick came forward. The king expressed pleasure that he'd escaped from Ridley and assigned him to advise Lord Maxwell, the commander of the forces.

Robert and Alex had merged their men with the rest of the Maxwells. Patrick joined a cluster of lords, Robert and Lord Maxwell included, who were discussing strategy. Patrick was coming to the game too late to be of much use and he would be resented if he tried to step in, so he decided to just listen.

Lord Maxwell detailed the plans to the men assembled. They were to attack the West March, laying waste to everything in their path, and push as far as Carlisle if they encountered little opposition. Meanwhile, the small force in the east would cross the border with bishops, find a church, and pronounce a papal interdict against King Henry. It was too late in the season for a prolonged campaign, so this was a warning to strengthen Scotland's position. They had promises of aid in the spring from France, and it was then that the king planned a large-scale campaign.

Everyone nodded thoughtfully at this plan.

"Our best weapon is surprise," Patrick said, unable to resist pointing out a potential flaw.

Everyone turned to look at him.

Lord Maxwell raised his brows. "Aye . . . that's the idea, Sir Patrick."

"Where do you plan to cross into England? We cannot take such heavy artillery across the moss, and if we cross just past it we risk trapping ourselves if the English become wise to us."

Lord Maxwell grunted. "Aye, but if we cross further

east we lose the element of surprise. They believe our forces are concentrated in the east."

"They have spies. I dinna believe they're ignorant of an army this size a dozen miles from the border."

"It doesna matter," Oliver Sinclair said, coming forward. He wore elaborate armor, far above his station, his plumed helm under his arm. "Even if they know, the English are guarding the east. They canna move men that fast."

"Aye," Lord Maxwell said, though he seemed displeased to be agreeing with Sinclair. "The most Wharton will be able to muster is some prickers, and they canna do much damage once we're across the Lyne."

Patrick held his counsel after that, though he had a bad feeling about the whole expedition. But surprise was their best weapon right now, and so they must move quickly.

With daylight still hours away, they mounted and headed south. As soon as they crossed into the Debatable Land, currently held almost entirely by English Grahams, the Scots went on a feeding frenzy, burning every cottage and field in sight and gathering up all the livestock. Dawn was approaching, but the world was bright from the fires raging around them.

As they neared the Esk they saw that beacon fires had been lit as far as the eye could see. Soon the English would arrive, and they still had the Esk before them. It was swollen from recent rains, roaring past.

A cold sweat broke out on Patrick's palms and the back of his neck. It was like Mohacs. He glanced at his brothers, both riding to his right. Robert was intent on something Lord Maxwell said, but Alex winked at him, the overflowing river obviously not worrying him in the least. Patrick mustered a grim smile in return, but it faded when the English came into sight. They drew up on the south bank of the Lyne, an estuary that ran nearly parallel with the Esk after branching off. As the Scots spurred their horses, plunging into the Esk, the English did the same. Their ford was easier, though, and while the Scots struggled against the Esk's current, the English quickly cleared the banks of the Lyne. Patrick had never been immobilized with dread before—especially at such a crucial moment—but when Scots were swept from their horses and the water of the Esk rushed over their heads, he found himself frozen on the north bank.

He could almost feel the water closing over his head, his armor dragging him down, the horses' hooves beating at him, keeping him from surfacing. There was a weight on his chest, crushing him, cutting off his air. He yanked on his horse's reins, trying to brace himself to enter the water, but he could not. Mohacs was there before him, the memories as fresh as if it had happened yesterday, not sixteen years ago.

His brothers had plunged on ahead of him, but Alex twisted in his saddle, realizing Patrick was no longer beside him. A fallen man grabbed at Alex. Alex tried to haul him across his horse's withers, but the river and the clamor around him spooked the horse, and Alex was distracted, still searching the river for Patrick, clearly worried. The man dragged Alex out of the saddle and into the river.

Panicked, Patrick dug in his spurs and splashed into the water, even as Robert tried to turn his horse to go back. Robert's horse reared, sending him into the river as well. Alex had not yet surfaced, and Patrick's heart was close to bursting. Water froze his thighs. His horse stumbled, almost losing its footing. Patrick couldn't slosh through the water fast enough. Already he'd shed his jack and helm, and unhooked his belt, letting his sword and latch rush away on the current.

When he reached the spot where they'd both gone down, horses crashed around him, churning the water. Men grabbed at his legs, trying to pull themselves out.

Then Robert surfaced. He'd shed his jack and helm as well, and when he saw Patrick he yelled, "I can't find him!"

Patrick dove off his horse, cutting through the water. It was not as deep as the Danube, though already bodies floated past him. None were Alex. The water was frigid and murky. When Patrick broke the surface again, he was east of the fording army. Robert was still in danger, searching frantically among the Scots still plowing across. A horse pushed him under, but he quickly popped back up again, unharmed.

Patrick looked to the south bank. English prickers had ridden forward, thrusting their lances at the Scottish flank as it emerged from the river. That's when Patrick saw the man crawl ashore.

"Robert!" Patrick shouted. "Robert!"

Robert turned and Patrick pointed. Alex stood on the bank, unhorsed and unarmed, trying to get his bearings. Robert swam for the shore just as Patrick did. A pricker came at Alex, lance leveled to pierce his heart.

"Alex!" Patrick called, but he couldn't swim fast enough.

Alex feinted, snagging the pricker and dragging him from his horse. He dispatched him and swung into the saddle, armed with the pricker's lance. By the time Patrick and Robert dragged themselves ashore, Alex had ridden into the fray.

Patrick pulled Robert up. "You're unharmed?"

Robert nodded.

They searched the riverbank for something to arm themselves with, but the prickers were no longer coming. Instead it was the Scots, retreating, riding like the devil was on their heels. Dornock stopped on the Esk's bank and extended a hand to Patrick.

"No! What's happening?"

"They've boxed us in," Dornock said, mopping the sweat off his brow. "They're pushing us west, where the Esk is dangerous—there's only the moss on the other side."

"What happened to Lord Maxwell?"

"I don't know, but Sinclair says he's in charge now and there was fighting amongst the lords. I wilna follow Sinclair, so we have no leader. I told my men to retreat."

When it was clear Patrick wasn't about to retreat with him he continued fleeing back across the Esk. Robert had gone in search of Lord Maxwell. Patrick ran through the retreating men, looking for his brothers. He managed to capture a riderless horse and swung into the saddle, searching from a higher vantage point. He spotted them to the south, battling the English on the ground, with Lord Maxwell and a dozen other Scots. The rest of the army was fleeing.

Damn. They didn't stand a chance, but Patrick wouldn't just leave them. He spurred his horse, bearing down on the fight, riding right into the middle of it and kicking an Englishman in the face. He reeled backward. Patrick leapt from his horse and captured another man's wrist as he brought his sword down. Patrick hit him and twisted his arm until it cracked, taking his sword. They came together, Patrick, Robert, and Alex, just as they'd trained, guarding each other's backs as more Englishmen attacked.

And then Ridley was there, before him, sword bearing down. He wore no helm, and his face . . . it was as clear and smooth as a babe's. In Patrick's surprise, he faltered, ineffectually blocking Ridley's cut. The blade skittered against his, cutting through his shirt and grazing his arm.

Patrick ducked and swung around to cut at him from the side, but he was there, grinning like a madman, his sword hissing past Patrick's nose. Patrick stumbled trying to back away, tripping over a body. He went down.

"I know what you're going to do before you do," Ridley said, laughing, his face flushed with triumph. He brought the blade down with enough force to cleave Patrick's skull. He rolled to the side. Ridley redirected his strike at the last minute to follow Patrick's movement.

Sparks burst in Patrick's face as another sword slashed down, blocking the fatal blow. Patrick still held his breath, waiting to die. It exploded from him now, burning his lungs, unable to believe he still lived. To Patrick's surprise it was not one of his brothers but an Englishman who'd saved him. He did not withdraw his sword but held it to Patrick's throat even as Ridley backed away, scowling with displeasure.

"You have your orders, Graham—we take prisoners."

"These are mine, Wharton," Ridley said, pointing to Patrick and his two brothers, unarmed and restrained by Grahams. "I claim the Annan Maxwells."

Lord Wharton, the warden of the English West March, removed his blade from Patrick's neck. "Very well," he said, his rough voice rumbling over them. "See they live long enough to ransom." He left, joining a cluster of Englishmen herding scores of captured Scots south.

Grahams descended on Patrick, forcing him to his feet. Patrick scanned the battlefield, looking for any signs of rescue, but the only Scots left on this side of the Esk were prisoners. Englishmen dotted the field, each with a group of Scots.

Patrick and his brothers' hands were bound and tethered to the horses.

"The battle was over before it began, eh, lads?" Ridley

called out. He was ebullient, grinning, his face flushed. Clean shaven, he looked like a prince, and likely fancied himself one now. Had the stone done that to his face? Somehow erased the scars? It had made him a formidable opponent as well. He'd known every move Patrick was going to make before he'd made it. How, then, could he be bested?

Ridley turned to Patrick and winked, patting his chest lovingly. "I cannot take all the credit. I had a bit of help."

Patrick was tethered to Ridley's horse. He had to jog to keep up with the horse's pace. For sport, Ridley spurred his horse to a near gallop periodically, dragging Patrick along behind him. Patrick's arm burned, and his mouth felt like sandpaper. His brothers were behind him somewhere and likely in no better shape. This did not bode well for any of them. The last time he was Ridley's prisoner he'd been left to rot. And now he had all three of them.

It was evening when they arrived at Graham Keep. Patrick was exhausted, his body aching from Ridley's torments, but he still fought instinctively at the rope, desperate not to be imprisoned here again. When the portcullis crashed down behind them, he feared he'd not escape Graham Keep this time, not with Mona gone.

Ridley laughed. "You're right there. No one here will help you. No one dares deceive me, even in their minds."

Patrick had spent the entire journey fighting not to think about Mona and Rosemarie, despairing that he'd never see them again. It sickened him that Ridley knew it, knew all his fears and weaknesses.

When they were led down to the dungeons, Patrick was stunned at how many prisoners Ridley had managed to take—at least twoscore. Patrick and his brothers were all shoved into Patrick's old cell.

"Welcome home!" Ridley said, smiling widely. He stood in the open door. "They'll come for you, you know. Your women."

Patrick felt his brothers start beside him, alarmed at Ridley's words.

"They're not stupid," Robert said. "Caroline would never do something so foolish."

"Oh, but she will. They all will. I've seen it, you see."

Alex ran for him, but Ridley was quicker, stepping aside and swinging the door shut. The lock clicked, and soon the sound of footsteps faded as the Grahams climbed the stairs and left them.

They had no candle, but the torches were still in sconces outside the bars of their cell, dimly illuminating the small room. Alex stood at the door, his forehead pressed into the wood. Robert leaned against a wall, a worried, puzzled look on his face. Patrick slid down the wall, crossing his arms over his knees.

"How does he know that?" Robert asked, his voice echoing.

Patrick closed his eyes. "The Bloodstone." Something nagged at him, something about his fight with Ridley. He'd not known everything.

"His face . . . ," Alex whispered. "It was ruined . . . I vow on my life he was dreadfully burned—I *saw* it. But do you see him now? Nothing. Not a scar."

Robert exhaled loudly and began pacing the small cell like a caged animal. "Are you trying to tell me the Clachan Fala is responsible for all this?"

"Aye," Patrick said. "It gives visions, is a window into men's minds, it apparently heals. . . . And who knows what else."

Alex turned, his face set angrily. "How can we win if he knows everything we plan afore we plan it?"

Patrick shook his head slowly, the memory of his fight with Ridley needling at him but the significance still hidden. He shut his eyes, trying hard to think, to remember. It felt important, and he'd never been so frightened in his life. Mona, Fayth, and Caroline were about to do something dangerously stupid, and Ridley knew they were coming before they knew themselves. And there was nothing he could do to stop it.

19

It was late afternoon when news began trickling in. The first to arrive was a boy, heading north. He'd been at the battle and reported that it was a complete rout. The Scottish army had barely made it across the Esk when the English sent them scattering. A handful of Englishmen defeated an army of fifty thousand. Scores of Scotsmen were surrendering to lone unarmed Englishmen.

The women sat before the fireplace, listening to the tale with growing horror, their sewing forgotten in their laps. Gaspar napped in a large basket at Mona's feet, and Rosemarie played with Fayth and Alex's dog.

"What of the Maxwells?" Caroline asked the boy.

"All captured or drowned."

When the boy was gone, Fayth gnawed at her thumbnail and said, "He's exaggerating. The Scots can't raise fifty thousand men—and even if they could, it would take more than a handful of Englishmen to send them running."

Caroline did not answer. She continued to sew a gown for the baby, her expression grim.

As the day wore on, Maxwell men returned home with

similar stories, though they gave more realistic numbers: twenty thousand Scots and a few thousand English. By full dark the men stopped arriving, and they had to accept the fact that their men weren't coming home.

When Mona had the children sleeping, she dressed warmly for travel and strapped a dagger to her thigh. She went downstairs to join her stepdaughters. She found Caroline in the hall, staring blankly into the fire, one hand absently stroking her belly, her sewing put away. Caroline looked up at Mona, taking in her cloak and leather sack.

"Where are you going?"

"To Graham Keep, to take the Clachan Fala back from Ridley and release our men."

"You said you'd wait. Two days."

"I can wait no longer. Everything I feared has come to pass."

Caroline stood. "I cannot let you go." She motioned to someone behind Mona. A light hand gripped Mona's elbow.

"Come along, Lady Graham," the guard said. "I'll see ye to yer chambers."

Mona dug in her heels, staring from the guard to Caroline. "What is this?"

"Patrick and Alexander would never forgive me if I let you and Fayth rush off like fools. You don't stand a chance against Ridley. We must write to our friends, ask for their aid. Lord Maxwell . . . perhaps even the king . . . will send men to fetch them."

Mona shook the guard's hand off. "Not if Lord Maxwell has also been taken prisoner. You heard what they're saying—a thousand men taken, hundreds of lords. Who does that leave to beg succor from? We must help ourselves. You stay here, but I must help Patrick."

Caroline wrung her hands now, her eyes wide. "But Ridley will not kill our husbands? Surely he will ransom them to us?"

"Like he ransomed Patrick? It was in your betrothal contract and still he didn't honor it. Patrick would still be there if I hadn't helped him escape."

Caroline looked as if she might cry, her throat tight, jaw rigid.

"Where is Fayth?" Mona asked.

"Locked in her room."

"She'll just climb out the window. But I suppose that's best. Perhaps I'm meant to do this alone."

The guard grasped Mona's elbow again. Mona gave Caroline a hard look, and she waved the guard away, looking more distressed by the moment. It had been refreshing to see Caroline so expressive, but this sort of lost anxiety worried Mona—it was bad for the baby.

She laid a hand on Caroline's arm. "I'll be fine, I swear it," she lied. "It's my fault Ridley has the stone . . . if I'd been a better Keeper this wouldn't have happened. I must rectify this." She paused. "I could use Fayth's help."

Caroline was truly alarmed now and sat on her bench.

Mona sat beside her. "I cannot promise any of us will live, but I can promise our men will not if we just sit here."

Caroline turned to Mona, calm now. "I'm going, too."

Mona shook her head and stood so she was higher than Caroline. "No, you are pregnant. That child must be protected."

"Why? Because of the foolish legend? No! We all know Ridley—but I have always been able to hide my feelings from him."

"It doesn't matter now that he has the stone, he'll know anyway."

"I don't think so. I didn't just fake it, Mona. Often I had

no feelings when I spoke to him. I didn't care about him—he'd killed any love I'd ever felt for him years ago."

The steward came forth uncertainly and cleared his throat.

"Yes, Henry?" Caroline said.

"There is a man at the gates, my lady. He says he's your brother. Wesley Graham."

"Wesley?" Caroline breathed, then stood. "Admit him at once." She sent another servant to release Fayth from her chambers.

Mona stood beside Caroline as the great double doors opened and Wesley entered, flanked by a handful of men. He strode across the hall to them and stopped before Caroline. He stared up at his sister for a long moment, opened his mouth as if to speak, then closed it, swallowing hard.

Then he dropped onto one knee and bowed his head. "Forgive me."

"I pray you, Wesley, rise," Caroline said.

But he didn't rise. "I didn't know . . . I didn't understand."

"Didn't understand what?"

"About Ridley . . . about Lord Annan."

Caroline stared at her brother, pain and sorrow clouding her eyes. Finally she sighed and said, her voice soft, "All is forgiven."

He rose slowly. His eyes were red-rimmed as if he'd been crying. Blood smeared his cheek, and his hands clenched tightly at his sides.

Mona went to him, moving the dark curls from his forehead to inspect a bruise. "What has happened, Wesley?"

He shook his head, but when Mona touched his shoulders and gently drew him to her, he embraced her, burying his head in her shoulder. Fayth rushed into the room, her face flushed and ready for a fight, but she stopped short when she saw Wesley.

He raised his head and whispered, "Fayth."

"Wesley . . ." Fayth ran to him, touching him with disbelief. "Where have you been? I thought Ridley . . . had you."

Mona found another bench, and they sat around the fire while Wesley told them all that had happened to him. How he'd fallen in love with Ridley's betrothed, Lady Anne Irvine, and she with him. Ridley had deceived him, promising him the tower of Gealach—Alex's home—once Fayth was wed to Carlisle, only Wesley had discovered he'd never intended to part with it. Determined to marry Lady Anne, Wesley forged a letter from Ridley, agreeing to break the betrothal and blessing the union between Wesley and Anne so her father, the earl of Dornock, would agree.

Filled with fury, Wesley had gone to Ridley at Gealach to confront him with his lies and betrayals, only to find him forcing Fayth into marrying Carlisle. He'd helped Fayth and Alex escape but had been unable to save himself. His men had been hanged and himself imprisoned. But Ridley had become a monster, hideous inside and out, and his men discontented. One had helped Wesley return to Dornock, only to find Lady Anne had traveled to Graham Keep in search of her husband.

"So he has them all," Mona murmured.

"Aye," Wesley said. "I was there at the Esk when the Scots retreated. I fought for the earl of Dornock, but I was not captured because I ripped off the St. Andrew's cross I wore. I saw Ridley take Lord Annan and his brothers prisoner . . . but that's not all."

Wesley turned to Mona, his face pale, bloodless in the firelight. "His face. The scars are gone."

"What?" Fayth asked, her voice a quaver. "That cannot be so!"

"But it is. There was no mistaking it—he'd shaved his beard, so it was plain for all to see." He looked at his sisters and Mona, the familiar angry determination gleaming in his brown eyes. "There was a time when the three of you were all the family I had. And you, Fayth," he gripped his sister's hand, "were my best friend. Much has changed." He swallowed, looking down at the ground a long moment before meeting their eyes again. "I have changed. I come to you now because I know you will not sit by while Ridley has your men. I bring men, once of Ridley's household, but mine to command now. Fayth and I know secret ways in and out of Graham Keep. I am surprised you have not already left."

Fayth snorted and narrowed her eyes at Caroline. "I would have left hours ago had Caroline not locked me in my room."

Wesley smiled. "Carrie, always looking out for us. Always trying to protect us."

"Someone needs to," Caroline said, brows raised.

Mona'd had enough talk. It was time for action. She stood. "You're right to believe we could not sit by. I was just leaving when you arrived. Please—join Fayth and me."

"And me!" Caroline said.

Mona frowned at her. "She is with child. She cannot go."

Wesley's face brightened as he looked at his sister, then he nodded. "Mona is right. A woman in your state should not leave the home."

"Thankfully I am not married to you, Wesley. I am going."

Fayth looked at Mona and her brother and shrugged. "Just let her come! Arguing will only waste time, and she won't change her mind."

Caroline smiled slightly and turned to Mona. "Have you a plan?"

"Yes, I do. The Clachan Fala has many powers. One is the sight, which I fear might warn Ridley of our coming. The other is the gift of knowing. But one can only know so much at any given time. The key is distraction. I will go in the front gates and give myself up to him. He will be so intent on me, he'll not pay attention to aught else."

"But if he knows what you're thinking," Fayth asked, "won't he know about us?"

"Well . . . maybe. I have been working on clearing all thoughts from my mind. There is no way to test myself unless confronted with Ridley, so I don't know if I will succeed. It's best if you don't tell me how you mean to get inside Graham Keep—that might protect you if I'm unsuccessful."

"You cannot sacrifice yourself in such a manner," Caroline protested. "Ridley is unpredictable . . . he might hurt you."

Mona looked at each of her stepchildren and said, "Of all of us, I am the safest from Ridley's temper, you must know that."

"She's right," Wesley said. "He wants her as much as the Bloodstone . . . he always has. And now that he has it, he likely wants her even more."

"That is what I mean!" Caroline cried. "What's left for him to possess but Mona? Don't you see?"

Mona had thought of that. He'd never been so forceful that he'd hurt her in the past, but he had the Bloodstone now and felt powerful. And he was angry and jealous about Patrick. It was a gamble she had to take. She would do whatever it took to distract him. For Patrick—and for her stepchildren. For all of them happiness had been hard won. Mona would not let Ridley take that away.

Patrick and his brothers had devised a plan for escape. The entire scheme hinged on the assumption that someone would return to their cell—to feed them, chain them to a wall, empty the chamber pot—*something*. After all, someone had come to Patrick at least once a day when he was imprisoned here before. But an entire day and night passed, and though servants came and went to the dungeons, they only tended the other prisoners.

Even when Patrick stood at the bars yelling at them, he was ignored. He was hungry and cold and knew that if not for his brothers he'd go mad locked in this cell again. Especially now, when everything had changed.

Patrick was surprised that he'd actually been able to sleep—he supposed it was because this cell *was* familiar to him. Terrifyingly familiar. And he'd been plagued with nightmares as he hadn't been in weeks. Alex had shaken him awake, concerned, but Patrick had refused to speak of it.

But hours later, Alex started in on him again. "You *do* still have the nightmares." He sat against the wall, his long legs stretched in front of him, crossed at the ankle.

The corridor outside their cell was ablaze with torches, giving them weak light through the bars of the door's small, square window. Robert turned from where he stared out through the window to look at Patrick.

Patrick sighed. "Aye."

"Have they gotten better?" Alex asked. "That one didn't seem as bad as the ones you used to have."

Patrick nodded, a deep sadness stealing into his soul. "It wasn't as bad. But just a month ago they were worse than ever."

"What happened?" Robert asked.

"Mona," Patrick said, throat tight.

It was not necessary to explain further; his brothers nodded their understanding. Patrick had not acknowledged until that moment that it was Mona who drove back the shadows. She'd forced him to talk about what had happened to his friends. And somehow that helped. He didn't try to understand it. It didn't matter. She'd saved him somehow and he loved her for it.

"She'll help Rosemarie, too," Patrick said. "She has this

way about her. . . . Mayhap she is a witch, for she has surely bewitched me."

Robert scratched at his temple, smiling slightly. "Perhaps if you told her that, she wouldn't have hid from you."

Patrick frowned. "She knows how I feel."

"Are you certain?"

"If not for Rosemarie, I would have asked her to marry me long ago. But I had to put Rosemarie first. She knew that."

Robert and Alex exchanged raised-brow looks.

"What?" Patrick demanded.

"Well," Alex said, "she might have understood your need to put your daughter first, but it's doubtful she understands anything else. Especially as ill as Rose is."

Patrick scowled. "Rosie's illness matters naught to me—she's my daughter, sick or no. It has nothing to do with why I wish to be with Mona."

"Patty . . . ," Alex said hesitantly, reverting to Patrick's childhood nickname. Alex's face was alight with humor. "You've never been . . . ah . . . verra . . . er, expressive."

Patrick scowled, but he realized his brothers were probably right again. When Patrick was with Mona again, he would tell her everything. Then she would marry him. If they ever left this place alive.

Alex's stomach growled loudly. "I knew he'd never let us live, but I didn't think he'd starve us."

"He wilna kill us," Robert said, irritation edging his voice. "Lord Wharton told him the king wanted prisoners and besides, ye canna ransom a dead body."

"He doesna care about the ransom," Alex said. "He wants Annancreag. He won't be happy until he destroys every last Annan Maxwell."

Robert sighed patiently. "Aye, ye told me this. But the English king would have to successfully invade and annex

Scotland for him to get my lands. They might have sent us running, but they never even crossed the Esk."

"You don't know that they don't plan to follow it up. Perhaps they are burning Scotland to ashes as we speak."

Robert stood and began pacing. "I doubt that very much. If the duke of Norfolk canna carry off an invasion in October, he bloody well won't succeed in December!"

Alex just shook his head.

"What do you think?" Robert asked Patrick.

Patrick exhaled. "I think Ridley is insane and we cannot anticipate what he will do."

Robert ground his teeth, striding to the door and staring blindly through the bars. "He would not kill us," he said angrily.

Patrick didn't want to die either, but thought it likely Alex was right. They'd never leave this cell. Patrick had never felt so hopeless. Ridley was an adversary that could not be bested. This was a prison that could not be breached from within. He'd gone over and over it in his mind—as he'd done for months when he was here before and come up with nothing.

The worst part was that he could not protect Mona or his brothers. Just like Julian and the others. Whether Mona came to Graham Keep for him or for the stone, it was still his fault. He'd given the stone to Ridley, believing her life was more dear than a piece of rock. It was, to him, but it mattered little now. And his brothers' wives . . . he could tell by his brothers' strained, worried expressions their thoughts ran parallel to his, miserable in their helplessness.

He pressed his fists into his eyes, unable to bear this line of thought. It couldn't happen, he couldn't accept it. Ridley was not all powerful. He was a man, and though the stone was enchanted it did not make him a god. Patrick was missing something here—it pricked at the edges of his mind, teasing him.

He stood, rubbing his jaw.

"What is it?" Alex asked.

"There's something I'm not seeing. . . . When I fought Ridley I could barely put up a defense—he knew every move I was going to make, even instinctive ones. But he still didn't manage to kill me."

"Aye, but that's only because Wharton saved you."

"That's it," Patrick said, frowning, hands on hips. "Why didn't he know Wharton would stop him?"

Robert turned from the door and leaned against it. "It seems he doesna know everything."

"Exactly. He was so intent on me, he was unaware of the thoughts around him."

Alex nodded thoughtfully. "That makes sense. He is only a man, after all, and can only do one thing at a time."

"Misdirection," Patrick said. "That is how we can best him. Two of us can engage him whilst the third comes upon him unawares."

"Aye," Robert said. "But if you're aware of this, then won't he be as well?"

Patrick sighed. "Aye, I hadna worked it all out yet."

"Keep working on it," Robert said, turning back to stare out the bars of the door. "It might be the only chance we have."

Mona sat on her horse, her heart hammering in her chest as she waited for the porter at Graham Keep to inform Ridley she was here to see him. She did not know where her stepchildren were or how they intended to get into Graham Keep. Her job was Ridley. To occupy him so they might get it in and rescue the others without Ridley's knowledge.

It wasn't long before the portcullis was raised halfway and Mona was admitted. She was ordered off her horse and led into the keep, flanked by two guards. The keep was unusually subdued, the servants watching covertly. The air was thick with fear. Mona was glad for her cloak to hide her trembling hands. She didn't know if she could do this. In spite of all her practice, she could not clear her mind now that she was here. All she could think of was Patrick, locked away in the dungeons, suffering. She couldn't bear it, and yet to think on it would be the death of them all. *Put it from your mind and stop being such a coward. Remember your duty.* Arlana's voice came to her, firm, demanding, and Mona relaxed. She could do this.

She was led into Ridley's private chambers. Ridley was there, sitting before the fireplace. He dismissed the servant. His face was in shadows. Mona approached him slowly. He did not speak, though it was clear he'd not taken his eyes from her since she entered the room. He wore the stone on an elaborate gold chain. It hung about his neck, resting in the center of his chest, where the ruby caught the candlelight, glowing a deep crimson.

When she was a few feet away she could see his face. His skin was clear and unblemished, pale where his beard once was, but already heavily shadowed with golden brown whiskers.

Her hand went involuntarily to her own face, touching where the hideous burns had once been. "It's gone."

"You are surprised. You didn't know it could heal?"

She shook her head. "Not until I held it. The healing was a rumor, unconfirmed . . . it's been threescore years since a Keeper held the stone, and then only briefly. Some of its properties are unexplored."

He leaned forward to frown at her, studying her face. She hoped that meant her thoughts were hidden from him.

He sat back, relaxing, and smiled. "Of course. A Keeper would not be so easily read."

"I have nothing to hide."

"Then why have you come?"

Mona removed her cloak. "Because you have the Clachan Fala."

"And you mean to take it from me."

"Can I?" She tossed her cloak onto a chest and went to him. He tensed but didn't move. She trailed her fingers over his arm and shoulder, moving around behind him. When she slid her hand forward to touch the stone, he grabbed her wrist. She'd expected as much, and when he stood, keeping a firm hold of her, she only smiled.

His frown deepened, his eyes narrowed on her face. "Only you could so trouble me." He pulled her close and she didn't resist, refusing to feel anything. "What to do with you? This is all surely an act, but such a pretty one."

"Are you sure it's an act? Mayhap I've changed my mind. After all, you've proven yourself worthy of the stone."

Something changed in his face then, as if her words were a balm, but he still did not act. "You know I want to believe you . . . if I discover you're lying to me, I will kill them all."

Mona blinked innocently. "Who?"

"The Maxwells. My sisters—it's too late for Wesley, I cannot let him live. He has aspirations of becoming the next Lord Graham."

Mona knew she couldn't play too cold or he would not believe her. She let some of her distress show. "Wesley has changed. Let him return to Scotland and live with his wife. He'll not trouble you."

Ridley considered her, the hand that clutched her relaxing to slide up and rub at her shoulder. "For you, I'll think on it." Even without the stone Mona knew that was a lie.

He stroked his thumb across her jaw, over her bottom

lip, then leaned down and kissed her. Mona willed herself to relax, to respond to him, to force the revulsion away.

When he straightened, his eyes had darkened. He licked his lips. "Better than I'd imagined." He urged her backward, one arm snaking around her waist. "You will tell me everything you know about the stone. Everything it is capable of."

When her thighs hit the side of the bed, she tried not to panic. She *must* do this. He was surely distracted now. He kissed her again, his arms around her, one stroking her hair. After a moment, she turned her head away and closed her eyes, fighting to clear her mind. He continued to kiss her jaw and neck. She gripped his shoulders and willed her fingers to relax, to touch him with desire.

"You want to do this now?" she asked, trying to keep her voice light. She stroked the hair at his nape. "Wouldn't you like me to tell you something about the Bloodstone? Let me wash and change?" He'd always been oddly fastidious about cleanliness—Hugh had harped at him about it, calling him a girl.

He raised his head, smiling. "You know me so well . . . but you are different, not like other women." He pressed his face into her hair. "You always smell lovely to me. I've waited seven years for this. I'll not wait another moment."

This was what she'd wanted—he was thoroughly distracted, submerged in lust, but she was afraid. Not so much of his touch—she could bear that, she'd borne many ghastly things in her life and she would do so again to save Patrick. What she feared was being unable to hide her unhappiness. Patrick would not want her to do this for him. He might not forgive her, even after, for allowing Ridley to use her. What did it matter? When all was finished and the others were free, Ridley would kill her.

He pushed her back on the bed, sucking at her neck, his

fingers working clumsily at the hooks of her bodice. When his hand closed over her breast she was unable to suppress the shudder of disgust or despairing thoughts of Patrick. Ridley's reaction was instantaneous. He dragged her off the bed by the front of her shift and shook her.

"You dare to think of him while I touch you?" He thrust her backward. "I should do it anyway, bitch." He shoved her thighs apart, pushing himself between them.

"Then do it," she said. She was determined to do this, to keep his mind full of her however she must. "Just because I've lain with him, doesn't mean I don't want you."

"You lie! You feel nothing when I kiss you, you are dead. You thought of him, not me."

"That's not true, Ridley."

His face was flushed, his breathing labored. He grabbed at her savagely, shaking her. Mona went for the dagger at her thigh, unsheathing it. But he caught her wrist, his grip punishing.

"You mean to kill me?"

Mona shook her head, unable to form a coherent thought.

His other hand clamped on her throat, and he squeezed. "You come here and think to use my love to kill me?"

Mona tried to gasp for air, clawing at Ridley's hand. His lips were drawn back from his teeth as his fingers tightened. Then suddenly he released her, backing away. Mona curled up on the bed, wheezing, her chest burning.

Before she could catch her breath he was hauling her up again by the hair. He brought her face close to his. His eyes were wild, crazed. "You will tell me what the stone can do—now!"

"Let me go and I'll tell you!"

He shoved her onto the bed and stepped back. "Tell me!"

"Well," Mona stalled, still trying to catch her breath.

She could not give its secrets away, not to him. "There is the knowing. It reveals others' thoughts and feelings."

His smile was sarcastic. "I know that one."

"It can give you visions of things to come."

He had calmed, the flush fading from his skin, but his eyes were still wild. "I know that, too—but I don't know how. It has given me several visions, but they just come over me. Damned inconvenient. How do I control it?"

Mona licked her lips. She didn't want to tell him this. He could discover all manner of things, thwart the rescue. She must think of something else to share with him. She could teach him how to be unseen. She immediately dismissed that. Too dangerous for everyone else.

Finally she said, "That's how it works. You can't control the visions."

He frowned at her, his fingers caressing the ruby. "You're lying . . . and there's something you're withholding from me. Unseen. What is that?"

Mona's breath hiccuped in her chest. It was becoming more and more difficult to conceal her thoughts from him. She shook her head as if confused. "Unseen? I don't follow you."

His lips curled back from his teeth as he glowered at her. "You dare lie to me?" He strode to the door and flung it open. Two guards waited outside the door. "Fetch Sir Patrick."

Mona's heart seized with dread. This was not going as she'd planned. What did he mean to do with Patrick?

He turned back to her, smiling darkly. "I had decided some time ago that I could not let you live. You are the Keeper, after all, and so long as you're alive I'll never be rid of your meddling." He sighed, strolling over to her with his hands behind his back. "But when you came to me, so beautiful and willing, well, my resolve faltered. It always does with you, love."

"Then what do you mean to do?" Mona could no longer keep up the ruse. Patrick was truly in danger now, and it was because she'd mucked things up.

"Well . . . though I can read little from you, I am certain this is part of some elaborate ploy to steal back the Blood-stone and free your lover. As much as I want to punish you for attempting to deceive me, there are other matters more urgent, and it won't do if you can't talk. You are the only one who knows all the secrets of the stone. However, I know you won't just tell me. I doubt torturing you would make you talk either."

Mona closed her eyes, panic gripping her. "I don't care about Sir Patrick. Torturing him won't make me talk." There was a wild note to her voice. She bit her lip and sat on her hands, knowing her feelings were probably clear to anyone.

"Really? We'll see."

The door creaked and Mona's eyes sprang open. Patrick was shoved into the room. He was barefoot, in breeches and a torn shirt. His hands were bound behind his back. His eyes locked on Mona as he was forced to his knees. Three men held him down.

Ridley circled him, smiling now. "This is so touching. So sad. He is terrified."

Mona didn't believe it. Patrick? Terrified? Never.

"Oh, but he is! He can think of naught but you, Mona . . . he loves you and cares only for your safety. Not a thought for himself." His behavior frightened Mona. It was as if he thrived on fear. His ability to use others' thoughts empowered him, twisted him.

He stopped in front of Patrick. "Do you know why you're here, Knight?"

Patrick said nothing, glowering up at Ridley.

"Together, we're going to make her sing."

20

Patrick didn't like what he was seeing. Mona sat on the bed, her hair and clothes a mess, her lips swollen—disturbing red marks and a love bite on her neck. Fury welled in him and he yanked at the bindings, tried to get to his feet. Guards on either side held him down, their hands pushing on his shoulders. Patrick would kill Ridley if he raped her or harmed her in any way.

Ridley laughed, but it was ugly, spiteful—humorless. "I pray you, Sir Patrick. Don't insult me. Does she look raped to you?"

Patrick only glared at him.

"I assure you she was quite willing." When Mona only sat there, wide eyed, mouth slightly agape, he said, "Weren't you, love?"

After a long moment she nodded jerkily. Patrick's jaw was rigid as he watched her rise from the bed and come up behind Ridley. She wouldn't look at Patrick, even as his gaze bore into her. What was she doing? Ridley turned, blocking her from Patrick's view, but he heard her voice.

"I was willing, Ridley, and I still am. Send him away so we can be alone." Her hands slid around behind Ridley's neck, drawing his head down. Sickness twisted Patrick's gut. *She was kissing him!* He knew what she was doing and why—trying to save his sorry ass. But not this way. Not like this.

With a growl, he surged to his feet despite the hands trying to force him back down. But when he tried to rush forward, to drive his shoulder into Ridley's back, the guard behind him caught him across the head with something solid, and Patrick sunk to his knees again, pain radiating through his skull.

When his vision cleared, Ridley had turned around. He had Mona by the hair at her nape. She clutched at his hand, grimacing in pain.

"Don't kill him, Ridley, please," she begged.

He shook her, veins standing out in his forehead. "You beg for his life? You distract me so he can attack?"

"Please, Ridley," she moaned.

He dragged her up, forcing her to look into his eyes. "I would have given you everything. *Everything.*"

She shrank from him, her hands trying to pry his fingers from her hair.

"Leave her alone!" Patrick said. "She doesn't want you—and you punish her for it? You're mad."

Ridley put his head back, glaring at Patrick, shaking. Then calm seemed to fall over him.

"You're right." His smile was thin and cruel. "I've wasted enough time on you, sweets." He shoved her to the floor. "You're too well used and getting a bit long in the tooth. And barren, at that. Practically useless."

Mona was on her hands and knees. When she looked up at Patrick, tears stood in her black eyes. "I'm sorry," she mouthed. Patrick couldn't stand to look at her, thought his

heart would break. She suffered for him and he could not
help her. He clenched his teeth, straining against the bindings. This couldn't be happening—he wouldn't let it.

Ridley paced away. "Now. What is unseen?"

Mona sat up on her knees, pushing black curls from her
face. Her eyes were helpless and wide. "It means—"

"No!" Patrick shouted. "Don't tell him anything!"

Ridley gestured to the guards. Patrick was hauled to his
feet, and the man behind him slammed his fist into
Patrick's back. White hot agony sliced through him, and
before he could gather himself for the next blow, it came
again, driving him into the floor. He lay there, his face
pressed into the floorboards, paralyzed by the pain gripping his back, unable to catch his breath.

"What is unseen?"

"It means others—"

"No!" Patrick rolled to his side, his back in agony, and
pinned Mona with a glare. "It's not worth it—I am one
man! You cannot tell him!"

Tears streaked her face. A guard kicked him, boot con-
necting with his back and arm. Patrick grunted, gritting his
teeth, but keeping his eyes on Mona. She shook her head
slowly, tears dripping from her chin.

"I've lived through far worse than this," he hissed. It
hurt to breathe.

"Have you?" Ridley said. "Get him on his knees again."
Ridley strode to a fat candle sitting in a bowl-like candle-
holder. He brought it to Patrick and knelt. A great pool of
melted wax surrounded the wick. Ridley tilted it slightly so
it dripped down the side of the candle.

"There's nothing quite like fire and hot wax. Do you
know, for days after Fayth burned me, I could still feel it,
like a fire in my skin? Roasting me. I could still smell it,
too, my burning flesh."

"Maybe that was brimstone you smelled," Patrick bit out. "Hell's gates opening wide."

Ridley's pale blue eyes narrowed. He brought the candle closer, the flame nearly blinding Patrick.

"Don't, Ridley!" Mona cried, rushing forward. "I'll tell you anything."

Ridley shoved her hard. She stumbled, sprawling onto the ground.

"Are you worried he won't be so pretty for you?" Ridley studied Patrick dispassionately. The seam at the shoulder of Patrick's shirt had ripped, exposing his skin. He tensed as Ridley eyed it. The idea seduced him; Patrick could see it in his eyes. He *wanted* to burn someone.

Patrick clenched his jaw and waited, watching as the candle wavered closer, closer, tipping. Melted wax splashed on his shoulder. It seared him, but he'd felt worse just moments ago, his back still throbbing with the memory. He kept his face neutral, even as Mona cried out, trying to push the candle away from Patrick.

Ridley rose and Mona was there, frantically trying to blot away the wax with her kirtle.

"It will be all right," Patrick whispered, though he didn't believe it, didn't even know why he said it except that he longed to wipe the pain and fear from her eyes. Her head was bent over him, and for a brief moment he pressed his forehead into her hair, inhaling herbs and flowers, a wave of longing and grief washing over him. "I love you."

She raised her head, her eyes meeting his, wide and sad, and then Ridley yanked her away. He had her by the throat, shoving her against a wall. He still held the candle, threateningly near her face. "Next it will be his face. Now tell me!"

The door creaked open behind Patrick. Ridley turned, and his eyes widened in surprise.

"Let her go, Ridley!" Wesley strode into the room with

a handful of men. "Where are you keeping Anne?" But he
didn't wait for an answer; he rushed at Ridley, drawing his
sword. Ridley flung the candle in his brother's face and
Wesley screamed, dropping his sword, hands over his eyes.
Patrick's guards had moved to engage Wesley's men and
Patrick acted instinctively, leaping to his feet and ramming
his shoulder into Ridley's chest, slamming him against the
wall. He reached for his sword. Patrick rammed his knee
upward into Ridley's crotch, but it only cracked painfully
into the wall. The element of surprise was lost.

Mona knelt beside Wesley but couldn't pry his hands
from his eyes. He moaned pitiably, and Mona feared Ridley had blinded him. Ridley came at Patrick with a sword.
Patrick was defenseless, his hands bound behind his back.
She could think of no way to aid him and so she ran at Ridley, throwing herself at his back. He stumbled, grabbing at
her, but she clung to him. Patrick kicked his ankle and Ridley went to his knees. He swung his sword at Patrick, but
he jumped back.

Ridley grabbed a handful of Mona's hair and tried to
yank her over his shoulder. He couldn't effectively fight
them both, and Patrick kept coming at him in spite of Ridley's waving sword. Ridley was succeeding in dragging
Mona over his shoulder when a glint of gold caught her
eye, and she knew that was the answer. The Bloodstone
protected him. Without it he was nothing. She released his
neck and latched onto the chain, throwing her body backwards. He kept hold of her hair, trying to twist around, but
Patrick drove another kick into his chest.

He fell back, Mona beneath him. He released her hair.
Patrick stomped down on his hand and Ridley made a
strangled sound, but he wouldn't release the sword, even as
Patrick's heel ground into his wrist.

Mona grabbed more of the chain, pulling and twisting, but it wouldn't break. He was smashing her, she couldn't breathe, but she couldn't let go or he would kill Patrick. She bared her teeth, grunting with the effort, and yanked harder. He made rasping sounds and clawed at the stone. The chain bit into her palms but held. She pulled harder, nearly screaming in despair. He was moving again, trying to roll off her.

"Mona," Patrick said. "You can let go."

Mona's eyes popped open. She could see nothing but Ridley's head.

"He's dead."

Mona's arms remained rigid. "It's a trick—I can't break the chain—he can't be dead!"

Ridley rolled heavily again. "It's not a trick. He's dead."

She loosened her grip but didn't release the chain, and Ridley rolled off her, aided by Patrick's foot. Mona sat up and looked down at Ridley's face. His wide eyes glistened in the candlelight, his mouth a rictus of pain. She'd killed him. Strangled him.

But how? Why hadn't the Bloodstone protected him—or healed him?

Patrick nudged her with his knee. Her scalp stung. Overcome, Mona turned to him, pressing her face into his thigh, her eyes burning, shudders ripping through her. She'd known it would come to this—it was Ridley or them, but she'd never wanted to kill him. Tears wet her face. Patrick went to his knees beside her, and she leaned into his chest.

"Dinna greet," he whispered. "Ye saved us all."

When she was snuffling, Patrick said, "Why don't you get that thing off his neck before it resurrects him or something worse."

Her hands shook as she took the chain and slid the Clachan Fala off Ridley's neck. She turned her face away from the mottled marks the chain had left and quickly backed away. Someone had cut Patrick's bindings. Mona looked around the room and saw that others had entered— Caroline, Fayth, Alex, and Robert—and other men she didn't recognize and a young woman who leaned over Wesley. Anne, Wesley's wife. She was crying.

Caroline knelt beside them. She spoke softly to Wesley and Anne, then looked up at Mona, her brow lined with despair. "He can't see."

Mona looked down at the Clachan Fala and back at Ridley's unblemished face. Just holding it, Mona felt power humming through her, alive somehow. She could place it around Wesley's neck and wait for it to heal him . . . days, maybe weeks. But Mona didn't want to do that. Couldn't trust with it. But she had to help Wesley.

She went to him and knelt.

Anne said, "Can you help him?"

Mona took Wesley's hands from his face and placed them over the Bloodstone.

He tried to draw them back. "What's that?"

"It is the Clachan Fala," Mona said, holding his hands around the stone with her own. "Ask it to heal your eyes."

Wesley's eyes were closed, the lids raw and swelling. "I can feel it . . . moving."

"Ask it, Wesley," Mona said, "and I will with you."

Anne held Wesley's head against her bosom and said through her tears, "Ask, Wesley, please."

And then Caroline was there beside them, placing her hands around Mona's and Wesley's. "Heal Wesley," she whispered. "Please."

Fayth knelt across from Caroline, her hands joining with Mona and her siblings, whispering the chant with the rest of them. Mona wished for it with all her heart—her stepson whole again, his sight restored. She tried to visualize it, the eyes healing.

Warmth pulsed in the stone. They all felt it, Mona knew by the way they stumbled over their prayers. It grew hotter, thrumming through their hands and up their arms. It was working—something was happening. They chanted louder and faster in their excitement. Wesley gasped, his hands tightening beneath Mona's.

Then it went still.

Mona opened her eyes and found herself staring into Wesley's brown ones. His hair was damp with sweat and his skin pale. But his skin and eyelids were clear and unblemished. Even the scar that had once marred his cheek was gone. They all drew their hands away until Wesley held the Bloodstone reverently in his palms.

"I can see," he said. "I felt it . . . inside me."

He stared down at it for a long moment, then gazed at Ridley's body.

He turned to Mona. "You saved us all." He placed the Bloodstone in her hands. "I am Lord Graham now and I will set everything to rights. I vow it."

"Oh, Wesley . . ." Mona touched his face, her heart swollen with pride at the man he'd become. He embraced her tightly.

He released her suddenly and turned, holding his hand out to Anne. She came to him, and he tucked her against his side. "This is my wife, Lady Anne."

Mona greeted her as Alex and Fayth came forth, clinging to each other as if they still might be torn asunder.

"I release Fayth's dowry and your tower of Gealach to you," Wesley said to Alex. "I might have some influence with the new Lord Carlisle, perhaps I can persuade him to sell it to you, or at least grant it to you in feu."

"My thanks," Alex said, shaking his brother-in-law's hand.

Caroline joined them, Lord Annan trailing behind her. Mona knew he still held a grudge against Wesley for the raid that had killed many of his people. But for his wife's sake, he was trying to be civil.

Hesitantly, Caroline reached out and touched Wesley's face where the scar had been. Wesley held very still, astonished that his sister was touching him.

"Wesley," Caroline whispered, then seemed overcome, unable to speak.

Wesley took her hand and squeezed, then looked up at Robert. "I will rectify the problems with the betrothal. Caroline's dowry will be paid to you immediately. And you all have my safe conduct back across the border."

Robert nodded his thanks.

Wesley turned to his wife now, holding her tightly, his face buried in her loose chestnut hair.

Mona felt a heavy hand on her shoulder and turned.

Patrick pulled her into his arms. "I'm never letting you go. I'll wear you down, Mona, I swear it, so you might as well just say yes and end it now." He drew back, gripping her shoulders and staring into her eyes. "You hold the Bloodstone, you are looking into my heart. You know I speak the truth."

The stone was still clutched in Mona's hand and she felt it, waves of warmth from him. Love. He did love her.

"Oh, Patrick," she said, great joy and sadness filling her. She touched his cheek. "I'm the Keeper. I cannot abandon my duty. I have many more years in which I must protect the stone and teach Caroline and Robert's son to use it. Can you live that way? There might be more Ridleys. This might never end."

Patrick's scowl was fierce, and she felt the impatience

rolling off him. He grabbed her hand, dragging her to where Robert and Caroline stood, and interrupted his brother as he chastised Caroline for putting herself and the child in danger.

"Robert—Mona has brought you the stone. It is yours to do what you will with, but I think you should destroy it. You've seen all the trouble it's caused. It's dangerous."

Robert stared at the stone, then to Ridley's body, frowning. Then his gaze rested on Wesley's healed face, and his frown deepened. "I cannot decide this now. Mona, as you are the Keeper, you will bring the Clachan Fala to Annancreag. I'll decide there."

"Damnit," Patrick said. "This cannot wait!"

"It will," Robert said in a tone that brooked no opposition. He turned to his wife, sliding an arm around her. "Right now, I just want to go home."

They all gathered in Lord Annan's inner chamber at Annancreag, closeted up tight so no servants could bear witness to what was said. Alex and Fayth sat side by side on a bench, hands clasped beneath the table. Caroline sat across from them and beside Mona. Patrick was on Mona's other side, his arm firm around her waist. The children were with Father Jasper.

Robert stood before the fireplace, the Clachan Fala, removed from its golden chain, in his hands. He'd had it for several days now. Mona had caught sight of him wandering the gardens with it alone or with Caroline. They were often closed up in their chambers for hours.

Mona's heart raced as she waited for Robert to speak. She and Patrick had discussed it at length as well. He'd not changed his mind that it was evil and should be destroyed, but he'd also said that whatever happened, he wanted Mona. He didn't care if she was the Keeper.

This comforted her, though she longed for a normal life. As the Keeper she'd never be free. Ridley might be dead, but there would be more like him. It would never be over.

Robert finally spoke. "I've thought long on this problem. And I know you all have, too." He frowned down at the ruby, staring into its depths. "That is the most troubling thing. That I know what goes through each of your minds. Patrick is right that it is dangerous." He looked to Caroline, and she smiled encouragingly. He went on. "I came upon a servant yesterday who was filching grain. He's done much worse than that, and I never suspected."

"That's good, then," Alex said. "Who can deceive you now?"

"Is it?" Robert said. He shook his head. "In some ways, perhaps. But it made me sore angry. Made me want to do more than turn him out."

He looked at his wife again, and they held each other's gaze. "There are other things I learned . . . about others. Visions it gave me, that I could use." He sighed deeply. "I like to think of myself as a man of honor, but I dinna know if even I am honorable enough to use it wisely."

"What about the healing?" Mona said. "There is no evil in that. No wrong in that."

Robert nodded again, his eyes on the stone. "I've thought of that, too." He looked at Patrick, his face grim. "I've thought of Rosemarie . . . but I also thought of Mona. This is not the life I wish for you and my brother. The Clachan Fala is mine now, to do with as I please. The first thing I do is release you as Keeper. There will be no more Keepers. Your last charge is to record what you know of the stone, its history, its powers. From now on the secret of the Bloodstone will be protected by the Lords of Annancreag."

Mona blinked, unable to believe what she heard. This was not something she'd considered. She'd assumed

Robert would either destroy it or she'd be forced to continue on as Keeper. The tension drained out of Patrick's arm, though he still held her tightly.

"Mona has been a fine healer all her life," Fayth said. "She can take care of Rosemarie. She doesn't need magic to heal her."

Mona smiled at her stepdaughter. "I thank you for your confidence, but Rosemarie's illness is grave." She looked at Robert, her smile fading. "I would ask that whatever you decide, you allow me to use it one last time. I don't know that the stone can heal an illness such as Rosemarie has. Perhaps it only works on flesh wounds, but I must try."

"Of course," Robert said.

Patrick was frowning hard at his brother. Mona knew this didn't make him happy. He wanted the stone destroyed, gone forever. Mona wasn't sure how it made her feel. Relieved and yet frightened. Robert may well say he released her from her duty, but if anything happened to him, it would be back in her hands.

"However," Robert continued, "I think it's unwise to have it within easy reach. The well in the garden is very deep, and since we use the cistern more and more of late, that is where I will drop it."

"It will be very hard to fetch should we need it," Alex said.

"That's the idea."

Alex shook his head. "Mayhap impossible. The last time something fell in the well a lad died trying to fetch it."

"You see why it's a good place for it? The situation will have to be desperate for us to take such a chance." He looked at them all, his face grim. "This must never leave this room, else we'll have scores of fools falling in our well and dying trying to retrieve it."

They all nodded agreement.

* * *

Later, alone in Patrick's old tower room, he asked Mona, "Are you sorry?" He held Gaspar on his lap. The lad never seemed to sleep and adored his new papa. Rosemarie had fallen asleep beside him, his sleeve still clutched in her hand.

They'd returned from Graham Keep to find Nadine gone and the children in Father Jasper's care. They loved the old priest, but Rosemarie had been frightened at everyone abandoning them. Patrick was still warmed by the child's joy and relief at seeing him. He'd feared she would never love him as she had Gaspar de Aigues, but now he had hope that he could make up for all the years they'd lost.

Mona sat beside him on the bed, smoothing her hand over Gaspar's silky brown curls. The children had taken to her immediately and she, of course, to them. Patrick still wondered that someone who so loved children should be destined to have none of her own. He only hoped Gaspar and Rosemarie would be enough for her. If she ever said yes. It rankled that she still hadn't accepted his proposal, even after Robert had released her from her duties as Keeper. Everyone assumed—himself included—that they would be married as soon as possible, but Patrick still wanted to hear her say yes.

"I'm not sorry," she answered. "I feel a bit sad . . . as if I let Arlana down. And a bit . . . odd, that it's truly over."

Gaspar's warm, soft body leaned heavily against Patrick's chest. The lad inspected his chubby fingers with sleepy fascination.

"Why, then, have you not said yes?" he asked somewhat sullenly.

Mona laughed, leaning forward and sliding her hand up his arm to his shoulder. "I thought you understood. Of course I'll be your wife, Sir Patrick Maxwell. I love you."

And when she kissed him, he knew that she would not just banish his nightmares but give him back his dreams.

Epilogue

の

Maxwells came from miles around to attend the baptism
of Caroline and Robert's first child, a son. At Mona's sug-
gestion they held off forty days and combined it with Caroline's churching so she could be present. It was a grand
affair, with Father Jasper presiding over the ceremonies, a
feast, and later music and dancing.

Pleasantly tired and sweaty from careening about with
Patrick and the children, Mona joined her stepdaughters by
the fire. The men gravitated to one end of the room to discuss the treaty with England, and Scotland's promises to
wed the infant queen of Scotland to the English prince, Ed-
ward. Shortly after the disaster of Solway Moss, King
James had died, but his queen had given birth to a daughter
and now Scotland must endure a regency. The country was
weakened, and the English king was trying to use this to
his advantage. The Maxwells, of course, didn't like it at all.

Caroline sat between Mona and Fayth, cradling her son,
named Rowan for Robert's father, unable to take her eyes
from him. He was a long child, sure to have his father and
uncles' exceptional height. Fayth stared down at the lad,

too, a dreamy haze to her eyes, her hand smoothing over her own well-rounded belly.

Mona heard a squeal, drawing her attention back to the men. Patrick swung Rosemarie in circles until her shoe fell off. When he set her on her feet, she toddled for a moment, almost falling, giggling all the while.

Gaspar tugged at Patrick's breeches, hopping up and down. "Me, Da! Me!"

As he swung Gaspar in circles, Rosemarie shrieked as if it were her. "I'm next, Papa!"

"I cannot!" he gasped, setting Gaspar on his feet. The boy promptly tumbled backward onto his bottom. Patrick picked him up and settled him on his shoulders. "My knee is paining me—you know what that means?"

Rosemarie raced across the room to Mona, Patrick and Gaspar trailing her. "Mama—it's going to rain! Does that mean we get to stay here?"

Rosemarie was a quick study and already spoke English very well, though she sometimes lapsed into French when speaking to her father. But the greatest miracle of all was that she'd not had the falling sickness since Mona had asked the Bloodstone to heal her. Mona knew it was too early to be certain. The falling sickness was unpredictable. But deep down, she believed her daughter healed.

They'd been at Annancreag more than a month, since Mona had been midwife to Caroline and brought wee Rowan into the world. Though she loved being with Fayth and Caroline, she was more than ready to return to her own home. Much work needed to be done to their small tower house, but Patrick loved the repairs and had many plans for additions. It made him happy, and that was enough for Mona.

Alas, it was not yet time to return home, much as they wanted to. Fayth's confinement was drawing near, and Alex insisted their child be born at Annancreag with Mona as midwife. It was more than the desire to be surrounded by family, Mona knew. Everyone wanted to be near the Clachan Fala in case something went wrong. And Fayth was so very small—Alex would take no chances with his wife. He'd fashioned a winch to descend into the well himself if necessary.

But they needn't worry. Annancreag had been blessed with the miracle of health. Not long after Robert had dropped the Bloodstone in the well, they'd gone several weeks without rain and had been forced to use well water. Not one inhabitant of the castle had been ill since. Not even a runny nose. It had since rained many times and the cistern was again full, but the Maxwells continued to drink from the well.

Rosemarie had moved to stand beside Caroline and peer over her arm at the baby.

"I want to stay with the baby," she said. "Why can't *we* have a baby? Not another brother, though." She wrinkled her nose at Gaspar. "I want a sister this time."

Mona felt Patrick's hand on her shoulder, squeezing comfortingly. He thought she was still barren. He leaned down, plopping Gaspar in her lap and planting a kiss on her neck.

But Mona had been drinking from the well, too. Her courses were nearly a month late, and there was a heaviness to her breasts. At times she could barely drag herself from bed in the mornings, and when she was up, she was queasy for hours.

Mona took Patrick's hand and smiled up at him. Tonight, she promised herself, she would tell him of the stone's latest gift.

Visit the
Simon & Schuster Web site:
www.SimonSays.com

and sign up for our
mystery e-mail updates!

Keep up on the latest
new releases, author appearances,
news, chats, special offers, and more!
We'll deliver the information
right to your inbox — if it's new,
you'll know about it.

SIMON & SCHUSTER
A VIACOM COMPANY
www.SimonSays.com

POCKET BOOKS

POCKET STAR BOOKS